THE FACE OF THE ENEMY

THE FACE OF THE ENEMY

CAROL BALIZET

Chosen Books

A Division of Baker Book House Co
Grand Rapids, Michigan 49516

Library of Congress Cataloging-in-Publication Data

Balizet, Carol.

The Face of the enemy.

I. Title. PS3552.A4536F3   1984   813'.54   83-26176

ISBN 0-8007-9186-X

Published by Chosen Books
a division of Baker Book House Company
P.O. Box 6287, Grand Rapids, MI 49516-6287

Second printing, April 1995

Printed in the United States of America

For Suzanne
    Cynthia
      Shirley
        Bonnie

I have no greater joy than
to know that my children
walk in truth.   3 John 4

Contents

The Intruder

From the door of the hospital room the sleeping young man somehow looked out of place. Ruddy, tough, muscular, too healthy to be in Brookshire Memorial—yet so vulnerable as he dozed on the crisp white sheets. One huge arm lay strapped to a board and a plastic tube carried liquid nourishment into his vein.

His stats were not unusual. *Twenty-six years old. Hernia post-op patient. Repair of injury suffered at warehouse where he had worked.*

There were no medical personnel around when the intruder slipped quietly into the patient's room. An injection of the deadly fluid into that plastic tube was done in a few seconds.

The muscular young man tossed once in his sleep, but he did not wake. Now, would not wake.

At the far end of the corridor a day nurse was preparing her tray of medications. An empty cup fluttered to the floor. As she turned to pick it up, she saw a blur of something moving at the end of the corridor by the fire stairs. Later, after the emergency, she would wonder what it was she had seen.

Book I

The Open Door

The call over the hospital public address system was urgent: "Code 99, Six North! Code 99, Six North!"

Even after twelve years as a nurse at Brookshire Memorial Hospital and hundreds of emergency calls like this, Sue Dunn still responded to the summons with a rush of adrenalin. She grabbed the crash cart and wheeled it rapidly down the hall toward Six North.

As she entered the emergency room, five uniformed people were moving with precision and purpose around the still form on the bed. A technician from inhalation therapy was ventilating the male patient, while an orderly was compressing the chest, mechanically emptying the heart muscle by pressing it between the breastplate and the spine. An older nurse was placing monitor electrodes on the patient's chest; a much younger one was nervously trying to start intravenous (I.V.) fluids. There was still no sign of life in the patient.

A doctor was standing by the bed, hands on hips, his dark eyes studying the scene. Dr. Charles Fortuna, a specialist in Internal Medicine, was a new addition to the hospital staff.

He turned to Sue Dunn. "Want to push an amp of bicarb?" he asked.

"Want to wait till we get a vein open?" Sue returned calmly. She knew as well as the doctor that soda bicarb was a routine part of the treatment for cardiac arrest, but the order

11

was meaningless until they had succeeded in starting the I.V.

She put her arm around the thin shoulders of the young nurse who was still fumbling with the I.V. "I'll do that. You get the fluid ready." The patient's arm was surprisingly young. Huge veins stood out like a garden hose. Sue eased the Jelco in and felt the immediate satisfying "pop" as it entered the vein and blood surged back. "Get the bicarb," she ordered.

"He told us he was going to die," the young nurse whispered. "And he's only 26."

"Straight line," said the older nurse laconically as the bright blip marched across the screen, unchanged except for the gentle surge that coincided with the chest compressions. "No 'P' waves, no complex, no nothing."

"What's this guy's history?" Dr. Fortuna asked. "Any cardiac problems?"

"Nothing," the young nurse sobbed. "There's nothing wrong with him but a simple hernia."

"Well, don't look now but his heart ain't beating."

Sue felt her spirit sag. A 26-year-old patient with no history of previous heart trouble, "coding" without apparent cause. How tragic! And this one would mean a stink. As area supervisor, she would be caught in the middle of it.

"Want some epinephrine?" she suggested tactfully to the doctor.

"Right," he agreed, evidently grateful for the suggestion, and she prepared the injection. He stabbed the four-inch needle into the patient's chest probing for the heart muscle.

"His pupils are fixed, Doctor," the inhalation therapist said. "They have been since we found him."

"This wasn't a witnessed arrest, then?" the doctor asked in annoyance. "So he might have been like this for hours."

"I found him like that," the new nurse whispered. Sue held on to her patience. It seemed each year these young nurses were less competent, knew less about the real world of patients and hospitals. "I'd been talking to him earlier.

When I came back, he was just lying there, not breathing, and I couldn't get a pulse."

"So he could have been like this for hours?" Dr. Fortuna persisted.

"Lay off," Sue said. "It's not her fault." The doctor grunted and turned away. He's uptight too, she thought with sudden empathy. Like the young graduate, he was new at Brookshire and probably very sorry he'd responded to this code call.

Sue turned back to the patient. The medical technicians were still doing all the things they knew to do, making every effort to restore the vanished spark of life to the virile-looking young body. Sue had a feeling of despair; she knew somehow it would all be to no avail.

She flipped the pages of the patient's chart. As supervisor, she would be expected to notify the family. "His name's Juan Hernandez. Next of kin is a brother, Luis. I ought to call him."

"Look at his legs." The staff nurse pulled back the sheet. The strong, muscular legs were no longer warm and tanned. They were cold and lifeless, blue and mottled in color. "This guy's just plain dead."

"You're right," Dr. Fortuna said suddenly. "Stop the code."

Sue looked at her watch, noting the time of death. She was relieved in a way; no sense in prolonging the inevitable. The new graduate was crying softly. Sue led her to the far side of the room and spoke gently.

"There wasn't anything more we could do."

"But Juan didn't need to die! He just gave up!"

"What made him say he was going to die? Tell me about that."

"Juan said he had a visit this morning from a sorcerer who told him he was going to die. And then he did."

"I've heard about such things in connection with witch doctors. But that's in Africa, not America."

"Juan believed he was doomed. It was like a curse or something. He just accepted it without fighting back."

"Well, there's nothing we can do about it now. Things sometimes happen here we don't understand, but you can't let it get to you. You still have to function."

The girl sniffed and squared her shoulders. Sue watched approvingly as she took hold of herself and joined the others in cleaning the area and preparing the body. Sue walked out of the room with Dr. Fortuna.

"Sorcery, huh?" he asked. "I heard what she said, but we'll need something more concrete for a cause of death. Get permission from the family for an autopsy."

"I'll ask," Sue agreed. "What shall I tell them? Cardiac arrest?"

"That'll do until something better comes along."

Sue went to the nurses' station and picked up the phone. Somewhere a man named Luis Hernandez was in for some bad news.

The doctor unwrapped the nameplate and put it on his desk: Charles F. Fortuna, M.D. A gift from his father, it had always been given a place of prominence. This new office was beginning to look familiar: the jade paperweight was in place, the diplomas hung discreetly on the wall behind him, everything just like the old office back in Springfield, Massachusetts. Everything except Margie's picture. That was left behind, along with Margie herself and all the memories of their painful marriage.

For years, her picture with her sleek blonde hair and dazzling white teeth had sat in front of him. His new office seemed bare without her overseeing eye. He shrugged and turned his thoughts to the present situation. At the perfect moment, just as Margie had won her divorce and he felt he could not endure Springfield for one more day, Brookshire had offered the ideal position of respect with a princely salary, a reason to leave town without appearing to be in retreat and a totally new environment to take his mind off the past.

He stood with hands on his hips, looking around the room. A smallish office, but well-furnished and suitable for his needs. Brookshire was not a new hospital but it had been built with a grand disregard for costs, and the thirty years of its existence had done little to dim the luster of its lofty ceilings and marbled floors. Swarms of decorators descended periodically, armed with paint samples, swatches of material and big budgets, vainly attempting to alter the atmosphere of Brookshire Memorial Hospital. But Brookshire had been designed and built by men who considered it a temple of healing and in many ways it did resemble a cathedral. It was large, stately, uncomfortable and, in a strange way, very hallowed.

Charlie nodded in satisfaction. He was a confident-appearing man, stocky, of medium height. His dark skin, eyes and hair spoke of his Italian heritage, as did the pattern baldness just discernible at his temples. At 38 he was attractive and virile. Margie had often told him that he looked more like a truck driver than a doctor, and only gradually had he realized how insultingly she had meant it. Now he knew that his M.D. degree was the only thing about him Margie had really respected.

Settling into his office had been simple. By the time he started his official duties as a staff doctor for Brookshire's new government-funded research program, he would be ready. But getting his personal things unpacked in his new home was less appealing. A mobile home, for crying out loud! A trailer! He, who owned a riverside condominium in Springfield, would be living in a trailer! But it was convenient, on the hospital grounds actually, and he would make do with it for a while.

Effie MacAllister returned to the nurses' station from the last round of her patients and stood leaning on the counter.

She shifted her rather considerable weight from one foot to the other, easing temporarily the discomfort in her legs and feet. Effie suffered the cramping, swelling and pain that are the result of varicose veins. In every other way, she was perfectly suited for the role of licensed practical nurse.

It had been a bad day, and she was glad it was almost quitting time. Not just a busy day, but a bad one because they had lost a young patient. This unexpected, unexplainable death had put the whole floor under a gray and oppressive weight.

A thin, dark, very agitated young man approached Effie. "I'm Luis Hernandez," he said in a barely accented voice. "I was called about my brother."

The young patient who had died, Effie knew, and her heart reached out in compassion to this grieving, bewildered young man. "Yes, I know. I'll call Miss Dunn. She's the supervisor."

Thank God, Sue Dunn was on duty today, she thought. Sue had some kindness left in spite of her years in the hospital. Her dealings with the young man would come from her own spirit and her own personality, not based on techniques taught in some course called "Dealing with the Needs of the Grief-stricken." Sue was a tough, no-nonsense nurse, but she was *real.*

Sue took the young man into an empty treatment room to steer him through the maze of red tape that accompanied death in a hospital. Effie completed her charts, waved goodbye to the on-duty nurse in the office. Now for the thirty-minute drive to the little town of Sandy Ford where all the MacAllisters lived.

Effie was a widow. She had five grown sons, plus eleven grandsons, all of whom lived near her. Beyond that ranged an almost unlimited number of nieces and nephews, cousins, in-laws and old friends, all of whom were enormously important to her. This large, happy, confusing family comprised most of her life and most of her conversation.

She smiled as she left the hospital, the happy thoughts of

an evening with members of her family, driving away the depression and fatigue of the day.

Josh Kingston stood in the doorway of his bedroom and stared with near affection at the sparse furnishings of his living room: a 30-year-old heavily stuffed red couch, one comfortable armchair, an ancient mahogany desk, assorted tables, lamps and an Oriental rug, severely worn in three spots.

Rudimentary, he thought. *Someday I'll upgrade these.* He could certainly afford a new sofa and several more comfortable chairs, plus a new chest of drawers for his bedroom. Proceeds from his new book were accumulating so fast in the bank it was almost embarrassing.

Then a feeling of heaviness settled over him. He had to put things out of his mind. Probably forever. Josh stared at his battered brown suitcase standing by the front door, packed and ready for a trip that could take months—or whatever.

He walked over to his desk and reluctantly picked up the three-page letter from Brookshire Memorial Hospital. It had arrived registered mail six weeks before and since he was almost never in his apartment when mail was delivered, it was necessary to make a special trip in the rain to the post office to sign for it.

That inconvenience was only the beginning. From the first time he picked it up, the letter had seemed charged. Fateful, somehow. It was signed by the head of the hospital—a man named Don Oliver Franklin—who invited Josh to participate in some psychic experiments to be conducted at the hospital. Josh's doctoral dissertation on the occult and his new book on healing from demonic possession had come to Mr. Franklin's attention.

Ridiculous! was Josh's first thought. *I don't want to be mixed up in anything like that!*

He had tossed the letter aside, wondering if he should

even grace it with a written refusal. Then began a period of inner disquiet that was to last for ten days. After this period of anguish, Josh had finally concluded he had to accept.

Now he stared long and hard at the face of the letter. Across the top he had written four words in large letters: *Bind the strong man.* Almost angrily he thrust the letter into the inside pocket of his coat. Then he picked up his bag, placed a light topcoat over his arm and walked out of his apartment. Josh couldn't escape a nagging sense that, for some reason he couldn't fathom, he was going to his death at Brookshire Hospital.

"Sue! Wait up!" Isabel Nebo waved an expensively manicured hand at Sue Dunn. "I'll walk to the trailer park with you."

Sue smiled politely and wondered again why Isabel was drawn to her. They were totally unlike: Isabel was a doctor, a psychiatric resident; she also had undetermined wealth, was passionately devoted to feminist causes and possessed of a driving ambition that dominated her totally. Sue was none of these and possibly it was that very difference that attracted Isabel.

"Quite a day, I hear. Lost your code patient, right?" Isabel asked.

"And he should have lived! I hate to lose the young ones."

"You hate to lose anybody. You can't be so subjective, Sue. You mustn't get emotionally involved."

"Don't tell me that, Isabel. I seem to have the opposite problem. It seems like I get harder and harder and less caring every day. Like the milk of human kindness in me is drying up."

"Don't be silly."

"No, really. When I was talking to the dead man's brother, the poor guy was wiped out, totally at a loss to handle this situation. All I could think of was how tired I was and how quickly I wanted to get it over with. Isn't that awful?"

"Not particularly," Isabel said calmly. "You have needs, too."

"I wish I could be gentle and loving like Effie MacAllister. When we don't care at all, we must come across as monsters. If I were in a hospital alone and scared, I'd want people to care."

They were walking slowly along the path that wound through the woods toward their mobile homes. The sinking sun highlighted the rich autumn colors. Sue glanced a bit enviously at her friend.

Isabel Nebo was 41 and looked 30. She was tall, slender and attractive in a tailored, aloof kind of way. She gave considerable attention to her image, dressing with care, spending large sums on her hair which was carefully tinted in shades which ranged from white through beige to brown. She wore sunglasses indoors and out and owned many different pairs. Sue felt tacky in her tired white uniform pantsuit and her old lab coat.

"We're getting new neighbors. Lots of them." Isabel changed the subject abruptly. Isabel always seemed to know everything that happened at Brookshire. It was a point of pride with her to be informed. "The three trailers in the row next to you will house some of the people coming in for the research project. One, I know, is a doctor, and one is a clergyman."

"Why is a preacher involved with a medical project?" asked Sue.

"Because his books are psychological, I guess."

"I met the doctor today. Dr. Fortuna. Seems nice enough. Has a way with women, I hear."

Isabel shuddered delicately. "One of those," she said with distaste. "Well, the preacher has a reputation too— he's a famous author. Maybe we'll be getting a little class around the place."

"About time," Sue chuckled. "By the way, what are you wearing to the press conference tomorrow?"

"It's a press *party*, Sue. When there are drinks and food and a lot of people to mingle with the reporters, it's a party." Isabel spoke with just a touch of superiority, and as usual, Sue ignored it.

"I'm wearing my flowing white wool; it's a bit decollete but still stately," Isabel continued. "Perfect if they take pictures."

"You're going to prove that a career woman can still be one very sexy lady, right?"

"I'm going to try, anyhow," Isabel laughed.

They came to the end of the path where a rustic sign proclaimed *Brookshire Mobile Home Compound*. This was the official name given the small encampment of mobile homes, but it was known throughout the hospital complex as the trailer park.

A pleasant place to live, Sue thought. Its proximity to the hospital made walking to work easy, and since one's neighbors were all hospital employees there was an easy sociability among the residents. A clubhouse nearby had a snack bar, game room, pool and a large recreation room that had been the site of many parties. And the park was lovely, nestled in the woods, removed by trees if not by distance from the turbulence of Brookshire.

As she closed the door of her trailer behind her, Sue realized suddenly what she was feeling and it surprised her. She was feeling *safe.* How very strange! Why should she feel safe inside? Did that mean she was *not* safe outside?

"Thanks for coming so promptly, Mal." Don Oliver Franklin sat enthroned behind his pristine-clean, virtually untouched desk. Only an ebony telephone, an unmarked desk calendar and a small, sterling silver bud vase containing three perfect roses marred its hand rubbed fruitwood surface. To Malcolm Rodney Brown, local pastor and hospital chaplain, the lack of paraphernalia on Franklin's desk always seemed symbolic of a life without problems. No half-done tasks, no reminders of future obligations touched Franklin; only a broad expanse of expensive, uncluttered perfection lay before him.

"Always glad to oblige you, Don Oliver," Malcolm answered. The double name was a vestige of Franklin's southern heritage; only recently had the pastor realized that the names had achieved the status of a title. Like a Mafia chieftain, Franklin had somehow become a Don. No one knew his age. Brown guessed he was about 55.

Franklin drew a long, thick and very black cigar from an inside pocket and rubbed it slowly between his large pale hands. Brown hated cigar smoke, but he knew that Franklin could hardly talk without one. It was used as a prop: he flashed and gestured with it to punctuate his conversation; he stared at its drifting smoke to emphasize his pauses; and the huge cigar, clasped in his fleshy hand, was as familiar a part of his image as the genial smile, the expensively tailored black suits and the diamond Masonic ring.

He spoke. "I've received a letter of acceptance from the man I've chosen to head up the religious section of the Project. I think you'll be impressed with my choice. He's Dr. Joshua Kingston, the author. How about that?" Franklin was smiling, expecting approbation from his friend.

The chaplain felt his stomach knot. Josh Kingston was one of those fanatical Christians he'd always tried to avoid. He fought to keep his countenance expressionless. One of Malcolm Brown's skills was his ability to mask his true feelings. It had evidently enabled him to survive many a storm as a pastor in a city church, then as an administrator in the denomination's headquarters in New York City. When the offer came to serve as chaplain at Brookshire Hospital, to everyone's surprise, Brown promptly accepted although it meant less pay and status.

Malcolm was a small, rotund, balding man in his late 50s, with ruddy cheeks and a genial smile. His plump little wife,

Fern, matched him exactly. They were like twin bookends; and seemingly had enjoyed a tranquil marriage of many years.

"I've heard of Kingston, of course. Everybody has by now. Someone even gave me a copy of his book, but I never found time to read it." He paused, seeking from Franklin's face some clue as to how he should proceed. "You're familiar with his work?"

"Yes, I did read his book." Franklin opened a drawer of the fruitwood desk and withdrew a slim, hardbacked volume. "It's fascinating. He documents twelve case histories of hospitalized psychotics labeled hopeless. They were all healed, Mal. Know what his method was? He claims he cast devils out of them! Now I ask you, doesn't a man like that promise exciting things for us in this Project?"

Brown nodded perfunctorily. When Don Oliver returned the book to his desk drawer, the chaplain let his eyes move around Franklin's office, the most lavish and prestigious in the hospital. The dark paneled walls were covered with degrees, awards, citations, publicity releases and photographs of Franklin with famous people. There were mementos of Franklin's years on the more respectable fringes of politics as undersecretary of Health, Education and Welfare, and more recently his expanding roles as philanthropist, statesman, humanitarian and guiding light behind Brookshire.

Only one thing was missing in this pictorial history of the rise of Don Oliver Franklin: there was no picture or memento of Franklin's wife, dead the past ten years and seldom mentioned by him. How foreign it seemed, to be discussing Kingston's bizarre ideas in such surroundings.

"You realize he's opposed to what we're doing here." Brown gestured toward the entire medical center complex that housed the Brookshire Foundation, the university and its medical school, four hospital and eight research buildings. "He pretty much says we don't need all this."

"He does march to a different drummer, I'll grant you

that." Franklin smiled benignly and drew on his cigar. Don Oliver Franklin could be indifferent to opposition, entrenched as he was in the power structure of Brookshire. As Chairman of the Board of Trustees, he sat at the very heart of everything. Mal Brown was sure nothing could ever give Franklin the pounding pulse and knotted stomach which he himself often experienced.

"Is this why you called for me, Don Oliver, just to tell me you'd selected Josh Kingston to head up the spiritual aspect of your research project?"

"No, actually, I called you here to ask a favor. Kingston won't be arriving for a day or so, so he won't be here for the press party tomorrow night. Will you fill in for him, represent the religious side of the project for us?

"I'll be happy to."

"And there's another little favor you can do," Franklin continued. "When Kingston arrives, will you help him get acquainted, introduce him around the hospital, show him the town?"

Brown peered intently at Franklin. The smooth, distinguished face across the desk smiled placidly. Surely he was joking! Don Oliver couldn't seriously expect him to join forces with the likes of Joshua Kingston!

"Well, anything I can do to help," Brown murmured.

"That's fine, Mal." Franklin smiled in satisfaction. "I think we'll all have an exciting time here at Brookshire in the weeks ahead."

As he bid his employer farewell, Chaplain Brown's round face was relaxed and genial. Inside, his stomach churned and his thoughts were awhirl.

Sue Dunn watched from the window of her trailer as Charles Fortuna wrestled three large leather suitcases up the steps to the front door of the mobile home opposite her own. Despite the fact that she considered him a bit unprofessional with nurses, she was glad to see him moving in. She lived in the final row of trailers, and several near neighbors had recently moved out. After the strange death on Six North this morning, she felt lonely. The heavy forest which lay between her and the rest of the medical center complex seemed oppressive.

As the new doctor opened the door and went inside, she considered a moment, then walked across the yard to his trailer. The compound was lovely at twilight. In the last rays of fading sunlight, the huge trees, dwarfed the puny mobile homes, overshadowing and covering them in an ancient, woody embrace. There were neat plots of flowers, full now of the waning autumn gold of mums and marigolds.

"Hi, neighbor," she called through the screen. "Anything I can do to help?"

The door was opened and Sue stepped inside. Fortuna's expensive luggage was piled in the center of the living room.

"I had to carry this stuff all the way from the parking lot." He was breathing hard.

"You should use one of those grocery carts they keep in the clubhouse. Perhaps some day they'll cut a road through the woods so we can drive in." She paused a moment. "I hear you'll be working with the research project."

"So they tell me. But getting details about it is like trying to grab a puff of smoke." He paused and looked at Sue uncertainly, as though doubting his wisdom in revealing his uncertainty to this stranger. "Perhaps we'll get some information tomorrow night at the press conference."

Sue smiled. It amused her that Dr. Fortuna also didn't know the difference between a press conference and a press party.

The doctor's countenance suddenly changed and he smiled warmly, his brown eyes studying Sue as he moved closer to her. "Say, how about a drink? I have a bottle of rum. Maybe we could party a little while I unpack."

She stepped back instinctively, shaking her head. "Thanks, but I can't stay. If I can help, like with a cup of

24

coffee, or the use of my phone, let me know." She wiped a finger across the surface of the end table leaving a trail of dust. "Or some cleaning supplies."

The doctor laughed. "I'm not very domestic," he admitted. "I never notice that kind of thing."

"See you tomorrow," Sue said and walked back to her own trailer in the deepening twilight.

There is an ebb and flow to hospital life, a living pulse. Like the country squire walking the borders of his land, Don Oliver Franklin enjoyed strolling down the halls of Brookshire Memorial Hospital, feeling that pulse. Since he had a comfortable apartment in the main hospital complex, he was a familiar figure to all, friendly and pleasant, but disconcerting to most because of his sudden, unexpected appearances and disappearances.

He enjoyed making his rounds at night with fewer staff members about, patients sleeping, doctors and visitors gone. Then the lights were dimmed and the novels, forbidden playing cards and radios came forth; nurses talked, smoked, dozed, rousing every two hours to make the compulsory rounds and chart the routine findings.

At 5:00 a.m. the pace quickened. Personnel roused patients to prepare them for X-ray or surgery. Kitchen workers arrived, huge stoves were lit and the enormous procedure of preparing breakfast for 1500 people began. Phlebotomists and laboratory technicians began their rounds, drawing blood, marking notations with orange grease pens on their glass tubes full of the precious substance of life.

At 7:00 the day shift arrived, a large, white-clad army taking the field. Nursing Service, the largest of the hospital's many departments, took control and began the frenzied, often chaotic routine of the day shift.

At 8:00 they were joined by the business office staff. The

Admissions Office opened, busily pre-processing those unfortunates already committed to a hospital stay.

At 8:30 the doctors began arriving, making hospital rounds before office hours. They clustered around the various nurses' stations, each assured of his own importance, of his own rights and privileges.

"I ordered a glucose tolerance on Mrs. Jones, so how come she's eating a regular breakfast?"

"503 had a brain scan four days ago. Where the hell's the report?"

"I need Miss Booth in the treatment room right away. I'm going to lance that abcess. Be sure you get a consent signed."

At 3:00 p.m. the shift changed again and the evening crew took control. The flavor again was slightly different. Supper was served. Then the flood of visitors came, laughing, bringing gifts, consoling the patients but filled with secret gratitude for their own freedom to walk out, body and dignity preserved.

And finally, night again. The surviving patients carefully sedated, sleeping the drugged, artificial slumber that overrode the strangeness of the environment, the discomfort of the narrow beds, the loneliness. The quiet, the lack of activity, lent a semblance of peace to this building, but underneath was turbulent, raw emotion.

The halls were haunted by the residue of recent activities; the fear, pain, anger, lust, nudity and death that had run rampant through the hospital throughout the day still lingered in the quiet of the night, ready to strike out in an unguarded moment. Only the traditional compliance of the patients, their drugged submission and their unquestioning faith and trust in this system to heal, kept the emotions under control.

Sue Dunn had lived alone since graduating from college nearly twelve years before. By now, her routines were set and predictable—the morning rituals, especially. For years she had awakened early, taken a brisk run, then a quick shower. After a breakfast of one egg, one piece of whole wheat toast, juice and tea, she usually spent a few moments with a book of short readings that gave her an inspirational thought for the day.

Sue awakened early and looked out on the crisp autumn scene with interest. There was no sign of life in the trailer opposite hers. This didn't surprise her. Dr. Charles Fortuna had all the earmarks of a late riser.

Had he really started coming on to her last night? Was the invitation for a drink really more than just a casual gesture of hospitality? In a way, she regretted her hasty flight, her fear of the possible consequences had she stayed on. Now she would never know what the young doctor's intentions had been. She wasn't the least offended by the idea that he might have considered seduction. Actually, the idea was rather flattering. Here of late she'd been more and more aware of the passing years, of a vague dissatisfaction with her job, her life.

Sue had never been a part of the underworld life of Brookshire, with its sexual intrigues, affairs, seductions and betrayals. She really wasn't interested. But if she were not to be involved, she'd rather have it because she chose not to be, rather than because no one wanted her.

She returned to her bedroom and exchanged her pajamas for the gray sweatpants and tattered jacket that were her running outfit. The routine morning run always boosted both her metabolism and spirits.

Sue had a tolerant affection for her body; it functioned well. She still longed, occasionally, for a more attractive model though she had adjusted fairly well to her appearance as she had to her single state in life. Nevertheless there was a deep ache within her for love and tenderness. It seldom rippled the surface of her peace; she accepted solitude. When she was with beautiful women, she felt a gentle regret that such was not her lot, but mostly she accepted things as they were. She was just good old Sue Dunn, a good nurse, a good sport, always a buddy to the men in her life, seldom a serious interest in theirs.

She stared for a moment at the reflection of herself in the mirror over the dresser. Freckled face, attractive warm eyes, small breasts and a too-thin body. Streaks of gray in her unruly hair did nothing to add to her appeal. At 32 she was acquiring that indefinable stamp of spinsterhood. By an act of will, she set aside her regrets. Nothing negative could long survive in the cheerful good humor that was Sue's greatest charm.

She shrugged her thin shoulders and grinned at herself in the mirror. "That's the breaks, kid," she said aloud. She hung her pajamas neatly on a hook and left the trailer for her morning run.

The night nurse was fighting off the bone-deep ache of sleepiness as she rattled off a summary of each patient's condition and activity for the past eight hours. Her indifference was so monumental that Effie MacAllister found it difficult to follow her facts.

"Room 621, cholecystectomy, eighth post-op day. She's fine, no complaints. Possible discharge today.

"622, vag hyst, first post-op day. She's been bellyaching all night, her I.V. hurts, her throat hurts, her bottom hurts . . . you know the type. She was medicated for pain at midnight and four and she's been on the intercom for the past hour wanting more. We gave her some Visteril to hold her but it didn't help. Oh yeah. Her Foley's draining all right but her urine's bloody."

This was Mrs. Dale, Effie remembered. A dependent, fearful woman not used to discomfort, let alone real pain.

The night nurse moved on down her Kardex file of patients. Her knowledge of them was only fair; she evidently shared the idea held by some night nurses that because the hours they worked were so difficult, less was required of them in the way of concern or effort. Effie felt sorry for her.

The woman was a divorcee with three small children who never had enough money, rest or emotional satisfaction.

"630-B. Empty. That lady died on three-to-eleven."

"What?" Effie sat up in astonishment. "That was Mrs. Carroll, 24 years old, right? Tonsillectomy?"

"Right. She sprang a bleeder and died about supper time." The night nurse flipped another page of the Kardex. She showed no interest in discussing the death but Effie refused to be sidetracked.

"What happened? How could she just bleed to death? Did they take her back to surgery or try to tie off the bleeder here? For heaven's sake, what did they do?"

The night nurse looked resigned. "Look, I really don't know. I wasn't on duty. I think they called the resident and he tried to do something but the headlight wouldn't work and he couldn't see what he was doing. And she was already shocky when they found her."

Effie was stunned at a second senseless, unexpected death of a young, basically healthy person.

When the night nurse finished her report, Effie turned her attention to staff members now milling about the smoke-filled lounge. She could see the effects of this death mirrored on each face. It wasn't just the fact that a patient had died. They handled death every day and were unaffected by it. This was different; it was a death that shouldn't have happened, a senseless, unnecessary death.

What they couldn't handle, Effie realized with a sudden clarity, was the fact that the system had broken down. It was all right to lose the old ones, the really bad ones, the ones with cancer or massive trauma or some serious defect. But it was an affront to lose a young, healthy patient who had every reason to expect a simple, uncomplicated, rapid recovery.

The whole massive, complicated, authoritative, expensive, entrenched system had not helped. A young woman who should be alive was now dead simply because she had trusted herself to the system and the system had failed.

This was the truth they found so hard to handle.

A wit from the public relations department had once commented that it was a shame Brookshire was not as successful at healing its patients as it was at conning the public. Like all large teaching hospitals, Brookshire was less than ideally efficient, but its reputation was excellent. Like Johns Hopkins, Mayo and Walter Reed, Brookshire enjoyed enormous prestige as an institution of healing. Much of this high regard was due to the efficiency of the public relations department.

Don Oliver Franklin strode through the doors of this little-understood but most powerful department just before nine o'clock in the morning and boomed out a question. "Everything set for the press party tonight, Givens?"

"Ready to roll. You'll be pleased with the turnout, Don Oliver." The clean-cut, cliche-ridden young man who headed the department was always effusive. "Almost all your people will be there with bells on, and the press is planning to do right by us on this thing. I have your statement printed for distribution and the food and drink will make you proud of us."

"Fine," Franklin nodded. "But I'm mainly concerned that this Project be launched with suitable fanfare."

"You'll have it in spades, sir," the young man replied earnestly.

"Very well. I'll see you tonight."

The Reverend Malcolm Rodney Brown closed the study door, flipped the television switch and sat in silence as the screen warmed to life. He seldom watched morning shows, but like the mongoose with the snake, he was fascinated by what he suspected might be a dangerous form of life. Joshua Kingston was an early morning talk show guest, and Brown was irresistibly drawn to watch.

In contrast to the wholesome attractiveness of the television host, Kingston appeared somber. He was taller than average, very thin and dark, with a narrow face and piercing dark eyes. He had an unruly shock of black hair that seemed in constant disarray. His expression and his voice were intense and he made what Brown considered shocking statements, but to Malcolm's astonishment, this trait seemed to captivate the press. He was constantly interviewed and quoted by the media, helping to make his book a bestseller.

"Where did you get the idea for this book?" the host asked, displaying for the camera a copy of Kingston's *The Children and the Powers*.

"These were real life healings. I thought people ought to know about them." The author's dark eyes peered so directly into the camera that Brown found himself drawing back from their intensity.

"And these young people in your book were all confirmed psychotics, right?"

Joshua Kingston nodded firmly. The straight dark hair fell across his brow and he brushed it back impatiently. "I think most mental illness is caused by demonic harrassment."

"So you're what's called a demonologist?"

"I'm just a Christian using the power given to us," Kingston replied.

The talk show host turned to the camera and spoke to his audience. "This book, titled *The Children and the Powers*, written by our guest, Dr. Joshua Kingston, is a surprising bestseller. People everywhere are taking sides in the controversy it has sparked, especially in the medical, psychiatric and religious fields. I understand the author originally aimed this book at a rather narrow market, at Christian parents who had children suffering from psychiatric disorders, but to the surprise of his publisher it caught on in the secular market. The author has treated twelve teenage psychiatric patients and in every case there was a total reversal of symptoms, with each patient returning to a healthy, normal life. And his method is one which might be called— well, unorthodox."

The author spoke again into the camera. "I believe that a lot of the evil that's happening in this world is not accidental or coincidental. I believe there's an intelligence behind it all. I think there are evil forces—a whole organization of them—moving among mankind. Their purpose is to kill, rob and destroy. I also believe there is a whole arsenal of weapons which we can use to disarm and control this evil. If we use these weapons properly, we can have victory over disease, oppression, despair, fear, bondage and affliction. I also believe there's a good power working among men and it has a name. That name is Jesus."

After a rather awkward silence the host asked, "So you performed an exorcism?"

"I have what is called a ministry of deliverance."

"I know a lot of Christians, Josh, but you're the only one I've heard who talks so openly about evil spirits."

"There are many thousands of Christians who not only believe as I do but are operating in the same power I do. It's just that I seem to be one of the very few today who's listened to by non-Christians."

"Can you tell us how you treated these young people?"

"A doctor treats, a pastor ministers. What I did was take authority over the demons who were oppressing them and commanded them to leave. They left."

"There's got to be more to it than that." The host's interest was genuine.

"Yes, there are other factors. These young people needed to commit themselves to the Lord, straighten out relationships with their parents, and learn how to keep the demons from coming back."

As Malcolm sat and listened, his insides twisted again. Did this strange, dark, intense man, Joshua Kingston, have any idea how foolish he must look to the millions of people watching him? Casting out demons! It sounded like the dark ages. And this was the man Don Oliver Franklin was bringing into Brookshire to be a part of his new research project!

32

The press party was held in the doctors' dining room. On hand were representatives from local papers, two news services, plus a stringer for a big-name news magazine. Local television stations had also sent reporters. Two long, linen-draped tables held an offering of exotic and delectable food. Nearby, a bar did a brisk business. The room's lighting was subdued and genteel; as Isabel summed it up, the whole affair had class.

Don Oliver Franklin tapped a glass politely and waited as the room quieted. He looked handsome in a well-cut black suit, the soft lighting gracious to his gray hair and his benign smiling face.

"Be seated, please," he directed. "I'd like to make a few remarks after which you may ask questions and mingle with our staff members." Franklin stood behind a small table and spoke without notes; though he was delivering a prepared speech, it seemed spontaneous.

"In 1868, at the ancestral home of Lord Ashley, outside of London, England, a gentleman named D.D. Home floated out of a third-story window and back in through another. The reality of this event was affirmed by a number of well-educated, socially prominent people. This was one of the first documented, witnessed incidents of psychokinetic phenomena."

He paused and looked around the silent room. "What was it? Trickery? Delusion? A genuine happening that contradicted the known laws of physics and violated the scientific theories regarding space and time and the properties of matter?"

He was effective, Isabel thought. He had captured their total attention as he stood erect behind his table, arms outstretched, the long black cigar clasped in one large hand and the cold blue fire from his diamond Masonic ring winking on the other.

"That's what we intend to find out! Ladies and gentlemen, the Project we unveil tonight will involve an intensive, multi-disciplinary scientific investigation into the causes and effects of parapsychological phenomena by means of controlled, methodical testing. The results will be calculated and evaluated according to standard statistical formulae. In short, we're going to take this weird stuff apart, study it and find out how it can help.

"Just what am I talking about? Just what is this realm of the paranormal, the psychic, the occult? Is it superstitious mumbo-jumbo or a new frontier of science, an odyssey into unexplored regions of power and knowledge that we can bring into our own experiences?

"In general there are two divisions: the physical, which is called psychokinesis, and the cognitive, which includes telepathy, clairvoyance and precognition. And these two aspects of paranormal phenomena, when truly understood, will prove to us that there are truths about the nature of reality that we have understood only dimly until now.

"The marriage of science and the psychic goes back a long way. In the dark and disreputable history of science, there was many a merging of the occult with the clarity of reason. Johannes Kepler, the astronomer, supported himself by casting horoscopes. Actually science first began with the systemization of knowledge by Babylonian astronomer-priests and they were also involved in the dim and hidden side of life.

"At least half of the forefathers of modern science were sorcerer-magicians. The ancient Greeks brought the myths of metaphysics into the clear light of reason, as did the huddled alchemists who murmured enchantments as they categorized the properties of metals. As da Vinci and Vesalius opened doors that led into realms previously shrouded in secrecy, so we now open the door into the realm of the paranormal."

Franklin paused and took a puff from his cigar. His listeners were hushed, attentive, somewhat numbed.

"The word science comes from a root which means *to know*. And no realm is safe from her unquenchable curiosity. But why? Why bring in men and women from every field of scientific study? We have here at Brookshire, biophysicists, physicians, psychologists, statisticians, psychiatrists, sociologists . . . the tops in their fields from every discipline. Why? To what purpose do we explore this controversial subject?

"Well, we want to form a theory. A lot of people believe in 'psi' factors; from respected doctors of psychology who research extrasensory perception right down to the gambler who is sure he can control the toss of the dice by 'willing' them to fall in a certain way.

"Many people are convinced there is something here, something beyond our ability to understand. They might believe it's the result of a collective unconscious, a common source of knowledge that the paranormal mind can tap. Or they might ascribe to the physical theory that there is some form of energy we haven't yet discovered that accounts for the phenomena. Or could it be an extra-added power that some minds have and others don't, which ranges beyond the normal? We don't know, but we must learn.

"And here is why we must learn.

"Time is running out for us all, ladies and gentlemen. And so are our resources. In the physical realm, our days are numbered. Clean water, pure air and fertile productive land are diminishing rapidly. Even worse are the social problems: overpopulation, aging, disease, world hunger, diminishing energy sources. I deal daily with men and women at the top in government, business, medicine, education and religion, and believe me, they realize as I do that there seem to be no answers at all to these problems.

"So in this realm of the paranormal—the extrasensory, the gifted ones with additional powers and skills—in here lies our hope. If we can develop and control the talents they've been given and use these gifts for the good of mankind, then there may be hope for our race. We may not have to file off the stage like the ancient dinosaur, our hour spent and our chapter ended.

"These special ones may have our answers. They may be our saviors."

Franklin paused again and picked up a sheet of paper

from the table in front of him. His audience was mesmerized.

"I believe in our poor, benighted world. Oh, we may bite and snarl and rise up in anger against our brother, but we also build schools and hospitals and churches. We enter an arms race with our brother, but we share our scientific and technical knowledge with him, and if he needs help, we're there to share the burden.

"I believe that if man is to save himself from the disasters that loom even now in the shadows, we need these special gifted ones among us.

"Within the next few weeks, we will be bringing to Brookshire three young men and a set of twin girls. Among them they represent the full range of paranormal talents. They will be tested and analyzed in every possible way and through them we will find answers.

"And that is our Project, ladies and gentlemen. A lofty, glorious, hopeful Project, one I'm proud to be a part of. We are calling it, very simply, Project Truth."

Franklin stood in silence, gazing around the room with an expression of pride, and there followed a generous burst of applause.

Isabel settled back in her chair as the soothing voice ceased. *What a crock!* she thought in some amusement. *Hope for mankind indeed!* What was happening here was much simpler, if the truth were known: it was a matter of money. A matter of hundreds of thousands of dollars of government funds looking for an outlet. She was convinced Franklin had dreamed up this Project to qualify as a recipient. But if he wanted to camouflage his motives for the public that was his privilege.

The reporters had a few questions that Franklin fielded easily, then they broke ranks for another trip to the bar and a good deal of note-taking as they interviewed the various staff members.

As the reporters questioned her, Isabel Nebo found herself echoing the high-flown phrases and altruistic sentiments Franklin had spouted. This amused her, too. Maybe this kind of concern-for-mankind talk was to be part of the Project. If so, she could talk it as well as the next guy.

As Joshua Kingston drove into the Brookshire Memorial Medical Center complex, he looked about him. The view was lovely. The winding red brick streets curved softly around the gentle hills, blending beautifully with the red brick buildings. The setting was wooded and rustic, rural, yet only a half-hour's drive from the center of the metropolis.

He passed several large buildings and read their names aloud. *Jocelyn B. Cannon Memorial Psychiatric Hospital, Dedicated to Troubled Youth.* A block further on, he passed the children's hospital, then the main nurses' residence that had the flavor of an old Southern mansion. At last he reached his destination, the largest of the buildings, a big H-shaped red brick structure, eight stories high. He read Brookshire Memorial Hospital and below the name, *A Helping Hand Extended.*

Josh parked his car, trotted up the stone steps to the hospital entrance, crossed the vaulted marble lobby, received directions from the information desk and found his way to the office of Don Oliver Franklin. He entered Franklin's office the way he did everything: aggressively, confidently.

Franklin and Kingston faced each other. They were totally different. Franklin was regal, impeccably dressed, blending to perfection with the lavish room and expensive decor. His manner was gracious and charming, the epitome of breeding and culture. Kingston was tall, raw-boned, dressed in inexpensive clothing, indifferent to the impression he made. His thick black hair was unruly, badly in need of a trim, and seemed to reflect the electricity of his personality.

His expression was intense, serious; he seldom smiled. His eyes were direct, brooding.

Franklin greeted Josh with warmth. "Dr. Kingston. How good it is to meet you. I'd like to introduce you to Dr. Malcolm Brown, hospital chaplain and a dear personal friend of mine. He'll be helping with the Project."

Josh worked his way through the formalities of greetings then sat down in an armchair across the large fruitwood desk from Franklin, his legs crossed awkwardly, showing an expanse of tooled leather boot. Malcolm Brown sat in the companion chair.

"I have read and reread your book," Franklin began. "Fascinating."

"Yes, and also true."

"You're a very eloquent spokesman for your sector of Christianity," Franklin pursued. "You've sent its message into areas where no one else with your beliefs dared to tread."

"The book did better than anyone thought," Josh acknowledged. "I hope people are ready for its truth. The Lord has much to tell us if we'll only listen."

"I agree." Franklin still smiled. He seemed to delight in remaining smiling in the face of Josh's stern intensity. "Now Mal and I want to welcome you to Brookshire. Our little Project will be getting underway soon and we're delighted to have you heading up the religious team. You'll be responsible for input regarding the spiritual significance of psychic phenomena."

"I don't understand what you mean by a team. How many others are involved?"

"With Mal's help I've already made the selections." Franklin gestured toward Brown with a graceful hand. "There's a Jesuit priest from one of the local parishes. He's quite active in politics. We also have an Orthodox rabbi, a Moslem and a man who represents transcendental meditation. All very qualified, well-educated."

"I'm sure they're learned men. Do you really believe we could agree on anything?"

Malcolm sat up straight, his ruddy face struggling for control. "What are you implying?"

But Franklin spoke quickly, smoothly averting a confrontation. "I think there's strength in differences; we welcome the balance of many opinions. Surely you aren't saying that we don't need other viewpoints?"

"Sometimes it's better to have one solid, strong viewpoint than six scattered ones," Josh said bluntly.

"Well, I admire confidence, and I admire a man who has the courage of his convictions, but I wouldn't discount the input you may receive from your peers," Franklin said.

Josh frowned, opened his mouth to say something, then closed it tight.

"You're a young man, Dr. Kingston," Don Oliver continued. "You will learn the importance of compromise. In fact, we may have quite a few things to teach you."

Josh stared at Don Oliver intently. "I'm puzzled about something, Mr. Franklin. Why did you select me for this project of yours? You must have studied my credentials enough to know I'm not a compromiser."

"I did study your credentials, Dr. Kingston. You have all the qualifications. Solid training in psychology, theology, even some science courses at which you excelled. Plus a national reputation now as an author."

"Many people in medicine consider me hostile, a critic."

"That doesn't bother me," said Franklin quietly. "Differences of opinion can be the yeast that improves and flavors a scientific work."

"Then don't expect me to compromise."

The strained silence lasted only a moment before Don Oliver's calm voice continued. "May I ask why you agreed to come to Brookshire, Dr. Kingston?"

For the first time a wry grin cracked Josh Kingston's frosty visage. "A good question, Mr. Franklin. I've been asking it of myself for days now. When your invitation first arrived I started automatically to turn it down. But something stopped me."

"You knew that coming to Brookshire would help the sales of your book," Malcolm Brown offered suggestively.

"That never entered my mind," Kingston replied coldly. "What stopped me was the realization that I should pray about such a decision before making it."

"Tell us what happened, Dr. Kingston."

"Something very surprising. I prayed and waited. Nothing came, so once again I started to draft a letter of refusal. But I couldn't do it. I began arguing with the Lord, presenting my case for not accepting. There were many good reasons and I gave them all. When I had finished the Lord seemed to agree with me. Yet there came this one question from Him."

"What question?"

"Are you My disciple?"

Josh was now staring intently at Don Oliver Franklin. "The question seemed off the point to me, but of course I said yes. Then came the words 'Go to Brookshire.' So here I am."

For a long moment the two men locked eyes. Then Don Oliver chuckled. "If the Lord wants you here, Dr. Kingston, that's good enough for me. How about you, Mal?"

Malcolm Brown made a strangled noise that Don Oliver accepted as agreement. The three men arose and said polite goodbyes.

Josh returned to his car and followed the directions leading him to the Brookshire mobile home compound which would be his new residence for some time. Aloud once again he asked the question, "Lord, are You sure You want me here? I make such a hash of my relationships with people like these."

Isabel Nebo stepped off the elevator on Eight Central and

waited for the ward secretary to open the closely guarded door leading into the psychiatric unit. It was a lovely fall morning and she felt exhilarated. This small, short-term unit, accommodating a maximum of ten patients, was her own domain.

The Brookshire Medical Center had other more notable areas for this type of care. There was Jocelyn Cannon Memorial, a 150-bed privately endowed psychiatric facility whose detoxification program had an international reputation for excellence. The children's hospital had a 30-bed unit of its own for psychiatric patients. Isabel preferred her own little bailiwick. Low-key and unpretentious, it handled its small patient load exactly as she prescribed, and the sensation of being in charge was most satisfying.

"Everything quiet?" she asked at the nurses' station.

"No problems. Two transferred out early this morning so our census is down again."

"Any admissions waiting?" Despite the low profile maintained by Eight Central, there was always a waiting list for admission. Isabel found this implied compliment from her peers a great satisfaction.

"Several. We'll be full by tonight."

Isabel left the nurses' station and wandered around the patients' recreation room, observing and greeting those who were reading, watching television or just sitting quietly. There was a free period each day after breakfast when their rooms had been tidied, and the patients could do as they liked until 10:00. Then Isabel took them for therapy. The nurse's report was right. All was quiet and peaceful.

Isabel was a strong believer in drug therapy. Her patients all received heavy doses of tranquilizers and mood elevators, and several were nodding. But this was all right. Quiet and peace were maintained. All turmoil and hostility had been quenched under the steady doses of Meprobamate and Valium. Isabel was free to begin organizing her plans for Project Truth.

It was almost upon them.

Josh Kingston stood outside his assigned trailer and looked around with interest. The grounds were lovely, rustic and restful, the trees giving a feeling of privacy and distance from the crowds and activity of the hospital. In midafternoon, the whole park seemed deserted.

He unlocked the door to his trailer, opened it and was greeted by the smell of dust, stale air and marijuana. He dropped his battered suitcases on the floor and an armload of books on the couch and viewed his new home.

It was adequate, superficially clean and well-furnished. There was a front kitchen, then a fair-sized living room with a couch, two chairs and a small table under the window. One small and one larger bedroom and a bathroom completed his tour and he nodded in satisfaction. Not lavish, but at least private. He opened the windows and despite the nip in the fall air, he relished the brisk breeze that flowed through.

Even before unpacking, he took a seat at the small table, got out his pen and turned to a new sheet in his little pocket notebook.

1. Name and bind the Strong Man.

2. Stake claim to present territory.

3. Get the leaven out!!!

He looked at his little notebook for a moment. Another battle, another set of enemies to encounter. He felt a flicker of excitement, tempered by that sense of destiny.

He rose from the chair and took from his pocket a small bottle of olive oil. He unscrewed the top, tipped the bottle until several drops fell on his middle finger. Then he began at the kitchen door. " . . . I claim this trailer for the Lord Jesus Christ and I take authority over any power of darkness. . . ."

Afterward, Sue was never able to remember why she had

turned left instead of right. Brookshire was shaped like a huge H; the connecting bar formed the central floors and the twin long uprights the north and south floors. As she walked briskly from Four Central into Four South, instead of turning right toward the nurses' station, she went left where there were only patient rooms.

She was opposite 4055, one of the few private rooms on Four South, when she heard a powerful, authoritative voice issuing from within. She stopped to listen. The words were indistinguishable, but the force and cadence and power with which they were spoken interested her. She opened the door quietly.

The room was brightly lit; the curtains were open and the blinds slanted to admit a maximum of golden autumn sunshine. The patient lay back on his pillows, eyes closed, a gentle smile on his face. He was a large black man with grizzled gray hair. But Sue only glanced at him; her attention was immediately caught by the room's other occupant who stood by the bed.

He was a tall, rangy young man with pale skin and a shock of unruly jet-black hair. He was dressed in worn Levi jeans, so faded they were now a light grayish-blue, and a large sloppy red sweatshirt. He wore scuffed black boots, not farmer's boots but what Sue always thought of as cowboy boots.

But the clothing was only the frame on the picture; the thing that captivated her interest was the man himself. He stood by the bed, his head so erect it was tilted backwards, a floppy black leather book under one arm, his eyes closed.

He was praying.

Sue had attended church occasionally and, if asked, would have identified herself as a Christian. If pressed she would have stated that this meant she was not Jewish, Moslem or Hindu. She knew little of the Bible and seldom prayed. Never before had she heard such a prayer as this one.

It was bold, loud, aggressive, and she listened with fascination.

" . . . since You gave us dominion over everything that creeps and crawls, Lord, I now exercise that dominion over every disease germ and virus that's trying to attack this man's body. I ask for his healing in the name of Jesus. It is written that You, Lord Jesus, have given us authority over all power of the enemy and I claim that right now. . . ."

A muffled sound escaped from Sue and the patient opened his eyes and peeped at her. He pursed his lips and shook his head slightly to warn her to silence.

As supervisor of all the surgical floors as well as the emergency department, Sue was used to handling strange situations. But this was something new to her. She had never encountered anyone quite like this unkempt young man who spoke so powerfully and she had no idea how to deal with him.

" . . . and we consider it done. We thank You, Lord, for Your love and Your healing power . . . Thank You, Lord. . . ."

As he wound down, a steadily diminishing series of *Thank You, Lords* falling from his lips, Sue cleared her throat. The stranger opened his eyes and looked at her.

Like most Americans, Sue was used to smiles. Almost invariably it seemed, people smiled or at least softened their expression when making eye contact with another. As this young man looked at her, she drew back instinctively, because he did none of this. He did not smile; his expression remained serious and his dark, somber eyes seemed to pierce her with intensity.

"I'm Sue Dunn, area supervisor," she stammered, growing uncomfortable and a little angry under his steady gaze. "I wondered what was going on."

"I was praying," he answered simply.

"Well, that's very nice, but perhaps you'd better go now. I know Mr., uh, Mr.—" Infuriated, she realized she didn't know the patient's name.

"His name is Harry Owens," the young man supplied, expressionless.

"Yes, well, I'm sure Mr. Owens appreciates your time, but he needs to rest now."

"He needs what I have to offer a lot more than he needs rest," the young man contradicted.

"Really, I don't want to be insistent, but actually there are rules about this kind of thing. Only ordained ministers or our chaplains can, uh, are supposed to do what you are doing. And then they can only meet with members of their own congregation."

"I am an ordained minister," he said matter-of-factly. A picture rose in her mind: one of those street ministries down in the inner city, staffed by intense, unsmiling young men like this one. "I don't have a church, though," he added. "I have a specialized ministry."

"Well, in any case, I'm afraid I'll have to insist you leave now." She moved toward the bed and began straightening the covers, her actions proclaiming her authority here, her right to control events affecting this patient.

"All right," he agreed, still without smiling. He turned to the patient and now his voice did soften. He spoke with warmth and compassion. "Remember, Harry, God loves you and is healing you right now. The Word of God says so. Read Isaiah 53, I Peter 2, James 5—those are the Scripture passages I gave you." He tucked the Bible under his arm and walked out. Sue stared after him in disapproval.

"That old Josh, he's really something, ain't he?" the patient asked in delight.

He was climbing from the bed, modestly tugging at the skirt of his hospital gown. He crossed to the closet and dragged a suitcase from its shelf. He opened it on the bed and began rummaging through the drawers in the bedside table.

"What are you doing?" Sue demanded.

"I'm leaving," he replied cheerfully. "Don't need to be here."

"You don't know that," she protested. "You may still be sick." She realized with sudden chagrin that she had no idea what was wrong with him. It was a surgical floor, but he showed no evidence of having had an operation.

"I'm not sick any more," he said firmly.

"But you can't just walk out!"

"You mean I really can't, legally or something?" The man had stopped in his packing and Sue could tell he was really seeking information. And she had to tell him the truth.

"No, of course you have the legal right to go. But I mean you shouldn't—you might get worse."

"Then it's really my business, isn't it?" His voice was gentle and she shrugged her shoulders in defeat before its calm, dispassionate logic.

"I suppose so. I'll go fill out the release form. You'll have to sign that."

"No, ma'am. I don't think I'll sign anything. I'll just go." He looked around the room. Despite the sunshine and the brilliant blue sky outside the windows, the room was not cheerful. There was nothing about it comfortable or warm or welcoming. And Sue saw it suddenly through the patient's eyes. The room was cold and alien with its rails around the bed and its dingy tan walls. Like a prison. Any desire to argue with the patient and try to change his mind died within her.

"Well, I hope you get along all right," she said.

"I'll do fine," he assured her.

As he closed the bathroom door behind him, and she was alone again, Sue felt a surge of resentment and frustration. The whole situation offended her professional outlook. The patient was almost certainly doing a very foolish, risky thing by leaving. And now she faced a mountain of paperwork to tie up the ends of this little episode: calling the doctor, signing off the chart, filling out an Incident Report, writing up the whole thing for the Nursing Office, with a carbon for the malpractice carrier. Such a lot of paperwork to raise a hedge of protection around herself and Brookshire. It would almost certainly mean she would be late getting off duty.

Sudden anger rose in her against the dark, intense young man. He was to blame for this irresponsible act. *If I ever see him again, I'll— I'll—*.

The nurse sidled up to Dr. Charles Fortuna. "I appreciate your helping here. I know it's not your responsibility." She handed a chart to the doctor and smiled gratefully. Her dark eyes and smoldering expression seemed totally at variance with her white uniform and professional demeanor. "You'll need to sign the Incident Report and make an entry on the Progress Notes," she added.

Dr. Fortuna took a seat at the nurses' station and flipped through the chart, still not familiar with Brookshire's routine. Progress notes were pink here; he was used to blue. He found his place and began writing.

The secretary from Six North approached hesitantly. "The lab called. Hemoglobin is five point eight and the crit is sixteen. Looks like we found her in time."

"Yeah. Thanks." Charlie refused to encourage the well-it-could-have-been-worse attitude. Things were slipshod enough without allowing that comfort.

"You want to run through it again?" he asked the nurse. "I want to be sure I know what happened."

The female patient referred to had been posted for surgery, and because she was to have nothing by mouth all day, intravenous fluids had been started. Because the surgeon thought he might need to administer blood, the needle used had been of a large gauge. Sometime during the morning, in some mysterious way, the tubing had separated from the needle and the fluid ran out rapidly, soaking the bed. Because the patient was sedated, she hadn't been aware of this, and nobody else had noticed. The fluid wasted on the bed had caused no harm; the bed linens could be changed without trouble.

The harm had come from the fluid that had drained unheeded from the other section of the broken connection:

the patient's blood. It had dripped steadily from the needle, a needle large enough to maintain a steady flow that did not clot. It was hours later, almost 3 p.m., when the crew from surgery arrived with their stretcher to transport the patient to the operating room, and they had pulled back the soaked sheet to see pools of dark, clotted blood around the patient's now comatose body.

Vital signs indicated shock, and Charlie had been called to assess the situation. Plasma expanders were started until blood was available and the surgeon would be on the scene shortly. It was fairly certain now that the patient would survive, but Charlie knew the situation was too serious to dismiss it lightly.

"How did it happen?" he asked the nurse. She dropped into the chair next to him and ran a distraught hand through her hair. She spoke softly, drawing him to her in privacy despite the turmoil in the nurses' station.

"Look, I was really busy. I had a whole team by myself, thirty patients, with only a med nurse and one aide. I had 17 I.V.s and this one was just a 'keep vein open.' You don't usually have to watch a KVO real closely. On top of that, I had four admissions and I had to be off the floor an hour for an Inservice Education class. I just didn't catch it."

Fortuna shook his head. "No vital signs at noon? No rounds? Nobody even went in to see if the patient was still alive, for crying out loud? All you had to do was open the door; the blood was all over the bed!"

"There wasn't any reason to check her," she said defensively. "She was pre-op."

"No reason except she was here, and your responsibility."

The nurse nodded, still defensive but too prudent to say more. Her dark eyes held his, steady and knowing and old beyond her years, and his mind veered suddenly from the problems of medical ethics. Something about this girl reminded him of Margie; she was also tall and athletic, and totally self-confident. He dropped the chastening tone and smiled.

"I'll finish the Progress Notes and that'll take care of my part. You get off at three?"

"Three-fifteen. It's nearly that now."

"Like to go somewhere for a drink?"

"Sure, I could use a drink. I could use a lot of drinks. Where shall I meet you?" She assumed their date would need to be secret.

"I'll walk down with you." *The great indoor sport,* he thought, *begins with eye contact.*

Charlie watched as she walked away, obviously aware of his interest. She swayed her hips and stood a little taller, very conscious of him. From somewhere a phrase dropped into his mind—Angel of mercy. *Sure, honey,* he thought. *You're some angel.*

"Effie MacAllister! How are you? I haven't seen you in weeks!" Don Oliver Franklin clapped a friendly hand on Effie's pudgy shoulder and beamed at her. They stood in the alcove by the elevators on Six North at the end of the shift. She was leaving for home and he was making one of his frequent rounds of the hospital.

"I'm just fine, Don Oliver." Many of the old-timers at Brookshire addressed him thus, by first name. This never meant a disrespectful or a casual attitude toward the great man. It was an expression of their affection.

"How's the apple crop in Sandy Ford? I may come out there one of these days, spend an evening with you and the boys."

"We'd love to have you, Don Oliver. My youngest son butchered this fall; we're up to our ankles in beef. And my other son raised some mighty good pumpkins. I could whip up a pie."

"It would be good to get away from Brookshire for a

while," Franklin said wistfully. "Sandy Ford is always so quiet and peaceful."

The elevator had arrived and most of the departing day shift piled on but Effie stayed, too polite to walk away from Franklin who always seemed genuinely to enjoy their talks.

"Things have been pretty grim here the past few days," she said hesitantly. "We've had a couple of deaths that were upsetting, young people who shouldn't have died, and today we almost lost another one."

"Sorry to hear about these deaths," Franklin said.

"Normally it's a good floor," Effie said loyally. "We have a good crew. Some of your best nurses are on Six North, Don Oliver." She nodded her gray head firmly.

"I'm sure things will straighten out," he said cheerfully. "Get some rest and give my regards to those grandchildren."

Franklin walked away down the hall, nodding and smiling at the people he passed. Effie stepped on the elevator and sagged against the wall. She would take his advice, she decided. Give her feet a rest, and make every effort to get her mind off Brookshire.

It was almost 10 p.m. when Charles Fortuna returned to Brookshire, tired and more than a little tipsy. He was also annoyed. He'd spent sixty dollars on drinks and dinner and nearly seventy for a motel room, and while he wasn't tight with money, he regretted the expense. In no way had the nurse been worth it.

He bypassed the hospital and walked a trifle unsteadily along the path into the woods to his new trailer home. Once inside he realized there was no food in his new kitchen and he was suddenly very hungry.

Then he remembered. This trailer park had a clubhouse only a short distance away. They'd have something, if only a pack of potato chips.

The clubhouse building was larger than he'd supposed and as he opened the door, he was surprised at how attractive and cozy it was. The decor was reminiscent of a ski lodge, complete with stone fireplace in one wall, rustic, chunky furniture, waxed wood floors with bright rugs and a roomful of cheerful, friendly people. There were two pool tables, a bank of various electronic games, a large television set and several card tables and chairs. A smooth black counter with black leather bar stools ran along the right wall, and Charlie spotted Sue Dunn among the people sitting there. He crossed the room to join her, even though she was not alone.

"Hi, neighbor." He greeted her with the charm born of an afternoon of rum sours.

"Oh, Dr. Fortuna. Hello." She looked friendly and cheery, with her pale blonde hair a mass of curls around her freckled face. "This is my friend Dr. Nebo. She's major-domo on Eight Central. Isabel, this is Dr. Fortuna."

"Let's skip the 'doctor.' I'm Charlie."

"I saw you at the press party, Charlie. You seemed bored stiff. Want to join us for some coffee?"

"Is there anything to eat?"

Sue gestured toward the bank of machines behind the counter. "Soup, cheese crackers, junk food. I'll get you something if you're desperate."

"I am. Get me anything."

As Sue left to get his food, Charlie turned to view his new acquaintance. The lady doctor was wearing a soft beige dress, vaguely Grecian in style, which flattered her tall, slender frame. The dark glasses she wore despite the dim lighting were framed in copper and her frosted hair was carefully tousled. She sipped her coffee gracefully, eyes locked on Charlie.

"It's a nice game room," he said.

"It's where all the swinging Brookshire people meet, not just the ones who live in the trailer park. And all levels, too. That older man playing pool is the Chief of Pediatrics, and

51

the girl with him is a second-year student nurse. So you can see there's no caste system here."

"Everybody's welcome but wives, right?"

"Something like that. It's called the happy hunting ground. Our own private singles bar except you don't have to be single."

Sue returned with a steaming cheeseburger, heated in the microwave oven, and a cup of beef boullion. He thanked her and began eating heartily.

"Remember that cardiac emergency the other day, man named Fernandez?" Sue asked. "I read his autopsy report. There was absolutely nothing wrong with him. He shouldn't have died."

"That just shows the power of suggestion," Isabel said. "He probably had a death wish. That sorcerer planted it."

"I don't understand these things," Sue protested. "They're spooky."

"I know who could explain it," Charlie said, gulping down a bite of cheeseburger. "Our new neighbor, Josh Kingston. He wrote a whole book about that stuff."

"Is he here now? I've heard a lot about him." Sue was excited.

"He's very famous," Charlie agreed.

"The man's a fraud," Isabel said coolly. "I've read his silly book. He's just a religious fanatic."

"He may be a rank amateur but he did what the professionals couldn't do," Charlie replied. "Every kid he worked with got well."

Sue laughed. "Would he talk my language instead of scientific mumbo jumbo like Isabel?"

"No, he wouldn't," Isabel snapped. "He'd probably say it was demonic. That's his answer to everything."

"Well, don't get mad," Sue said calmly. "I'd like to talk to him, maybe read his book. So he's a neighbor now."

"We'll all meet him soon enough. And we can ask him about the Fernandez case." Charlie had finished his supper

52

and was now sleepy. "I'm going home now. Nice meeting you, Isabel. See you girls tomorrow."

The brisk, clean air cleared Charlie's head somewhat as he walked back toward his trailer. He smiled at Sue's interest in Josh Kingston. As he passed the trailer next to his own, he was disappointed to see it dark. He'd hoped to get a look at this fellow Kingston. He was certainly not your usual next-door neighbor.

"I can't believe you want to quit, Brandt. You've been here longer than I have." Sue refolded the head nurse's resignation and returned it to its envelope. "Five North will fall apart without you."

"I can't stand it any more." Lois Brandt lit a cigarette and leaned back in the chair opposite Sue's desk. "It's been piling up a long time and it finally got to me."

"Lots of people get fed up, get the 'burn-out' syndrome. Take a few days. . . ."

The head nurse was shaking her head emphatically. "It's not just the pressure and the frustration, or even the hard work. I'm sick and tired of this whole business and I want out."

"Was there any special thing?"

"Well, yes. It was what happened to old Mr. Lindley." Lois sat back and spoke quietly. "You remember him? A nice old gentleman, bright as a penny. He was a patient of Dr. Harris. That man's a butcher, has been for years. Well, he posted Mr. Lindley for an exploratory lap, said he had a pelvic mass. They took him to surgery and the orderly put a Foley catheter in his bladder and drained off twenty-three hundred CCs of urine and there went his so-called tumor. He evidently had some kind of stricture or an enlarged prostate, I don't know, but the old guy's tumor was nothing but a full bladder.

"Dr. Harris never did an abdominal X-ray, did no kind of

work-up at all. Anyhow, that wasn't the bad part; I could have stood that. The thing I can't handle is this, Sue. They took that old man into surgery anyhow and cut him open. Called it a 'lysis of adhesions' and charged him a big fee. It makes me sick and I don't want to be part of it anymore."

"What about the tissue committee? The surgical suite committee?" Sue was horrified. Mike Harris' reputation was poor; most of the staff had no respect for his ability or his ethics. But this was a new low, even for him.

"Nothing will be done. He's too rich and too influential. But I don't have to stay here and watch these things happen."

"You've been a nurse a long time, Lois. You'll miss it."

"Oh no I won't. I've been doing some research and I'm finding out stuff that surprised even me, and I thought I knew it all. For example, did you know that last year there were over two million unnecessary surgeries performed in this country? And they're estimating now that way over fifty percent of all surgery is totally without value! Value to the patient, that is. The doctor gets his value, naturally."

"I saw those stats. Hard to believe."

"Oh, there's more, much more. Did you realize that every time doctors go on strike the death rate goes *down*? Fewer people die when the doctors aren't working! There's a message in that. And when the doctors go back to work, the death rate goes back up. This whole system is falling apart, Sue. I just don't care to be a part of it any longer."

Lois Brandt leaned forward and crushed out her cigarette. She peered at Sue hesitantly, then spoke, her voice confidential.

"You know my vision now about this place. I see this big old ugly pagan god, demanding his blood sacrifice. He has all those altars down there in the operating rooms. We wheel in the sacrificial victims, strip them and lay them on the altar. Meanwhile, the priest is making his ceremonial preparation, donning the priestly garments—the scrub gown—and going through the ritual purification ceremony of scrubbing up. The sacrifice is bared; he takes the priestly knife and cuts. Then you have the blood sacrifice, and later, after pathology does its thing, you have a burnt offering."

Sue stared at her in astonishment. It was silly talk, of course, but she still felt a rising of goose bumps along her arms.

"You see, this thing is almost like a religion, Sue. It has its priests, its temple prostitutes. It operates on faith and it even has a collection."

Sue sat in silence, thoughts racing. Part of her agreed. Things had changed a lot in the twelve years she'd been a nurse, and few changes had meant an improvement. But part of her was concerned for her friend's emotional stability. It sounded as though she were on the verge of collapse.

"Can I help you Lois?"

Lois shook her head, gave a short laugh. "I'll be fine as soon as I get out of here."

As Lois Brandt left the office, Sue felt a sudden rush of envy, and it surprised her. She had always liked her job; why should she envy someone who was leaving? Was the whole medical system in a process of decay? Sue shook her head angrily. There was nothing wrong here that more efficiency and dedication couldn't correct.

Sue took her mid-afternoon break with relief and headed for the staff dining room. She found a table by the window and sat with her hot tea, waiting for Isabel. What a day it had been! What a week!

Isabel joined her, carrying a green bottle of ginger ale. She was dressed in a tailored suit of pale green tweed with a snowy white silk blouse. Her multi-colored hair was in a cunningly contrived disarray and she looked, to Sue, perfectly groomed.

"Doesn't your hair ever get messed up?" Sue asked in annoyance.

"Almost never," Isabel laughed.

"How come we call this a coffee break when I always drink tea and you drink something that matches your outfit?"

Isabel laughed again. "Why does it bother you?"

"I don't know. Everybody else can get irritated, but not me. Why's that?"

"Because you're not the type, that's why. Now, what's wrong?"

"I just had a talk with Brandt. She's quitting."

"She's a good nurse. Why's she leaving?"

"She says this hospital is the temple of a pagan god who demands blood sacrifices. She also talked about burnt offerings. Weird."

"There have been some strange things around here, all right. But if you want something really spooky, wait till the Simmons twins get here for the Project."

"What can they do?"

"Well, let's see," Isabel mused. "Where do I start? They're fourteen-year-old identical twin girls. They have a total telepathic communication, for one thing. Almost like they have one mind between them. And they have a common, unlearned language they've used since they were eight months old. They can sometimes see through solid objects, too, like living bodies."

"They're from the planet Krypton, I suppose."

"They're from Wichita, Kansas," Isabel answered patiently. "They'll be here in a few days, staying right in the trailer park."

"Like they say, there goes the neighborhood."

"They ought to be on Eight Central," Isabel confided. "They have a lot of behavior problems. The mother is about out of her mind, too, from trying to cope with them. A sister will be coming with them as guardian."

"And you think you can cure all their strangeness?"

"Oh, we don't want to stop these things, Sue! They're very rare psychic talents. We just want to bring them under control. If the Project works the way we want it to, then everybody will be able to do the things these kids can do."

"That's not what Don Oliver said at the press party."

"What he stated as Project goals and what we really intend to do are quite different."

Sue was so shocked by this deception that she found a reason to excuse herself, leaving her tea unfinished. It had been a bad day all around. She had awakened late, which meant she had to forego either her usual jogging or her breakfast. She decided to eat instead of run and had later regretted it. The day had worsened after this dismal start.

On just her floors, fourteen staff people had called in sick, and help from the float pool was never very efficient. There were two narcotic errors. The morning count was off on Five North, and that meant a big hassle with crying nurses and the usual mountain of paperwork. And later on Four South a student had given a quarter grain of morphine to the wrong patient. What a mess that had been!

Then they'd dropped a patient off a stretcher on the way to X-ray and broken his collar bone, and to Sue's dismay, his attorney appeared on the scene before his doctor. Then had come the blow of Brandt's resignation. She could hardly wait for her shift to end so she could sit alone in the trailer and sulk.

At 6 p.m. Sue was brushing her hair, contemplating its many deficiencies and wondering how she'd look in one of the new, very extreme hairdos. This rather dreary reverie was interrupted by a brisk knock on her kitchen door. It was Dr. Fortuna, who entered cheerfully in a bluster of chilly air. "I need some old rags or some paper towels. Got any?"

"I have both," Sue said, pleased at this trivial evidence of her efficiency.

"Well, I'll take the rags then," he decided.

I haven't said I'll give them to you, she thought tartly, but she nodded and opened a cabinet under the sink and pulled two clean but ragged towels from a box. "I wash my car a lot," she explained.

He took the towels without thanks and walked into her living room. "I'm fixing up my back room," he offered. He looked around, his dark eyes alert. "You haven't done much redecorating, have you?"

"I like it just as is!" she retorted.

Charlie sat down on the couch and grinned mischievously at her. It was a little awkward to remain standing, so she sat in one of the chairs and smiled at him uncertainly.

"What kind of redecorating are you doing?" she asked.

"I have two bedrooms; I guess all the trailers do. Well, I'm taking the little one for my real bedroom and I'm fixing the other one up to, well, entertain, if you know what I mean." He smirked.

"I guess I do."

"You know what a motel room costs in the city?" he asked.

"I have no idea."

"I had to pay sixty-eight bucks the other night, and it's not that I'm cheap or that I don't have it, but the way I figure, why drive all the way into town and pay all that money if I got a place right here handy, for crying out loud?" He spread out his hands in a very Italian gesture.

I don't believe this, Sue thought in amazement. *What am I supposed to say?*

He went on, ignoring her silence. "I got my stereo in there and I'm painting the walls dark red, and I got a couple mirrors—"

"Stop," she interrupted, embarrassed. "I don't want to hear any more. I'm not the least bit interested in your plans or your room." She sat up very straight, angry at her discomfiture and avoiding his amused eyes.

"Too bad. I was kind of hoping you'd help me fix it up."

There was a long silence. *Why don't you go home*, she thought furiously.

"Look, we're neighbors, we work in the same place, we have a lot in common. Don't you ever get lonesome? I thought maybe we could just be friends, help each other pass these long, chilly evenings. Don't tell me you don't ever get a little lonely."

In spite of her anger and frustration, there was a sudden appeal in his words. Of course she got lonely; she was often alone at night and the years were creeping by relentlessly. The job was never enough to fill her whole life, and the idea of belonging, of being loved and desired, of mattering to someone in a special way—all this had deep appeal for her. Then, too, it was flattering that he'd want her when there were so many younger, prettier girls around.

And who would care? No one, anymore, would call it wrong. This kind of thing was accepted by everyone these days. He was a doctor, well-educated; maybe there could be long talks, discussions of things that really mattered, a meeting of the minds, the souls. . . . She raised her eyes and looked at him.

And the sight of his face killed every trace of the appeal. He was grinning like a mischievous child, delighted at her discomfiture. He showed not one vestige of tenderness or concern for her as a person; he obviously cared nothing for her. He cared for one thing only: the conquest.

"Why don't you come over with me now," he suggested slyly. "I have some rum—"

"No," she said flatly. "I'm not interested. Find yourself another girl."

"You're sure?" he persisted. "Not the least bit interested?"

"I am absolutely positive I'm not the least bit interested in you, or your room, or anything else you might have in mind."

"O.K." He rose to his feet, still smiling, no trace of rejection or disappointment. "Just thought I'd give it a try. What about your friend Isabel?"

Sue shook her head in amazement. It was as though he'd

offered her a cigarette and she'd declined. There was no emotional response in him at all. And he evidently thought this exchange should have no effect on their new and fairly superficial relationship. This was truly the modern man, the hedonist, who lived only for the satisfaction of the moment.

She rose, too, with a feeling of having just escaped a great danger. "I don't know about Isabel," she said. "But I don't think she'd be interested in a man who goes to such great lengths to save sixty-eight dollars."

Charlie laughed with every indication of genuine amusement. *He's got skin as thick as an elephant,* she thought.

"Well, thanks for the towels," he said cheerfully. "I'll go home and start my painting. Let me know if you ever change your mind. I'm real handy."

"Well, let's put it this way," Sue replied. "If I were in the market, I don't think I'd be a convenience shopper."

She followed him and stood watching as he trotted down the three steps from her kitchen door. It was almost dark; a few lights were shining indoors and the sky was a deep purplish-blue. A single star twinkled over the roof of Fortuna's trailer. A beautiful night.

A sudden sound caught her attention and she turned to look at the trailer next to the doctor's. Someone had opened the back door and was coming out. As he stood silhouetted in the light from his kitchen, she saw him clearly and gasped.

He was tall, very thin, with tousled black hair and a somber face—the man she had encountered in Four South who'd prayed so intently for the black patient. The intense young minister in faded jeans. This must be Joshua Kingston!

She stepped hurriedly back inside and shut the door.

So this was what her situation had come to! A predatory doctor as a next-door neighbor and a religious fanatic one trailer up the row! Within a few days the weird Simmons twins would arrive and before long the three psychic men the Project had invited.

There, indeed, went the neighborhood!

Maybe she'd do like Brandt and quit.

But it wasn't just the job, it was everything. And you couldn't quit everything.

Luncheon in the staff dining room was suddenly interrupted.

"Code 99! Emergency Room! Code 99! Emergency Room!"

As the paging system became louder and more urgent, the room fell silent, each one listening for his or her designation. As the emergency and location were given, several people rose to hurry from the room.

Sue Dunn and Isabel Nebo left their meal and walked swiftly toward the door. Joshua Kingston abandoned his meal in haste and followed quickly behind the others. Malcolm Brown eating with Don Oliver Franklin, stared at Josh's retreating figure, his cheerful expression gone for the moment. Don Oliver never paused in his eating during the emergency call.

As the code began sounding, Dr. Charles Fortuna was leaving the emergency room thus removing himself from the tragedy that was working itself out in Cubicle C. *They don't need me*, he told himself. *The emergency room doctor seems competent enough.*

The side door opened and the inhalation therapist bustled in, wheeling a pediatric-sized ventilator in front of him. *Blasted waste of time*, Charlie thought. He spotted Sue Dunn and Isabel Nebo and nodded to them.

"What's going on?" Sue asked.

The drawn curtains around Cubicle C were billowing out from the activity of the professional people who had crowded in. Charlie gave a terse resume.

"A three-year-old came in with a bad cold, nothing serious, no temp or anything. They gave him a shot of penicillin and he went into anaphalactic shock. Had a raging allergy to penicillin nobody knew about. And they gave him a whopping dose. He only weighs about thirty pounds and they ordered six hundred thousand units."

"The poor little thing!" Sue was instantly sympathetic. "You think he'll make it?"

"I doubt it," Charlie shrugged.

"Why are you here?" Isabel asked suspiciously. "You don't work in this department."

"I just answered the code," Charlie said. "But they don't need me and I'm more than ready to disappear. Seems like every room I've walked into lately has a big neon sign reading *Potential Lawsuit*."

Suddenly their attention was drawn toward a small frightened woman who stood hunched against the wall. Her eyes were wide with fright as she stared intently at the curtain surrounding Cubicle C.

"Probably the child's mother," Isabel murmured.

Sue crossed the hall and put her arm around the woman's thin shoulders. "Would you like to come with me?" she asked softly. "I'll take you where you can be alone and they'll let you know as soon as there's any information."

"No, I want to stay here," the woman answered fiercely. Sue nodded with understanding. The woman opened her purse and withdrew a large wooden rosary and began muttering under her breath as her thumb pulled the beads one by one across her forefinger.

Sue was suddenly aware of a tall, dark young man standing beside them. Joshua Kingston. He spoke directly to the mother.

"I'm a minister of the gospel. Do I have permission to pray for your boy?" he asked abruptly.

The woman looked up, startled, and spoke uncertainly. "I guess so. Yes."

Kingston turned on his heel and moved to the cubicle. He grabbed the encircling curtain in one strong hand and pulled it open.

The tiny form on the stretcher was surrounded by white-clad figures. Sue knew the routine: I.V.s, benedryl, steroids, endotracheal tube if possible. Opened so suddenly to the eyes of the mother, the scene could have the appearance of vultures gathered around a fresh kill. She gasped aloud and clutched the beads to her breast.

"I'm going to pray for this boy," Kingston announced in a firm voice. "Would you please step aside for a moment?"

"Pray if you like," the emergency room doctor said. "But we can't stop. The kid's dying."

"No." The young minister's voice was calm. "He is not going to die."

"Hey, somebody," the doctor protested. "Get this guy out of here!"

"I have the mother's permission," Kingston replied firmly. "If he dies and you have refused to allow me to minister to his spiritual needs, she will have a grievance against you and against this hospital."

The word *grievance* made the doctor turn around and face Kingston. "All right then, dammit! Pray! But be quick about it!" The doctor stepped back in obvious anger, while the rest of the people around the stretcher, who had watched the exchange in silence, followed his lead. Kingston was left alone by the child's body.

He placed one thin dark hand on the child's head, closed his eyes and spoke aloud. Almost immediately, everyone within hearing distance fell silent listening to the loud, firm, bold words he spoke.

"Father, I know when Jesus raised Jairus' daughter, He sent away all those who doubted Him. I can't do that. This room is full of doubters because this is their place. I know, Father, that You sent me here as Your instrument. And I know it is Your will to heal. So I ask You now, Father, in the name of Jesus, to heal this child. Spirit of allergy, I command you to loose this child now and be gone. I command you to yield to the power of Jesus. . . ."

Every eye in the room was on Josh Kingston and no one else spoke a word.

Sue Dunn found the whole scene unbelievable. Something deep in her admired the man's courage; he wasn't afraid of making a fool of himself.

And because they were all watching the intense young preacher, nobody noticed the little boy. The first indication of any change came from the mother, who suddenly gave a little scream and dashed forward to clutch her son to her bosom.

The doctor, broken out of his trancelike absorption in Kingston, pulled her away and looked at the boy. The child sat up on the stretcher, frowning at the people around him, breathing normally, color restored to a healthy pink. Suddenly he began to cry and reach toward his mother piteously.

"I wanna go home," he wailed.

Throughout the emergency room there was sudden clapping, then a hubbub of loud voices. In stunned amazement the doctor stared at the small boy who was upset by the noise around him and by his mother's hysterical tears, but showed no sign of the coma produced by his reaction to the drug.

"Isn't it marvelous?" Sue grabbed Isabel's arm and squeezed it, her pale face streaked with tears.

"I'd like to know how he did it," Dr. Fortuna said, his face a study in bewilderment.

Josh Kingston was heading for the elevator. As people moved toward him, he brushed by almost as though he were unaware of them. Only when the boy's mother approached did he stop. He looked at her seriously, dark eyes intense.

"Thank you, sir. You saved my boy." Fervently, she grasped his hands.

"No. Jesus did. I just said the words." He stared at her a moment. Again the room was quiet. "You can pray directly to Jesus, you know. Just your own words coming from your own heart."

"Mama, I wanna go home." She turned to her son, and Kingston watched her soberly. He seemed to consider following her to say more, but he shook his head briefly, turned abruptly and walked out the side door. The room gave a collective sigh and settled back into normalcy.

Charlie chose coffee, Sue hot tea and Isabel, apple juice. Together they sat down at one of the long tables under the windows. Sue was full of questions, amazed and challenged by the episode in the emergency room. To her astonishment, neither Isabel nor Charlie wanted to discuss the event.

"Don't you even care what happened?" she asked finally.

"I'm glad the child is all right," Isabel said calmly. "But I don't think it matters exactly how it happened."

"I'm more interested in telling Isabel about my decorating plans," Charlie grinned.

Sue drank her tea in silence as the two doctors chattered away.

Isabel leaned closer to Charlie. "Red walls, you say? Have you read the latest findings on the effects of color on the psyche—or should I say the libido?"

"Did I read them?" Charlie smirked. "I was part of the research!"

Sue stared at Isabel in dismay, wondering how a competitive and ambitious woman could so quickly regress into a giggling, flirting schoolgirl.

Sue made an excuse to leave and walked from the dining room in a state of dejection. *I'm some kind of a mess,* she thought in disgust. *I can't stand Isabel and Charlie's conversation because it's too sensual. And I don't like Joshua Kingston because he's too spiritual. What's the answer?*

Joshua Kingston stopped and looked around him. This

part of the pathway from Brookshire Hospital to the mobile home compound was already a special place to him. In only a few days he had discovered that right here, around a curve from the hospital and down a little slope from the clubhouse, there was no sign of civilization. Here he could feel totally isolated from the cares of life, alone in a still, hallowed forest of giant trees. He loved to stand under their soaring branches and bow his heart before the God who made both them and him.

He heard footsteps along the path behind him. It was almost 4:30, late for a day-shift worker from the nursing staff and still early for anyone on the business staff who would work till five. He watched.

Sue Dunn turned the corner of the path and stopped suddenly at sight of him. She wore a coat of forest green, and it was most becoming to her. It was the first time he'd seen her in anything but white. She was staring at him strangely. Without preamble, she said, "You're Joshua Kingston and I'm Sue Dunn. I was in the emergency room today. That was wonderful, what you did."

"I'm just glad the boy is all right." He had no idea how to talk to her about this episode. He was afraid of being too blunt; she had been obviously offended at their first encounter.

"Do you do a lot of that, praying for people that way?" she asked. It was a little chilly in the woods, shaded from the late afternoon sunlight, and Sue put her hands in her pockets. Without discussion, they began walking slowly toward the trailer park.

"I only do what I'm told," he said. "Miracles happen at God's initiative. When He says to act, I do."

"Do they stay healed? Like with Mr.—ah, that other man, the fellow on Four South?"

"Harry Owens," he told her for the second time, this time with a trace of amusement in his voice. "And yes, he's just fine. I've seen him twice."

"I was a little angry about that," she told him.

"Yes, I know. Most people react as you did."

"You must have a lot of faith," she said awkwardly.

"No. Just enough to do what the Lord tells me to do. I'm accused of acting too much on faith, but nowhere in the Bible do I see where it's wrong to have too much faith. Jesus was bothered by those who had too little faith."

"I remember that," she said with childlike pride. "O ye of little faith."

"You went to Sunday school?" he asked.

"Oh, yes. I still go to church when I can, but I only get every other weekend off."

They had reached the fork in the path, one branch leading on to the rows of trailers, the other leading to the clubhouse. The nurse stopped and hesitated before speaking. "I'm going to the clubhouse," she told him, a note of defiance in her voice. "I've had a bad day. Really this whole week has been bad and I intend to fix myself a drink."

Josh stared at her a moment. "You think I'd look down on you because you want a drink?"

"You don't drink, do you?" she challenged him.

"Well, no, but that doesn't mean I'd pass judgment on you if you do."

Sue was silent for a long moment. "You say some strange things," she said finally.

"I'm peculiar," he admitted.

"One other thing." She continued to look at him intently. "Do you ever smile?"

Josh was annoyed. He had been pleasant to her, and all she noticed was this same old thing he'd heard so often before—that he didn't smile.

"Yes, I smile. But never on purpose."

"I see," she said. "Well, nice to have met you again. And I'll say one thing for you: you sure have guts."

She headed off toward the clubhouse and he walked slowly down the other fork toward his temporary trailer home.

Book II

Oppression

In many ways, Brookshire was like a small village. It housed, bathed, fed and cleaned up after hundreds of people, and it was just as truly a self-contained and autonomous entity.

It had a government and men and women in a hierarchy of authority. It had rules, regulations, ordinances and armed men to keep the peace. It had commercial enterprises such as gift shops and concessionaires, as well as dietary and pharmacy centers. Goods were bought and sold every day, with a profit-making motive.

Like any small town, Brookshire had its educational system, too, with medical curricula prescribed and teaching strictly regimented. It had a well-developed communications system— several of them, in fact—from the monthly house newspaper, and a public address system to the latest in computer technology, right on down to the grapevine of gossip that fed on rumor and slander. Brookshire was held together by many networks of communication.

One could live there for months without leaving the confines of the medical center and suffer no deprivation. Within Brookshire, you could get your hair cut and styled, washed and set. You could cash checks, make bank deposits and pay utility bills. You could buy almost anything: clothing, drugs, books, flowers and plants, cosmetics, reading material. You could have your shoes repaired. You could worship the God of your choice in any of six different chapels, two Protestant, two Catholic and two that aimed at offending no one. Once a month you could eat a three-course luncheon while you watched the younger and more attractive of the doctors' wives model new fashions, and you could pay a great deal of money for this privilege. You could enjoy a workout, a steam bath and a rubdown. There was even a branch post office.

You could have your clothes laundered and, if necessary, mended or altered. You could play a game of cards in either the residents' quarters or the doctors' lounge and you could lose a lot of money. You could get sound advice on investments and money management and the latest quotes from the big board of the New York Stock Exchange. You could have eyeglasses prescribed, the lenses ground and the frames fitted. You could have your photograph taken with proofs available the next day and prints mailed within a week. You could be fitted for a brace, a prosthesis, or corrective shoes. You could meet, court and marry another consenting adult and arrange your honeymoon trip through the branch office of a travel agency.

All this without leaving the hospital.

In selecting the subjects for his research Project, Don Oliver Franklin did most of the investigating, and made all the decisions himself. He read through hundreds of reports ranging from articles in tabloid newspapers to weighty scientific studies. He used his own criteria. He wanted young people, those who had not yet commercialized their gifts. And because he wanted the full range of prophecy, telepathy, telekinesis, healing, clairvoyance, psychophotography and all the rest, he decided it would be wiser to select those with multiple talents. He read, studied, deliberated and pondered. And for the final judgment, he relied on his instincts.

Out of the hundreds of people he'd considered, he contacted the five who were his top choices. The letters went out over his signature, impressive, persuasive, prestigious.

All five accepted his offer.

His very first choice was LeRoi Williams, a nineteen-year-old black man from Alabama. LeRoi was the most promising American talent in the field of psychokinesis. His mind had a remarkable ability to affect the material world; he could heat metals, move objects, open and close doors, rearrange furniture and levitate bodies with only the power of concentration. He also had manifested multiple personalities, which fascinated Franklin. He selected LeRoi for these abilities despite certain drawbacks, for this young man had a rather unsavory reputation. Besides some fairly serious social maladjustments, he had had a few run-ins with the law. But to Don Oliver his gifts offset his drawbacks.

Next, Franklin chose Wanda and Glenda Simmons, fourteen-year-old identical twin girls. While LeRoi was gifted in the realm of what the parapsychologists called PK, or pyschokinesis, and could manipulate the material world around him, the Simmons twins were gifted in the cognitive or thought realm. The name for these gifts was extrasensory perception, commonly called ESP. These young girls had enormous mental powers; under certain conditions they could see into the future and into the minds of others. Like LeRoi Williams, they had defects of personality and adjustment, but again Franklin overlooked these qualities in view of their remarkable gifts.

Don Oliver's next choice involved a subject that had fascinated him for years. Even before committing himself to a study of psychic phenomena and its various manifestations, Franklin had been a UFO buff. He had studied unidentified flying objects from every aspect, from science fiction to the archives of classified governmental studies of sightings. He was extremely interested in the subjects of flying saucers, extraterrestrial encounters and the likelihood of life on other planets. It was a delight for him to discover Wallace Graham.

Wallace was a 28-year-old Southerner, the scion of an old, genteel, and just a shade decadent Louisiana family. He had dropped out of college several years before, after an alleged encounter with the inhabitants of a space vehicle. He claimed to have been abducted by these extraterrestrials and he gave interviews freely to anyone who would listen. Like all true fanatics, he was disconcertingly singleminded, but underneath his warped personality and the strangeness of his claims, there appeared to be a foundation of reality. It would be a fascinating exercise to investigate his experience.

The last of the five psychics given top choice by Don Oliver Franklin was a twenty-year-old musician from Omaha, Nebraska. Vincent Ponder was the only one of the five who appeared to be without serious personality defects. Indeed, from all Franklin read, he seemed quite normal aside from his unusual musical gifts. He was a good-looking, boyish charmer who conducted interviews with the press or with scientific investigators with good taste and modesty.

For Vincent Ponder, music was more than a hobby; it was a vocation. And he seemed almost chagrined and distressed by the fact that upon occasion he would fall into a trance state during which he could compose music that gave every evidence of having been written by the old masters. He was not the only psychic with whom this had happened, but, as with Franklin's other four, young Ponder seemed to be at the top of his particular field.

So these were Franklin's five: two young girls and three young men under 30. Four Caucasians, one black. One poor, three middle-class, one quite wealthy. The girls and LeRoi Williams had only nine years of schooling, Vincent Ponder was a high school graduate and Wallace Graham had completed two years of college. LeRoi Williams was from a broken home, the others had a reasonably normal family life.

Franklin shifted their files around on his desk, comparing, evaluating. So many differences, so few similarities. The only common factor he could see so far was their ability to perform in ways which other human beings could not.

He smiled in anticipation.

As Brookshire Memorial Hospital prepared for the arrival of the five psychics, Don Oliver Franklin continued to feed news items to the press on a daily basis. He watched in pleasure as interest in the Project grew and publicity spread.

Isabel Nebo spent several frustrating afternoons with her section of the Project staff. There were two psychologists, one old and quite charming statistician and the parapsychologist. They proposed to plan the initial testing on the five subjects, but they had trouble arranging a meeting. The testing location was finally set up in two rooms at the end of Eight South, former classrooms used by the Inservice Education Department.

When Charlie Fortuna was handed medical records on all five of his patients, he read through them dutifully. He had no idea what kinds of examinations or tests would indicate the physical aspects of paranormal behavior, which was what he was supposed to determine. He hardly even knew where to start, but he kept his doubts to himself.

Joshua Kingston attended one session with the men and women selected by Don Oliver Franklin to delve into the spiritual aspects of psychic behavior. He considered it a disaster. Josh felt he had little in common with those selected as his associates. They couldn't even agree on when to meet.

Although Sue Dunn was not directly involved in Project Truth, she soon absorbed all the gossip, since it had become the number one topic of conversation at Brookshire. What she heard troubled her. Too many things were happening at Brookshire that left her puzzled and disquieted.

Project Truth seemed at the root of them all.

"Let me get this straight," Josh Kingston said slowly, peering at Don Oliver Franklin. "I'm being reprimanded for praying for that little boy? Even though he was healed?"

"No," Franklin said gently. "Not for what you did, but for the way you did it."

"And of course, we're all delighted that the boy wasn't as ill as the doctors had thought and was able to go home."

Josh whirled to face Malcolm Brown, seated in the other chair facing Don Oliver's massive desk. The chaplain was smiling cheerfully. Josh controlled himself with an effort.

"I wondered how you'd explain it away. Now I see: the doctor was just mistaken, right?"

"The point is, you offended Dr. James," Don Oliver interjected. "He says you were very abrupt and disrespectful."

Josh shook his head in disbelief. "You mean it's more important to cater to that man's inflated pride than to obey the voice of God and allow His power to move?"

"Nobody is trying to curtail your ministry, Dr. Kingston. But there are rules and procedures." Don Oliver gestured regally with his cigar and continued. "You see, in a hospital, the doctor is the captain of the ship, the head of the team. The rest of us must defer to him and to his expertise, especially in time of crisis."

"You have a very low opinion of the medical system, don't you, Dr. Kingston?" Malcolm Brown asked slyly.

"The Hippocratic Oath that doctors take when they begin their practice is a vow sworn to four false gods—Asclupieus, Apollo, Hygiea and Panacea. That ought to say something to you," replied Josh. *Control yourself,* Josh thought firmly. *They'll never receive this and you'll just make them more angry.*

But Don Oliver laughed. "Those are just myths, my son. They have no bearing on medical practice."

"They are false gods," Josh said firmly.

"You think you know a lot because you've written a best-seller," Malcolm continued. "Well, you're not the only author here."

"Yes, I know one of your books: *God Helps Those Who Help Themselves.*"

"That's a principle that works today," Brown explained.

"It's not true and it certainly isn't Scripture." Josh replied calmly.

"What do you mean?" Malcolm snapped.

"That phrase isn't in the Bible. It was quoted by Benjamin Franklin in *Poor Richard's Almanac* in 1757. And he got it from Algernon Sidney who wrote *Discourses on Government;* and he probably got it from Aesop's Fables, because it was in them. As far as I'm concerned, God helps those who ask Him, those who trust Him."

Again Don Oliver spoke soothingly into the breach. "Let's not argue among ourselves. We must respect other people's opinions, Dr. Kingston. You should not be so intolerant. Surely you agree that God gave us doctors, and gave them their wisdom."

"There are two kinds of wisdom spoken of in the Book of James," Josh replied. "Wisdom from above and another wisdom that is earthly. Do you know what the sign RX at the beginning of a prescription means? Back in the days of the Roman Empire prescriptions began with a prayer to Jupiter. They're still often written in Latin, and the RX is what's left of the prayer; it's Jupiter's astrological sign."

"We've talked enough," Don Oliver said firmly. He pointed his cigar at Josh like a weapon. "Consider that I have passed along a reprimand and in the future try to be a bit more accommodating of the doctors. After all, when people come here, it is to receive help from this medical system you seem to oppose. It's not your place to stand in their way."

77

"Right," Josh said stiffly. "When in Rome, do as the Romans. If that's all, I'll leave now." The room was utterly silent as he walked out.

Effie MacAllister's feet hurt again, which meant it was time for a break. She decided to take it in the staff dining room on the first floor, rather than in the nurses' lounge on Six North, because she wanted to be alone to think. She chose one of the dining room's small tables for two in the hope that no one would join her, but before she had time to add sugar and milk to her coffee, Sue Dunn put a cup of tea on the table and sat down in the chair opposite her. "All right if I join you?" she asked.

Effie smiled a welcome. If she had to share this precious free time with another, Sue was the best possible choice. Despite a difference in age and professional status, they shared many opinions and attitudes.

"We haven't seen you all day," Effie commented.

"I haven't been anywhere yet but Five North," Sue said in annoyance. "That place is a zoo this morning. You know Lois Brandt is leaving?"

"I heard. I'm sorry for your sake."

"Yes. She's the best head nurse we have. Without her, Five North will be—." Sue paused in sudden embarrassment.

Effie laughed. "I know. With Brandt gone, Five North will be like Six North. And that's why I'm sorry for you."

"How are things up there?"

"Well, it's funny you should ask. I've been trying all morning to put my finger on exactly what's wrong. It's not that it's too busy or disorganized or that everybody's cutting everybody else's throat; that's normal. It's something else here lately. Something really strange."

"What do you mean?"

Effie spoke carefully, choosing her words deliberately. "There's a lot going on you can't explain. People die who shouldn't and people who should die don't. You get the Incident Reports. Have you ever seen such a rash of errors and mistakes?"

Sue was listening intently. "Anything else?"

"Well, I guess it's more an atmosphere than anything. Like we're not as much in control as we ought to be. Does that make sense?"

"Not really. The word I keep using is spooky. I find I'm sometimes just suddenly afraid and I don't know why."

"I haven't been actually afraid," Effie said. "But I have been disturbed. And I think it may get worse when the psychics get here for Don Oliver's project."

"Now there's a happy thought. Why do you think that?"

"Oh, Sue, I don't know. In a way I envy Brandt. Nursing's getting to be such a burden."

"Don't let's start on that. I may cry."

Effie knew Sue's feelings about nursing; they'd talked often on the subject. In twelve years as a registered nurse, Sue had seen many changes, and almost always they meant less satisfaction for the nurses. Third party billing, government regulations, increased malpractice litigation, steadily growing paperwork requirements, adjusting to computers—all these and many other factors made nursing a different career today than the profession they had selected years before. These changes were driving more and more nurses from the profession in disillusionment.

Effie glanced at her watch. She would enjoy a few more minutes off her feet, then return to the demands of the job. If Sue was concerned by the changes she'd witnessed in twelve years, Effie's experience spanned thirty years. She was one of the few nurses at Brookshire who had no formal education in nursing; her license had been acquired by waiver when practical nurses were first licensed.

She could remember back before the days of hospitalization insurance, before the development of allied health care fields like inhalation therapy, physical therapy, nuclear medicine and the like. She could even remember the days before the age of specialization, when doctors were usually just doctors. Now the general practitioner was often scorned by the specialists as a "country boy." Effie had viewed the institution of medicine from within for a generation, and, like Sue, was more and more disenchanted by it.

"I need to get back," she said regretfully. "My fifteen minutes are up." She walked slowly from the room on painful feet, obedient to the call of duty.

Talking didn't solve the problems, she mused. Too much paperwork and doctors concerned only about money, inaccurate lab tests, and the drugs that interacted with each other doing more harm than good. The current imperative of the medical system was, "Don't just stand there. Do something! Intervene!" This new cardinal rule had replaced the older one: "First, see thou do no harm."

These things were all part of the package now, but there was something else on Six North—something that indicated even more than a loss of control. It seemed to indicate that new factors had entered the picture. New, and as Sue said, spooky and frightening.

Malcolm Brown liked the idea of being head of Brookshire's chaplains, but he found the routine of visiting patients tedious. Being cheerful to them hour after hour was not only tedious; it was hard work.

At Six North a nurse described the case to him while shaking her head. "You might want to take someone along with you," she cautioned. "The things she's saying are real weird." The chaplain declined the offer and walked with some trepidation toward the patient's room. He reviewed the little he knew. The woman was hearing strange voices and was possibly psychotic, but the attending physician had decided to explore the spiritual aspects of her problem before seeking psychiatric help. Brown's task was to make an evaluation and then call the doctor with his opinion.

It was a private room, dimly lit despite the bright afternoon sun. The blinds and drapes were tightly shut and the patient lay quite still, eyes fixed on the wall opposite her bed. She was younger than he'd expected, probably about 30. Her face was sullen and she didn't acknowledge his presence.

He coughed delicately and spoke with a smile. "Good afternoon, Mrs. Spillman. I'm Chaplain Brown. Your doctor asked me to stop by and see you."

She said nothing and he continued, overriding his embarrassment. "I notice you're listed just as Protestant. Do you have a denominational preference?"

She remained silent and he stood awkwardly. His counseling techniques usually served him well, but most were based on reaction to the other's words; it was hard to get started when he drew only silence. She finally blinked once, studied him carefully and spoke.

"Where is my little boy? Nobody can give me a decent answer. You're a minister; you must know. Where is he?"

"Suppose you tell me about it," he suggested softly and she nodded. Her gaze was now set upon his face as it had previously been fixed on the wall.

"He died, you know. Not long ago, in a car wreck. He was six, going on seven. I want you to tell me where he is."

"Where do you think he is?"

"I won't play that game. I want to know where you think he is. If you won't tell me, get out."

Malcolm was acutely uncomfortable. He'd read the proper books on death and dying, knew all the stages of grief and understood how the human psyche reacted to loss, but he was still uncomfortable in the presence of bereavement. "Well," he said hesitantly, "Would you like to think he's in heaven?"

"I need to *know*. Can you prove he's there?"

"No, I can't give you any proof. You have to have faith."

"I need to know because I think he's still around. I hear him."

"Maybe it's just your mind—."

"No." Her face was masklike in its control but her voice trembled, and Malcolm could sense a load of emotion in this woman that was almost unbearable.

"I'm sure he's just with the Lord," he said soothingly.

"I hear him calling. Other people have heard it. Some of the nurses, too. He keeps calling, 'Mama, come get me.'"

"You must not dwell on your son's death. He's all right now. It's time for you to get on with your life." He made his voice deliberately cheerful and avoided looking into the patient's deep-set, haunted eyes.

"Yeah, sure," she said dully and fell silent. She withdrew her gaze and turned toward the opposite wall. Malcolm relaxed, no longer pinned by those eyes like a butterfly pinned to a board. He'd most certainly tell the doctor she needed psychiatric care; voices from the dead, indeed! He classified her problem neatly and slipped from the room.

He was relieved the visit was over, and then felt a pang of guilt that he always seemed to feel this way after seeing patients. He shoved aside his dissatisfaction with the visit and consoled himself that nobody could have helped her except a trained professional. After all, this wasn't his field.

The whole day had gone wrong. Sue hated working the evening shift, but because she'd been asked and because she didn't have enough gumption to say no, she had changed shifts to accommodate another supervisor. Now she was angry with herself for being so spineless. She was comfortable working the emergency room and her own surgical floors, but she knew little of the evening shift routines and was sure she'd be less than adequate as supervisor. To make it worse, it was Saturday, the emergency room's busiest day.

She took the house report in the supervisors' office at 3:00 then began her first rounds. She made a swing through the three outpatient clinics and things seemed under control.

She walked slowly through the emergency department, finished her tour in the large receiving area. It was a huge room, noisy, full of activity. Three large plate-glass double doors opened onto ambulance ramps, and with an appalling regularity they swished open electronically to admit stretcher loads of injured, suffering, wounded, painful humanity. The personnel here, inured to the shock of blood, pain, disaster and trauma, worked with calm, dispassionate purpose to evaluate, classify, record and relegate these pitiful cases.

"Miss Dunn? We need your signature." A young paramedic approached respectfully. "We have a DOA, a knife wound."

Sue followed his quick steps through the doors into the trauma section, mentally reviewing the legal requirements for patients who are "dead on arrival." Would the attending physician sign the death certificate? Was there a question of foul play? Was an autopsy required? She reviewed all the detailed ramifications of this system's tenacious hold on death, birth, illness and their legal aspects.

"It's the first time I've seen a murder," the young paramedic confided. "I've been on lots of accident calls and I can handle 'road pizza.' But this is something else."

He led her to Cubicle C, and her mind flashed back to another Cubicle C, over in the medical section of the emergency department, and the incredible events that followed Josh Kingston's bold prayer. No such reversal of the natural course of events seemed possible this time. As the curtain was pulled back, Sue saw the bloodied, clammy, pasty-white dead body of the victim.

A short, chubby nurse in tight blue jeans and a dirty lab coat was speaking to the police officer who stood beside the body, making notes on a yellow pad. She turned as Sue approached.

"You're the relief supervisor? We need you to sign the medical examiner's form. This is a legal case, foul play."

Despite her youth, the nurse seemed to know the proper

procedures. Sue signed her name on the two indicated lines and handed the form back to the nurse, who ripped out the second copy and gave it to the policeman.

"We'll put this guy in the cooler and they'll autopsy him Monday. But the cause of death is pretty obvious. Knife wound, right lower quadrant."

"We need it official," the policeman responded.

The nurse filled out a small cardboard tag with the patient's information and added a big red "M.E." before attaching it to the patient's big toe with a wire twist.

"O.K. He can go." She explained the evening shift procedure to Sue. "Cart him back to the morgue and log him into the morgue book. There isn't an attendant there over the weekend. They'll find him Monday." She covered the patient's face with the sheet and whipped open the cubicle curtain. "Need a couple of orderlies here," she bellowed.

Sue pulled the sheet off the patient's feet and read his cardboard tag. "Joseph William David, age 26, male, Caucasian. . . ." How bland it sounded. A life summarized, all pertinent facts catalogued. She covered his feet again as two big orderlies joined her and began wheeling the stretcher out. She trailed after them.

The hospital morgue was at the end of a long, dim hall. The rooms and offices along the hall were closed and locked on this weekend evening. On one side was a small laboratory used by the outpatient department on weekdays; on the opposite side were offices and receiving areas for the purchasing department. There were no signs of life and no sounds except the swish of stretcher wheels and the footsteps of Sue and the orderlies, the trio forming an honor guard for the dead body. At the end of the long hall, a locked door labeled *Morgue* faced them and Sue found to her distress that her hand shook slightly as she withdrew her master key.

The room they entered was the receiving area for the morgue, with a desk and filing cabinets and an ancient brown leather couch. Sue turned on the light but its chill blue rays did nothing to dispel the clammy eeriness of the cold little room. The orderlies, more familiar than Sue with the routine for this shift, wheeled their burden past the desk and through a second door, into the morgue itself. She followed them.

This second room was bitterly cold, the walls and floor a dirty tan concrete that oozed moisture. There were three autopsy tables, each with a hanging flourescent light over it, and three walls banked with retractable slabs, holding places for bodies awaiting shipment to funeral homes. She stood by the door, shivering with cold and with a feeling of trespassing on alien territory. In her twelve years at Brookshire, she had never entered this room; on the day shift, this area was staffed and bodies were *sent* to the morgue, not *taken* there. The men wheeled the stretcher next to the first autopsy table, locked the wheels and walked back into the first room. It seemed almost cheery now, in contrast to the morgue itself.

"There's the log book," one of the men told Sue, pointing to a large bound book on the desk. She found the current page and filled out the proper columns concerning Joseph William David. Some lines she had to leave blank, but she did what she could, signing the last column with her official signature, "S. Dunn, R.N."

She turned to leave and found to her annoyance that the orderlies had already gone, leaving her alone. She snapped off the lights, locked the door and walked back down the long, deserted hall, and found she had to slow her steps deliberately. She kept telling herself there was no need to run, nothing to be afraid of; there was no evil force behind her, following her. How strange that she, who was usually so practical and matter-of-fact, should now be the victim of a fevered imagination. Without logic or reason, she was thoroughly frightened. For despite the calming words she spoke to herself, she felt that they had disturbed something in the morgue. Her imagination took over and she could literally sense something flowing silently down the hall toward her unprotected back; a powerful, evil, destructive "thing" that hated her.

By the time she reached the main hall she was almost running. And she was angry with herself for yielding to imagination.

Time for a break, she told herself. Time for a room full of people.

She headed toward the staff dining room and an early supper.

"Who in the world is the 'Peeper in the White Coat?'" Charlie asked. He took a sip of his rum and cola and smiled at Isabel. She was sitting next to him on one of the cozy sofas in the clubhouse.

"He's some kind of a sex pervert who gets his kicks in hospitals. He's got nerve, I'll say that for him. First time he just showed up in the labor wing of obstetrics, dressed like a resident, a neat, nice-looking young fellow. He went into a patient's room, introduced himself as a resident and said her doctor had asked him to check her progress. Then he did an examination. The only way anybody knew he wasn't kosher was when the patient complimented him to the attending doctor; she said he had a nice bedside manner. The doctor knew we didn't have a resident by the name she gave and the story came out."

Isabel adjusted her dark glasses and went on. "He's been around a couple of other times. We're getting a pretty good description of him. That last time was a couple of days ago in E.R. He waltzed into a cubicle and told the patient that she was supposed to have a complete physical and he'd been assigned to her case. The only problem was, she was a nurse from Children's Hospital, an off-duty L.P.N. who had just come in for a flu shot. She knew a complete physical wasn't required and she started yelling and he ran out."

Charlie chuckled. "That's nerve, all right. You know, this

is quite a hospital. Seems to have more than its share of strange things."

"You heard about the roach in O.R.? They had a young boy in for an appendectomy, got him all prepped and draped on the table, the crew was scrubbed, gowned and gloved, the usual routine. Conner was just ready to make the incision when this big cockroach crawled out from under the drapes, right across the patient's belly. The scrub tech screamed and knocked over her Mayo stand and Conner hit the roof. He's the type who gets mad if you just blink wrong. Well, you can imagine how he felt about a cockroach invading *his* case."

"Brookshire's O.R. must be even dirtier than the average. Roaches, for crying out loud!"

"Probably came in on the E.R. stretcher," Isabel replied. "That whole wing is full of bugs and I don't think they ever clean their stretchers."

"Emergency rooms are always dirty," Charlie agreed.

Isabel took a healthy swallow of her beer. She looked better tonight, not so bandbox perfect, and Charlie had always liked women who enjoyed beer. If it hadn't been for his long-standing determination to dislike psychiatrists, he might have found her quite interesting.

"There's always something unusual happening at Brookshire," she said thoughtfully. "But nothing as strange as Joshua Kingston."

"He is far out," Charlie agreed. "Have you formed a psychiatric profile of him?"

"Let's forget Dr. Kingston, okay? I'm sorry I brought him up."

"Fine with me. I can take him or leave him alone."

"Good, so can I. And right now I prefer to leave him."

He grinned again, always pleased to see a chink in the armor of a psychiatrist. Something about Josh Kingston made her nervous and that amused Charlie.

Only an hour to go, Sue thought with relief. *And I'll never work 3-to-11 again.* At 10 p.m., it was time to collect her house reports and compile the shift consensus.

"Sue Dunn, Extension One-One-Four. Sue Dunn, Extension One-One-Four."

One-one-four? That was security. Why would they want her? Sue dialed the number and a brisk male voice answered immediately.

"Supervisor? We got a problem, or maybe just a situation. There's somebody hollering on first floor down at the end of south hall by purchasing. We need to go investigate."

"Hollering?" she repeated pointlessly. The man was describing the hall to the morgue.

"Yes, ma'am. Yelling. Shouting."

"I know what the word means," she replied tartly. "I thought maybe you'd explain a little more."

"I don't know anymore. Just hollering coming from the end of that hall, and I think my department head would like you to be with me when I check it out."

"I think probably my department head would, too," Sue said. "I'll be right down. Meet me at the south elevators."

Sue took a deep breath to stop the shivers shooting through her body. She had battled a number of fears during her life, including being confined in small places. Her feet were leaden as she headed for the elevator.

The appearance of the security guard reassured her. He was husky-looking, a barrel-chested middle-aged man with an intelligent face. "Just the two of us?" she asked. "Maybe we should take another guard."

"Can't spare them, ma'am," he apologized. "Too near shift change and we have to cover the parking lots. Don't worry. I can handle it."

As they talked, they were walking again toward the long hall Sue had traversed earlier. The guard explained briefly that only a few minutes before, two maids from housekeeping had reported hearing the cries and shouts from the deserted hall. The guard had called Sue right away.

They turned off the main hall in the south wing of the

building and entered the long, dim hall past the outpatient laboratory and the purchasing department. Sue heard a strong male voice shouting, muffled by closed doors but still unmistakable. The voice was coming from the morgue. The guard began trotting toward the locked door, answering loudly.

"Hold on! We're coming!"

Sue felt shivers again and only an iron will kept her trotting along behind the guard. She'd been in that room about six hours ago, and there was no sensible, logical, normal way anyone could be screaming from within. An overwhelming dread filled her, but she continued hurrying toward the voice.

The guard stopped at the door into the morgue receiving area and as he fumbled with his key, Sue tried to understand specific words in the screaming. Now that their footsteps were stilled, she could hear more clearly.

"Get me out of here! Help! Somebody help!"

The guard opened the door, rushed through the first room into the morgue itself. Sue followed more slowly, flipping on lights as she passed. She was standing at the doorway to the second room as the flourescent lights flickered into life above the autopsy tables and she and the guard stood still, frozen at the sight they beheld.

In a way, Sue was not surprised. In fact, she'd known from the time the guard paged her that this was the explanation. Sitting up on the emergency room stretcher, clutching the sheet to his bare chest in fear and cold, yelling in fright and anger was Joseph William David, no longer gray and stiff with death. He was shivering with cold, obviously frightened and angry but also full of life.

She rushed toward him, ready to assess his vital signs, to check again the knife wound that had spilled out blood and vicera and eventually his life. But as she reached for him, he drew back.

"Lay a hand on me and I'll flatten you," he threatened. His teeth were chattering and his eyes glittered.

"I want to help you," she protested. "We need to get you

out of here, get you warm and check you over. You've been hurt."

"All's I want is my clothes. I'm getting out of this place."

"You know who he is, ma'am?" the guard asked.

"Well, yes. He's the body we brought in here about four o'clock this afternoon—I mean the patient we brought in. We thought he was dead. . . ."

Her mind suddenly boggled at the maze of red tape, explanations, reports and legal hassles that faced her. Such an error, such a colossal *blunder*, would require a lot of fence-mending. Her mind centered on her own accountability. She'd signed the medical examiner's form, logged the so-called body into the morgue. And, of course, she was stuck now with handling this current situation: a very lively, angry patient instead of a cooling dead body.

Certainly the real onus would be on the physician who'd pronounced the patient dead. His was the obvious responsibility. But Sue, as area supervisor at the time, was the hospital's agent and she'd have her own share of grief.

As her mind was busy with these thoughts, and trying to determine her next proper move, the young man jumped down from the stretcher and draped the sheet around his naked body like a Roman toga. He was continuing his harangue, anger overtaking fear now that lights and human company were present. He was increasingly profane in his anger.

"I'm leaving this place. *Now!* You show me the door or you'll wish you had!"

The guard looked at Sue doubtfully. "You're the boss," he said.

"Well, of course he's not a prisoner. We can't hold him against his will." She appealed to the patient hopefully. "Won't you please come back to the emergency room and let us check you over? Then we'll get your clothes and you can sign a release and leave."

"Lady, I'm not going anywhere with you and I'm not signing any release. I'm leaving! Right now!"

He strode purposefully through the door into the receiving area, then out into the hall, his bare feet leaving dark prints on the moist floor.

Sue and the guard followed, Sue still pleading with the patient. "You can't go out in just a sheet. Please just let us check your abdomen. You were wounded."

He stopped and faced them, holding his sheet firmly in one fist, the other hand gesturing wildly. Despite being upset, Sue could see both humor and pathos in his posture.

"You aren't touching me again. Ever." He walked more rapidly, and at the junction with the main hall made the proper turn, by chance selecting the quickest route to an outside door. There was a seldom-used exit next to the purchasing agent's private office, almost hidden behind a stairwell. The patient headed directly toward it and stood tapping his bare toe as the guard unwillingly unlocked the door. Sue wondered where the cardboard tag had gone, the corpse tag that had been attached with a wire to that same toe.

Sue and the guard stood in silence watching the sheet-clad figure as he hurried away, heading toward the taxi stands next to the ambulance ramps.

"Maybe he can catch a cab," the guard said. "He doesn't have any money, though."

"Or anything else."

"You suppose he'll sue?"

"He probably couldn't collect," Sue answered. "He wasn't actually damaged. They usually have to prove we did some real damage."

"Lots of folks would consider being locked up in a pitch-black morgue for six hours at least an unpleasant experience."

Sue looked at the guard sharply, but his face was bland and she decided he wasn't being sarcastic. "It's going to be bad enough just to have the word get around. The papers and all. And he'll tell; he's really mad." She suddenly chuckled. "He was about as mad as anybody I've ever seen."

"I need to make my rounds and call in a report."

"And I need to do *something*. I don't know what. I think I'll call the director of nursing. Maybe she'll know what the proper procedure is." They separated and Sue started back toward the south elevators.

Suddenly she remembered. They'd left the lights on and the door unlocked to the morgue. *No way,* she thought. *Security can handle this. I wouldn't go back in that room for a million dollars!*

Few of her co-workers knew how much Effie MacAllister hated working on Sunday. She always enjoyed attending the First Baptist Church in Sandy Ford, sitting among her family. But nursing personnel at Brookshire usually had to work every other weekend and when she was scheduled for duty she tried to be as cheerful and uncomplaining as possible.

This was a light day even for a Sunday. By 10:30 she had finished most of her morning's work and decided to take her coffee break in the staff dining room. She bought coffee and a sweet roll from the cafeteria line, spotted a dark, serious young man sitting alone at a table for two. Josh Kingston. She had heard many reports about this newcomer. He was rude, arrogant. A fanatic. Nevertheless she walked over to his table.

"Mr. Kingston, I read your book this week and if I wouldn't be intruding, I'd like to talk to you about it."

He didn't smile, but he nodded toward the chair across the table and made a gesture to get up as she sat down. She continued talking as she scooped sugar into her coffee.

"After I finished your book, I went back to the Christian bookstore and got some other books on the subject. I've read *Satan on the Loose* and *Deliver Us from Evil* and a couple more."

He still said nothing, so she took a sip of her coffee and continued. "You're about the same age as my middle boy, I think. How old are you?"

"Thirty-three."

"Oh, you don't look that old! I thought you were about 28. My middle boy is like you; he always looks at things from a different point of view, you know what I mean? Then he'll explain it to you, and after you see what he means, it's all so clear and makes such sense you wonder why you never saw it before."

He spoke at last. "You think I'm like that?"

"Well, certainly!" She nodded so enthusiastically that her gray curls threatened to dislodge her stiff little organdy nurse's cap. "I've been aware of things around here for quite awhile now—strange things that nobody could explain. There was no connecting link I could see except they were abnormal and they made me nervous. Then I read those books and now it all makes sense. It's like I found the link that connects them all up together."

"And that link is?"

"Well, you know. Supernatural activity. I've really had my eyes opened. I've been a Christian for over fifty years, but I never knew much about any of the things you were writing about. But I believe you."

"It's been a long time since the church taught about spiritual warfare," Kingston replied. "There's rampant satanic activity against God's people today and most of them don't have any idea what's going on."

"Well, praise God for people like you who are telling us!" She smiled again and he nodded his thanks. "Look, explain to me about the prayer of authority."

He leaned toward her, his face now alive and intense, his voice urgent. "That's the kind of prayer that has the authority to *command* things to be done. Like the Bible says, 'We're seated with Christ in the heavenlies.' We've been given power over the enemy. 'Fever, go in the name of Jesus.' 'Spirit of fear, stop tormenting this person.' 'Satan, loose your hold on this body right now.' That kind of prayer."

"That sounds glorious," she breathed in excitement.

"It's very scriptural. Jesus addressed things like demons and storms and fever and all."

Effie drank her coffee automatically and munched her

sweet roll, her mind busy on the things the young man was saying. She'd never met anyone with his intensity and power. Suddenly a suspicion formed in her mind, and she asked tentatively, "Are you a, ah, Pentecostal?"

"I was born and raised Church of God, but I'm not really in any denomination now. If what you want to know is, am I filled with the Holy Spirit, well, yes, I am."

She was a little embarrassed. She'd been so impressed with his book and excited by his presence, it was awkward now to feel a barrier rising between them. And she suddenly tore it down by an act of her will. *I don't care if he claps and dances and rolls on the floor,* she thought firmly, shoving aside her traditional teaching and prejudices. *He knows something of God that I don't know and I want to learn about it.*

"One of the things that's been bothering me is this Project of Don Oliver's. It's all wrong, according to your book. That ESP stuff is all demonic."

He nodded. "Absolutely."

"Then things are going to get worse around here when it really gets started, aren't they?"

"Almost certainly."

"Then what should we do?"

"Pray. Wait on God. When He says move in a certain direction, move. It's not really our battle, you know. It's His."

"Can I ask you something personal?" As he nodded, she continued, "Why are you part of it? You know it's wrong."

"The Lord told me to come. When they asked me, I started to say no, but when I prayed, the Lord said I was supposed to come."

"That's remarkable."

"Not really," he contradicted. "Remember the story of Daniel. He was right there in the palace. God's man in Babylon."

She laughed. "And Ezekiel was with the slaves." She might not be as knowledgeable as young Mr. Kingston, but Effie knew her Bible. "They were both doing God's work."

94

"I'm glad you're here," he said. "You're the only real Christian I've met." His voice was almost humble and Effie felt a maternal tenderness toward him. He was so young and alone. She wanted to hug him and take him home and feed him a good meal. He was very thin. But there was nothing in him to encourage such behavior on her part. He was far too stiff and serious.

"If there's ever anything I can do for you, let me know," she said. "I work on Six North on the day shift."

"I may stop by to see you. At least it'll be a comfort to know you're there." He smiled suddenly and she was astonished at the transformation it wrought in his thin somber face. The smile changed him into a charming little boy, and she beamed back at him in utter delight.

"Time for me to get back on the job," she said. "I've enjoyed meeting you."

"Thank you, Effie."

She walked back to the elevators, smiling. God's man in Babylon, for all of his spiritual power, was quite a pussycat.

Barbara Simmons at 24 had a dainty but voluptuous body and she coddled it shamelessly. Her face was a small, flawless oval with perfect, even teeth. She had smooth, unblemished skin and a surrounding glory of long, black, gently curling hair. Her most striking feature was her eyes: large, framed with thick black lashes, a brilliant cobalt blue. Bebe, as she was known to the family, set off all this natural beauty with a tasteful selection of clothes.

Barbara felt sorry for her younger sisters, Wanda and Glenda, because the twins were so unattractive. At fourteen they had developed no flair for clothes or makeup and no interest whatsoever in the opposite sex. Their lives and prospects for the future seemed utterly dreary to Barbara, who derived what satisfaction life gave to her from her youth, beauty and success in attracting men.

The twins pitied Barbara because she was so limited.

They made jokes to each other about her shallow mind that had been poorly educated and never challenged to grow. Furthermore, she had no paranormal abilities at all. In the twins' opinion, she was almost a cripple, deprived and handicapped in comparison to them. What a tiny compensation was her beauty in light of all this lack!

Still, they viewed one another with a certain tolerance. The twins could be not jealous, but rather proud of Barbara's attractiveness, and Barbara made allowances for her sisters' lack of femininity and appeal. These tolerances didn't always mean they got along well; there were frequent skirmishes, but not nearly so many as might be expected considering the selfishness and willfulness of all three.

At Brookshire they would be alone, away from their parents for the first time.

The departure date was now almost upon them. Each of the Simmons reacted in a different way. The father was delighted; he planned to enjoy a rare time of peace and quiet while his three daughters were away. Their mousy little mother was hopeful that somehow this exciting, prestigious scientific study would produce more submission and obedience in her children.

Barbara looked toward the time at Brookshire as an escape from the boredom and tedium of her daily life; the twins were only the means toward a truly important end—that of meeting her own needs for excitement and change.

The twins were also eager to be gone. Even though Barbara was harder to manipulate than their mother, the testing, experiments and interviews should be fun. And, like their sister, they were eager for change and the excitement of a new environment.

The twins packed quickly. They dumped everything they owned into two suitcases and a number of brown paper sacks. After adding a stereo, sketchpads and paint box, two stuffed frogs and two books of poetry, they were finished. It had taken less than twenty minutes. They piled their belongings in the front hall and went upstairs to watch their older sister pack.

Barbara favored a more traditional approach to packing, considering each item and even referring to a list. The twins watched her in amusement.

"You'll be all day, Bebe."

"But I'll have what I need when we get there," their sister replied calmly. "I wish we had some idea how long the tests will take. I suppose at least a month."

"Suits me," said Glenda.

"As long as we're there, we don't have to go to school," Wanda laughed. Although the twins were avid students in areas that interested them, they disliked formal schooling.

Barbara stood in thought, tapping her long, brightly colored nails impatiently. "I guess the only safe approach is, 'When in doubt, take it along.' "

The twins lay on the bed and watched Bebe with interest. They considered their sister the most beautiful girl in the world, an opinion they suspected Bebe shared.

"It's going to be a blast," Wanda said gaily.

"We'll take them by storm," Glenda agreed.

Then they spoke in unison: "It's almost time to go!"

Barbara nodded absently, thinking how much more she would enjoy the trip if only they could leave behind the two black pit bull terriers which belonged to the twins. At first Barbara had refused to take them. Wanda and Glenda had rebelled: "If the dogs can't go, we won't go." No arguments could persuade the two girls. As usual, the rest of the family capitulated to them.

There were three farewell parties for Brandt, who had been a supervisory nurse at Brookshire for fifteen years. There was a tear-filled, emotional little get-together given in the nurses' lounge on the floor. They gave her a $25 gift certificate from a local department store. Then followed the obligatory reception held in the staff dining room where Carleton Phillips, gimlet-eyed hospital administrator, presented her with a Cross pen.

There was also a big party at the clubhouse of the trailer park, with food and drinks. They gave her a fifth of Johnnie Walker Black Label scotch and a T-shirt that said, "Love a Nurse P.R.N."

Charlie had never met Brandt but that didn't keep him from enjoying her party; he was fast becoming a familiar part of the clubhouse social life. It was almost midnight before he spoke to the guest of honor. She sank down next to him on the sofa, a can of beer held loosely in one hand. Sue Dunn joined them, sitting on Charlie's other side.

"Brandt is a nut on statistics," said Sue. "She'll quote them on most any subject."

"Shall we try doctors?" Brandt asked Charlie, grinning like a mischievous child. Then without waiting for an answer, "Your suicide rate is twice the national average. Over half of American doctors are divorced, and one in twenty is under psychiatric care. Want some more?"

"Not particularly."

"Did you know that a third of all doctors abuse amphetamines, barbiturates or narcotics? And these are only the ones who get caught!" She leaned toward him, and he could smell the beer on her breath.

"For crying out loud, you just hate doctors." Charlie was still forcing a smile, but he was irritated. "No wonder you want to quit."

"Like I say, it's a good week to quit. We had more deaths this week than any other I remember. Some pretty weird deaths, too."

"Like what?" Sue asked.

"Like a drowning on Three South. The resident put a feeding tube into the patient's lungs instead of his stomach so the nurses poured eight ounces of Isocal into his lungs. He didn't make it."

"The whole eight ounces? Why didn't they catch it?"

"They hung the bottle, didn't stay around to check. We had a strange death in O.R. Guy just died, for no reason." Brandt upended her beer can and drained it. Charlie suddenly realized he wasn't having any fun. A depressing conversation with two women who weren't even possibilities for his new back room.

"A young fellow, only twenty-six," Brandt continued. "Came in last Saturday night with a hot appendix. They rushed him to O.R., everything seemed perfectly all right, but when the doctor made the incision, he died. Just like somebody flipped a switch and turned him off."

"Saturday was horrible," Sue agreed. "I worked 3-to-11 for a change. Had one awful—"

"This was on 3-to-11," Brandt interrupted. "He died about eight p.m. They had trouble finding an acceptable cause for the death certificate. I mean, on the surface, it looks like he died of a knife wound, because there was nothing else wrong with him."

Sue was now staring at Brandt. "He died of a knife wound, you say?"

"Well, the surgical incision. They did a post-mortem and there wasn't anything wrong with him but that incision."

"He died Saturday, right about eight p.m., of a knife wound. And Brandt—" Sue's eyes grew enormous as the color drained from her face and she spoke in a strained voice. "That knife wound was in the *right lower quadrant?*"

"Well sure, Sue. That's where the appendix usually is."

"Brandt, I checked in a young man D.O.A. with a knife wound in the *right lower quadrant*. Saw him deposited in the morgue myself. And he came back to life about eight p.m." Sue looked from Charlie to Brandt seeking their understanding. "Don't you see? One died who shouldn't. One who was dead came back to life. Both had a knife wound in the right lower quadrant. Both at eight o'clock."

Charlie looked at Sue suspiciously. She appeared to be

almost in shock. Then she gained control and began speaking in a calm, deliberate voice.

"Just a series of coincidences, that's all." She rose to her feet and smiled a little unsteadily. "It's late and I've had all the hospital talk I can stand for one day. Goodnight."

She walked off and Charlie turned to Brandt. "You think she knew the guy who died? She seemed strange."

"I don't know. But I think she's right about one thing. We need to find something different to talk about."

Vincent Ponder spent the Sunday night of his last week in Omaha at his parents' restaurant. In a town full of excellent steak houses, the Ponders had achieved a moderate success with theirs and for years this building had been as familiar to Vincent as his home. Many nights he had spent, doing homework in the kitchen, clearing tables, playing his guitar for the customers. It was a familiar and beloved place, but tonight he filled a new role. Tonight he was an honored guest, sitting at a table with the customers instead of at the little table in the kitchen.

His mother smiled lovingly as she served him a fourteen-ounce sirloin, onions, buttered mushrooms, a large foil-wrapped baked potato and his father's famous green salad. It looked and smelled delicious, but Vincent had no appetite.

"I hope they feed you good, Vinnie," his mother worried. "You're still growing."

"I'll do fine, Mama. I can always go to a fast food joint," he teased. His parents had an understandable dislike for the growing number of hamburger and chicken establishments.

"Got a little present for you, Vinnie." His father joined them and handed Vincent a small gift-wrapped package.

"Oh, Dad, you didn't need—"

"I know. I wanted to." Both parents were now smiling at him.

They think it's some big honor or something to be invited

to this Project, Vincent thought to himself. *I guess they figure if I have ESP, it must be good. They don't even question it.*

He opened the gift with shaking hands. It was a camera, small but obviously expensive. How typical of his father!

"Dad, I have a camera. You shouldn't have—"

"You don't have one like this. You don't need a flash, and it focuses automatically." His father pointed out the various features of the camera. "We want lots of pictures of Brookshire."

They think it's a trip to summer camp, Vinnie mused. *They don't* really *understand why Project Truth chose me.* "Thanks a million, Dad. I'll send you a picture of everything."

Being an only child, born when his parents were older and almost despairing of a child, being extraordinarily gifted in looks, charm and ability, it was only natural that Vincent Ponder should be spoiled by his parents. Despite their permissiveness, he had grown up unspoiled, sensible and extremely popular.

Vincent had graduated from high school two years before, voted most popular boy in his class, offered a number of scholarships in both athletics and music. He had turned down the educational offers and spent all his time with music—studying, practicing, composing. The little boy who at age ten had been the guest soloist with the Omaha Symphony was still a serious student of music, and nothing short of perfection would satisfy him.

He might have continued on, blissfully wrapped in a protecting cloud of music, had there been no publicity about his talents. But his skills were so extraordinary, and his explanation for his achievements so remarkable, that there had been considerable publicity. Perhaps now the project at Brookshire could undo some of the harm done by irresponsible journalists. That was his hope, at any rate.

Vinnie choked down his tender steak, unaware of its flavor. He loved these two old people so much he was close to tears. They were so good, so unquestioning in their love for him. How could he ever repay their devotion?

He hoped he could, for their sakes, be normal. That

much they deserved. And soon. Before they discovered how very abnormal he really was.

Bright and early, Sue dressed in her jogging clothes and stepped out her kitchen door. The fall air was brisk and clean; her breath hung in a cloud before her. The first rays of golden light were filtering through the forest, making huge shafts and beams in the lingering early morning fog, and she smiled in pure joy at the sight.

"Hello." The voice startled her and she whirled around. Joshua Kingston stood beside her.

"Oh, good morning," she replied. "You're out for some exercise, too?"

"Not physical exercise. Bodily exercise profiteth little, but godliness is profitable unto all things."

She stared at him blankly. The few times she'd talked with this intense young man, she realized he occasionally spoke in Scripture.

"That's from Paul to Timothy," he explained. "A lot of modern-day Christians need to learn it. The body doesn't need to be coddled. It isn't going to heaven. We spend too many hours perfecting the body, thus neglecting the spirit."

"Well, I love to jog. It gets the blood stirring and then my spirit rises."

There was a slight tremor at each end of his mouth. For a moment she thought he was about to smile. "If it works that way, Sue—fine. May I call you Sue?"

"Of course. And you're Josh, right?"

He nodded and was silent a moment. Then he suddenly gave an expansive sweep of his arm, indicating the scene around them, the colorful trees still glistening with dew, shimmering in the golden rays of the morning sun. "Isn't it beautiful!" Then the smile broke forth. It transformed him. He was at once younger, handsomer, more likable. She smiled back spontaneously.

"Glorious!" she agreed.

"Somebody on the planning board for this complex must have been an ecology buff. They've preserved the natural flavor remarkably."

"Do you have an extra copy of your book? I'd like to read it." Her abrupt change of subject didn't seem to surprise him. He nodded slowly.

"Yes. Walk home with me, and I'll get one for you." They crossed the grassy area between the rows of trailers, passed Charlie Fortuna's home—no signs of life from it yet, although he was almost certainly at home and probably not alone—then came to Josh Kingston's dwelling. He opened the kitchen door and led her inside.

It was spotlessly clean, the only signs of his occupancy being several neat stacks of books on the little table near the doorway between the kitchen and living room. Sue sat primly on the couch as he went into the bedroom to get a copy of *The Children and the Power.*

She felt uncomfortable but not sure why. She hoped Josh wouldn't consider this encounter any kind of a commitment on her part. She had no desire to become like him, but many things were happening that she couldn't explain. Strange things that somehow she felt sure Joshua Kingston did understand. Or at least he thought he did.

Josh returned and handed her a slim paperback volume. The cover illustration was of a small silhouette standing between two tall figures, one dark and one light. Sue smiled as she took it.

"That reminds me of an old cartoon where the character had a little devil whispering in one ear and a little angel whispering in the other. Remember?"

"Yes," Josh agreed. "A pretty good illustration of temptation, I suppose."

"What kind of illness did these young people have? I know they were classed as psychotics, but what specific diseases?" She tucked the book under her arm and shoved both hands in the pockets of her jacket.

"Schizophrenia, manic-depression, you name it. They were suicidal, homicidal, some totally out-of-touch with reality. The only thing they had in common was the fact that they were all in a position to be delivered from bondage."

"How so?"

"Their parents were Christian."

She was silent for a moment, then began again. "You include twelve cases in your book. I assume there were others who did not respond to your treatment?"

"Yes."

"Psychotherapy wasn't helping any of them?"

"Not really. Maybe some decrease in symptoms while they were being medicated, but nothing approaching a cure."

"And you cured them?"

"No. Jesus did."

She looked at him searchingly. "Do you really believe they were all possessed by the devil?"

"Not all were possessed. Some were obsessed. And to explain the difference would take awhile. And it wasn't the devil, not Satan himself, but demons. But why don't you read the book? A lot of this is in there. Then we can talk."

"You realize I don't agree with you about these little men in red pajamas and pitchforks. But I do want to know more about what it is I don't agree with."

"Well, I don't believe they're little men in red pajamas either. You're just seeing them the way their public relations wants our society to see them." Josh leaned toward her intently. "They've been around at least six thousand years, and they're the same satanic strong men Paul warned about in Ephesians, the same principalities and powers and thrones and dominions. You see, they react differently in different ages, but they're still the same entities. Only the names have been changed to deceive the innocent."

Josh sat down in the chair next to her and continued. "Take the spirit that stirs men to war. He's a very violent, hostile fellow, and he has lots of guys in his department

104

working for him, like Hatred and Anger and Murder. They all have one goal, to drive men to violence. Maybe one society called this fellow Mars, one called him Ares and another Tyr. Still another pretends he doesn't exist, or calls him by some scientific, psychiatric name, but he's still the same guy."

"You're into mythology?" Sue asked in bewilderment. "What's that got to do with it?"

"The myths were just one way humans recognized evil spirits, one way the unseen realm broke into the material world. False gods are empowered by demonic forces. Like another one—he's been called Apollo, Balder, Frey, Phaethon, Baal and Ra. He's supposed to be the sun god; he's been worshiped ever since he was called Tammuz by the Babylonians. Don't you see, he's robbed the true God of honor and glory, and tried to supplant Him."

"So you think the old mythological figures were real?"

"Sure. That's why cosmogonic mythologies are so similar in every culture. Probably one of the most powerful is the Babylonian virgin-mother goddess; they called her Ishtar or Astarte. She's found all over the world in almost every society. She was Shingmoo to the Chinese, Aphrodite to the Greeks, Isis to the Egyptians, Isi in India, Hertha in Germany, Disa in Scandinavia, Venus in Rome, Virgo-Parbitura to the Druids, and she was Diana of the Ephesians. She is a real being, a supernatural evil spirit. Jeremiah called her the Queen of Heaven."

"You're a strange one," Sue said with a shake of her head. "Imagine anybody saying mythology is real; and not only real, but demonic."

"But I've found it works. If you're praying for somebody who's in bondage to alcohol, start binding the spirit of Bacchus or Dionysus. A satanic prince is involved in addition to alcohol; if you know his name and you bind him like the Bible says, his power is broken. And that's just one example."

Josh gave a short, humorless laugh. "Believe me, I know

how weird this must sound to you. You've been conditioned all your life to look at reality a certain way, and I come along with a totally different viewpoint. But that doesn't mean I'm wrong."

"I accept that."

"There are some evil spirits, some satanic strong men right over this hospital, too, and I know some of them by name." He paused. "How about the spirit of Pharmakia? That's drug-taking, and it's also sorcery. And of course, Asclupleus; he's the strong man over the whole system." He looked at her, gauging her willingness to hear more. "He's a snake, incidentally. The snake on the staff of the cadeusus. A snake, Sue."

Suddenly he relaxed and smiled and again she was astonished at the difference it made in him. She wondered suddenly how he was around his own friends, people who thought as he did. Then he could relax and be himself. She decided he was probably a very human person under those circumstances. But his ideas were unreal, totally unacceptable. It was hard not to laugh in his face.

"You think I'm a real fanatic, don't you?" he asked, almost a teasing tone in his voice.

"Well, yes. I guess I do," she admitted.

"There's another word for fanatic, Sue. It's overcomer. And there's another word for satisfied. And that's lukewarm." His face was somber again, his eyes intense and probing. "I know I've gone too far and said too much, but it matters so much to me."

Suddenly she realized he was trying to change her, to affect her with his beliefs, and she was angry. How dare he assume this superior role? She spoke firmly.

"Well, I'm quite satisfied the way I am. I don't want to be a fanatic." She was eager now to be gone, away from him and his intensity and his wild ideas and his unspoken assumption that he was totally right and anyone who differed was totally wrong.

He stared at her in silence, almost sadly. She was suddenly aware of her unflattering apparel, unruly hair, lack of makeup. *You're no prize yourself*, she thought tartly.

"Thanks for the loan of the book," she said, rising. "I'll have to go now if I'm going to have time to run a mile." She hurried out the front door.

It was raining in New Orleans and some of the Crescent City's residents were depressed by its cold, gray pall. Wallace Graham, however, was never influenced by such trivialities as weather. He had a singlemindedness of purpose and a power of concentration that dwarfed such minor concerns. He stood now in the bedroom of his apartment, putting the last of his shirts into his suitcase. A short, neat, ordinary-looking young man, he was dressed as usual in quiet but expensive good taste.

He was well-organized. He'd had the car serviced; the map had come from the travel club marked with the best route to Brookshire Medical Center; now his clothes were packed. There were traveler's checks and cash in his wallet. There was only one thing remaining: He must decide what to take along of his Zoran lore. He must be very sure about this.

Wallace had been a mostly unnoticed young man for the first 22 of his 28 years. Often moody. A loner, since his wealthy parents traveled so much. There was still a lot of controversy about exactly what had happened to him at age 22. A few people believed his story, most did not. But there was a continuing interest. The press, government officials, certain free-thinkers among the scientific world continued to listen as Wallace updated his accounts of his life among the aliens. No one offered an explanation, but an increasing body of irrefutable evidence indicated that *something* had happened to Wallace Graham that could not be explained away.

According to Wallace he had been chosen, chosen from the whole of the human race as an American contact with the Zorans, who appeared regularly in this country in their spaceships. From that time on he had been totally absorbed in them. He was never lonely; he was always busy, his time totally occupied with his interest in the Zorans.

Although their language was alien, he thought he could understand them a little. He knew what they wanted. They wanted to be heard, to have their influence and opinion valued by our younger, less developed race. Wallace knew very well that they liked his publicity; they were pleased by his television and radio appearances, the newspaper articles. Even if he was merely the object of ridicule, it seemed to serve their purpose somehow. And they were gratified by his acceptance into the scientific world.

What should he take along? The sketches of the spaceship, of course. The papers still insisted on calling it a UFO. He tried to tell reporters that the Zorans' ship had been identified, but the journalists were too interested in using catch phrases that would attract readers and sell their papers. These sketches had made quite an impression on the astronomers and engineers who'd seen them. Aerodynamically perfect, they'd said, impossible to fake.

And the star charts. They also revealed a knowledge not available to him in the usual way. Maybe they'd like his notes of the first interview with the Zorans. He'd jotted down all he could remember, right after being returned to earth, and the investigators usually found them interesting. He continued his list, pausing thoughtfully at each item, ready to respond immediately to that mental prod that meant his contacts from Zora were displeased. They said nothing and he accepted the negative confirmation.

He began gathering the material, putting it carefully into his briefcase. He'd been very prudent with his things; copies were in the bank vault, other copies hidden here in the apartment. The people at Brookshire might destroy what he submitted to them; he certainly wasn't going to be foolish enough to trust them.

He locked the briefcase and put it with the suitcases by

the front door. He'd be ready to leave first thing in the morning for the long drive to Brookshire.

"What do you know about suicide, Mal?" Don Oliver Franklin asked the rotund, smiling chaplain who was accompanying his friend on a tour through Brookshire. Franklin was striding majestically and Brown almost trotted to keep pace.

"Well, just what everybody knows. Why do you ask?"

Franklin gestured grandly; for once there was no cigar in his big hand. "We've had so many lately. Young fellow in Four overdosed; some friend must have brought him the drug. An old man on Eight Central cut his wrists; of course that is the psych floor where you expect that kind of thing, and I don't think there's any family to raise questions. But this last one, on Six North, that one might be trouble. She'd been hearing voices and the family might claim we should have watched her more carefully."

Malcolm suddenly felt his stomach tighten. "On Six North, Don Oliver? A surgical floor?"

"Yes, Mal. As a matter of fact, you talked to her yourself." They took a stairway from the seventh floor down to the sixth and emerged at the east end of Six South. This was pediatrics and the walls were decorated with larger than life paintings of cartoon and story book characters. Malcolm stared at a picture of Snow White and wondered briefly if he could recall the names of all the dwarfs. Then he pulled his mind back to Don Oliver Franklin and the suicides.

"I remember," he said, as casually as possible. "Young woman. She was mourning a child who had died?"

"Right."

"Yes. Her doctor asked me to visit her."

"What did she say to you? She speak of suicide?" Franklin asked.

"No. She was unhappy, mourning her little boy, but she didn't mention suicide. Why?"

"She just jumped out the window, fell six floors. A couple of nurses are trying to say she was enticed out, somebody calling her name from outside on the ledge. Pretending to be her little dead child."

One of the pediatric nurses spoke to Don Oliver and he turned aside to chat with her, leaving Malcolm with his own thoughts. He understood Franklin's concern. If the patient had been genuinely psychotic, the hospital might be liable for leaving her on a general floor without benefit of constant observation. But his thoughts moved quickly to his culpability. He'd seen the woman and never even called the doctor back to give him a report. He hoped desperately no one would make a point of his negligence.

Franklin spoke a cheery goodbye to the nurse and resumed his conversation without looking at Malcolm. "Two nurses claim to have heard the voices. I don't like it. Could give bad publicity to our Project."

"What can we do about it, Don Oliver?"

"Well, for one thing, we can be sure this death is classified as a straight suicide. Not let any information slip out about her hearing voices or any of that."

The Chairman of the Board turned into Six Central. "We have a dilemma, Mal. We can't give people the idea she was truly psychotic and we failed to protect her. Remember, when patients come into our temple of healing here, they're ours. We're responsible for them."

"Could you call it an accident?" the chaplain suggested.

"That doesn't really help, Mal. Whether she jumped or fell, it was our responsibility to protect her."

"Maybe there won't be any trouble, Don Oliver. Maybe you're worrying unnecessarily." The chaplain spoke with a hearty encouragement he didn't feel. "After all, there may come a time in any life when suicide could be the only answer."

Franklin looked at his friend in surprise. "You think so, Mal? That's hardly the usual pastoral position, I should think."

110

"This is advanced thinking, I realize, but in this woman's case perhaps she reached the limit of what she could endure and took the easy way out. No spirit voices, no psychosis, just a human being exercising her right to determine her own destiny. If we took that stand, it would keep things from getting, well, messy."

Franklin looked at his friend, eyes probing. "Is that so important, Mal? To keep things from being messy?"

"Well, certainly. We have to protect the hospital, don't we?"

"And you, Mal. We certainly wouldn't want anyone to think you'd seen a depressed patient and so failed to offer any real help that she took her own life shortly thereafter. We have to hit the precise balance between suicidal depression and genuine psychosis. She had to be just a little too far gone to receive help, but not so far gone as to require a locked ward. A very delicate balance."

"What are you saying, Don Oliver? Do you think I failed with that woman?"

"What do you think, Mal?"

As they walked briskly toward Six North, Malcolm Brown's thoughts churned. It was essential that he reject the idea of failure. How could he live with himself if he admitted his visit to the woman was worthless? He pushed aside this thought. A depressed and grief-stricken patient was a psychiatric problem not a spiritual one.

Sue laid the book down on the coffee table and went into the kitchen to fix a cup of herb tea. Josh's best-selling book, *The Children and the Power*, was exciting and disquieting.

She returned with her tea but didn't pick up the book again. There was already so much to absorb and consider there was no room for more.

It would have been simple to discount it all as hoax, to simply assume it was wrong. But there were too many proofs, too much documentation that the psychotic children Josh wrote of had really been healed of their various mental illnesses. And she was too logical to consider the cures a result of coincidences or accidents. No, there was undoubtedly something here, and that something might mean that all her life she'd been mistaken about the nature of reality. The idea overwhelmed her.

She picked up the book and reviewed the first case history. The patient was a fifteen-year-old girl, the youngest child of well-educated, loving parents. She'd been a behavior problem for years, increasingly emotionally disturbed. Then she'd become more and more involved in destructive and antisocial behavior, finally deteriorating into genuine psychosis. She was diagnosed as a manic-depressive psychotic, with repeated suicide attempts. She was given the routine treatment for this type of problem—chemotherapy, psychotherapy, none of which was effective. She had grown worse and worse until she was finally classified as hopeless by the psychiatrists in charge.

In desperation, her grieving parents had allowed Josh a free hand. He had led the family quickly through instruction about spiritual warfare, and the child through deliverance. She had been set free and returned to her delighted parents. She went on to become an honor student in her school, a cheerful and obedient daughter, no longer a problem. It was almost too good to be true, Sue thought. Too much a fairy tale. If it were that simple, surely more people would know about it, take advantage of it.

She turned the book over and read the biographical notes by the rather unflattering picture of Josh. This was quite a man, she thought, radiating power and confidence like no one she'd ever known. He certainly didn't fit her picture of the meek and mild Christian. Josh was uncompromising. She was repelled, but still fascinated by him.

She turned the page and continued to read.

When the plane ticket arrived, prepaid, first-class, LeRoi

Williams was tempted to sell it and hitchhike to Brookshire. A neat way to make a few extra dollars. But he was cautious; if they found out, they might ask him to leave and he didn't want that. In his 19 years, he had completed nine years of formal education and held 27 different jobs, all of which he had hated. The trip to Brookshire promised to relieve him of this kind of life. He dare not jeopardize his position with Project Truth.

If his formal education had been limited, his street knowledge of the black section in his town was excellent. He was most proficient with a knife; only once had he come off secondbest in a knife battle and a long, ugly scar on his cheek was a reminder of this defeat. The sparse little beard he'd cultivated only partially succeeded in hiding it. LeRoi could also open the door and start the engine of any car; keys weren't necessary. No undercover policeman could deceive LeRoi. As he walked the streets of his native Huntsville, Alabama, he could tell with unerring accuracy who was "holding," who was "strolling," who was "cruising" and who would make a profitable target for muggers.

His preparations for the trip to Brookshire took little time. He packed his extensive wardrobe of bizarre, avant-garde clothing into cardboard suitcases and told his friends goodbye. He was very proud of his psychic talents; there was little else in his life to encourage pride. He often performed, using his paranormal skills to gain attention and approval. It was the high point of his life to be sought out by Project Truth at Brookshire. His friends were properly envious and he was satisfied.

He took a bus to the airport, not sorry at all to be leaving Huntsville. He had no great affection for his hometown, what little family he had left, or his ties to the past. He was ready for new horizons.

"I've read your book. Now tell me, what in blazes is going on around here?"

Josh smiled at Sue and set a cup of tea in front of her. She had come to his trailer to return the book and had stayed for refreshments. Now possibly a door was opening in her to receive some truth.

"What makes you think I know?" he countered.

"Don't play games. I'm really serious."

He put the sugar and a carton of milk on the table and sat down opposite her. He looked deep into her eyes. His spirit could evaluate people much better if he could see their eyes. Sue's were a soft brown, gentle and harmless as a fawn.

"Let's start with a few facts. There is a supernatural realm, things that transcend the natural laws as we know them and operate outside the five senses. Agreed?"

She nodded. So far so good.

"There are only two sources of supernatural power. It is not inherent in man. No ESP or anything like it is a natural property of human beings. If it's supernatural, there are only two sources, one good and one bad."

He took a sip of tea. So far he sensed no resistance. "Now the good side is always done in accordance with God's Word, and brings you closer to Him. And up until very recently, the bad side, the devil and his fallen angels and his demons, felt their cause was best served by remaining hidden. So they did everything they could to convince mankind that they didn't exist. They saw to it that the devil appeared comical, the sort of a joke or fairy tale only a child or a half-wit would believe in. They promoted the idea that if you were intelligent, you must be materialistic and humanistic."

Sue signaled for him to continue.

"But here lately, Satan and his friends have begun to change their policy. They're exposing themselves, allowing us to see some activity. But get this now. They're trying to disguise themselves. They're reaching out for other labels, either medical or scientific like ESP. Or 'force.' It's acceptable now to believe in the supernatural, as long as you keep

114

it scientific and not religious. Religion is getting less supernatural while science is getting more so. That's the devil's
current strategy."

"So you think all the weird things in the hospital, the
deaths, the bizarre happenings are being caused by the
devil?"

"Maybe not directly. But he has a lot of channels he can
work through, human and demonic."

"Do you know many people who believe in demons?
Like you said in your book, disembodied spirits? That's
hard to swallow, Josh."

"Because you can't see them? You can't see a virus, either,
but you believe in it because you see the results of its activity
and because the experts in the field say it exists. Well, the
same is true of demons. You've been conditioned to think a
certain way. It's hard to change."

"I'm not at all sure I want to."

As Sue sipped her tea thoughtfully, Josh reassured himself that in all his dealings with unbelievers, whether about
salvation, or healing, or deliverance from evil spirits, he
had found the most effective weapon to be truth. It had a
way of confirming itself to all those who listened with an
open heart.

"What does astrology have to do with it?" Sue asked.
"You said in your book it was dangerous."

"Well, there are a lot of ways demons can get into a
position to harass people. Through sin, drugs, satanic music, but probably the main way is through the occult. That's
a wide open door. The occult is just about as dangerous as
letting a baby play with a basket full of snakes."

"Most people read the horoscope! I do, just for fun. I
don't really believe it though."

"It's dangerous whether you believe it or not. It's also
forbidden by God."

"That's silly. I've been a Christian all my life, and I've
never heard anything like that."

"You're hearing it now. And the Bible is full of it. Deuteronomy 18, Isaiah 47—I have a whole list if you're interested. But horoscopes are just part of the occult. They're certainly not the only way demons can get at a person."

"Are you trying to frighten me?" she asked angrily.

"You're already frightened, Sue. Not by me but by what you're seeing around you. And you don't need to be scared! If you're properly armed and know what you're doing, you can control *them!* Jesus said, 'I have given you power over all power of the enemy.' But there *is* a battle and we *do* have to fight."

Sue drained her tea and nodded, her eagerness to be gone very obvious. "Well, thanks for the tea. I really need to go." She rose.

"I'm glad we can talk this way, Sue. Hope I didn't offend you." He went with her to the door and stood there as she walked down his steps. As she turned around to say goodbye, she looked young and totally vulnerable.

She nodded at him, smiling uncertainly. As she walked away, Josh watched her tenderly. *She called herself a Christian*, he thought. *Lord, let's make it true.*

A brisk wind swirled around the corner of his trailer, rustling the fallen leaves on his little concrete slab. He shivered and stepped back inside, shutting the door firmly.

"Are you in right standing with the law again, Mal?" Don Oliver Franklin asked slyly. He puffed at his black cigar, a look of bright-eyed interest on his genial face. His office was the scene today of a department meeting for the Project. The ministers and spiritual leaders were gathered in his office to discuss the religious aspects of paranormal talents, and yet Franklin had started off with an exceedingly embarrassing question for his friend.

Pastor Malcolm Brown sat up straight, flustered. "Why, of course, Don Oliver. There was never any problem, really. They just asked me about the patient's suicide." He forced his mind to return to his frustrating visit to the depressed young woman on Six North. How he wished he'd never been asked to see her!

"The investigation is closed?"

"Yes, no problem at all." Malcolm sighed, remembering. There should have been no investigation. The suicide should have passed as routine, but the strange stories of ghostly voices persisted despite all they could do. Two nurses had made a trip to police headquarters to make a statement about the voices; an inquest had been ordered. What distressed the chaplain most was the linking of his name to this rather sensational event. He wanted badly for the affair to die down, be settled once and for all. And now to have Franklin bring up the subject at a meeting of the religious leaders of his Project, that was embarrassing.

"The woman who heard voices and jumped from her room?" Josh Kingston was suddenly interested.

"Yes," Malcolm answered. "She was obviously deranged by grief. Her young son had died recently."

"I heard about that. Lord, I wish she'd talked to a Christian before she died! There was no need for that to happen."

Franklin chuckled slightly. Brown whirled to face his old friend, hoping he would say nothing, but his hopes fell as Franklin spoke softly. "I suppose it would require a certain type of Christian, Josh. One with a more fundamentalist viewpoint than our friend Mal. Because, you see, Mal did visit her. Made a pastoral call on her."

Josh looked at Malcolm intently. The other ministers followed the exchange with interest. "What did you say to her?"

"I tried to be reassuring. She was under a doctor's care."

Josh shook his head in sudden anguish. "That poor, poor woman! She was under a supernatural attack and there was nobody to tell her about a supernatural God."

"And you, of course, would have saved her?" Malcolm asked icily.

"Not I. But Jesus. He's shut out of this hospital."

Franklin's smooth voice flowed into the silence. "Let's not

117

argue among ourselves. The woman is dead, so the question at this point is academic."

Malcolm sighed in relief as Josh was silenced. What accusations! The others were on his side; he could tell by their faces. Once again Josh came across as a rude fanatic.

It was the first really cold night of the year. The clubhouse was cozy and warm with a huge fire burning away merrily in the big fireplace. The glow reflected off the wooden floors, making the room seem smaller and more cheerful than usual. Sue Dunn sat in a big armchair near the fire, shoes off, feet tucked warmly under her, watching the dance of the flames. With half an ear, she listened to Isabel and Charlie as they talked.

They shared a plump sofa facing the fireplace. Isabel had the coffee table in front of them spread with newspaper clippings, letters, resumes and notes. She talked excitedly to Charlie, who sipped a rum sour and listened placidly.

"Now look at this, Charlie," she said, waving a newspaper story under his nose. "This fellow Wallace Graham is unreal, incredible. He's been up in a flying saucer twice, and he talks to aliens all the time."

"Sure, Isabel. And I'm the Queen of England."

"No, Charlie. There's proof. When he started telling his story nobody would believe him; they laughed, naturally. But he has proof! He can draw star charts, yet he never studied astronomy. He made a sketch of the spacecraft and the engineers at NASA said it was aerodynamically perfect. They've tested him at Princeton and MIT, and nobody can shake his story. He really was in a UFO."

"Isabel, you're as nuts as he is." Charlie was mellow from his drinks, teasing her gently.

She ignored his response. "I'm setting up interviews for him with some of the university people. Want to see the rest of his file?"

She handed Charlie a manila folder neatly labeled *Wallace Graham* but Charlie laid it in his lap, unopened.

"So we've got the twins, and this musician who's coming this week, and now the space traveler. Who was the other one?"

Sue was drowsy, mesmerized by the play of firelight and the comfort of her chair, but something was nagging at her mind.

Isabel drew another folder out from the untidy tumble of papers on the coffee table. "LeRoi Williams. This boy probably has the most exciting range of telekinetic powers in America. He's no Uri Geller, but he's close. He's nineteen, black, from Alabama. He can do amazing things—heat water, open doors, tip tables, just with the power of his mind. And he has multiple personalities, too. I can't wait to see him."

Charlie gave a snort of derision and took a healthy swallow of his rum sour. "I can't believe you. You're really hooked on this, aren't you?"

"Aren't you, Charlie?" Isabel asked in surprise. "Don't you believe in it?"

"I believe in two grand a week for caring for five patients who aren't even sick. That's what I believe in." He laughed in delight. "The good old American motive, the profit motive. I couldn't care less if they're psychics."

Isabel took the folder *Wallace Graham* from Charlie's lap and put it and *LeRoi Williams* carefully beside her and began straightening the other papers on the table. "At first, I was only interested in what it would do for my career; that was my motive. But now I am kind of hooked. I mean, I'd want to do this even if it did nothing at all for me professionally. I find it fascinating, Charlie."

She looked up at him, the firelight glinting off her dark glasses. "There's something special here, something they all have in common. Like some kind of power that's just starting to show up among humans. I've never experienced anything like it, and I want to know all about it."

Sue turned to watch her friends as they talked. Her mind recalled what Josh had said, a power that had been hidden, that was beginning to expose itself, pretending to be scientific. She spoke for the first time.

"Isabel, do think this power, whatever it is, is good? Or is it evil?"

"Lord, Sue, I never thought about that," Isabel chuckled. "All I know is, it's real, and it exists, and I want to find out about it."

"It exists," Sue repeated. That's what Josh had said. But there seemed to be no pattern to all the different manifestations. Yet somewhere there must be a common denominator. Josh would say they were all evincing a power that was evil.

"They'll all be here by the end of the week. Then the fun will start!" Isabel finished straightening her papers and slipped them into a slim brown briefcase. "It's getting late. Want to walk me home?" She smiled coyly at Charlie.

"Why not go to my place? I've finished my back room, and it's worth seeing." He smiled like a sleepy Buddha.

"All right. After all your talk, I'd like to see it," Isabel agreed.

As they walked away together, Sue turned back to watch the firelight. *He's fickle as the wind,* she thought. *I hope Isabel comes to her senses before he hurts her.* The fire was warm and the room cozy, but Sue felt disquieted. The question of whether the power was good or evil had seemed silly to Isabel, irrelevant. But it seemed very important to Sue. If Josh were right, and any supernatural power that did not come from God was evil, the Project Truth might be a very dangerous thing.

When the taxi pulled up in front of Brookshire Memorial Hospital, Barbara Simmons stepped daintily out of the front seat. "Wait here," she told the driver. "Someone will come for the luggage. Glenda and Wanda, you come with me."

"What about these dogs?" the young driver asked. Because Barbara had the unconscious arrogance of those who are always admired, he had been intimidated into allowing the dogs to ride in the taxi. Though it was a large vehicle, the three passengers, piles of baggage and two large dogs made it a tight squeeze. The dogs were now nervous, whining and slobbering. "If you three girls are all leaving the cab, you must take the dogs with you."

"I don't know where we're to stay," Barbara pleaded. "Couldn't you watch them just a few minutes?"

"Sorry, lady, I made a concession to let you even bring them."

While Barbara stood in thought, Glenda opened the taxi's rear door and jumped out. "Come on, Castor," she called.

Wanda opened the opposite door and clapped her hands eagerly. "Come on, Pollux! Come on, boy!" Both dogs lunged from the car excitedly.

They entered the building together, the dogs making a swirl of noise and confusion around the twins.

Suddenly the twins drew back in distaste. *Oh, Glenda, I don't like it here*, Wanda thought.

Me, neither, Glenda returned. *This is a terrible place.*

Without speaking words, they reached out and grasped hands. Then they crossed the lobby behind Barbara toward the information desk as many eyes turned to watch them.

"I'm Barbara Simmons," Bebe spoke to the information clerk. "My sisters are here for Project Truth. Psychic talents, you know." The clerk turned to stare at the twins.

She acts like we got horns or something, Glenda thought.

No respect at all, Wanda agreed. *We ought to sic the dogs on her.*

Okay, Glenda nodded. *Let's let the dogs have a little exercise.*

Hand-in-hand, the girls began to concentrate deeply, their blue eyes squinting behind their thick, steel-rimmed glasses. The dogs, as though goaded by some unseen prod, began to move about in agitation, whining and nervous. Only after the dogs became truly frenzied and nearly emptied the lobby of people did the twins relax. They stood together, smiling in secret pleasure.

They won't stare at us like that again, Wanda thought.

121

We can be in charge here just like at home, if we want to, Glenda thought in triumph.

Vincent Ponder was tired and his hand numb by the time he and his two companions, LeRoi Williams and Wallace Graham, had traversed the pathway into the Brookshire mobile home compound. He switched his heavy suitcase into his other hand and looked around. It was just as it had been described to him, rustic and woodsy. The homes were identical, medium-sized and nearly new. Each had a concrete slab outside the front door, equipped with redwood furniture.

"We're third from the end of this row," Vinnie said, leading his two new roommates along the pathway to their new home. "They tell me that our mobile home has been enlarged to include three bedrooms!"

Falling leaves blew over their patio as the three young men crossed it. A small placard was taped to the door:

Wallace Graham
Vincent Ponder
LeRoi Williams

Vinnie unlocked the front door and they staggered in, dropping their bags in relief. They were in the living room, furnished neatly in a nondescript style with one sofa, two chairs and a small dining table. To the front was a small kitchen, and to the rear a narrow hall led past one small bedroom and bath to a second, larger bedroom, and then to the newly added third bedroom at the end. Vinnie opened a window and the crisp fall air dispelled some of the mustiness.

"Not bad," LeRoi Williams commented.

Wallace Graham merely grunted. He had hoped for separate quarters.

"I guess the first thing is to decide how we bunk," said Vinnie. "I have no preference."

"I'll take the end room," LeRoi said. He picked up his

bags and headed down the hall as the other two men stared at his long, shaggy hair and jet black jacket and pants.

"I'll take the middle room," said Wallace indifferently and carried his expensive bags down the hall without further comment.

Vinnie shrugged and placed his bags in the smaller bedroom. Soon he and LeRoi were back together in the living room.

"I brought my stereo and guitar," Vinnie remarked. "Hope you like music."

"Yeah, sure," LeRoi nodded. "Music your thing, man?"

"Well, yes. Some things about my music aren't strictly normal." Vinnie spoke hesitantly, always at a loss to explain his psychic talents.

"I got what they call telekinesis," LeRoi said proudly. "I'm the onliest one they got which can boil water by my mind." He seated himself on the couch and stretched his long legs out in front of him.

Vinnie smiled uncertainly. "Ought to come in handy when the stove won't work."

Wallace appeared from his bedroom. "The electricity's not on. I plugged in my clock and it won't run."

"Think you can handle that, LeRoi?" Vinnie asked, but the other two simply looked at him blankly. *This is really going to be great*, Vinnie thought. *We have nothing in common at all, except we're all weirdos.*

"Don't you think it's a little strange that things are going wrong already?" Wallace asked.

"Hey, man, take it easy," LeRoi said. "Things bound to need some fixing right at first."

"I just thought you'd want to know," Wallace said stiffly and returned to his bedroom.

"Rich guy," LeRoi said knowingly. "Too much college. Betcha I know things he'll never learn in college."

"I'm sure you do," Vinnie replied.

"Where you from, man?" LeRoi asked.

"Omaha."

"What do you do?" LeRoi's eyes were very black and he fingered his wispy little beard constantly.

"I told you, I'm a musician."

"That's neat. You in a group?"

"Not right now. I work alone, usually. Sometimes I teach, do scoring and arranging."

"Oh, you play classical stuff." LeRoi looked disappointed and Vinnie was suddenly very weary of the inquisition.

"If you really want to know, I play every kind of music and I play it perfectly. I can play every musical instrument ever made and almost every composition ever written. I have perfect pitch and absolute pitch and total recall. I am your ultimate musician."

LeRoi was a bit surprised, but not at all disconcerted by Vinnie's outburst. He nodded. "Great, man. I want to hear you."

Vinnie relaxed and the tension left. *We're gonna make some team,* he thought. *LeRoi's a fugitive from "Motown"; I'm the "all-American boy" with psychic overtones, and Wallace is a cold fish from the bayou.*

"The young men are all here. I met them before they left for their trailer." Isabel dropped into the chair opposite Charlie Fortuna and began to organize the food on her lunch tray. "Vincent Ponder looks fairly normal, but those other two are something else."

"You should be used to strange people, being a head shrinker." Charlie was wolfing down a double helping of meatloaf and mashed potatoes that were almost submerged in thick gravy.

"They're strange in a strange way," she explained. "Not just neurotic-strange; they're more weird-strange."

"That makes it all crystal clear." He was beginning to like Isabel. In spite of his basic prejudice against what he called pushy women, and his irritation with her sunglasses and her bandbox perfect grooming, he found her amusing. Her personality was sufficiently complex to keep him from boredom. And their night together had been more than satisfactory.

"Now that they're here, it's time for us to start producing." She was eating lima beans one at a time, spearing them delicately with her fork.

"I wish you hadn't said that," Charlie said ruefully. "I have no idea how I'm to evaluate the medical aspects of paranormal activity. Everybody else in the Project has help, but I'm the only one in the medical area."

"Poor baby," she grinned. "No help at all?"

"Well, I could probably get a nurse," he admitted.

"I hear you do a lot of that . . . "

He smiled indulgently, having no objection to his growing reputation as a fox in the hen house. "Seriously, Isabel, I can't get any kind of specific instructions from the top."

"I'm no better off, actually." Isabel's face showed some strain. "We've had several meetings, but nothing ever gets done, nobody ever makes a decision about anything. I'm the only one who has actually *done* anything! I made some appointments for Vincent Ponder and Wallace Graham. But, Charlie, we really don't have a game plan yet for the Project."

Charlie shook his head. "Well then, the door is wide open for you to take over; show these male chauvinists who's running things."

"I just may do that," Isabel retorted.

Charlie finished the last of his food and lit a cigarette. "Where are the psychics housed?" he asked.

"Right down the row from you. There's you, then Josh Kingston, then the three guys. Hope they don't mind being in the same trailer. I got an extra bedroom added. Don't think that wasn't a hassle."

"Isn't it kind of tacky to put them all in together? I thought this was supposed to be a high-class operation."

"It is. And each was to have his own place, but the two trailers that were supposed to be vacant had occupants that we couldn't move."

"And the Simmons girls? When are they arriving?"

"Sometime today," Isabel answered. "They'll call for me when they get to Brookshire."

"Dr. Nebo, dial operator. Dr. Nebo, dial operator.

"That may be them now," Isabel said excitedly. "See you later."

When Isabel arrived in the hospital lobby, she saw a scene of wild disorder. Two large, untidy dogs were dashing madly around the lobby, scattering patients, visitors and assorted luggage.

A small, dark-haired, beautiful young woman stood by the information desk, calling to the dogs: "Castor, Pollux, you stop right now and come to me." The dogs ignored her.

At the end of the counter two young girls in thick, steel-rimmed glasses stood giggling at the confusion, holding hands. The Simmons twins, Isabel decided. They were identical, small for fourteen and appeared awkward in their baggy blue skirts and pink shirts. Their straight black hair was worn in an uneven, shoulder-length bob.

Isabel approached the counter, speaking in a take-charge voice. "Here, now, we can't have this. Those dogs will have to go outside."

"I can't make them mind me," Barbara Simmons complained. "I don't want them here, either, but the girls wouldn't come without them. The dogs are twins, too." She offered this last as though it explained the whole situation.

"Don't you have leashes?" Isabel asked.

When Barbara shook her head, Isabel turned to the operator. "Call security. Tell them we need help."

The twins walked toward Isabel, still holding hands, and stared at her.

"Leave our dogs alone," one said to her.

"They go everywhere with us," the other added.

"They can't stay inside the hospital," Isabel said firmly. "Maybe at the mobile home compound; we'll see. But there

126

are sick people in this hospital, and we can't have a disturbance like this."

Two uniformed men from the security department arrived and began chasing the dogs around the lobby. Soon they were caught and, to Isabel's great relief removed from the building.

"The guard will take you to the mobile home park," Isabel explained to Barbara Simmons. "The porters will bring your luggage and you can get settled. I'll take the girls up to our testing room on the eighth floor and show them around."

"The dogs go wherever we go," one twin said insistently.

"Surely not everywhere. How about to a movie? Or a party?" Isabel tried to make it light but there was no answering smile from the twins.

Isabel turned to the sister again. "There are health laws. You can understand that. We can't have dogs in a hospital."

The twins drew closer together and began to speak in a strange language, vaguely Oriental in sound, both speaking at the same time yet obviously communicating. Isabel felt uneasy. She knew from their resume that this was their "common, unlearned language" they had shared since they were babies. She also knew they had a total telepathic communication and other paranormal skills. After a while, they were silent and one said to Isabel, "O.K. They can go to the trailer."

Isabel was annoyed that they seemed to be granting a concession rather than yielding to authority, but she was glad the matter was settled. She spoke again to the sister, giving her a house key and explaining the setup in the trailer.

"I'm sorry about the dogs," Barbara said without conviction. Isabel nodded tersely. She already disliked this young woman intensely.

"If they stay at the trailer, maybe that'll be all right," Isabel said doubtfully.

She turned to the two little psychics. "Would you like to see where we'll be working?"

The twins nodded without smiling and followed Isabel to the elevator.

Don Oliver Franklin varied his walks through Brookshire Hospital. On this day, he took an elevator to the eighth floor and worked his way down. Shortly after 4 p.m. he stepped off the elevator on Three Central to face closed double doors marked *Surgical Suite. No Admittance. Authorized Personnel Only.* He pushed the doors open and entered.

Only ten of the 28 operating rooms were in use. There was always a lull as the dinner hour neared; things would pick up a bit later, then settle down again for the night, open for emergency cases only. He walked slowly through the PARR area (post-anesthesia recovery room). There were six patients, all sleeping soundly. Two registered nurses were sitting at the desk, punching charges into the computer. A licensed practical nurse was checking blood pressures. A fatigued surgical resident was dictating his operative report, speaking into the dictating phone linked directly to medical records.

Second North was obstetrics; twelve rather primitive delivery rooms, a huge newborn nursery and a smaller neonatal intensive care unit, plus six private and 32 semi-private rooms for mothers. The labor wing was one of the few places Franklin avoided.

There had been problems here of late. The young man who had posed as a doctor and examined patients in labor had caused a stir; despite all they could do, it did get into the papers. What had they called him? Oh, yes, "The Peeper in the White Coat." And now there was this flap about the number of Caesareans being done; the rate at Brookshire was over sixty percent and still rising. The press was taking an interest. To Franklin it was unhealthy for the public to begin questioning the doctors or the hospital, presuming to judge them or their actions.

The public should have an unquestioning faith in the medical system. He was disturbed by Dr. Kingston's attitude and wondered if this choice had been a mistake. No, it would prove out, he decided.

He cooed through the plate-glass viewing window at the newborns. The statistics for the day were bad; 32 babies, 16 born by Caesarean Section and 19 had an infection. (Nosocomial infections, those which the patient contracted because he was in the hospital, were an increasing problem also.)

Several of the administration offices were on the central wing of first floor. He knew almost every employee here and greeted each of them by name. Young Mr. Givens of public relations grinned and boasted, "The dinner tomorrow night for the Project is really shaping up." Franklin nodded.

He finished his tour in the doctors' lounge behind the emergency room. Though a small and somewhat ratty little room, it was handy to the action and was used a great deal. Two young men on the house staff were sitting on a sagging brown sofa watching a local news show. Franklin poured himself a cup of coffee from their battered pot and joined them without an invitation. He lit a long black cigar and settled down for a little visit.

Sue stood by the window in Isabel's kitchen, watching the colors change in the twilight as her friend prepared a special for dinner. While Isabel tossed chunks of green pepper, onion, celery and pineapple into a shiny copper wok, Sue wondered how well Isabel could see in the dark glasses she wore everywhere. She watched as Isabel opened a can of boned chicken and tossed the contents into the strange mixture she was concocting.

"I've read Josh Kingston's book," Sue said, a little defensively. As she'd expected, Isabel looked up with disapproval.

"Why? The man's a fanatic, Sue."

"Well, there's just so much queer stuff going on around here: people dying, people coming back to life, accidents and strange incidents. I've been trying to see some kind of pattern to it all. I think Josh knows a lot about this kind of thing."

"Well, before long I'll know a lot, too." Isabel was adding liquids to her mixture—molasses, catsup, vinegar and the juice from the can of pineapple.

Sue watched suspiciously; Isabel always cooked only one dish. If it wasn't good, there was nothing else.

"I'm planning to learn everything there is to know about psychics," Isabel continued.

"Where did Franklin find them? I mean, how did he know what rock to turn over?"

"Sue, that's not fair." Isabel turned up the heat under the wok and began adding spices—ginger, nutmeg, coarse ground black pepper. "Like with Vincent Ponder. The compositions are excellent and experts say they're genuine, really written by Brahms, Liszt, Handel."

"A real ghost writer, huh?"

Isabel ignored Sue's humor. "Will you pour the wine and light the candles? I'll be through here in a minute."

The table was set for two, done in Isabel's usual style, with a fresh arrangement of bright autumn leaves, real silver and candles. She carried in plates heaped with her strange dinner and set them on the table. Sue tasted the food; it was delicious.

"I heard about your twins and the dogs. They made quite an entrance."

"It was something to see," Isabel agreed.

"Was it really the twins making the dogs act that way?"

"I think so. They seem to have some psychic control over those animals."

"Who has control over the twins?" Sue asked.

"I don't think anybody does." Isabel laughed. "But we don't expect children like Glenda and Wanda to be well-adjusted socially. After all, they're bound to look on the rest of us as a little inferior. You and I can't see inside a person's body. Nor can we read minds."

"I don't want to," Sue declared. She grew thoughtful. Often she'd envied her friends who had children; if she allowed herself to dwell on it, her heart would ache with longing for a child of her own. *But I wouldn't have kids like that,* she mused. *They'd mind me, by golly, or they'd have to eat a few meals standing up. Their problem isn't just because they're psychics. It's also because they're brats.*

"Shall we go to the clubhouse after dinner?" Isabel asked.

"I don't think so," Sue replied. "I'd like to go back through Josh's book."

Isabel shook her head. "Don't get caught up in all that, Sue."

"All what? The supernatural? You're just as interested."

"Yes," Isabel agreed. "But I'm studying what science has to say, not the ideas of some religious fanatic. There's a big difference."

"Just offhand I'd say religion is better qualified to deal with the supernatural than science," Sue retorted.

"Well, don't let's argue! Finish your dinner and go read your book while I head for the clubhouse to meet Charlie."

Sue cleaned her plate, but she was still annoyed. *The Simmons twins weren't the only ones around with a bit of the brat in them,* she thought.

Josh was his usual intense self. "It's natural for man to cry out for supernatural help in times of crisis. Yet modern novels and television and movies today mostly present a godless world. That's misleading. For the reality is that man's basic urge is to seek help from his Creator."

Though Josh's eyes were probing hers, Sue was no longer

upset by his unsmiling intensity. She had been given a small glimpse of the gentle spirit behind the gruff exterior.

"I can accept that," Sue replied. "When my father had a heart attack, all I could do was keep saying, 'Don't let him die.'"

"Yet if man is left on his own to find God, he makes mistakes. He ends up with a very wrong idea about what God is like, and it generates fear and guilt and self-condemnation," Josh added.

They were standing outside Sue's kitchen door in the dawning of early morning. It was chilly but clear, the beginning of a beautiful day. Their chance meeting as Sue returned from her run had quickly turned into another lively discussion.

"So, because his ideas of God are wrong," Josh continued, "man is repelled by God, not attracted to Him. But still he knows he needs somebody bigger and smarter than he is on his own, so he finds other gods. And every man has a god, at least one. Maybe his god is from outer space come to change the course of history and straighten us out. Or his god may be humanism; it may be another person, or drugs, money, Buddha, Krishna, science, education. There are all kinds of false gods running around, but in the long run they always fail to satisfy. Nothing really works but the real God." He paused and smiled slightly. "There's an old saying about that: *There's a God-shaped hole inside every man, and nothing will fill it completely but God.*"

"That's cute," Sue smiled. Usually she resented any intrusion into her privacy at this special time. Morning always seemed so clean to Sue, the air and the forest untouched by human contact. Somehow Josh didn't seem an intrusion.

"But God didn't leave us on our own, to try to figure Him out in our own reasoning. He has revealed Himself to us through His Son," Josh continued. The sun warmed the intense face opposite her, revealing red glints in the unruly black hair.

Sue nodded a little uncertainly. She was still not sure how to react to Josh's conversation.

132

"It's just wonderful to know what God's like!" Josh said suddenly, clapping his hands together in delight. She drew back in surprise. "Do you realize we have a source of absolute wisdom, absolute power and absolute goodness available to us any time we want? Isn't that great?"

"I suppose so," she murmured, now uncomfortable.

Josh suddenly relaxed. "You're very patient with me. You listen to me go on and on and never complain."

"That's because you're different from anybody I've ever known," Sue replied. "But right now I'm getting hungry. I think I'll go find some breakfast."

"I'll see you later, then," Josh answered. She halfway hoped he'd ask her to join him, but things like that never seemed to occur to him. And she was hesitant to invite him.

Sue waved goodbye and walked into her trailer, thoughtful. She wondered if her own ideas of God were solid. Did they need rethinking? It seemed that there was a lot that required rethinking.

The private dining room with its fine linen, candles and silver was lovely, obviously designed and furnished for doctors and not patients or staff. The separate tables for two and four had been rearranged by order of Don Oliver Franklin to form one long table.

"We need to determine what makes these people different," he had explained to the Project staff. "Why are they gifted and others not? I think one way to the answer is to find out what traits and experiences they have in common; what attributes they share that may have a bearing on their psychic talents. To discover these common denominators all of us need to spend time together, just talking and sharing, getting to know one another. The key word is togetherness. We'll start out with all of us at one table, like a family."

Guests arrived for dinner one by one. Isabel Nebo stood by the door welcoming them as hostess, remembering each name and smiling graciously. Journalists, doctors, scientists, educators, psychics, family members and officials stood around the luxurious room and began conversations.

Dr. Charles Fortuna, showered, shaved, scented and dressed in a chocolate-brown suit that flattered his complexion, paused at the door and assayed the situation. The well-furnished room resembled a private room at some expensive club or restaurant. It was quiet and dim. The sparkling chandelier and tapered candles lent a soft, rich glow to the table. The group was elegant, richly dressed, appropriate to the gracious setting. Charlie started to join Isabel, then stopped in his tracks.

He saw Barbara Simmons.

Her loveliness hit him like an electric shock. She stood at the far side of the table facing him. As he beheld the vision of her—hair, face, form and features—he longed to draw nearer, to savor each detail, for he knew the total perfection could only be the result of many smaller perfections. Barbara's dark, curling hair framed a face as untouched and lovely as a Madonna. Her figure was small and dainty; her clothing complimented her without being diverting. She had small, slender hands with long, red nails. Without conscious thought, he walked toward her.

He introduced himself and she smiled slightly. "I'm Barbara Simmons, usually called Bebe. These are my sisters, Glenda and Wanda."

He dragged his eyes from Barbara and smiled at the twins, noting how unlike their sister they were. "Welcome to Brookshire," he said, wishing he could think of something less inane.

"Take seats now, all of you," Isabel said loudly. Charlie glanced at her and suddenly she seemed all wrong; too tall, too angular and entirely too old.

He guided Bebe to the table and held her chair. The twins sat on her left and he took the seat on her right. Others found places at the table and all turned expectantly to Isabel. Charlie met her eyes, almost invisible behind her dark glasses, but he knew somehow they were disapproving and he turned away quickly.

The rest of the group found places at the table and looked up expectantly as Don Oliver Franklin rose and smiled at them. Then he launched into a prepared speech, explaining the purposes of the Project, how the subjects had been selected and some of their plans. As Franklin droned on, Charlie looked around the table, examining the five famous psychics. All in all, not a very impressive lot. Franklin was now introducing the young people in turn.

"First, on my right, is Wallace Graham. Why don't you give us a little bit of your background?"

"You've probably all read about me," Wallace began. "I was taken in an alien spacecraft by the Zorans, visitors from another world, and I have been out of our solar system."

When he stopped for breath, Franklin interrupted quickly. "Thank you, Wallace, that's very interesting. Wallace is from New Orleans and he was a student at Tulane for two years. He left to pursue his interest in UFOs."

Charlie stared at the well-dressed Wallace. He had seemed fairly normal before starting into his harangue.

Meanwhile Franklin had turned to the next young man. "Vincent Ponder is a truly remarkable musician. Tell us about yourself, Vincent."

The young man smiled and began a rather self-conscious recital of his abilities. Charlie knew little of music, but it sounded extremely impressive.

"Thank you, Vincent," Franklin said. "Now we meet our youngest guests, Glenda and Wanda Simmons."

The twins said nothing, staring at the group without smiling. Barbara Simmons patted Glenda's shoulder gently, like a trainer soothing a skittish horse.

Charlie then turned his attention to LeRoi Williams who was almost unintelligible in his jive talk. As the introductions were completed, waiters entered with the salad course.

The food was far better than the usual hospital fare and the company was delightful; Charlie was prepared to endure the strange behavior of the twins if it meant he could enjoy the sight and sound of Barbara Simmons. He kept his back turned away from the head of the table and ignored as much as possible the waves of disapproval radiating from Isabel. But as the meal ended and the diners rose, she walked over to him.

"I see you've met the Simmonses," she said brightly. The twins were whispering together and Barbara was chatting with Vincent Ponder, so he could reply to Isabel without their hearing.

"That's some gal, Isabel. I'm thinking about taking a crack at her."

"Well, of course you will, Charlie. That was predictable."

"Any objections?"

"What you do is of no concern to me. Just don't let your hobby interfere with scientific research."

"Isabel, I'll do my best." He grinned at her.

"She's very shallow, you know," Isabel warned. "There's nothing below the surface. Just a sex object, perfectly willing to be some man's plaything."

"Glad to hear she's willing." He laughed. "I've been wanting a plaything."

Bebe turned from Vincent Ponder and addressed herself to Isabel. "Can you get somebody to take us back to the trailer park? If not, I think we can find the way."

"I'll be glad to escort you," Charlie interjected. "Dr. Nebo is too busy to leave yet. She's really in charge of this Project, you know. Franklin's right-hand man."

He chuckled again as he led Barbara from the room with the twins trailing after them. He could feel Isabel's eyes on his back until the door closed behind them.

It was dark when Barbara awakened. The room was cold and very still. She lay there for a moment wondering what had roused her. A soft knocking came from the twins' room and Barbara frowned, trying to identify it. Then she flinched, startled to realize the twins were standing just inside her bedroom door, linked together by tightly clasped hands, heads bowed and shoulders hunched.

"Girls, what is it?" Barbara asked softly.

Glenda rushed toward her, and Barbara moved over in the narrow twin bed to make room for her. Wanda was right behind, her small body shivering as she crawled in next to her sisters. Her cheeks were wet with tears. They both seemed very young, no longer the confident, arrogant young girls who viewed the world with such superiority.

"Oh, Bebe, they're back," Wanda moaned and Barbara felt a certain dread.

"Who's back?" she asked, hugging them close to her, one under each arm. They were so seldom willing to admit a need or allow affection.

"Them. The phantoms."

"Oh, girls, there aren't any phantoms," Barbara protested. "It's just the PSI factor you have that's not yet under your control. Don't you see? We're with this group now and Dr. Nebo and the university people will be getting to the bottom of it all."

Glenda sat up suddenly and Bebe could see her face in the glow from the outside lights. She was ashen and shaken but resolute. "They woke us up talking. They're *glad* to be here, Bebe. They don't feel the least bit threatened by Dr. Nebo. They're having fun!"

Wanda wiped her tear-stained cheek and continued, "The curtains started moving like there was a breeze, but we had the windows shut. Then they started tapping on the wall. Hear it?" She fell silent and cocked her head. From the other room they could hear the soft tapping, rhythmical and steady.

"It may be a branch hitting the side of the trailer." Barbara suggested.

"We know it's them," Wanda said firmly.

"I can even *smell* them," Glenda echoed.

"Would you like to sleep in here the rest of the night?" Barbara had given the larger bedroom to the twins, the back one that stretched the full width of the trailer. They had so many belongings: books, stereo, stuffed animals, sketchpads. This second bedroom was much smaller but neither girl wanted to leave. They snuggled together and listened to the *tap, tap, tap.*

"Glenda," Barbara asked hesitantly. "Do you hear them speaking out loud or just in your head?" Barbara had never been able to understand their gift of clairaudience, or clear hearing.

Glenda and Wanda were silent a long time. They had never encouraged questions about their ESP and usually refused to answer, but this night was different. They were in a new place, among strangers, and Barbara was all they had of security or home.

"Both." Wanda finally answered softly.

"Why does it frighten you so? They haven't threatened you, have they?"

"They're mean, Bebe!" Glenda said.

"They always have been, but they're getting worse," Wanda agreed.

"But they're just voices. They can't really do anything," Barbara protested.

"I don't know. It's just they're so excited about being here, like it's going to help them somehow," Wanda said uncertainly.

"Well, maybe they're glad the doctors will find out more about ESP."

"I don't think so, Bebe," Glenda shook her head.

The tapping stopped abruptly and they waited for a long moment. Then they relaxed with a sigh. "It's not what they say that scares us. It's not even what they might do," Glenda explained. "Bebe, what if everyone of us in this Project has phantoms? What if we're bringing them all together?"

Wanda leaned toward her older sister, nodding intently. "That's right. What if it isn't us who'll be learning things and gaining control. What if it's *them?*"

Book III

Possession

Like most government-sponsored endeavors, there was a lack of organization in Project Truth, with red tape, committee meetings, memo-writing and rhetoric replacing purposeful action. In such a power vacuum, a bold, resourceful person can take authority. Isabel determined to be that person.

With that end in view, she awakened very early the morning after the dinner, something she almost never did. She dressed with her usual care and by 7:30 she was knocking on the door of the trailer assigned to the Simmonses. She greeted them with deliberate charm and walked with them through the still-dewy forest to the staff dining room. They worked their way through the food line and took seats at the end of one of the long tables under the windows.

With the Simmons, at least, Isabel had been established as the person in authority.

This breakfast quickly solidified her feelings in one area. Barbara Simmons was insipid and bland, without personality or accomplishments. It infuriated Isabel that Barbara was so confident of herself. She took none of the bait Isabel offered but merely sat there eating daintily, calm and assured, contributing little to the conversation.

The twins were quite a contrast; they were full of questions, bright-eyed and sly, chattering away as they ate.

Halfway through breakfast Sue Dunn joined them. Isabel

141

made introductions; the twins then became interested in Sue's role as supervisor.

"Do you enjoy being a nurse?" Glenda asked.

"Tending to sick people?" Wanda added.

"Well, I like being a nurse, but I don't do much tending to sick people. My job is to make sure the other nurses do that."

"Yes," Isabel laughed. "Sue is too good a nurse to waste on patients. She's been promoted beyond that."

Sue started to protest when Josh Kingston suddenly appeared and slid his tray next to hers.

"I thought you ate at home," he accused her.

"I usually do, but this morning I didn't feel like cooking. I thought you never ate breakfast at all."

Their conversation was interrupted by the twins. "You wrote *The Children and the Power*," Glenda said eagerly.

"We read a review of it in *The Kansas City Star* and wanted to read the book," Wanda continued.

"Why didn't you?" he asked, peering at them.

The twins laughed, not at all discomfited by his unsmiling intensity. "Oh, we don't have much follow-through," Glenda said.

"We have a lot of ideas that never get anywhere," Wanda agreed.

"Why are you interested in a book about demonic possession?" Josh continued.

"Whoa! Hold it!" Isabel held up a hand, shaking her head. "I think it would be real confusing for the girls to get involved in your ideas right now, Josh. They're here for a scientific study."

"We can read anything we want to," Glenda stated.

"Nobody bosses us around," Wanda declared.

"And I will never relinquish my right to present a viewpoint," Josh said firmly.

Isabel reddened at this three-part defiance and clamped her lips together tightly. Barbara continued to eat placidly, taking no part in the conversation.

"Are those your three psychics?" Sue asked, pointing to the three young men who stood indecisively at the end of the food line.

"Yes, I'll call them." Isabel stood up and waved a hand. Soon Wallace, LeRoi and Vincent had joined their table.

"Room for one more?" Charlie Fortuna had appeared and to Isabel's disgust he forced a chair between Barbara and Glenda. "Hi, Sue. Josh, I didn't know you did anything as human as eating! Good morning, Bebe."

Isabel turned from him in annoyance and addressed Vincent Ponder. "You're set up for an interview at the university at 10:30, Vinnie. At the music department. Some musicians from the symphony in town will be there; they'll have everything you need, instruments and all. Wallace, you're to go to the astronomy department at the university at ten. I think I can get free and go with you. They've invited some engineers from NASA, too. I have photocopies of your sketches and star charts. The twins and LeRoi will begin medical testing with Dr. Fortuna this afternoon at two. That clear to everybody?"

A jumble of questions followed. Isabel answered them smoothly, delighted that the Project was finally underway.

At 9 a.m., Sue Dunn stepped off the elevator on Eight South and bumped into Malcolm Brown. Literally. He recovered his balance and straightened his vest as Sue apologized.

Then Sue had a new thought. "Are you busy, Rev. Brown? I'd like to talk with you a few minutes."

When he nodded in cheerful agreement, Sue led him down a side corridor to a small, seldom-used waiting room. They sat down in two plastic chairs.

"Dr. Brown, do you believe that demons exist today?" Sue's voice was intense and eager.

His face went blank, his answer began hesitantly. "What makes you ask that?"

"Well, strange things have been happening around here. And I've just read Joshua Kingston's book."

"Oh, I see." His face was expressionless, but his voice managed to convey his disapproval.

"Well, do you think he has the right explanation?" Sue persisted.

"I think we're all too eager to blame things on the devil. I believe most of our troubles can be laid right at our own feet. In a way, I think we make our own devils."

"But things have happened in this hospital that seem to be frankly supernatural." Then she told him of a dead man restored to life, running angrily down the hospital corridor clad in a damp sheet; of six suicides in one week; of 42 medication errors in one day; of a little boy sitting on an emergency room stretcher, crying to go home after being instantly healed of symptoms of anaphalactic shock.

"Have you read Dr. Kingston's book?" she asked.

"Well, no. I've been too busy. I understand it's quite radical and controversial."

"I just want to know if it's true," Sue persisted. She peered closely at Malcolm Brown. This man was as familiar to her as the halls and rooms of Brookshire itself. He was also a prominent clergyman, a true representative of established Christianity. His outlook should be practical, orthodox, safe.

"I'm sure you have more important things to worry about than that," the pastor chided gently. "You don't need to be concerning yourself with the devil's activity, even if he does exist. Keep a smile on that pretty face. That'll chase away any demons." His face was so full of good humor that Sue was afraid for a moment he was going to pinch her cheek. She felt like a little girl being placated by a nice old uncle, being told politely that she should go play with her doll and not bother the grownups anymore. She took a deep breath and made another attempt.

"Dr. Brown, I've seen very strange things here. If an evil

supernatural power does exist, then surely we ought to do more than ignore it."

Malcolm shook his head. "We all have too much to do helping the sick to start looking for demons behind the trees."

"But if there are demons behind the trees, shouldn't we know how to deal with them?"

He made no response and Sue saw Malcolm Brown suddenly with absolute clarity. He had no knowledge about the subject upon which to base an opinion. He was expressing to her not a position he could defend with facts; he was merely telling her what he hoped was true.

"Then your advice is just to forget it, right?" Sue pursued.

The chaplain nodded. "We have to put our emphasis on the good that is in the world and in people. Not on evil."

Sue rose from her chair, nodding with a new understanding. "Well, I appreciate your time," she said.

As she watched Malcolm Brown wend his way cheerfully down the hall, Sue reviewed the facts in her mind: science doesn't have an answer. Now it seems that traditional Christianity doesn't have an answer. And I know my own experience doesn't provide an answer. So the next step is Josh and his fanaticism.

I will get an answer, she determined. *From somewhere, I'll get an answer of some sort.*

Effie MacAllister closed the door of the linen room behind her and leaned against the wall. *Put a guard around me, Lord,* she prayed. *Don't let anybody come in.* She took a deep breath and steadied herself.

Within a few minutes she would have to go back onto Six North and face the admission of a new patient, a transfer from surgery, and she desperately needed these few minutes to calm herself and prepare for the battle she would face as soon as the patient arrived.

They gave such cute names to the operations: they called them a T.O.P. or a T.A.B. But the cute names couldn't disguise what they were doing; T.O.P. was termination of pregnancy and T.A.B. was therapeutic abortion. In Effie's eyes it was murder. Most of these patients went home a few hours after the operation; it was a quick, simple procedure, relatively safe in the physical realm. Of course, she knew the statistics about the psychological and emotional problems that often followed, but rarely did an abortion surgery cause such problems that the patient had to be admitted to Six North, one of the surgical floors.

Now one was coming, on her way from surgery. Something had gone wrong during the procedure; perforation of the uterus or some such. The girl was in serious condition and had been assigned to Effie's care. The problem wasn't so much the actual care; that was routine. The problem was in relating to the patient non-judgmentally, treating her with dignity, respect and consideration regardless of what had brought her to the hospital. This was a real problem for Effie.

With surprise and annoyance, she saw the door opening. This was usually a safe place to hide from interruptions. Since it wasn't a hiding place where one could grab a smoke, Effie was almost the only one who ever used it. She straightened up, composing herself to face the intruder.

It was Josh Kingston.

"Are you all right?" he asked. "I was walking by, saw you come in here and you looked pretty upset."

"I am upset. They've assigned me a new patient who's just had an abortion. Something went wrong. I have a little trouble handling that kind of patient."

Josh leaned against the opposite wall, his dark, somber eyes piercing hers as she spoke. "What's so new about legal abortions?" he asked. "Except that they make the medical profession a profession of legalized killers."

"But as a nurse I'm supposed to be non-judgmental, and as a Christian I'm supposed to be loving. Still I get upset. I've had five babies, five little boys, and I wish now I'd had ten. These women let doctors kill their babies and then expect a nurse to comfort them and rub their backs and make them feel less guilty. I just don't know if I can do it."

"How do you think God feels about these women?" Josh asked her.

It had never occurred to her to wonder how God felt about the girls. "He loves them, of course. He wants me to be loving."

"Does that mean approving of everything they do?"

"Well, no, I guess not."

"You're a good parent," Josh said. "A loving parent. Does that mean you always approve of everything your kids do?"

"No. Of course not. My baby son is buying a new tractor and he's going to have to make these huge payments for four years and he doesn't need that tractor at all. He only has about ten acres under cultivation and his second brother has a tractor he could use any time. But what can I do?"

"Well, as far as a tractor is concerned, I don't know. The point I was making is, God may love us, but that doesn't mean He always approves of us. Certainly He hates murder. For heaven's sake, don't feel guilty for seeing murder as a sin!"

"What do you think I ought to do?"

"I think you ought to tell them you don't want to care for this patient because it offends your religious belief. Let somebody else have her."

"But what if I'm supposed to be witnessing to her, trying to lead her to the Lord?"

Josh shrugged. "Then you'd feel differently. You'd have an anointing and God would give you a love for her."

Effie's mind was a whirl: not forced to manifest love to this girl? Not obliged to take the servant's role? Justified in her anger and offense at the killing of a baby? It was all a totally new point of view. As these new thoughts whirled around in her mind, the door opened and Six North's head nurse spoke with some vexation.

"Well, here you are! Effie, I've been looking for you everywhere. I wanted to tell you, the transfer from P.A.R.R. isn't coming up after all. I hope you didn't fix the room yet." She looked at Josh in curiosity.

"This is Josh Kingston, he's a chaplain," Effie said, reddening with embarrassment. Josh nodded brusquely.

The head nurse continued, "The patient started bleeding pretty bad in the recovery room and they took her back to surgery. They'll be sending her to S.I.C.U. if she makes it off the table."

"What's that?" Josh asked.

"Surgical intensive care unit. Anyhow, Effie, you don't need to get her room ready." She walked slowly out, staring at Josh's cowboy boots.

"I'm sorry for the girl, but I'm glad I don't have to refuse the assignment." Effie said with relief. "It can get very sticky; they call the supervisor and you have to sign a paper. Supervisors can make it tough on you, unless it's Sue Dunn. She's the nicest supervisor we have."

"Yeah, she's nice," Josh agreed. "Look, be praying for her, hear?"

"I've been praying for Sue Dunn for twelve years," Effie replied.

"You have?" Josh asked in surprise. "Twelve years?"

"I have a list of people who work for Brookshire; I pray for all of them."

He stared at her with open-mouthed astonishment. Then he shook his head, dislodging even more of his unruly black hair. "I guess that explains why she seems willing to listen to me."

"I have to get back on duty," Effie said. "Maybe you ought to page Sue and ask her to go for coffee."

Again Josh looked surprised. "I never thought of that. You think I ought to?"

"Of course," Effie reassured him. "It's almost 10 a.m. Break time. Go call right now."

The small examining room was bright with flourescent light, clean and professional. Dr. Charles Fortuna, in lab coat and stethoscope, kept his professional calm despite his frustration.

"It's a requirement," Charlie explained again. "Every single patient that's admitted to Brookshire has it done. And all the subjects for the Project do, too."

The Simmons twins sat together on the examining table, holding hands, glaring at him. They weren't really angry, certainly not frightened, but they were as unmovable as a mountain. They refused to allow the laboratory technician to draw their blood for a routine analysis.

"It doesn't hurt but a little bit," the lab technician said encouragingly.

"We don't have anything wrong with our blood," said one twin.

"And we don't want anybody to stick us with needles," her sister finished.

"Let's see," the technician said, looking at her requisition slips. "Which one is Wanda and which one is Glenda?"

"We never answer that question," from one twin.

"Because it doesn't matter," from the other.

"You're too old to be acting like this," Charlie rebuked gently. "When we have little babies, we have to hold them down to take their blood. You don't want that, do you?"

"You'd better not try it."

"Not if you know what's good for you."

The twins' eyes were very strange to Charlie, a brilliant blue, yet curiously lifeless, like shiny buttons or dolls' eyes. The doctor had seen their physical records and he knew something the twins tried to hide. As soon as they walked into the room, he could tell which was which. One twin was a half inch taller than her sister, and the larger twin had the

149

longer name. To establish his authority he now used this knowledge and addressed them by name.

"Glenda, you're first. Hold out your arm for the lady to take your blood or I'll call the attendants and we'll hold you down. Make up your mind; I don't have time to wait."

The twins looked at each other, surprised. They spoke intently to each other for a few minutes, using some language other than English. Then they turned again to the doctor and spoke in unison.

"No."

"Okay, you made the choice." Charlie went to the wall phone and pretended to dial. Without a nurse, with no chaperone present, he was not about to physically restrain these adolescent females, especially since he was going to make every effort to impress their sister. Better to bluff them, if possible. "I'll need two attendants," he said over the phone. "Right away." He looked back to the twins.

Glenda stood up and slowly held her arm out stiffly. "You'd better do it right," she threatened the lab technician.

The woman smiled in relief, fastened a rubber tourniquet tightly around Glenda's biceps, and inserted the needle. Glenda screamed. The needle was in the vein, Charlie was glad to see, the blood flowing rapidly into the glass tube.

"There. That wasn't so bad, was it?" The technician held an alcohol sponge on the puncture site briefly, then folded Glenda's arm up, bending it acutely at the elbow. "Keep it tight for a few minutes."

"Now for you, Wanda," Charlie turned to the second twin, standing by the door. The child stood smiling wickedly, holding out her left arm. From a small puncture wound in the soft tissue on the inside of her elbow there flowed a steady stream of bright red blood. It ran around the curve of her arm and dripped off her elbow onto the floor. Wanda said nothing but her brilliant blue eyes glittered triumphantly.

The lab technician gave a strangled scream and covered

150

her mouth with her hand. Glenda chortled in glee and walked over to her sister and again they clasped hands.

"How did you do that?" Charlie demanded. "Do you have a needle?" Yet he knew they had no such weapon.

"You wanted blood; here it is."

"Come help yourself."

The lab technician had retreated to the far side of the room, staring white-faced at the twins.

Charlie thought quickly and told her, "Just do the one you have. We'll pass on the second one for now."

"Yeah, a rule of the hospital; gotta have blood from everybody," Glenda sneered as the technician rushed from the room. "Can't change the rules."

"Gotta make your blood sacrifice," Wanda chanted, her arm still outstretched, still bleeding.

Charlie spoke very calmly. "That's enough now. Let's get a bandage on your arm, Wanda. Then you two can go on back to the testing rooms."

They exchanged a look of victory and smiled at Charlie as he placed a Band-Aid over the puncture wound on Wanda's arm. The twins then nodded gravely and left the room in silence. Shaken, Charlie stared after them.

"Isn't it upsetting to know that so many people dislike you?" Sue asked.

Josh shrugged. "I'm used to it by now." He changed the subject. "This is terrible coffee. No wonder you drink tea."

They were seated at a small table for two in Brookshire's staff dining room. The room was nearly deserted; it was late for coffee breaks, a little too early for the lunch crowd.

"The coffee is probably left over from breakfast," Sue replied, then shifted the subject. "Tell me about yourself. Do you have much family?"

"Parents, one sister. They live in Tennessee."

"You don't talk like a Tennessean."

"I've been away so long I've lost my accent." He was

peering intently at his coffee cup, swirling the dregs of inky black coffee around the cup.

"Were you always a Christian?" she asked.

"Since I can remember. My folks were evangelists; we traveled all around the south holding revival meetings. I used to sing by myself or with my sister."

"How interesting," Sue said and hoped she hadn't sounded condescending. She could suddenly see the conditions that had produced this strange, intense, lonely man.

"My mother's nearly sixty and still wears her hair long," Josh continued. "She uses no makeup. Today some call this legalism and perhaps it is. But I never saw anybody else with the love she has, or the power, either. My dad's a great old guy; he's retired now, but he goes to nursing homes every day, preaching to anybody who'll listen. I love those two old people." He lifted his eyes and his look was disconcerting. "You'd find them really foreign, as alien as Wallace Graham's Zorans."

"Maybe not," she countered. "I meet all kinds around here. I might like your parents very much."

"Maybe so," he shrugged. "They probably wouldn't approve of you."

"Why not?" she bristled.

"Lots of reasons. But they'd love you even though they disapproved."

"Do you disapprove of me?" she asked.

He stared at her, thinking deeply. "No, I don't exactly disapprove of you," he said slowly.

"Thanks," she laughed shortly.

"I do think there's a lot wasted, though," he went on. "You could be so much more than you are."

"How so?"

"You waste a lot of effort and time on things that don't matter at all, like your job here—."

"I have an important position," she interrupted, stung again by his bluntness.

152

"But does it really amount to anything?" he asked, unaffected by her outburst. "It's mostly paperwork, isn't it? It's what the Bible calls 'vanity,' meaning vain, pointless. Don't you agree?"

And to her surprise, she did. She realized in a sudden rush of clarity that her job, the focus of her life, was mostly vanity in that sense and thus frustrating, annoying, unfulfilling, vexing.

"Yes, I guess I do agree. Nursing is not helping people the way I thought it would be. It's not what I planned for, trained for. But I suppose everything in life is a disappointment in the long run. Not what you'd hoped."

He leaned forward, touched her hand and said, "Don't be depressed. Things will get better."

It was a banal and superficial little statement, a gesture of comfort hardly above common politeness. Yet it moved her. And Sue was astonished at her reaction to his touch. A quick surge, like an electrical current, shot through her.

Abruptly Josh stood. "I need to go now. See you later."

Startled by his bluntness, annoyed by his lack of grace, her eyes followed him as he strode briskly out of the dining room. He was dressed as usual in boots, casual slacks and a worn flannel shirt.

Don't be a fool, she told herself sharply. *You have nothing in common with him; he's strange and serious and not at all pleasant to be with.* She shook her head in firm negation. Ever since this man had entered her life, things had been uncomfortable; she had become dissatisfied with her job and her lifestyle; and prospects for her future had somehow diminished in the groundswell of questioning that had arisen.

Lunch had not satisfied Charlie. Cottage cheese, fruit and skim milk were pallid fare to one raised on pasta, tomato sauce and red wine, and he feared he would find it difficult to reverse in a short time the effects of years of alcohol, tobacco, rich food and indolence.

153

He had frequently deplored his body type, its tendency to gain weight. But now the thickening around his waist could no longer be joked about as "love handles." Now it was part of twenty-five extra pounds, bad enough as a prelude to hypertension and a coronary within ten years, but intolerable as a possible hindrance to his plans to captivate and conquer Barbara Simmons. His infatuation with her was overwhelming and he was desperate enough to try both diet and exercise. He had eaten lightly and now planned to spend the remainder of the lunch hour running.

He tried to dress the part. He wore baggy red gym shorts and a frayed Adidas T-shirt. His bright blue running shoes were brand-new and would reveal him as a novice to any discerning eye, but he ignored that. He felt tough and macho as he stepped outside his trailer into the golden noon sunshine.

As he headed out along the faint trail that led into the deep woods, he heard the sound of guitar music from the men's trailer. *That must be Vincent Ponder,* he decided. Charlie liked Vinnie. They had talked a couple of times and he was the most normal of the group. Vinnie was embarrassed by his abilities, instead of being prideful like the others. He seemed like a nice, normal kid, friendly. Charlie deferred his run and walked toward the young psychic.

Vinnie was sitting in one of the redwood chairs on the concrete slab outside the front door of his trailer, strumming his guitar. He stopped as Charlie walked up. "See my new guitar? It's a Martin, the best you can buy. The best acoustic, I mean. Dr. Nebo bought it for me." He held it out and Charlie nodded in appreciation.

"What I know about music and musical instruments you can stick in you eye," he confessed. Charlie took a seat, his noontime run forgotten for the present. "How did it go with the symphony people?"

"They all conclude I can't do what I do on my own ability, but they're unable to agree on *how* I do it." He paused. "Do you know anything about Johann Sebastian Bach?"

When Charlie shook his head, Vinnie continued, "Well, he's just about the most magnificent composer who ever lived. His music is perfect mathematically; you can almost design an algebraic formula that will fit it. And he sometimes wrote in different keys, some instruments playing one key while others play in another. Some keys are compatible, but most aren't and each note has to be considered in relationship to every other one. And he takes many different melodies and weaves them together, then separates them and brings them back together."

"Go on."

"Well, I came up with a piece of music everybody says is Bach. Now I'm a pretty fair musician and I have some creativity, but I couldn't do anything like that." Vinnie's fingers continued to strum while he stared at the concrete slab, his face solemn. The one thing Charlie had noticed these psychics had in common, possibly one of Don Oliver's "common denominators," was that they all seemed rather sad.

"Does it bother you that some dead genius is creating music through you?"

"Now you sound like a shrink." Vinnie laughed and his fingers moved more quickly along the strings and the music seemed lighter. "Yes, it bothers me. It would bother you, too, if your knowledge of medicine came from some dead physician."

"That's true," Charlie laughed.

"Do you know what music is?" Vinnie was suddenly reflective. "Music is just organized sound. It is waves of motion in the air that hit your tympanum and cause it to vibrate. So why the big deal about how it is arranged? Why care if the particular levels of sound happen to come together as Bach might have done it? Well, I'll tell you why."

Vinnie hit a loud, powerful chord and leaned toward Charlie intently. "Because music gets right into your soul and changes you. That's why it matters. Music can make you happy or sad or warlike or sexy. Those who control

155

music control the souls of people. I really believe that. Can you imagine how I feel when something comes in and creates music *through* me? I feel violated." He stopped and stared off into the woods for a long moment as though he had forgotten Charlie was there.

"It used to be dictated," he continued. "I heard the music in my head and played it, then I would write it out. I was at least a link in the chain; I had some say-so about it. Now they just take over and use me."

"Vinnie, do you really believe that a great composer like Bach can come back from the dead and use you to write music? Do you honestly believe that? Couldn't it be that the same force that inspired him is inspiring you?"

"I don't know what to think! I've tried that 'eternal force' routine. I've tried reincarnation. I've tried anything I thought might help me make some sense out of it. Nothing helps. Whatever it is, it's real, and it's stronger than I am, and I'm not sure it's good. You know . . . has good intentions."

"Now you sound like Josh Kingston."

Wallace Graham stuck his head outside and nodded to them. "I'm going to drive into town, Vinnie," he said. "We have a little free time and I for one am sick of this place. Want to go with me?"

"No, thanks. I think I'll take a walk later."

"Suit yourself." Wallace withdrew his head and Vinnie grinned.

"Now he's a case for Josh Kingston."

It suddenly occurred to Dr. Fortuna that these psychics all knew about Josh Kingston. Charlie hadn't quite realized how famous his new neighbor was.

Vinnie was playing some bluegrass riffs, tapping his foot vigorously. Charlie patted his thigh in rhythm to the song. "You're really good," he complimented.

"Thanks. I know. The only problem is knowing for sure what's me and what's not me."

Suddenly Charlie began to see a little of what these

156

young people were facing. *Something*—what Isabel called a PSI factor, what Wallace Graham called aliens, what Josh Kingston called demons—was systematically invading the personalities of these young people. That must be terrifying. Charlie knew how destructive it had been to be manipulated by another person; what Margie had done to his ego and his self-image had almost wiped him out. What if he were being manipulated by unseen forces over which he had little or no control?

That, he could not have handled with a divorce.

Effie looked closely at the patient. He was young and quite sick. His skin was pale and grayish and there was a thin sheen of perspiration along his upper lip. He moved about restlessly; only his leg, heavily encased in plaster, remained still.

It took longer than usual to cut through the cast and spread it open. The orderly was cautious in the presence of the patient's two doctors because he'd heard this case was presenting problems. At last he was done and the cast lay in two halves along either side of the leg. He stepped back involuntarily; the odor was overwhelming and offensive.

"Whew," the resident said, also backing up slightly. "Something's rotten!"

The patient, a high school football player, moaned slightly, and reached down with a restless hand to feel the leg, open to the air for the first time in seven days. The surgeon caught his hand and held it. He cut away the gauze dressing with tiny snips of his scissors.

"Look there," he said softly to his partner. Instead of a healthy pink with skin intact and underlying tissue firm and healthy, the skin was blackened from the knee downward; in spots it was almost falling away from the bone. The stink from the putrefying flesh was almost unbearable.

"You cast this leg?" The surgeon turned to the resident doctor in fury.

"I don't remember. It ought to be on the operative notes." The resident had moved another two steps back from the bed. His face was an ash gray; he looked almost as ill as the patient.

The surgeon wheeled suddenly and snarled at the head nurse. "How come nobody reported this? This kid must have been screaming since surgery. But nobody says a word to me till you notice it's stinking and he's spiked a temp." The doctor stared at his young patient. "Now he's so septic he's comatose."

"He didn't really do that much complaining," the head nurse protested. "It's true he didn't seem to get much relief from his pain shots, but then some of these teenagers use drugs a lot and build up an immunity. You know how it is."

"I know how this is," the surgeon replied grimly. "I know if we can save this leg we'll be incredibly lucky, and there is simply no excuse for it."

He sagged against the wall and wiped his face in a gesture of fatigue. Effie liked this particular doctor; she didn't see him often since most of his patients were on the third floor or orthopedics, but he was what Effie considered a gentleman: quiet, polite, seldom aroused to fits of screaming anger as were so many doctors.

He looked miserable and there was room for sympathy for him, but her heart was breaking for the patient. Seventeen, and he would almost certainly be a cripple for life; if his leg could be salvaged at all, it would never be normal. All because the cast had been too tight; the immovable plaster had cut off the blood supply to part of his leg.

Who was at fault? The doctor who had applied the cast? The nurses who failed to report the steadily increasing signs of post-operative complication? The surgeon who received almost $2,000 for an hour-and-a-half's work, and therefore must be ultimately responsible? Not for the first time, she breathed a hasty little prayer of gratitude that she was just an L.P.N., too small a target to be cast in the role of scapegoat.

"Well." The surgeon stood up straight and began to make plans. "I'll have to tell the family; maybe I can convince them it was unavoidable. I guess we'll take him back to surgery and debride all the necrotic tissue. Let's do a culture of the wound, too. Maybe we ought to get a plastic consultant, see about a graft. Let's hope to God he doesn't have osteo."

"Anything I can do?" the resident asked. His face was still a mask of fear; almost certainly he had applied the cast, and his future, and the $50,000 he had borrowed so far to prepare for that future, were tottering in the balance.

"No, sir," the surgeon said hotly. "I don't want you around any of my patients again. If this thing goes to court, then maybe we'll have to talk, but until then, you better make an effort to avoid me."

He turned back to the head nurse and spoke, his voice still angry. "Get your supervisor up here, get the chart reviewed, fill out the incident report, call the malpractice carrier." He laughed shortly and it was an ugly sound. "Batten down the hatches, boys. Big storm's a-brewing!" He left the room. The resident slunk out behind him.

Effie moved toward the bed and began to clean the mess caused by the split cast, plaster dust and cut dressings. She peered at the leg; it looked dreadful. Was there any chance it could be saved? She touched the boy's forehead, her lips moving softly.

For crying out loud, she's only 24 years old. You're 38. Don't make a fool of yourself. Charlie brushed his hair carefully to cover up the encroaching baldness. He had changed shirts three times preparing for this evening visit with Barbara Simmons. He continued talking to himself as he fastened on his slim gold watch, almost $1,000 worth of metal and mechanism, which he hoped she'd have enough sense to appreciate.

Maybe it was just that she was so different from Margie.

Margie was tall and blonde and very liberated, while Bebe Simmons was little and dark and feminine. Bebe seemed very safe for a man who'd recently been bruised by a pushy wife. And his mind began to play a happy fantasy: he was introducing Margie to Barbara, proud of his new lady, reveling in Margie's distress that the new one was younger, prettier.

He followed the path in the shadowy darkness and found the Simmons' trailer. Barbara opened the door when he knocked and smiled at him as he took a seat on the couch. He accepted her offer of coffee and as she prepared it, he looked around the trailer. Like his own, it was neat, commonplace. On the room's only table a small black-and-white television was turned now to an old musical from the '30s. The sound level was too low to follow the dialogue. Music was blaring forth from the twins' room, however; pounding rhythm, no melody, lots of bass. Barbara returned with his coffee and sat beside him. They began to talk.

The conversation quickly turned to Bebe and there it stayed. She spoke on at length, telling a fairly routine life story; 24 uneventful years. A typical, middle-class family; the father stayed busy at his drugstore, the mother was a housewife. There was enough money, no great excess. Not a very close family. The story droned on; if she had been less beautiful, Charlie might have been bored, but he watched her in total admiration. She might have been reading a telephone book for all he cared.

It was only when the story moved on to the twins and their strange powers that he began to pay close attention to the words. As Bebe talked of her sisters, her hands twisted nervously, the long colored nails clawlike in their tension.

"They've always been smart. They did everything early, walking, talking, all that. They talked to each other in their strange language by the time they were eight months old."

The music from the back room throbbed through the trailer, more felt than heard. The thin electronic voice from

160

the television was a treble counterpoint, the old-fashioned music of the '30s a bubbly froth in contrast to the pounding, shuddering contemporary beat. Charlie watched as Bebe continued the story, oblivious to the music.

"They used to say there were strange beings who came to heckle them; they called them 'phantoms.' Now they believe like the scientists do, that they have some kind of extra faculty. They're really strange, though. It makes our whole family different from other people. I hope the Project can cure them."

Charlie remembered the trickle of blood from Wanda's arm, the inexplicable, eerie puncture wound. He hoped the Project would produce some control, at least.

Bebe, sitting on one leg, turned to face him. She wore tight black corduroy pants and a soft sweater the exact cobalt blue of her eyes. She was breathtaking. He put his arm along the back of the couch, moving gradually closer. She continued, "The psychiatrist at home said they were beyond his help. He as good as said he doesn't want to treat them anymore."

"And it falls on you? What about your parents?"

"They're not very close to the girls. I think they're frightened."

Charlie sipped his coffee and watched her. She had little play of emotion on her face, seeming calm and unconcerned, but her twisting hands revealed at least some emotion. "What do you plan to do all day while the twins are busy?" he asked.

"I brought a couple of books, although I don't read much. I like television. I watch my soap operas every day."

Charlie shuddered slightly. "Do you like dancing?" As she nodded, he continued, "Maybe we can go into town one night. Try some of the local spots."

"I'd like that," she agreed and his spirits soared.

"Do you play tennis?"

"A little. Not well, though."

"I used to play quite a bit." He remembered well. Margie

161

had been an excellent tennis player, tanned and blonde and in her element, savoring both the competition and the opportunity to display herself. He had never enjoyed the game. "I'm into racquetball now. That's more the thing today. But maybe we can play a little tennis some afternoon, before it gets too cold. There are some courts behind the residents' quarters."

"Maybe so."

"Well, I guess I ought to go. It's getting late."

"All right," she agreed. She rose and walked with him to the front door. He took both her hands in his and smiled into her wide-set blue eyes. "Thanks for the coffee and the conversation. I enjoyed it. Sleep well now. See you at breakfast."

As he walked home through the chill night, he wondered that he'd made no move. Very unlike him. A whole night filled only with talk. But it had seemed right. How right to be saying to this gorgeous woman, "See you at breakfast."

There were only five of them, yet it was remarkable the impact they had on Brookshire. Almost everyone knew all the psychics by name and the grapevine was full of gossip about them and their activities.

They settled into routine quickly; the forming of habits brought a sense of security in the new surroundings. For one thing, they ate together almost every meal. They had appropriated one of the long tables under the windows in the staff dining room and almost no one sat with them who was not a part of the Project.

Isabel Nebo had become the liaison between the five psychics and all the other staff members; people soon learned to contact her for appointments or interviews. She made her announcements each morning at breakfast and the days were full of testing, interviews, rap sessions and demonstrations for the various groups and members of the staff of Project Truth. The five were usually very tired by nightfall.

The thin, strangely dressed LeRoi Williams was not disappointed with the Project. He had never been so well-housed, well-fed and supported with so little personal effort needed on his part. The psychological and parapsychological testing were far easier than any gainful employment, and the test results were enormously rewarding. To make his contentment complete, a nurses' aide from Brookshire was a ready source of marijuana, which was LeRoi's main habit.

It was hard for an outsider to tell if short, slightly pudgy, expensively groomed Wallace Graham was happy with the Project. If one judged by the level of frustration and complaints Wallace evidenced, it appeared he was very dissatisfied. Yet following his successes with the astronomers and space engineers who interrogated him, he seemed even more delighted with the Project than his colleagues. He was never friendly and isolated himself from other people as much as possible. He frequently left Brookshire, driving into town for some private purpose of his own.

The boyishly charming Vincent Ponder was quick to make friends at Brookshire, just as he had in every other situation in his life. He often talked with and seemed genuine in his liking for Charlie, Sue Dunn and Isabel; even Josh Kingston succumbed to his charm when they met outside their next-door trailers and talked together.

The small, neurotic Simmons twins continued to be an enigma to the rest of the Project. They seemed to need no human companionship except each other and only occasionally did they reach out to include their older sister. The results of their tests were phenomenal; here was true, documented telepathy. Their scores on testing with Zenar cards, those marked with the five symbols of cross, star, rectangle, wave and circle, were almost perfect.

Sue Dunn became an unofficial part of the Project. Although she had no real function among them, she ate with the Project people and was soon considered one of them, breaking the habit of years to join the group at breakfast. She usually sat next to Joshua Kingston despite the fact that she was often upset by his outbursts.

At lunch, they were occasionally joined by the psychologists, behavioral scientists, chemists, exobiologists, statisticians, clergymen and the like who were a peripheral part of the Project. In this larger category were Don Oliver Franklin and Malcolm Brown who assumed the role of listeners at meals and sat quietly as the dialogue crackled back and forth between Isabel Nebo, Charlie Fortuna, Joshua Kingston and the five psychics.

As the tests and evaluations proceeded for Project Truth, throughout Brookshire Hospital there was a continuing increase in unexplained happenings, errors, accidents, mistakes, misidentifications, wrong medications and deaths.

Only the outspoken Josh Kingston firmly connected this deterioration to the coming of the five young psychics.

As they took the elevator to the sixth floor, Malcolm Brown marveled at Don Oliver Franklin's stamina. He was not even breathing hard after their quick march through the preceding five floors while the chaplain was panting from exertion.

"I issued your invitation personally to each one of them, Mal," Franklin said. "You didn't get a single taker."

"Well, that's all right," Malcolm said, allowing none of his disappointment to affect his tone. "I suppose they're still settling in." He had wanted at least some of Brookshire's psychic guests to attend his Sunday services in the hospital chapel.

"At least that gives me my first common factor," Franklin concluded. "None of them is interested in your brand of organized religion." The elevator doors opened and Malcolm was spared the necessity of responding.

Six North was in turmoil. The head nurse was speaking in a scolding voice to two young student nurses, both of whom were crying. Nearby two young men patients in pajamas were doing a little dance while laughing uproariously. One suddenly seated himself in a wheelchair and the other began to push him rapidly down the hall.

"Stop that right now and go back to your rooms," the head nurse shouted at them.

"Don't mind us, lady," one of them shouted. "We're just a little high."

The head nurse turned from them in disgust and spoke again to the sobbing student nurses. "Tell me where you found those cans of ether. If you don't, I'll have to call the narcotics men in."

"No, please don't," one of the girls begged. "We don't want to get in any trouble."

"It may be too late for that," the nurse said tartly.

To the chaplain's surprise, Franklin kept silent while watching the little drama intently. None of the participants seemed aware of their audience.

The second young patient jumped from the wheelchair and grinned at the head nurse. "Come on, give us a break. Didn't you ever get a little high on alcohol?"

"That has nothing to do with this," she returned shortly.

"They're just the same." The patient was giggling. "Jocose, bellicose, lacrymose, comatose. . . . Those are stages of intoxication and the same is true for anesthesia." He danced in a little circle around the wheelchair chanting, "Jocose, bellicose, lacrymose, comatose. . . ."

The nurse turned back to the students again. "Your in-

165

structor will be here in a few minutes. I'm giving you one last chance to tell me where you found the ether."

The girls exchanged a long look, then one of them spoke. "In OB. There's a bunch of cans back in the supply room. That's what they wanted." The girls shot a hostile look at the grinning, pajama-clad boys. "Aren't you glad we didn't get cyclopropane?"

"I'm not believing this." The head nurse threw up her hands and leaned against the counter weakly. "I'm not all that old; I was a teenager myself not too long ago, but I would never have dreamed of pulling a wild stunt like this."

The elevator doors opened again and discharged two instructors from the School of Nursing; their faces were grim. They bore down on the little group by the nurses' station like avenging angels and Malcolm felt sympathy for the young girls.

Effie MacAllister was sitting at the long desk on the other side of the counter, staring at the scene in dismay. Franklin approached her. "What's going on here?"

"We have a lot of teenagers here right now," Effie began. "Since most of them aren't seriously ill, they've been a real problem for us. They cut up a lot and are constantly in each other's rooms. One of the boys was found in a girl's bed the other night, but the night nurses were convinced that nothing, er, nothing really happened, so they just let it go with a scolding.

"Yesterday they persuaded the student nurses to bring them some beer. I don't believe the nurses drank any. Then this morning, they somehow found the ether, sniffed it and became 'stoned' as they call it. The nurse called their parents at this point."

"That was wise of her," Franklin said.

As they left the floor, Franklin turned to Malcolm with a sad smile. "I guess modern nurses see things that Florence Nightingale never dreamed of. We'll have to tighten up our procedures."

166

There was a breakthrough with the psychics during a discussion at lunch. They discovered the first common denominator: a hard fact, a common, unusual experience shared by all five and that was almost certainly connected to their psychic abilities.

It came out accidentally through something Glenda Simmons said. She and her sister had been teasing Vinnie Ponder. They were seldom playful, or indeed even friendly, and their teasing was quite heavy-handed. Vinnie as usual was good-natured about it, but after awhile he wearied of the annoyance and tried to ignore the twins. Finally, he rebuked them sharply. Enraged, Glenda lashed back, echoed by Wanda.

"Just cool it," Vinnie snapped. "Nobody's going to tolerate that kind of behavior, so just cool it."

Glenda suddenly burst into tears. It was very dramatic. Wanda began crying, too, and people from other tables in the dining room turned to look at them. Vinnie was now thoroughly flustered and he glared at the sobbing girls in dismay.

"Will you two shut up?" Barbara snapped in irritation. "You're embarrassing all of us."

Glenda spoke in a loud wail, "I just wish I was dead. Nobody loves me but Wanda. I think I'll kill myself."

When no one responded and Wanda added nothing to her statement, Glenda continued. "I'm not kidding, you know. We've tried it before. Ask Bebe. We can try again."

Vinnie leaned over and patted her awkwardly on the shoulder. "I didn't mean to hurt your feelings. Don't do anything foolish."

"The old saying that people who talk about suicide never try it is wrong," Wallace said quietly. He was in his usual place at one end of the table, and he spoke in a pontifical voice. "I've wanted to die lots of times. Once when I was younger, I cut my wrists. I was furious with my parents and it seemed like a good way to get back at them. The joke was on me, though." He laughed shortly. "My dad didn't even

167

come to the hospital, and my mother took almost three hours getting there. It didn't seem to bother them at all."

"We tried to kill ourselves with gas from the kitchen stove," Wanda explained. "But my father smelled it and stopped us. They kept asking us why we'd done it and they couldn't understand. There wasn't anything really wrong, but there wasn't anything really right, either. You know?"

The group turned with one accord to LeRoi, slouched in a chair next to Vinnie, fingering his beard. As they stared at him, he nodded slowly. "Yeah, me too. But it wasn't no show-off thing to lay guilt on somebody." He looked at Wallace with distaste. "I really meant it."

"You're not dead," Wallace snapped.

"Ain't my fault. I OD'ed three times. They always thought each overdose was an accident but I knew what I was doing every time." He said no more and all eyes now turned to Vinnie.

"I was ten when I tried it," he responded. "I'm not sure why, either, except something in me said, 'Do it.' So I took a whole bottle of tranquilizers. I still remember that stuff the doctors give you to make you vomit. It sure worked. Then afterwards my parents took me to a shrink. He told them I needed to be reassured that they loved me; he told my folks to show me I was important. From that day on, they were afraid to say no to me no matter what I did. I was a royal brat for years."

Vinnie told the story haltingly, a shadow of pain on his handsome face. "My folks have a little restaurant in Omaha. They're comfortable; they get by. But they couldn't afford me. I demanded the best stereo equipment you can buy, musical instruments, sound systems, and so on. They bought me a concert grand piano when I was only eleven. Then one day my old man got fed up. I asked for a new amp for my guitar and he said no. I started my usual squawling and bawling and he let me have it. I mean he just turned me over his knee and wore me out. Funny, I felt so relieved I

168

started crying. Not because he hurt me but because I finally got him to stop me."

They sat for a moment, digesting Vinnie's story. Suddenly, Isabel Nebo clapped her hands together, startling them.

"Do you see? Attempted suicide is a shared experience! This is a true common factor! Let's go into it a little deeper, see if the psychic factor has caused you to be more demanding of life, more easily disappointed. More sensitive, perhaps."

"You mean is it cause or effect?" Charlie asked.

Vinnie grinned and picked it up. "Are you psychic because you're suicidal, or are you suicidal because you're psychic?"

"It's unfortunate that our first common factor is one most people will find, well, undesirable," Isabel said regretfully. "But we need to educate the public to the fact that you people are not to be judged by the usual standards. What might be unfortunate for others, or wrong or whatever, may not be the same for you people."

"You're saying it's O.K. for them to want to kill themselves? Keep trying till they make it?" Charlie challenged her.

Isabel glared at Charlie. She was about to answer when Josh Kingston spoke. "You asked if the history of suicide attempts is a cause or an effect of psychic power. Well, Isabel, I'd like to answer that." Josh turned his head slowly around the circle of faces.

"The most common symptom of demonic activity is depression. And depression carried to its ultimate leads to suicide."

"You could find a lot of people who attempted suicide who aren't psychic," Isabel pointed out.

"But you can't find any who aren't under some kind of satanic oppression," Josh answered.

"Do any of you feel suicidal?" Charlie asked, suddenly

169

aware that he was responsible for the physical welfare of these young people.

"I don't think Glenda meant her little threat. I think she just had her feelings hurt," Isabel said. "But if any of you really want to die, let's get it out in the open and talk about it.

"I do, sometimes," Wanda said.

"Me, too," Glenda echoed.

"Oh, everybody does sometimes," LeRoi agreed and several others nodded.

"No, everybody doesn't," Sue said firmly. "I never do. I never have. I enjoy living and I will cling to life no matter what."

"I wouldn't try again, ever," Vinnie said. He laughed with some embarrassment. "I'm afraid of dying."

"Now there's no need for that kind of fear," Isabel said in a hearty voice. "Dying is just another life experience. I hear it can be a beautiful happening."

"I'm afraid, too," LeRoi admitted. "I know they say it's just like going to sleep, like a door into another plane of living, but what if it's not?"

"I'd like each of you to write out a little paper for me on how you feel about death." Isabel spoke quickly, almost as though she suddenly wanted to stop the line of thought Vinnie had started. "It will be confidential, of course."

"How about you, Dr. Nebo?" LeRoi asked suddenly. "You ever think of suicide?"

"I have an intense interest in the other world," Isabel replied, "but I'm not eager to hurry up that inevitable appointment."

"You don't think it's just going to sleep?" LeRoi asked.

"No, LeRoi, I don't. I know there's something beyond the grave. Reincarnation is a possibility. There have been too many messages from the other side not to accept some form of afterlife."

Vinnie was looking at Josh Kingston. "What do you think?" he asked.

170

"My opinion wouldn't do you much good, Vinnie," Josh replied. "Let me tell you what the Lord says in His Book. He says there definitely is life after death, and there are only two possible destinations. Every human being will live forever in one or the other of those two places, and we'll be either perfectly happy and fulfilled or else perfectly miserable. And the main purpose of this life is to determine where we'll be forever."

"Just another theory," Isabel said condescendingly. "We might more profitably consider what the experts say."

"You mean the thanatologists?" Josh replied. "What makes them experts? They just present more human wisdom in their rejection of God."

Isabel spoke with deliberate calm. "There aren't many people today who have your fundamentalist viewpoint, Josh. This is the age of the new consciousness, philosophies that give a new insight into life, death, the universe. People are tired of hearing about that dead Savior of 2000 years ago. There is new thought today that excites people."

Josh sat up straight and slapped the table with the palm of his hand. "Garbage!"

Isabel reddened. Charlie stifled a grin. Sue looked embarrassed. The others turned accusing eyes upon Josh.

"Your approach is too narrow, Dr. Kingston," Wallace Graham said in icy superiority. "We need a new way of thinking about ourselves, of understanding our own potential as human beings. . . ."

Josh interrupted. "Without Jesus you have no potential! The Bible says without Him you can do nothing, and—"

Wallace interrupted, matching Josh in force and fervor. "I don't happen to count the Bible amoung my source references!"

Josh made a deliberate effort to calm his voice and spoke more quietly. "I shouldn't blow up like that, Isabel, but what you say about a dead Savior hurts me. His words are fresh and alive today. More so. And all these supposedly new cults, they're not new; at least the message they preach isn't. They're as old as the human race. They're all saying we can become gods, march through some evolutionary process until we're divine. They have different names, sure. Buddhists call it Nirvana, Hindus call it Self-Realization, Scientology calls it being a Clear, drug-users call it Unity Consciousness. The Eastern cults, yoga, transcendental meditation . . . they're all basically Hindu, and say we shall become like—an image of—God, and worship ourselves."

Josh stopped to take a sip of water and there being no challenge he continued. "These cults have a strong appeal: they promise to get your life together without needing to encounter a personal God who might make some changes in you. So we have about thirty million Americans in Eastern cults, becoming Hindus without knowing it, or chanting the names of Hindu gods (which is what the mantras are), opening themselves up to every kind of evil spiritual influence. It's monism—all is one, all is god. But it doesn't work! It doesn't have real creativity. That you get from the true God, who is a true Creator.

"The 'new morality' isn't a new belief. It's the same old immorality that denies we have to meet God on His terms, not our own. Sin used to cause shame and then bring repentance. Now it's considered normal, healthy, legitimate. Society is beset now with the perfection of the body. That's more important than character or moral fiber. But the body isn't going to last. Sooner or later it will rot, no matter how careful we are about diet and exercise. Only the spirit is eternal."

As Josh outlined his beliefs, the faces around the circle were mostly hostile. But he had held their total attention with his intensity.

Vinnie was very quiet. "Josh," he said finally. "I wish I could believe in something as strongly as you believe in your God."

Suddenly they all began to rise from the table, eager to be

gone. The impact of Josh's words was swallowed up in a flurry of trivial talk.

Vinnie held the guitar in the manner of the classical guitarist, resting it nearly upright on his left knee. He finished the number with a flourish and smiled at LeRoi. "That's from Stravinsky's *Firebird*," he said.

"Man, that was great!" LeRoi grinned with pleasure. "I never heard no classical music like that."

Wallace joined them in the living room during their post luncheon break and spoke with annoyance. "There isn't any maid service here, you know. If we don't keep this place clean, nobody will. We've only been here a few days and look at it! It's a disaster area—beds not made and the bathroom's a mess."

"Sorry," Vinnie apologized. "I'm used to living at home where my mom does all that. Guess I've been spoiled."

"I ain't spoiled," LeRoi said. "I just don't give a damn." He laughed while Wallace shook his head in disgust.

A soft knock interrupted their talk. Wanda and Glenda Simmons walked in and looked around the room boldly.

"You guys want company?" Wanda inquired. The girls sat side-by-side on the sofa.

"Anybody got a reefer?" Glenda asked.

"Don't tell me we're going to have that stuff here," Wallace said in annoyance. "This is supposed to be a serious, scientific study. You'll get no marijuana from me. I don't use the stuff."

"You don't need to," LeRoi said scornfully. "With all them perscriptions you got in the bathroom, you got no room left for pot."

"He's got you there, Wallace," said Vinnie. "You do your own thing with Big V, don't you?"

"My Valium is a medication prescribed by a doctor," Wallace said stiffly.

"What's the difference? You still get off on it," LeRoi said. He turned to the twins. "I'd light one up, girls, but we got no time. We're to be back at the hospital by 1:30 and it's nearly that now. We can't get caught; they might send us home."

"Your sister know you're here?" Vinnie asked the twins.

"No. She's too busy with Charlie-the-tuna Fortuna," Glenda sneered.

"He's at our place all the time and they don't care where we go as long as it's away from them," Wanda added.

"They might not like you getting buzzed here with us."

"I agree with Vinnie," Wallace said firmly. "It would be better if you had Barbara's permission to come here."

"We run our lives," Glenda said bluntly.

"Not Bebe," Wanda finished.

Vinnie put his guitar back in its case. "Well, it doesn't matter now. It's time to go back."

"Sorry we couldn't accommodate you," LeRoi said.

"Maybe next time," Glenda answered.

Wanda added, "Yeah, next time."

Isabel walked the length of her trailer for the third time and stood staring out the wide kitchen window down the path. *Well, admit it,* she told herself firmly. *You're waiting to see if Charlie Fortuna passes by on his way to see Barbara Simmons.*

Isabel had finished an early, solitary dinner and the long evening stretched out before her. Only a short time ago, Charlie might have joined her to pass the hours, or he might have invited her to join him at the clubhouse, or even more excitingly, in his increasingly infamous back room. But not since the arrival of Barbara Simmons. That decorative but shallow young lady had captivated Charlie on sight. And Isabel was finding it more difficult than she liked to admit to put their brief encounter behind her and forget him.

She shrugged finally, tolerant and even amused at her own weakness. But no sense wasting any more time, she decided. Charlie had been an interest, his earthy masculinity had been exciting for a moment, and she had enjoyed the unfamiliar flurries of femininity he had roused in her. But he was not her only interest. Almost as exciting and certainly as time-consuming was her new interest in the psychic. With the singlemindedness that had seen her through medical school and residency, Isabel began an indepth study of every branch of the field. By now, her trailer was overflowing with books—secular, scientific and occultish—on all different aspects of the subject.

She categorized them roughly. She began with paranormal science, including extrasensory perception, telekinesis, hypnosis, clairvoyance, bioplasmic bodies, psychic photography, psychic healing and acupuncture. This led on to the occult, to witchcraft, sorcery, seances, enchantments and also to astrology, horoscopes, fortune-telling and precognition.

Next she found herself studying mysticism, including the Eastern thought forms, transcendental meditation, animism, reincarnation, magic. And several miscellaneous areas had cropped up, like unidentified flying objects, the work of Carlos Casteneda, pyramidology and the Atlantean Circle. On and on. The study seemed endless.

How could she have spent so many years involved in the area of mind science and be so ignorant of such a large subject? But no longer. Her reading was yielding a harvest of information and attitudes. She was absorbing the new ideas eagerly, but it was hard to know what was fact and what was speculation. She quickly realized that modern science was not able to handle the claims of the paranormal realm. Even with documented phenomena the classic hallmark of the scientific—the ability to repeat—was lacking.

So with her reading there was a tendency to slide away from the documented, the proven, the repeatable, into mysticism on the one hand and to the dark arts, the occult, on the other hand. But anywhere within the scope of the study, Isabel found fascination. It was a science in that it made a statement about the nature of reality, but it was more than a science. It was the door that opened after the intellect was spent.

The study was enticing, seductive. Two things it promised. Two things that Isabel wanted very much. It promised power on a new and awe-inspiring level, and it promised the revelation of knowledge unattainable in any other way.

She settled herself into a cozy chair and picked up a book on the Rosicrucians. Thinking about her new interests made Charlie Fortuna seem unimportant and Isabel was almost glad he no longer made demands on her time.

"You're really something, you know that?" Sue told Isabel with exasperation. "You not only get me involved in a picnic with these weird kids, you have it at my house."

"Well, my trailer's right in the middle of the park. You're here on the edge with all this room for the twins and the dogs to play." Isabel waved a hand, indicating the sweeping forest behind Sue's trailer home. Isabel was placing boxes of food on the redwood table. "There's fried chicken, potato salad, baked beans, all the usual!"

"Well, let's get it set out," Sue said, resigned to this uncomfortable use of her free Saturday. "There's more than enough food here for everyone in Project Truth. Who all is coming?"

"All the Project kids, except Wallace," Isabel said. "Barbara and Charlie are in town, I believe." Isabel answered in a neutral voice. "Josh may come by, which ought to stir your girlish heart."

Sue said nothing but covered the table with a cloth and continued to spread the food and picnic supplies on it. Glenda and Wanda Simmons were dashing around the lawn, the large black dogs running with them, full of excitement. They dropped in an untidy heap under a large oak tree and the twins began to whisper together conspiratorially. The dogs flopped down to rest beside them, tongues lolling.

Down the path beyond Josh Kingston's home, the door of the psychics' trailer opened and Vincent Ponder and LeRoi Williams sauntered down the path to join Sue and Isabel. Vinnie had his guitar, as usual, and he began to strum it softly. "What would you like to hear?"

"Play that thing from *Bolero* you did the other day," Sue responded. "That was great."

Vinnie nodded and began to strum. The lively music danced along the sunlit air; LeRoi tapped his feet in rhythm.

A tall, slender figure was walking slowly down the path toward them. Sue recognized Josh Kingston. He wore his faded jeans with a plaid lumberjack shirt open at the neck.

Please be a normal person, Sue thought. She hoped Isabel would soften her attitude toward him.

A sudden gust of wind grabbed the stack of paper plates and whipped them one by one into the woods like so many frisbees. The cups were knocked over and a cascade of leaves was showering down. Sue felt a chill as the sun clouded over suddenly.

The weather had been beautiful. Although it was early October, it had been very warm all week, and the afternoon sun had been brilliant. Now suddenly it was cold. The wind continued and Isabel, the only one wearing a dress, clutched at her skirt while the men fanned out to retrieve the paper plates.

Potato chips were being whirled around among the paper plates, cups and napkins swirling toward the trees. Sue caught sight of the twins, still under the large oak. They stood facing each other, arms outstretched like sleepwalkers. They had their eyes closed and Sue could faintly hear their chanting over the howl of the wind. The word *enchantment* appeared in Sue's mind, but she wasn't sure what it meant.

Sue did not fear weather of any sort; usually she found storms exhilarating. But not this storm. The thing that frightened her was its unnaturalness; it was obviously not just a storm. It had started too suddenly and grown too quickly.

The sky had taken on a curiously yellow hue and the wind howled even louder. The giant trees whipped and bent under its fury, scattering their brilliantly colored leaves like a snowfall. But the storm was only wind. There was no rain, no lightning or thunder; only the constant, fierce, cold, howling wind. Suddenly, she heard a loud crack sounding clearly over the noise of the gale.

She could see the limb falling. She watched as it fell like a bomb on one of the Simmons twins. She had seen perfectly; only one twin had been hit but both fell as though dead.

Sue stood spellbound, unable to move while all around her things were happening. Isabel screamed and ran toward the children, Josh, Vinnie and LeRoi at her heels. The wind was dying now. By the time Sue roused from her stupor and stumbled toward the children, the air was growing still again, the sun shining almost as brightly as before and the only sign of the whole bizarre episode were the shambles of the picnic lunch, the fallen leaves and branches, and the two stricken children.

Sue knelt beside Isabel who was making a quick examination. The twins were lying like discarded rag dolls. Their two large dogs stood over them whining in dismay, nosing them nervously.

"I saw it happen," Sue said. "The limb hit only one of them. I'm positive of that."

Vinnie spoke tensely. "Will they be all right?"

"We may need to get them to the hospital," Isabel answered. "We can call E.R. and ask them to send a litter." She added to Sue, "There's no way to get an ambulance in here and we can't very well carry them."

As they talked, the smaller twin moaned softly and stirred. Isabel turned to her and touched her forehead; Wanda shoved her away roughly. The youngster sat up, saw her injured sister lying unconscious beside her and clutched her limp hand.

Josh was squatting by the fallen limb and Sue moved closer to him. He looked up. "Strange wind."

"I never saw anything like it! Was it a small tornado?"

"Whatever it was, it wasn't natural."

"What does that mean?" Sue asked. Again she was feeling goose-bumpy chills.

"It just means the enemy is showing his hand a little. The girls tried to conjure up something to scare us, and it got out of hand. But it's over for now."

"Are you saying the twins caused all this?" Sue asked.

Josh shrugged, "Certainly." He straightened up and brushed the dirt off his hands. They both turned to the twins who were conscious now, standing, fending off Isabel's attempts to examine them further.

"You need to be checked over, especially you, Glenda," Isabel stated. "That's quite a goose egg. I don't know when Barbara will be back, but until then I'm responsible."

"No," Glenda said in a voice every bit as firm as Isabel's. "No examinations, no doctors. Nobody touches us."

"Don't try anything, Dr. Nebo," Wanda added. "We know our rights. Ever hear of 'informed consent'? Well, you don't have it."

Isabel stood in silence, her face betraying her indecision and her annoyance.

She's not used to people bucking her, Sue thought. *But the twins are just as stubborn as Isabel.*

Glenda had a large swelling on her right temple, and a very thin trickle of blood oozed from an abrasion on its summit. She touched it tenderly and a little sound of pain escaped her.

"At least let's put an icebag on that goose egg," Isabel urged. "And you both can lie down until your sister and Charlie get back." She took a twin under each arm, shepherding them toward Sue's trailer. "You both lost consciousness, you know. You ought to be lying down."

The twins conferred in their private language for a moment, then nodded in agreement. As Isabel herded them through Sue's front door, the others began picking up the litter strewn around the grounds by the wind.

Quite a party, Sue thought in disgust. *Everything weird: the guests, the weather, and the way it ends. And I'm so sick and tired of weird! Well, I don't care what anybody else does, I'm going to fix me a plate of potato salad and beans and sit down, eat and be normal.*

It was late when Charlie and Barbara returned from town, but it had been one of the best days Charlie could remember. They'd had lunch, strolled through a sidewalk art show, seen a movie, and on the way back to Brookshire stopped and had two drinks at the Roadhouse Inn, a picturesque little pub on the highway near the entrance into Brookshire. He was overwhelmed with pride as throughout the day, over and over, men looked with admiration and envy at his beautiful companion.

Bebe savored being the center of attention. She enjoyed sensual pleasures, too. She ate and drank with the relish of the gourmand, and she was extraordinarily aware of temperature, lighting, the noise level. She insisted on comfort, and Charlie catered to her whims with delight.

Although they had been together for over nine hours, Charlie was reluctant to part from her as they approached the Simmons' trailer about 7 p.m. There was still a hope that she might go with him to the clubhouse.

"What's this?" she asked. The trailer was dark and there was a note stuck in the screen door.

The twins are at Sue Dunn's, the note read. It was signed by Josh Kingston, and Charlie felt a rising disquiet. He and Bebe walked rapidly toward Sue's trailer. It was almost full dark and a cold wind was rising.

Sue and Josh were seated with Wanda when Charlie and Barbara entered. Josh was in one of the chairs, a Bible in his lap. The Bible made Charlie immediately uncomfortable; like a badge or sign, it symbolized Josh's different viewpoint.

The two newcomers stared at Wanda who was just perched there, not talking, not listening; stuporous, as if unplugged from her power source.

"It was strange, the way it happened," Josh began. He went on to explain the wind, the falling limb, the fact that both twins were affected although only one had been struck, that Isabel had examined them both before she left, that Glenda was resting in the bedroom. Barbara listened in polite silence while Charlie fought a rising feeling of fear.

What was it with those kids? he wondered. *Why did Bebe have to be kin to such weird sisters?* He ought to go see Glenda, check her over. Isabel might hold an M.D. degree, but what did a psychiatrist know about trauma? Yet he felt a real reluctance to walk down that hall and enter a room where Glenda Simmons lay in darkness.

She's just a kid, for crying out loud, he told himself in anger. *What can a fourteen-year-old kid do to you?* He looked at Wanda for reassurance. She wasn't even a very big fourteen-year-old.

Wanda shifted her eyes to Charlie and he felt suddenly like somebody had hit him in the stomach. She wore her thick, steelrimmed glasses but he could still see her eyes; too shiny, knowing, with a mischievous glint that somehow made him uncomfortable. He dropped his eyes, unable to meet her stare. She spoke. "Glenda is gone. I can't hear her thinking anymore. I can't wake her up, either."

"Do you want some supper, Wanda?" Bebe asked.

"No, I'm going for a walk. I want to see about Castor and Pollux." She rose and stared defiantly at them. Only Josh stared back. When she left by the front door, Barbara sighed.

"They're really a handful," she complained. "Too much responsibility."

"Bebe, you don't have to go on letting things happen this

way," Josh said softly. "There are things you can do to change the situation. Will you let me pray with you about your sisters?"

Barbara stared at him as though he had suggested something obscene, then shook her head. "We don't just let things happen. We plan. We planned everything, actually. My parents got married, had children, everything, according to their charts."

"You mean astrology?" Josh asked.

"Yes. They wanted a child born under the sign of Gemini. You know, the twins. So they did, and they had twins. They knew that was a sign that they were doing things right, that it was working. When they were just tiny babies, a friend of my mother's who's an astrologer cast their horoscopes, then read them their sign and all their characteristics. My folks have brought them up according to their horoscopes."

"Now don't take offense, but let me ask you one question." Josh was leaning toward her. "Do you and your parents enjoy the children? I know you love them, but do you like them? Do you have fun with them, enjoy them?"

Barbara said nothing. *It's obvious*, thought Charlie, *that nobody could possibly enjoy those particular children.*

They were interrupted by a noise from outside, a cacophony of strange animal sounds.

Charlie turned to Josh. "What's going on out there?" he asked. His voice sounded hoarse to his own ears.

"It's another manifestation. An attempt to frighten us. It could be insects . . . or owls . . . they're unclean birds. . . . I'll make them stop."

Josh opened the front door and went outside. Charlie would have preferred to stay inside, but with Bebe there he didn't dare. He had to appear brave in the presence of his lady love, so he followed Josh. Sue and Barbara stood in the doorway watching.

Postlights along the path illuminated the scene. The ground on every side was alive with frogs, leaping and

182

croaking, constantly in motion. Charlie felt the hair on the back of his neck rise in fear. Josh spoke loudly.

"In the name of Jesus, I command you to leave! Be gone from my presence! You may not manifest in my presence!"

Charlie would have laughed if he had not been so scared. To see a grown man, Bible in hand, solemnly addressing a bunch of frogs had to be ludicrous. Yet within a few minutes there were noticeably fewer frogs and the noise had subsided. Josh finally turned to go inside; then he stopped short, staring in the dim light toward the woods. Charlie followed his gaze and another sudden chill hit him.

Wanda Simmons stood in perfect stillness, eyeglasses glittering from the reflected rays of the light along the path. Around her feet there was a constant motion as the remaining frogs leaped and hopped.

"Wanda, come inside now," Josh called. She stood as though carved out of stone for a suspended moment, then slowly came forward. The frogs followed her till Josh spoke again harshly. Then they vanished.

Wanda walked past the men without a word and went into the trailer. Josh nodded to Charlie. "Let's get inside. I think things are quiet for now."

"Right," Charlie agreed. "I'll wake Glenda up and check her over, then we can leave. I want to get out of here."

"Yes, I know. It's haunted ground."

"You really believe that, don't you?"

"Yes. There's haunted ground and there's holy ground," Josh said matter-of-factly. "A deep woods near a hospital full of sick and disturbed people would probably be haunted without the addition of these so-called psychics, but there's no doubt about it now."

Charlie examined Glenda and was satisfied that she could walk back to the Simmons' trailer. On the way to his own, he noted that the ground was free of frogs and everything looked natural again.

He went inside and prepared himself a stiff drink.

What refreshment would you serve somebody like Wallace Graham? Josh studied the sparse larder of his trailer kitchen. Instant coffee and a box of teabags that he had bought for Sue Dunn were all he could find. No juice, cola or milk.

I guess it will be coffee or tea, he decided. *That's too bad, considering all the New Testament has to say about hospitality.*

This visit by Wallace would be the first of Josh's obligatory interviews with the Project's subjects. He was required to evaluate their spiritual background, their attitudes and approaches to the subject of religion. Josh had waited till he knew a little about them before beginning his interviews, and he would have preferred to start with Vincent Ponder, a far less formidable individual. Yet there were so many demands on the time of the five psychics that Josh was forced to begin with Wallace. And three o'clock Sunday afternoon was the only free time Wallace had.

Wallace was prompt to the minute. He was dressed in a three-piece suit of pale gray wool with a dark blue shirt and a red, blue and silver striped tie. His blond hair was neatly combed. He looked affluent, confident. Only his eyes seemed strange, disquieting. Josh knew that this was no ordinary young man, no matter how normal his appearance.

"Have a seat, Wallace," Josh said in what he hoped was a friendly, hearty voice. "Want a cup of coffee?"

"No, thank you." Wallace sat in the smaller armchair and crossed his legs. He didn't look relaxed; there was still a tension in his body almost as though he were poised for flight. "There's an association here in town called the Sky Watchers; they've just put on a little luncheon in my honor."

Josh responded amiably, spreading out his notes on his lap. He did not take time for small talk. "The religion department of the Project has put together some questions for me to ask you, Wallace. First, do you have any religious affiliation, and if so, what?"

Wallace answered the prepared question concisely and intelligently, but there was no interest in his voice or his expression. Obviously he was indifferent to religion.

Only when the questions touched on the nature of divinity was Wallace roused from his polite apathy. "Well, of course there is a higher being, or what I'd call a more advanced life form. But I don't think it has much to do with what people like you call God."

"Tell me about this advanced life form," Josh urged.

As though he had dropped a record onto a turntable, Wallace began his recitation. The record could have been labeled, "A Brief History of Unexplained Phenomena in the Sky."

"Unexplained aerial phenomena have been a part of human experience since the dawn of man. There are mentions of flying objects and fiery lights in the sky in the writings of many ancient civilizations—Roman, Tibetan, Japanese, Hindu, Egyptian, even American Indians from California. There are cave drawings of space vessels in the sky, complete with humanoid figures, some in China dating back to 45,000 B.C. And over seventy such cave drawings have been found in Spain and France."

Wallace cleared his throat and changed his position slightly. "Christopher Columbus spotted a UFO only four hours before sighting the New World; that's part of the record, still unexplained and still ignored for the most part.

"Hard data goes way back, too. The first photograph of a UFO was taken at the Zaticas Observatory in Mexico in 1883, and since then there have been literally thousands of photographs taken.

"It's not just a delusion or a hoax; something real is there. A poll of Americans was taken about ten years ago and it seems over fifteen million people claim to have personally witnessed a UFO and over fifty percent of the population believes they exist. Hardly likely if indeed they are merely figments of someone's imagination."

Josh leaned back and let the stream of Wallace's words

flow over him. The young man certainly had facts and statistics at his fingertips. In his spirit Josh attempted to fathom what lay underneath the facts and figures.

"The term UFO, or 'unidentified flying object,' has been in use since 1953 when the United States Air Force coined this phrase to replace the earlier term, 'flying saucer,'" Wallace droned on. "It's a fairly parochial term; other countries still use 'flying saucer' and the Russians say 'flying sickle.'

"The first official investigative body was formed in the United States by the Central Intelligence Agency in 1952, comprised of meteorologists, intelligence officers, engineers, astronomers, physicists, military men and others, under the directorship of Dr. H. P. Robertson of Cal Tech.

"There have been sightings in virtually every country in the world, and organizations have been formed in many countries for study. Russia has its All Union Cosmonautics Committee, and fifty countries are joined in the Aerial Phenomena Research Organization.

"Although these study groups explained away many sightings as natural phenomena like birds, hot gases, airplanes, balloons and such, or as meteorological phenomena like auroras, ion clouds and meteors, there was still a remnant left for which there was no natural, rational explanation. This inexplicable remnant spawned what is called the ETH, the Extraterrestrial Hypothesis."

When Wallace paused, Josh broke in. "Is this really going to answer the question concerning your ideas of divinity?" he asked.

"It will render the question inapplicable," Wallace replied calmly. "There is a great deal of human thought that just doesn't apply to me."

"How so?"

"It's just that I understand the universe in such a different way. I have a viewpoint so foreign to that of most people that there are no holding places in their minds or experiences for most of my thinking."

186

Wallace went on to describe Project Blue Book, the official investigative body of an Air Force study group, which has maintained files of UFO sightings. There were almost 13,000 by 1969. Computer analysis of 27 years of reported sightings indicated a sharp increase of UFO activity, up to 100 times the normal, every 61 months. These are called flaps and they occur in a west-to-east direction, touching earth approximately every 1500 to 2000 miles. Wallace then launched into a description of sightings and methods of classifying them.

Josh was wondering how these so-called UFOs related to the Christian faith. He agreed with Wallace that there was something here beyond error, lies and mistaken identity. But what?

His mind reviewed Scripture. Many references might apply to this phenomena. In Joel, God had said, "I will show wonders in the heavens and in the earth blood and fire and pillars of smoke." This same thought was repeated in the three Gospel accounts of Christ's teaching on the end of the world, found in Matthew 24, Mark 13 and Luke 21. And there was Revelation 6.

But were these "terrors and portents" of biblical prophesy the same as UFOs? He had previously thought the reference applied more to things like black holes, quasars, pulsars, white dwarf stars and such. Maybe both applications were true. . . .

His thoughts were interrupted by Wallace's shift in emphasis. "Of course, I realize I'm a pioneer. I was one of the very first to be chosen for the role of liaison, but I am not alone. There have been over 2000 carefully documented cases of contacts such as mine. These are not just sightings, these are actual contact. There are doubtless many others who have not as yet come forward to face the ridicule and harassment that the world heaps on any true prophet of a new age.

"Some of us will be martyred; I know that. But it'll be worth it! I have knowledge and experiences and a commitment that lesser men cannot even comprehend! I am fully willing to die for my beliefs to advance the cause of what I know to be truth." He was sitting very erect, the pride and passion of the fanatic transforming his face from its usual ordinary appearance.

How I understand that position, Josh thought with emotion. *I could apply almost everything he's said to my own position in relation to Jesus Christ for whom I would gladly die. But there has to be a difference; what I believe is truth and what he believes is deception. What I believe produces love, joy and peace. What he believes produces bondage and fear.*

As Wallace spoke on, sudden illumination came to Josh. He didn't need more facts. Wallace Graham's all-out involvement with UFOs exposed him to the occult, psychic control and astral projection, to mention a few. Josh knew that on these battlegrounds the prize of war was the souls of mankind.

The bright, intelligent, well-to-do young man who sat in Josh's living room now, speaking so intensely of his passion, was in total bondage to powers he understood not at all, powers who hated him beyond his capacity to understand. And he was totally ignorant of both his bondage and their hatred.

How could he be helped? Could truth penetrate his delusion? Probably not, not at this point. Wallace would almost certainly reject any ideas that countered his own convictions, until the soil of his mind was softened by prayer and by the binding up of the lying spirits who dominated his mind. Better to spend the time gaining Wallace's confidence.

With that in mind Josh began to ask questions. "Did the Zorans explain to you why UFOs can upset our electrical systems? Like an automobile, for example."

"Yes." Wallace leaned forward eagerly. "We have several sources of power on this earth: gravitational, magnetic, electrical. The Zorans have other sources that we have never even conceived. Way beyond nuclear fission or fusion.

Like the ERB force. It's almost exclusively mental and it apparently acts simultaneously in emission and effect. . . ."

Josh listened with every evidence of interest as his mind battled through prayer against the forces that had entrapped this earnest young man.

One of the things Sue didn't like about her job was the monthly meeting of head nurses and supervisors. For years she had sat through these meetings, listening as nurses discussed their problems, made studies, formed committees, filed reports, instituted changes, yet failed utterly to reverse the rising tide of dissatisfaction, errors and inefficiency. Being crowded into a room with a lot of people always gave her feelings of claustrophobia.

It seemed even worse on the Monday morning following what had been a most disquieting weekend.

She sat at the end of the long, wide table in the conference room of the In-service Education Department. The table and its chairs were the only furnishings in the room, except a wheeled cart from Dietary containing a large pot of coffee and stacks of styrofoam cups. There was no tea. So Sue sat in annoyance, watching as the others served themselves.

The head nurse on Six North dropped into a seat next to Sue and stirred powdered cream into black coffee.

"I hope we're not here all morning," she said. "I have 24 surgeries on Six North today. You'd think Five North was closed down or something the way we get all the admissions."

"I haven't seen an agenda," Sue replied. "But maybe it'll be short."

The Director of Nursing, a tall, heavy-set woman in her late forties, entered the room briskly. Like many nurses, she had a take-charge air about her and a notable lack of patience. She also had a deep, throaty voice and a tendency to casual profanity.

189

"Ladies and gentlemen"—she nodded to the three male nurses also in attendance—"get your coffee and let's get started. We're in something of a crisis situation. For that reason, we'll dispense with the routine business and reports. No minutes or any of that crap." Sue sat up with interest. This was unheard of; routine had always prevailed. There must indeed be a crisis.

"Yesterday afternoon I met with the department heads, administrator, representatives from the malpractice carrier and two gentlemen from the legal department. Public relations was there, some men from the Brookshire Foundation, even Don Oliver Franklin. What I'm here to report is absolutely confidential and must not leave this room. Understood?"

The nurses nodded, shocked into complete silence.

"There is something very wrong here at Brookshire," she continued. "Our death rate has risen over 600 percent in the past three weeks, and some of the causes of death have been mighty bizarre. For example, five suicides, one drowning, six drug-related deaths from overdoses or drug reaction. There was one electrocution down in nuclear medicine, two anesthesia deaths, one old fellow burned to death in physical therapy, three died in surgery and three more post-op. That's *in addition* to our usual deaths. All the deaths have been categorized by causative agent, patient's age, diagnosis, patient's location, time of day, all those variables; we're still trying to sort them out. All we can say at this point is, there are too many of them and too many bizarre causes.

"In addition," the Director continued, "we've had twenty cases of mistaken identity; that is, twenty we caught. But seven times this month surgery was performed on the wrong patient. Not to mention the innumerable X-rays, lab tests and other diagnostics being done on the wrong patients.

"The formula prepared for the newborn nursery was contaminated and there is a high incidence of gastro-enteritis. Again, no fatalities, but we're not out of the woods yet. There's an outbreak of staph among the personnel in Central Supply. It looks like staph aureus and that'll be a real hassle to bring under control. Central Supply, of all places!"

She looked around the table again, then back at her list. Sue was hardly breathing, so intently was she listening to the additional horrors being read out.

"There have been 17 major breakdowns in the computer, disrupting billing and delaying the inpatient lab by almost 36 hours. There have been five different bomb threats, all fakes as far as we could tell, but still something else out of the ordinary. When the fire marshal made his semi-annual inspection, he found every one of our fire extinguishers non-operational. They'd somehow been discharged and were absolutely worthless. Good thing we hadn't needed them.

"The vacuum system has failed twice; they may have to go into the walls to fix it and we don't have anywhere near enough portable vacuums to handle surgery and the acute care areas, let alone the rest of the hospital.

"There was a strange, apparently pointless theft of surgical specimens from the pathology lab. Who would want to steal a bunch of tonsils, uteruses and hernia sacs? But they are gone and it's caused an enormous amount of trouble and confusion.

"There were almost a thousand incident reports filed the past month, three times as many as we've ever had in a comparable length of time. I won't continue to detail the problems; suffice it to say, there is something very wrong here.

"Yesterday's staff meeting was the first effort to determine exactly what is happening. We brainstormed like some think-tank group and came up with all kinds of explanations, but no definitive action was taken. We discussed the possibility of hiring efficiency experts or a private detective, and there was even talk of closing the hospital for a while. But of course that isn't feasible. About the only thing

191

decided was that every department head was to discuss the situation with his supervisory staff and see if they had any light to shed on things. Do you people have any ideas?"

For a long moment the room was totally silent.

"I'd like to comment that we've pretty well proved that the errors in identification in surgery weren't really the fault of O.R. personnel." This was offered stiffly by the head nurse of surgery, a tall, horse-faced woman with noticeably yellow teeth.

"The allocation of blame is a secondary consideration right now," the Director said with a hint of sarcasm. "There will be time for that after we've made sure there won't be any repetitions."

"Do all your statistics date from the first of September?" asked a young male R.N.

"Yes. They were compiled by data processing."

"How do we stand legally?" asked one of the 11-to-7 supervisors.

"Pitiful. Almost every doctor on the house staff is involved in litigation, plus about thirty current suits against the hospital. And that's just so far. More are on the way."

"What percentage of the problem is really the business of nursing service?" another supervisor asked. "We always seem to get caught in the middle."

"I don't have an answer to that question."

"Is the problem still increasing or has there been a leveling off?" questioned a male nurse from infection control. "You make the hospital sound like a ticking bomb."

"That's a very good way of describing it," the Director nodded. "Something strange is going on, and it is not leveling off. It's almost like we're losing control of things."

Sue's heart was pounding in excitement. Of all those present, she might be the only one who had a real insight into the possible cause of the problem. Only she had been exposed to the ideas and philosophy of one Joshua Kingston, and only she had heard his prediction that the coming of the psychics would make something like this happen.

Namely: a loss of control, a rise in bizarre and unpleasant happenings, a stirring of people and events that the natural mind could neither explain nor effect.

But there was no possible way she could mention this to the Director and this group of nurses or they'd laugh her from the room.

At precisely twelve noon on Monday, Malcolm Brown took his tray of food from Brookshire's cafeteria line and walked with confidence toward the long table under the windows, which had become unofficially but unquestionably the property of the staff and subjects of Project Truth.

He smiled cheerily and nodded a greeting as he took a seat toward the end of the long table. A big crowd for today's lunch: Dr. Fortuna, Dr. Nebo, and two other staff members were in their accustomed seats, and all five of the psychics were present. Sue Dunn was sitting as usual toward the head of the table facing the windows with her back to the room, and Josh Kingston sat in his usual seat next to her.

"Looks like you're all suffering from the 'blue Monday blues,'" Malcolm said teasingly. "Not a smile among you."

"I've had a bad morning," Sue apologized. "Head nurses' and supervisors' meeting."

"I got a headache," LeRoi Williams said defensively. "Don't feel like smiling."

Wallace Graham, who customarily sat at the head of the table, favored the chaplain with a haughty glance. "It would be a bit artificial to smile in the middle of a controversy."

The Simmons twins, sitting side-by-side across the table, laughed together mirthlessly. One of them spoke up. "Just like always we have a meal together and an argument."

"Yeah," her sister added. "We get meat, two vegetables, salad and an argument."

Malcolm noticed that one of the twins had a large area of

swelling and discoloration on her temple that was not bandaged. "Any way I can be a mediator?" he offered cheerfully.

"I don't think Dr. Kingston would listen to you any more than to the rest of us," Wallace Graham replied. "He's convinced that what we're doing here is wrong and nothing we say will change his mind."

"That's right," Josh responded. "The rest of you are all sweet reason; I'm the only one who's stubborn."

The chaplain took a spoonful of gelatin. It was refreshing to have the authoritative Dr. Kingston disturbed.

"What you're doing is putting respectable scientific names on old occult practices," Josh continued. "The modern medical system is rapidly falling back into the dark ages, even teaching nurses at one university I know all about voodoo and witchcraft. It's getting worse and worse."

Sue Dunn who had been eating quietly, looked up at Josh in surprise. "You're kidding!" she protested.

"No. And did you know in 1973 the World Health Organization recognized witch doctors? I didn't think so. The medical system is changing, just like everything else in this world, harming more and more people, helping less and less. Evil is crowding out good."

"What really is happening is that the world is redefining what you call evil," Isabel Nebo inserted. "In short, changing your old-fashioned traditions."

"For the worse," Josh shot back. "What's happening is you're building another tower of Babel, blending an occult religion with science. The fact is, healing began as a religious ceremony, and in the final analysis, it still is. It works by faith."

Malcolm ate in silence. He had joined the discussions a couple of times in the past and had suffered embarrassment and wounded pride as a result. No, he wasn't going to join in, but he could enjoy listening to the others.

Vincent Ponder rose from his chair. "I'm going back to the trailer for a while. I want to relax before it's testing time."

"I'll go with you," LeRoi said.

"Anybody else?" Vinnie asked.

The Simmons twins rose together, stepped behind their chairs and pushed them under the table in perfect synchronization. *Like dancers in a chorus line*, Malcolm thought.

"Don't be gone too long," Isabel Nebo warned. "The tests are set for one o'clock sharp."

"We'll be there," Vinnie said reassuringly.

"And if we ain't, go ahead without us," LeRoi smirked.

Wallace Graham was eager to continue the discussion, leaning toward Josh Kingston. "At Notre Dame University, there's a priest who's favorable toward developing psychic powers. What do you say to that?"

Josh stared at Wallace for a long moment. When he spoke his words were gentle. "I've probably said too much already."

There was an awkward silence around the table and Malcolm Brown sniffed in disgust. What a phony show of humility! All done to disarm his opponents. Sue Dunn, Brown noticed, looked at Josh with an expression of approval. So Josh had her fooled.

One by one they got up to leave as Malcolm continued to eat, talking casually with Charlie Fortuna. The food was not especially enjoyable but there was satisfaction in seeing Josh Kingston discomfited.

The Project had been assigned a suite of rooms at the end of Eight South for use in parapsychological testing. There was a small outer office, furnished sparsely with a desk, two filing cabinets and some cast-off chairs. Beyond this outer office was a short hall leading to two larger identical rooms, dubbed A and B. Both rooms were perfectly square with fading gray tile floors, off-white walls and a built-in counter with sink and faucets along one wall. Each window opened onto the glorious view of the Brookshire Mountains. Into these two rooms had been brought a wealth of equipment and apparatus for parapsychological testing.

At 1:15 p.m. Charlie Fortuna slipped quietly into Room A, where the five psychics were standing in a group by the window, whispering together. Despite their differences, they were developing a certain degree of camaraderie being thrown together so often. Isabel Nebo hovered over them like an officious mother hen.

Others in the room included three visiting parapsychologists, two from California and one from Boston. A statesmanlike old gentleman, the statistician for the Project, stood among them. Charlie walked over to join the psychics, putting a friendly arm around Vincent Ponder's broad shoulder. "What's the hold-up?" he asked.

"The Boston fellow wanted to try some long-distance ESP between the girls," Vinnie explained. "Isabel thinks that's a waste of time, too easy and already documented. Now he's wanting to go into long-distance hypnotism."

"Is that possible?" Charlie asked in surprise.

"Oh, sure," Wallace Graham said with a certain amount of scorn. "In Russia they do it all the time; hypnotism is effective from as far away as a hundred miles."

"Without the subject's knowledge or consent," Vinnie added. "That's frightening."

"They want us to demonstrate with the ouija board again, too," Glenda Simmons said. "Blindfolded with the letters scrambled."

"I heard you could spell out messages blindfolded without knowing where the letters were. That's pretty impressive," Charlie said.

Glenda nodded. "Impressive maybe to somebody like you," she said.

"Not for us," Wanda's voice held scorn. Charlie frowned over their attitude of superiority. It was masked at times but never absent. They might say "Dr. Nebo" to her face, but behind her back she was "Isabel." And Fortuna knew they called him "Charlie-the-Tuna."

"All right, kids," Isabel called in a bright voice. "I think we've reached an agreement. We're going to do some testing in the Witches' Cradle starting tomorrow. All five of you."

"What's a Witches' Cradle?" Charlie asked. One of the men from California made a sound of irritation and looked pointedly at his wristwatch.

"It's a device the subject enters where there is no light or sound or outside stimuli," the Boston parapsychologist explained patiently. "It's kind of a platform, hanging loose, which negates even gravity's effect. It seems to encourage an altered state of consciousness and increases psychic powers." He chuckled and added, "It's called Witches' Cradle because we got the idea from something witches used to use."

Charlie wondered if Josh Kingston knew of such a device; he didn't need to wonder what Josh's opinion of it would be.

"What we're aiming for," Isabel continued, "is some strong documentation, scientific evidence of the existence of nonphysical bodies. Scientists have established the fact that the drop in temperature in the presence of psychic and occult activity is in direct proportion to the energy released."

"That phenomenon is also present with second-and third-kind encounters with UFOs," Wallace said excitedly.

Another of the parapsychologists spoke to Wallace. "There are many other similarities between UFOs and parapsychological phenomena and the occult. All three manifest levitation, for example, and unusual odors, occasional humming sounds, poltergeist effects, OBEs. . . ." He turned to Charlie as though he realized Charlie needed a translation." That's out-of-body experiences. We'll be examining some of these similarities."

"Thank you, Doctor," Isabel broke in. "We haven't tried

to explain all our thinking to the kids; we don't want to clutter their minds with extraneous details."

"Since it's their minds that are doing all this, maybe the more they know the better," the parapsychologist replied mildly.

"That's another thing I'd like to comment on," Wallace said firmly. Isabel gave him a brief look of annoyance; Wallace consistently refused to stay quietly in the position where she placed him. "You people are almost unanimous in believing that this power is in our minds," Wallace said. "Yet we all routinely deny that—the five of us here and almost all other psychics."

"That's pretty far afield from what we're going into right now, Wallace," Isabel objected. "But we can discuss it at dinner if you like."

Wallace turned away in irritation and Isabel continued, "The doctor is collecting data to present to some of his colleagues, all of whom are committed to proving the reality of psychospiritual manifestations with solid, tangible, reputable scientific proof."

"You've got your work cut out for you," Wallace commented. "Are you into the neutrino thing? Hyper-dimensionality? Or possibly the famous supraluminal particle, the Tachyon? I can't see any of this falling into your hands like a ripe apple."

The parapsychologist nodded. "You don't fail to take the first steps just because the journey is a long one."

It looks like Wallace has finally found somebody to talk to, Charlie thought.

"What's on the schedule for today?" Vinnie asked.

"Probably get the EEGs done, right?" Isabel turned to the visitors for confirmation. The three parapsychologists nodded in agreement and all the psychics groaned in weariness.

"Not like before," Isabel hastened to reassure them. "This time we want to store your particular brain wave patterns in the computer. There's a possibility they can be fed back to other people, enable them to function in the PSI realm just as you do. You remember, we've discussed this possibility."

"Yeah," Vinnie said wearily. "So call your EEG technicians and get your computer people up here. Let's get going."

No one but Charlie seemed really happy about the proposed plan for the afternoon. But he was delighted; this kind of thing did not require his presence so he could leave and spend the afternoon with Bebe Simmons.

Josh was surprised when Sue invited him to dinner. It was a bit unprofessional, but he accepted and she was pleased.

It was Josh's first home-cooked meal in some time, and it would have been an occasion on that account if no other. She promised chili—"even if it isn't very healthful." He could smell it in his own home an hour before he was due. When she greeted him at the door, her face was flushed from the heat of the kitchen and her hair was fluffed rather nicely around her face.

She excused herself to tend to her cooking, and while she was busy in the kitchen, Josh wandered around her living room. She had been in his home several times, but this was his first visit to hers and he was curious. A tall bookcase stood against the back wall. He studied the titles of her collection.

"You read C. S. Lewis?" he asked in surprise.

She peered at him from the kitchen door. "Yes. I love his books. Does that surprise you?"

He ignored the question and looked further. Most of her books were popular fiction, some poetry, and a few lightweight books he labeled "inspirational." In Josh's opinion, nothing else there approached the level of Lewis' trilogy.

The rest of the room showed her touch: restful, quiet,

cheerful. There were plants all around, growing and prospering. A watercolor landscape hung over the couch and reading lamps stood by each chair. A framed copy of "The Desiderata" hung over the table. This was the sort of thing that irritated Josh—an ancient bit of prose which sounded good on the surface but had in reality only an illusion of faith in God. *I guess it's better than a poster that says, If it feels good, do it,* he thought.

Sue came in from the kitchen, sat on the couch and leaned forward eagerly. "I have a thousand questions."

"Fire away." Josh sat down in a chair opposite her.

"First of all, if all you say is true, why aren't more people aware of demonic activity?"

"Good question. And I suppose the answer is because we've gotten too smart. We've been persuaded to use different names: neurosis, psychosis, compulsions, obsessions, and so forth. And we started handling their manifestations by humanistic means: drugs, psychotherapy, counseling. When the supernatural power of the Church is disregarded, there is no other way to fight demons. But the power is coming back. There are people all over the world who now really believe the last few verses in Mark."

Sue looked blank so Josh quoted for her: "And these signs shall follow them that believe; in my name they shall cast out devils."

"How does a person get a demon?"

"There are many different ways it can happen, different degrees—influence, harassment, control. Demons get ground from which to torment a person when that person has given in to some sin, or when he's taken drugs—that's a wide open door—or if he's been involved in the occult. False religions or cults are an opening; also certain types of music. Christians are primary targets for attacks by these creatures, but if you're not Christian, you're really wide open, what the Bible calls a city without walls."

"And you think these psychic kids are like that?"

"They're influenced and occasionally controlled by demonic forces. Yes, I believe that."

"Tell me, exactly what is a demon? I know it's in your book but I want you to tell me." She clasped her hands together and leaned forward again. Josh plunged in, telling her as simply and factually as he could the things he'd learned about the spiritual realm.

Sometime during the discussion they moved to the little table and she served the chili. It was excellent and Josh interrupted their talk to compliment her. She smiled.

"I have a secret, but I always tell everybody. I use V-8 juice instead of tomato paste. It gives it a better flavor. Now, what do you mean by 'feeding a demon and making it grow'? What does it eat?"

"Some of them eat drugs; I can almost tell what spirits are bothering a person by the drugs he takes. For example, a spirit of depression loves Valium. The spirit of epilepsy feeds on Dilantin and Phenobarbital. I sometimes get a picture in my mind of a caged beast. If you keep it fed constantly, it'll stay quiet, but if you miss a feeding, it'll pitch a fit. Other spirits feed on whatever aligns with their nature. . . ."

She interrupted. "Epilepsy is a demon?"

"Yes. You might not accept that, but if we find a Christian with epilepsy who'll receive the teaching and put himself in a position to hold a deliverance, I think I could prove it to you."

"I feel like all my life I've been looking at things a certain way and now you're trying to change all that." She was frowning.

"Well, check it out. Matthew 17, or even better, Mark 9. What that kid had was epilepsy and Jesus cured him through deliverance."

He watched Sue as he spoke. They had finally come to the center, the core of the matter. How she reacted to this one point would determine the eventual outcome of all his sharing with her. Would Sue accept the Bible as proof? Would the fact that the Bible described epilepsy as demonic in origin persuade her? He knew it would be hard to convince her of this truth in opposition to the clamoring voices of traditional training.

He spoke urgently. "Read the Bible. That's the only safe place for your faith."

"You're going too fast," she protested. "I need time to let it settle in."

"I understand, but remember the Bible says the natural mind can't receive spiritual truth. You'll have to take some of it on faith." He smiled. "That's really it, Sue. Taking things on faith. The world may say, 'Seeing is believing,' but the Lord says, 'Believing is seeing.'"

"All right. I'll think about it. Now, let's talk about something else."

He smiled again. He really liked this woman. She was one of the few people at Brookshire with whom he felt comfortable. They moved from the table to the chairs of the living room and continued to talk; natural, easy, relaxed talk about many things— their education, families, Josh's career.

"Do you have any special friends?" Sue asked.

Josh thought a moment. "A few. I never seem to have enough time for friendships."

"What do you look for in a friend?"

"Common interests, I guess."

"Someone who believes exactly as you do?"

Josh smiled to himself, aware of the little trap. "I'm not afraid to have a friend who doesn't agree with me."

He saw the relief in her eyes. "I'd like to be your friend, Josh, but I'm no good at pretending. You interest me, then scare me. At times I root for you, and at times I want—"

"To kick me," he finished with a smile.

"Well . . . yes. It's not so much that you come on strong. I like the depth of your conviction. It's that you can be— abrasive when it isn't necessary."

Josh felt wistful, wondering how open he could be with Sue, hesitant, yet wanting to probe the matter. "I admit that, Sue. I hate myself at times for my intemperate remarks. I wish I had Don Oliver's poise and aplomb, but I'm not made that way."

"Which means that you don't really want to change," Sue pressed.

Josh sighed. "I wish I were more likable. Yet if I were that type, I probably couldn't do what I'm supposed to do."

Sue's eyes so reflected the pain she felt for him that Josh's heart was warmed. Yes, he did like this young woman whose honesty shone through like a bright stone at the bottom of a clear stream.

"Oh, ho," said Glenda, impressed. "She's wearing the red dress."

Wanda added, "Isn't that a bit grand for just sitting around watching television with Charlie-the-Tuna?" They plopped on the bed and stared at their sister.

"Well, actually, we're going out for dinner. You'll be all right, won't you?" Bebe spoke without looking at them; she was admiring herself in the mirror.

"Maybe so, maybe not."

"Sue Dunn will be home if you need anything."

Barbara's dress was a wine-red velvet, simply cut, a classic style that flattered her figure. She brushed her hair back from her face. "I wish I had a fur stole," she complained. "The weather is perfect for one. I just hate to wear an old cloth coat over this dress."

"Maybe if you stick with old Charlie, he'll get you one," Glenda suggested.

"He's rich, isn't he?" Wanda asked.

Bebe smiled slightly. "I guess he does all right. Most doctors do."

"Do you really like him?" Glenda probed.

"He'll do. And he's a doctor."

Glenda looked disapproving. "Is that all you care about?"

"I think he's kind of cute for an old guy," Wanda smiled.

"He's only thirty-eight, girls. That isn't old."

"It's fourteen years older than you are," Glenda said firmly.

Bebe made a sudden decision. "I don't think I'll wear a wrap at all. I'd rather be cold than wear that old coat."

With their sister gone, the twins looked at each other and smiled.

Let's get the dogs and go, Glenda thought eagerly.

I'm ready, Wanda thought back.

They pulled on their heavy sweaters, called Castor and Pollux from the back bedroom where they had been sleeping and the four of them left the trailer.

We'll go see the boys, Glenda thought with excitement.

Maybe LeRoi'll have some grass, Wanda thought back hopefully.

They walked toward the trailer shared by the three young men. Their older sister's supervision was cursory and seldom hindered the twins' activities, but this was even better. Now there was no one to check on their movements.

Shortly after midnight a front of cold, damp Canadian air moved in over the Brookshire hills, dropping temperatures into the low 30s. Then came freezing rain, beginning about three and lasting till dawn. By 7 a.m. the rain had stopped but the air was still damp and penetrating as the personnel of Brookshire Hospital met for breakfast.

At the long table under the windows all the psychics were present. Wallace Graham ate his breakfast in silence, aloof from all the trivial chatter, while Vincent Ponder talked quietly with Charlie Fortuna. LeRoi Williams looked ill; his eyes were red-rimmed and he had the sniffles.

The Simmons twins had come to breakfast alone. Barbara, they explained, had been out late the night before. Isabel Nebo was dressed in a woolly green suit that had the unfortunate effect of making her resemble a caterpillar; her glasses were a darker green and she wore chunky jade earrings.

Josh Kingston ate rapidly. He was involved in a study project and wanted to get back as soon as possible to his books. It centered on Vinnie Ponder's strange powers, which had touched Josh. The inexplicable intrusion of foreign intelligences, forcing on Vinnie a creative drive in the area of music, was very interesting. A familiar spirit, of course, but what else was involved? Automatic writing?

Josh knew a little about this kind of thing and was learning more. Many psychics had been gifted—or, more properly, cursed— with this ability. Edgar Cayce wrote what was dictated to him in trance states. Such famous writers as Kahlil Gibran and Richard Bach had apparently written what had been given to them by others, by "voices," "spirits," "guides." And Ruth Montgomery had seemingly carried things a step further in writing *A World Beyond*, employing what amounted to automatic typing. This was at least similar to what was haunting Vinnie, and Josh planned to spend this day in deeper study, seeking clues to the answer.

Sue Dunn had no idea at breakfast that she would spend almost six of the next eight working hours involved in a frustrating, tiring and unsuccessful conference on the hospital's current crisis. She was still thinking about her evening with Josh and had little interest in Brookshire Hospital and its problems this cold, wet morning.

Don Oliver Franklin was scanning the computer printout, reading the statistics for the 24-hour period that had ended at midnight. As he expected, there were more deaths, many of them unaccountable.

He folded the paper with its condemning figures and shoved it into a pocket. It was about time to visit the kitchen, help himself to toast and a couple of rashers of bacon.

Effie MacAllister leaned over the counter at the nurses'

station on Six North and spoke as gently as possible to the head nurse.

"I'm afraid Mr. Anton is dead."

"What!" The young head nurse sat up in astonishment and glared at Effie. "What do you mean he's dead? There isn't anything wrong with him!"

"Nevertheless, he's dead," Effie responded, still speaking softly.

"Well, why didn't you call a code? Maybe we can save him." She rose from her seat where she had been busy ordering supplies.

"He didn't just die," Effie explained. "He's been dead quite a while. He's cold as a wedge and already stiff. A code wouldn't do anything but cause a ruckus and cost his family a lot of money."

The head nurse sat back down, staring at Effie with glazed, stricken eyes. "He was just here for a 'vas,'" she protested. "Band-aid surgery. Lunch-hour surgery. He's only thirty!"

"Thirty-three," Effie corrected.

"Whatever. Too young to die. What was wrong?" The head nurse reached behind her to the chart rack and drew out the chart for Mr. Anton. She thumbed quickly to the nurses' notes, the running record of the patient's activity and condition. "He was only admitted because of the kind of hospitalization he had," she mumbled. "He sure didn't need to be here for a simple vasectomy."

"I know," Effie said soothingly.

"Nothing," the head nurse said triumphantly as she read the notes quickly. "Slight nausea last night, normal vitals. For discharge today. Nothing to indicate he was going to die!"

"It looks like he vomited," Effie offered. "Right on the bed. Maybe he aspirated or something."

"Why didn't he put on his call light?"

"I don't know." Effie's voice still calm and gentle. "I just went in to say good-morning and tell him I'd be back later to get him ready for breakfast and he was dead."

"Well, here we go again." The head nurse stood in silence a moment, her face reflecting the distress she felt. "I'll call the supervisor, call the resident, call the surgeon, call the family, and—oh, yes. I think I'll call the employment agency. Maybe they can get me a job somewhere as a waitress. That sounds mighty appealing right about now."

Charlie drained the last of his rum, set the glass on the coffee table and rose to click off the television set. The news, as usual, ranged from boring to bad and he had no interest in the game show that followed.

The long night stretched before him. Almost certainly he would traverse the chilly pathway to the clubhouse before too long. An entire evening alone was unthinkable, and Miss Bebe was in one of her moods and had refused to spend any part of it with him.

There was a sharp, authoritative knock on the door and Charlie opened it. Isabel Nebo stood on his steps, wrapped in a voluminous cape of purple wool, her face almost hidden in the folds of its hood.

"Charlie, Bebe's been hurt, cut on the forehead. It may need stitches and she wanted you." Her voice was brisk and businesslike.

Charlie felt a rush of alarm. Not that beautiful face! Suddenly he was excited that Bebe's thoughts had turned to him.

"I don't have my bag," he said. "I can't do any suturing, but I'll come, of course." As he spoke, he was donning his leather jacket. "What happened?"

"I don't know. I was outside, carrying some things to the trash bin when I heard her scream and went right over to her trailer. She asked for you." Isabel was not happy with her present assignment.

They hurried down the pathway, hunching against the chilling wind, and within five minutes arrived at the Simmons' trailer. All seemed peaceful within as Charlie mounted the steps and knocked, Isabel huddled close behind him. Barbara Simmons opened the door, holding a handkerchief to her forehead.

Barbara took a seat at the table and Charlie flipped on the overhead light to examine her injury, his professional side taking charge. The twins sat on the couch, holding hands and singing softly in their private language.

"This is going to need a couple of stitches," Charlie told his patient. He was heartsick and angry at the desecration of this beautiful face. "I don't have anything here, but we can walk over to Brookshire. I can get a needle holder and a piece of suture and fix you up in no time. And you ought to have a tetanus booster." Should he suggest a plastic surgeon? he wondered. A scar on that face would be an abomination.

"No. I can't leave." She was emphatic. The twins' two large, angry-looking dogs walked into the living room from the back hall and made a deliberate circle of the newcomers, sniffing suspiciously. Charlie was a dog-lover ordinarily, but these particular dogs roused no feelings of affection.

Isabel handed him a dish towel wrung out in cold water and he cleaned off the area around the wound. "How'd it happen?" he asked, relieved as the dogs lay down by the door.

"I hit my head on the freezer."

The twins giggled together, and Charlie felt a tingle go up his spine. "That's where she keeps the ice cream," Wanda declared.

"*Her* ice cream," Glenda added.

"They're putting on weight," Barbara said defensively. "I thought they ought to cut out sweets for a while. We had a scene. They usually do what I say and don't get mad and lose control."

"You're still bleeding," Isabel said. "I can stay here with the girls while you two go to the hospital."

"No!" It was a chorus. Bebe and both twins responding loudly.

"Just leave me; I'll be all right," Barbara said in a dull voice.

208

They remained at an impasse for several minutes. Then in helpless frustration Charlie left to get his medical kit. By the time he had walked to his office, packed the equipment in his black bag and returned to the Simmons' trailer, fifteen minutes had passed. He opened the door without knocking.

Something had happened. The room was filled with an electric tension that made his insides squirm. He looked around the room quickly. The same people there with one addition—LeRoi Williams.

He walked toward Barbara and placed his bag on the table in front of her.

"You don't need that now," Barbara said in a muted, uncertain voice.

"What do you mean?"

"Look at my forehead."

Charlie's eyes turned to the wound. His knees began to tremble and his mind whirled.

Bebe's forehead was smooth, unmarred by any sign of a wound.

"I did it. I closed the wound." Charlie's head snapped around toward the voice. LeRoi! The unkempt psychic was pale, his face drawn and tense, his hair in total disarray.

"Is this some kind of a joke?" Charlie's voice was hardly audible.

"No, Charlie. LeRoi did his chant, standing before Barbara, and the wound closed up. It was a psychic healing." Isabel's voice was excited. "It was incredible. Better than Josh could do."

Charlie could think of no reply whatsoever. Somehow he had been duped. Yet the wound had been there; he had touched it.

LeRoi had nothing more to say. He looked totally drained. Isabel was chattering away, the twins seemed bemused, and Barbara was embarrassed.

"Want me to stay a while?" He turned to Barbara and made his voice as casual as possible.

"No. We're fine," Bebe answered.

Charlie squeezed her hand, picked up his bag and started back to his own trailer, his mind reeling.

Sue Dunn had broken a long-standing habit when she began eating breakfast with the Project people. This morning she carried her tray to the long table under the windows and greeted the others: Isabel, the Simmons twins, Charlie Fortuna and the three young psychics. There was no sign of Josh Kingston, she realized with disappointment.

She arranged her food and began to eat, listening without interest as Wallace and LeRoi bickered over the relative nutritional value of their selections.

"You're swimming in a sea of carbohydrates," Wallace said, appalled. He gestured toward LeRoi's tall stack of pancakes covered with syrup.

"Yeah, guess I'd better watch my weight," LeRoi scoffed, patting his bony chest.

Wallace appealed to Sue. "Do you think we could get some honey instead of syrup? And maybe some orange juice that hasn't been pasteurized?"

"Just don't mess with my grits," LeRoi warned.

"Did you hear about last night?" Isabel interrupted.

"Come on, Isabel," Charlie Fortuna protested. "Let's just drop it."

"Yeah," LeRoi agreed. "The less said the better."

Isabel glared around the table. "I don't understand you people," she said with a shake of her head. "Why doesn't anybody want to talk about it?"

"We have talked about it," Glenda Simmons contradicted.

Wanda nodded. "We've said everything there is to say about it."

Sue's curiosity was aroused. "What *are* you talking about?"

"It was an honest-to-goodness psychic healing!" Isabel leaned forward excitedly. "Barbara had cut her head on the freezer door and LeRoi healed her." And she repeated the astonishing tale to Sue.

"Don't make it such a big deal," LeRoi urged.

"It was a big deal," Isabel countered. "It was a paranormal psychic healing and you should be very proud of yourself."

"Well, I ain't," LeRoi said rudely.

Josh suddenly appeared, sat down quietly next to Sue and listened carefully as Isabel repeated the details of the healing.

"So you see, Josh," Isabel crowed, "you're not the only one who can heal."

"I can't heal, Isabel," Josh corrected sadly. "Neither can LeRoi. You are talking about supernatural activity that happens through us."

LeRoi was watching him, his smoky eyes fastened intently on Josh's face. "Yeah," he agreed. "It just happens through you."

"Well, you two ought to know. You're the ones with the power." Isabel laughed, her glowing excitement in sharp contrast to LeRoi's embarrassment and Josh's sadness.

"Just for the record," Josh began wearily, "what we have is different. No offense, LeRoi, but we're on opposite sides, each of us with a different source of power."

"You don't even seem to be happy about Bebe's healing," Isabel accused. "That isn't very Christian."

"Non-Christians always seem to know how Christians are supposed to behave," Josh commented mildly.

Isabel's anger spilled over. "Will you please tell me the difference between what LeRoi did and what you did for the kid in the emergency room?"

"What I did was done under the power and direction of the Holy Spirit and for the glory of God. What LeRoi did was done under the power of Satan who has powers forbidden by God."

"But you both did a good thing; both resulted in healing," she snapped.

"Isabel, a thing isn't good or evil because of its nature but because of its origin. And it isn't a good thing to heal a cut on Bebe's face if the end result moves her toward the enemy's camp."

"What makes you think that happened?"

"I don't know; I can only guess. But the enemy's main purpose is to make God unnecessary, and LeRoi's psychic way of healing—" he hesitated, then spoke firmly—"and Charlie's medical methods both operate without God's power, making Him unnecessary."

"That's just ridiculous," Isabel said stiffly. "You have to argue about everything, don't you?"

Josh shrugged and shook his head. "Isabel, I'm sorry we get into these arguments. I'm afraid they don't help anybody."

"They sure don't," Isabel replied. "And I have too much to do to continue them." She arose and left the table. The others also departed one by one, except for Sue.

Josh turned to her, a quizzical look on his face. "Afraid I did it again."

Sue seemed numbed by the exchange. "I guess you have to say what you believe, Josh."

Josh nodded, reflective. They walked out of the dining room together.

Outside LeRoi was waiting for them, his eyes squinting with intensity. "Hang in there, man," he muttered to Josh. "Don't let Isabel rock you."

When both Josh and Sue looked at him in surprise, LeRoi flashed them a grin, turned and swaggered toward his trailer.

The twins took the elevator with LeRoi and walked with him down the long hall toward the testing rooms, chatting cheerfully. They weren't particularly fond of LeRoi; they weren't really fond of anyone but each other. But with Vinnie and Wallace away on special assignment, only the three of them were scheduled for testing this morning. They had each latched onto a skinny brown arm and smiled up at him in companionship if not friendship.

Together they entered the outside office of the rooms on Eight South that had been assigned to the Project. Most of the routine testing was being supervised now by the two young students from the university, graduates in psychology, who had been hired to help the professional staff. The young woman was a quiet and inoffensive person in the twins' opinion, who at times seemed almost frightened by the tests and the uncanny results they were getting. The young man had a thinly veiled dislike for the psychics and his work with them.

"Come in and take your seats," he said to them impatiently. "We have a lot to cover this morning."

"What we gonna do?" LeRoi asked.

"Sit down and wait for instructions," he replied shortly. LeRoi frowned.

"Telekinesis again today," the young woman said. "You'll see if you can move or alter the objects on the table without touching them."

"Get me a pan of water," LeRoi said. "I'll make it boil."

"We have to do the tests the way they're set up," she answered.

"You don't think I can do it," he countered.

"It's not that. We have to stick to the program," she said firmly.

"I'm the onliest one you got can boil water," LeRoi said again.

"Well, these are the 'onliest' tests we're gonna do," the young man said with a sneer, shaking the test form in LeRoi's face.

The twins frowned. *He's being nasty,* Glenda thought.

Wanda nodded. *And mean,* she thought back.

LeRoi rose to his full height, his face radiating anger, and spoke in slow, deliberate tones. "You are a very stupid young man. You have made a very serious mistake."

The twins stared at LeRoi in astonishment. The voice was clear, the diction perfect. The expression, posture, tone and gestures were totally new; the personality now before them was not LeRoi Williams.

The pale young student shrank back in surprise; he too could recognize the metamorphosis in the person before him. LeRoi himself had always been jittery and nervous, hands and body in constant motion, his voice and language usually pure Alabama black. The stranger now housed in LeRoi's body was icy calm, his speech clipped and precise with a noticeably British accent. The tall, thin body seemed even larger, held erect and still.

"I'm sorry," the graduate student stammered. "I didn't mean to be rude."

"That is a lie. You spoke as you did for the very purpose of rudeness. You thought LeRoi too stupid to recognize your intention. However, it is not LeRoi you will deal with; it is I."

"Who are you?" the young woman asked in awe.

"We are a very long way from the Carribbean but my power is not limited geographically."

"Look, I'm sorry," the man said. "Let it drop this time and I'll never hurt your—er, that is his—feelings again, okay?"

"I will let it pass for the moment." The tall figure turned toward the twins. His glittering eyes took them in slowly. They drew back as he stared at them without expression. They had heard a great deal about multiple personalities, but this was their first encounter with one and they found themselves longing for the old LeRoi in all his jivey, uncouth, boastful personality. This being was totally alien to them.

He sat down suddenly and for a moment slumped across the table. Then he drew himself up and looked around. It was LeRoi again. Just as surely as they'd known it when his personality had changed, now they knew the old LeRoi was back.

"Okay. I'm ready," he said.

The tests proceeded without further incidents. But the twins kept looking secretively at LeRoi.

He's like a time bomb, Wanda thought.

You never know when he'll go off again, Glenda agreed.

At least we don't do that, Wanda thought back gratefully.

Since Sue had some time off coming to her, she decided to take a half-day and go shopping that afternoon. It had been many months since she had last bought any new clothes.

The local department store was not crowded so she looked through the selection of dresses, skirts and blouses leisurely. Somewhat to her surprise she selected a low-cut bright blue cocktail dress that she thought looked becoming. Then she purchased an attractive turquoise blouse with brown flecks in it and a brown skirt that matched. Next came a new pair of shoes.

When she passed the lingerie section, she paused and fingered the silk nightgowns. On impulse she bought a pink one, plus a new green dressing gown.

She left the store with her arms full of packages, feeling a little breathless, a little extravagant, and more girlish than she had in years.

Sue put on the new dress that night as she prepared dinner for Josh. She had been to the hairdresser that afternoon and spent an hour fixing her nails and putting on makeup. Honest with herself as usual, she admitted it was all for Josh. *You're falling for the guy.* Then she sighed, wondering if she would be hurt as she had been several times before.

Josh arrived at 7:00 drawn and tired. He didn't notice anything different about Sue at first. He watched the news on television as Sue prepared the food. Finally she called out to him, "You know, I can talk as I fix dinner."

He turned off the television and joined her in the small kitchen. "Do you like to cook?" he began.

"It depends."

"On what?"

"On who I'm cooking for."

"I see. Are you enjoying it now?"

"Yes."

Josh smiled at her. "Can I help?"

"Yes. You can set the table." She showed him where the silver, glasses, napkins were.

He did it casually, carelessly, as he launched into the subject of most concern to him. "Sue, I think I'm the only one here who truly understands the spirit realm. This whole Project reminds me of a bunch of kids playing with matches in a shed full of dynamite. There are things going on in the unseen world that are deadly. LeRoi has no idea what he's messing around with, or he'd run away screaming like a Banshee." He dropped a spoon on the floor, picked it up absently and put it by his place. "Glenda may know the truth," he continued. "I think she's in complete bondage to the dark powers."

"Why Glenda and not Wanda?"

"Because Glenda's the dominant one. She controls." He paused a moment to reposition the napkins. "Take Wallace Graham. Do you know much about his background?"

"A little."

"In my opinion he is in great danger. He's tied up with these so-called aliens, who are of demonic origin, and he's also involved in a lot of other garbage like astrology and all the Eastern thought forms. Ever notice the charms and things he wears around his neck? Supposed to bring good luck? Italian horns, golden idols. I don't suppose anybody ever told him what those things really attract. It's sure not good luck."

"You can't tell him much. He's pretty independent."

"And stand-offish," Josh agreed. "His parents are in Europe most of the time. I think they're afraid of him."

"Vinnie told me Wallace spends hours in the bathtub, up

to his neck in hot water," Sue added. "Says it increases his sensitivity to the Zorans. But what I can't understand is why, out of our whole planet full of people, the Zorans picked him as a contact. They may be light years ahead of us in technology, but they have very poor taste in contacts."

"Wallace is on drugs, too," Josh continued, ignoring her remark.

"Really? I thought maybe LeRoi was, but Wallace seems too snobbish to lower himself to make a connection."

"I don't mean street drugs, Sue. He's on prescription drugs, but his bondage is every bit as real. You can be hooked on pharmaceuticals. A lot of people are unaware that even prescription drugs are a wide-open door for enemy harassment."

Sue had broiled a small steak to which she added a salad and broccoli, plus hot rolls. Reluctantly, she decided not to open a bottle of red wine. Josh had indicated once he didn't drink. *Did this mean wine, too?* she wondered. She guessed she shouldn't press it on him.

They sat down together. Josh said a long blessing while Sue worried for fear the food would get cold.

Josh ate several bites of steak, then looked up at her suddenly. "You look different tonight."

Sue felt her cheeks redden. "How so, Josh?"

He studied her a minute. "Well, your hair, for one thing. And that dress. I haven't seen it before."

"Do you like it?"

"Yes. It makes you look more—well, different." Josh squirmed on his hard chair.

"Thank you, Josh. You don't usually notice things like that."

Josh smiled again and Sue felt the warmth of it. *If only you would do this more often,* she thought dreamily.

But her guest wanted to get back to the main subject at hand. It wasn't until after dinner and they were sitting side-by-side on the couch that Sue got the conversation off Project Truth.

"Stop me if you think I'm too nosey, Josh, but have you ever been married?"

"No."

"Engaged?"

"Well, not really."

"Meaning that there was someone?"

"Yes, but it couldn't work out because we didn't believe the same way."

"I see. This is very important to you if you were to get serious about a woman?"

"Absolutely."

Sue sighed and put her hand on his arm. "Josh, I'm going to be my usual blunt self with you. I've come to like you; sometimes I'm not sure just why. You know I'm rooting for you with your work here. But I don't believe like you do. Maybe it's because I don't understand your beliefs, but it's also because I'm afraid of them."

Josh looked at her intently. "I like that kind of honesty, but I would never expect you to believe exactly as I do. Then there would be no room for growth in our relationship."

Sue was warmed by this statement. She leaned back on the couch, hoping he would pursue this line of talk.

Josh disappointed her. Instead of relaxing, he became tense and uncommunicative. Then he arose, thanked her for dinner and bid her goodnight.

Charlie Fortuna felt he was being forced to think about things that distressed him. He had no desire to make a decision or even form an opinion about the psychic healing LeRoi had performed on Bebe. At the time it had shocked and disturbed him, and at breakfast the next morning he'd been irritated that Isabel kept talking about it. Underneath his calm exterior was an enormous anxiety which he did his best to ignore.

After returning home from the Simmons' trailer, he'd spent the remainder of the evening with a bottle of rum, a six-pack of Coke and a blurred succession of television shows. He went to sleep late and by morning the reality of the experience had dimmed somewhat. The wound on Bebe's forehead had been more superficial than he first thought. There was a natural explanation for it all somewhere. He was pretty sure he could forget the whole thing if Isabel would only shut up.

At lunch that day Vinnie was back but Wallace was still on special assignment. LeRoi ate in silence while the twins communicated in their private language. Bebe and Sue ate silently while Josh Kingston and Isabel Nebo talked.

"I want to reiterate the fact that I consider this a serious scientific investigation," Isabel was saying to Josh as Charlie carried his tray to the table and took a seat. "I hope you won't bring in any of your superstition."

"I can guarantee you, no superstition," Josh replied mildly. "But I can't promise not to talk to them. These kids deserve to know what's happening around here."

"You be careful how you spread your beliefs among these young people." Isabel was firm. "Before I'll let you corrupt an important investigation like this with your unscientific methods, I'll close down the Project. I mean it."

Charlie smiled to himself. The lady doctor was really getting delusions of grandeur, he thought. She had no authority to make such statements.

"These methods helped cure twelve children whom your scientific brains called hopeless," Josh answered bluntly.

Suddenly LeRoi confronted Josh in clipped British accents. "You will accomplish nothing here. You are outnumbered and you are surrounded by unbelief."

Everybody stared at LeRoi, whose dark eyes were fastened imperiously on Joshua Kingston.

"Oh, you know who I am, do you?" Josh asked softly.

"You might as well leave. You cannot succeed here."

Josh gazed back intently at LeRoi. "Greater is He who is in me than he who is in the world. You can't discourage me and you won't be able to frighten me."

Isabel reddened with anger. "This is what I won't tolerate," she railed at Josh. "You cannot set yourself against these young people this way. It is totally unprofessional."

"I wasn't setting myself against LeRoi," Josh replied, "but with another personality inside him."

The group around the long table became silent. LeRoi changed personality again and centered his attention on his food. Charlie ate mechanically, his mind busy with what he had just seen. Like the healing of Barbara's laceration, he could not explain it satisfactorily and he resented being forced to consider the evidence here of a whole realm of experience about which he knew nothing.

"I just hated it," Vinnie said between clenched teeth. "It made my skin crawl." He fell silent and then grinned at Josh. "I guess you hated it, too."

They sat at the dining table in Josh's trailer; Vinnie was softly strumming his guitar while Josh completed his Project interview. Then the matter of LeRoi's divided personality had come up.

"Yes, everything in me is repelled by that kind of manifestation," Josh replied.

"It showed me something," Vinnie said. "Did LeRoi know what was going on?"

"Probably not. Most times when a demon acts through a person like that, the person just thinks it's a part of himself. Thinks he's lost his temper, or had a sudden fit of depression, or had a big mood change. He might even think, 'I don't know what possessed me to do that,' but he doesn't realize that another entity *is* possessing him."

Josh gazed at Vinnie thoughtfully and continued, "Parents seldom face up to this sort of thing. When they notice something wrong with a son, for example, they'll tell me, 'He's like two different people.' But they don't realize how true that is."

"Well, I learned something," Vinnie said. "I never thought LeRoi could talk that well in his own power."

"It's not in his own power. That's what's so hard for people to understand. I think the main reason I'm here is to expose the enemy who has this power." Josh ran a hand through his tousled hair and added, "You might say I've been called to wake up some sleeping virgins."

"What?" Vinnie asked, startled.

Josh grinned. "I'm speaking figuratively; there's a parable in the Bible about ten virgins—and *virgin* here means they were believers—five wise and five foolish. And it says, 'While the Bridegroom tarried they all slumbered and slept.' I'm going around, grabbing a sleeping virgin by the shoulder, shaking her and saying, 'Wake up! It's getting late!' "

"That's interesting. Not many virgins of any kind in our little group," Vinnie reflected.

"I expect you're right. But still I'm called to expose the enemy."

"And demons are the enemy?"

"They're part of it, certainly not all." Josh leaned forward. "You need to see the big picture. It's really a war. There are two armies. Our side has the Lord, two-thirds of the angels, a small part of the human race. Their side has Satan, his demons, a third of the angels—the ones who fell—and most of the human race. The enemy has quite an army."

"Seen and unseen."

"Yes. All we can see are the humans. Most of them are on the enemy's side, although not many are even aware that they've made this decision."

"You mean that most people don't know what side they're on?"

"Right. Few have any understanding of spiritual warfare," Josh continued. "And even fewer are willing to take part in the battle."

"On both sides?"

Josh stared at Vinnie. "Yes, on both sides. And it's surprising you should say that. I think there may be somebody on the other side who is an active, purposeful agent of the enemy. Right here in Brookshire Hospital."

"You know who it is?"

"Not yet."

"You think it's one of us psychics?"

"It could be."

"This is just like a who-done-it," Vinnie laughed.

"Yeah, or a who's-doing-it." Josh turned an unsmiling face toward Vinnie. "Just remember this. Nobody in this whole world can be neutral today. The Lord says if you're not with Him, you're against Him. Whether you know it or not, you're on one side or the other."

Vinnie drew back instinctively from Josh's intensity, then looked at his watch. "Got to leave now. I'm due at the hospital for more tests."

Josh watched sadly as Vinnie departed, walking swiftly back down the path toward Brookshire.

When Wallace Graham found himself alone in the testing room with the Simmons twins one morning, he immediately took advantage of the privacy.

"Would you girls like to go with me to meet the Zorans?" he asked in a soft, confidential voice.

"Where?" from Glenda.

"When?" from Wanda.

"Some night this weekend; they'll set it up," he answered. "That kind of thing is at their initiative."

"Why?" Glenda persisted.

"They want to meet you," he answered simply. "They've heard about you, know your abilities."

"So they want to meet us?" Wanda asked dubiously.

"They want to get to know you, study you. Are you frightened?"

"No," Glenda said. "Of course not."

222

Wanda looked less confident, Wallace noted. Usually the twins were so alike in their responses. Now there was a slight difference of opinion.

"What have you got to lose?" he continued. "Millions of people would give anything to meet an alien. A third-kind encounter."

"That means we'll see these people from outer space?" Wanda asked.

"Yes. A close encounter of the first kind is just a sighting of a spacecraft; the second kind involves demonstrable effects on the environment or objects; and the third kind involves occupants. In this case, Zorans."

"What'll they do to us?" Wanda asked.

"Nothing painful or upsetting. They'll probably examine you, physically, I mean, and do some mental probing. But that's no worse than being hypnotized. Very similar, as a matter of fact. They aren't enemies, you know."

"How can you be sure?" Wanda asked.

"I guess we can go one time," Glenda said. "Not make any commitment but just go once."

Wanda was silent.

Wallace leaned toward Glenda and whispered, "I'll check with the Zorans and get back to you."

They were calling it The Task Force, and it was supposed to be a secret. Of course it wasn't, but that was one of the few things Sue had been told when the Director of Nursing informed her she was to be a part of it. The meeting was called for 2 p.m. and when Sue arrived, the room was already crowded. She was one of only three present below the level of department head.

The meeting was being held in the medical library—a dark, wood-panelled room that had been patterned after an English men's club; it had the flavor of pompous, weighty solemnity, steeped in tradition. The room contained several leather couches, some matching chairs, two lengthy

223

tables backed against the end wall and on the three walls that held books there were high-backed, uncomfortable benches. Today, in addition to the usual furniture, stacks of folding chairs had been provided. Sue took a seat on one of the benches and studied the invitees.

Four men stood in a little knot in front of the windows; Sue recognized the Chief of Staff, the Chief of Surgery, the Chief of Medicine and the Chief of Pediatrics. They were in soft, serious conversation; probably discussing their golf scores or the recent bearish trend on Wall Street, Sue thought wryly. Other doctors present included the Chief of Pathology, two from the laboratory, a young man with a full beard, whom Sue thought was an epidemiologist, and an aged cardiologist who had retired from active practice to lecture at the medical school.

How did I ever get included in this crowd? Sue wondered.

The Director of Pharmacy was present, laughing boisterously with a young bacteriologist from Infection Control. He was a tall, blond, Nordic-looking man with an active, aggressive friendliness that was exhausting to his colleagues.

The head dietitian was there, a scrawny, pallid young woman who looked so undernourished as to be almost emaciated. There were also representatives from Housekeeping, Radiology, Nuclear Medicine.

The Director of Nursing took a seat on the bench next to Sue and whispered an apology. "Sorry I didn't have a chance to brief you about all this. Try not to say anything foolish."

"My stars," Sue responded in horror. "In this bunch? I'm not going to say a word!"

Don Oliver Franklin, the big boss himself, appeared and the buzz of conversation began to die down. His face lacked its usual geniality. Sue felt a tension grow inside her. If Franklin was upset, things must really be bad.

"Let's take seats, everybody. We have a problem to resolve and need to get started." Don Oliver stood there impassively until all had settled down and the conversation had ceased.

"Many of you met last Sunday afternoon to discuss the unacceptable rate of incidents, accidents and deaths. I appreciate your giving of time and thought to this, but there has been no improvement. As a matter of fact, things are worse.

"We're not here today to talk and argue. No, we're going to listen to a report and then see if we can come to some decisions. I'm turning the meeting over to Mr. Phillips."

Carleton Phillips, the hospital administrator, was a tall, thin man with thick glasses. He stood up before the group, opened a manila folder, took out several typed sheets, and peered around the room. "First, a few recent case histories.

"Anne Brazzo, age 29, divorced, no children. Admitted at 8 a.m. yesterday morning for a mammary augmentation at noon." He paused in his businesslike delivery to grin mischievously. "Went from a 32A to a 34D in just a couple of hours. Seems she felt a new bustline would solve all her problems."

It's not funny, Sue thought to herself.

The administrator continued, "There was a delay in surgery, she didn't get in till almost 3 p.m. and it was after seven when she was brought to Five North. She'd missed supper, so one of the nurses fixed her a tray from the nourishment room. Mrs. Brazzo rang for a nurse at about quarter to ten, asked for either a sleeping pill or a pain shot and the nurse, in her strong desire to keep the patient from bothering anybody, gave both. She had 75 milligrams of Demerol I.M. and 30 milligrams of Dalmane P.O. The nurse checked her over superficially; the dressings were dry, vitals were stable and the patient wanted to go to sleep.

"The next thing we hear is when the night shift takes midnight vital signs and the aide went into Mrs. Brazzo's room. She was dead. The surgical wounds were still intact, there was no indication of any problems of any sort; she was just dead." He paused and jerked his glasses off to peer around the room. No one spoke.

Sue began to see why she had been selected to join the Task Force; it wasn't a happy thought. As the day shift supervisor of Five North, she knew about Mrs. Brazzo. And also of Six North, which had its own unexplained death. These things had happened on Sue's floors. But when Mr. Phillips began reading again, he was describing a patient Sue had never heard of.

"John Anthony Marshall, aged 22 months. Diagnosis acute gastroenteritis with dehydration. Admitted to pediatrics for I.V. therapy. He was here three days; we got his fluid level back to normal, regulated his electrolytes. The vomiting stopped, he was put on P.O. fluids and by yesterday he was taking a soft diet. The I.V. had been discontinued.

"The child was found dead in his crib at 4 a.m. No adverse signs at all, no one heard him cry. Just dead."

The room was in total silence. Sue's heart was pounding in reaction to the tightly controlled but harsh words she was hearing.

"Mr. Rufus B. Anton. Thirty-three, married, father of four. Attorney-at-Law. He came in last Tuesday for a vasectomy; he was admitted to the hospital instead of having the surgery done at the doctor's office because he had the kind of hospitalization insurance that won't pay unless you're admitted for 24 hours. While he was here, his doctor ordered some tests, an EKG, a blood profile, chest film, just routine things since he was available.

"The surgery went fine, less than twenty minutes: you know, tie, tie, snip, snip. Local anesthesia, and I understand he was up walking around by suppertime. He had no visitors; his wife couldn't get a babysitter, so he watched the movie on Channel 11 and went to sleep. He slept well; they checked him every two hours, opened the door and flashed a light in, and since he wasn't complaining they figured he was fine. The day shift nurse found him dead at ten of eight this morning. Dead and getting stiff; he'd been dead at least five hours. Again, no sign of anything really wrong.

"Three deaths, ladies and gentlemen. Three people who should not have died. We can find no cause of death and for that reason we can't say with any assurance that it's going to stop with these three. We need to know the cause of death and we need to stop it.

"I invite your comments."

Sue shrank back on the bench. She sure wasn't going to say anything.

"We need a breakdown of common factors," suggested one of the younger pathologists. "Then feed all the data into the computers and see what we get."

The administrator nodded. "We're trying to break down the common factors and finding darn little. Two were surgical, one medical. Two had I.V.s, Mr. Anton didn't. Big age difference. And so on and so on. No single employee came in contact with all three." He hesitated, then spoke carefully. "We are considering every possibility, believe me."

"So all they had in common was the fact that they died," the young pathologist said thoughtfully. "Plus the fact that none of them really needed to be here."

"Good point," the administrator nodded. "But I don't see it gets us anywhere."

The Chief of Surgery then spoke. "How about the post mortems? Have there been any histological studies done yet?"

"No final report yet, but everything so far is negative."

The Chief of Staff rose to his feet and spoke ponderously. "I think it was a mistake to bring this group together; this should be kept as quiet as possible."

Sue looked for Don Oliver Franklin's reaction to this. He had obviously called the group together. But the big man was no longer in the room.

They should have asked Josh, she thought suddenly. He would have an opinion to offer. Then she shook her head, amused at herself. She surely was thinking about him a lot these days; even the news of three unexplained deaths hadn't succeeded in driving him from her thoughts for very long.

As the discussion heated up, Sue realized that this group wasn't any more effective than the one of head nurses and supervisors. Just a little more arrogant.

"No, thanks," Wallace said primly. "I'm fasting."

"How 'bout you, Vinnie?" LeRoi held out his open bag of pork rinds.

"I guess I'll pass," Vinnie smiled.

LeRoi grinned at them amiably. "That just leaves more for the kid." He snapped on the television and took a seat on the couch.

"Not cartoons again," Wallace groaned.

"Man, these the good cartoons," LeRoi protested. "Bugs Bunny, Road Runner, all them guys." He stretched his long legs out before him, crunching his pork rinds loudly, the picture of a fulfilled man.

Vinnie put his guitar in the case. How he missed the quiet retreat in his parents' garage! There was nothing there to interfere with his playing music whenever he liked.

Yet there was a choice. He could join LeRoi for cartoons—at this point Daffy Duck was antagonizing Elmer Fudd—or he could talk to Wallace Graham. What a choice! He sat down next to Wallace.

"Going out tonight?"

"Yes, at seven." Wallace was sipping a tall glass of water. He put it down on the table and turned it slowly between his hands. "Would you like to go with me?"

"Where?"

"I'm attending a meeting of the Sky Watchers. They know of you and many of them have asked to meet you. They also know about our gifts. They've studied psycho-energetics. They know about the Brotherhood of Cosmic Enlightenment."

"Good for them," Vinnie said shortly. "I don't."

"You're serious?" Wallace asked in surprise. "The Great White Brotherhood? The Messiahs of Cosmic Evolution, of our expanded awareness, the revelation that within each of us is the spark of God, a fiery core of cosmic consciousness that is the real self, the God-self—"

"I have no idea what you're talking about."

"Oh, come on, I mean your soul, that eternal and indestructible part of God that can lift itself in a state of altered consciousness to know truth. It is that God-principle in all of us, the principle of life energy of the cosmos."

"Sure, I've heard it. You can't hang around psychic researchers as much as I have and not hear that talk. But I never could make heads or tails of what it's supposed to mean." Vinnie nodded toward LeRoi. "He has as much psychic ability as I have and he doesn't understand all that jargon, either."

Wallace nodded. "I've seen some of the things LeRoi can do. He can move the hands of a watch, control laboratory equipment, set Geiger counters off, alter electronic circuitry. I know. Yesterday he erased some videotapes by his ESP, just to annoy the tester. Dr. Nebo said they were able to measure changes in the electromagnetic field when he was doing his thing. But none of it seems to touch him. He's proud of his gifts and shows off like a kid, but none of it touches the real him."

"Maybe that's true of me, too," Vinnie said thoughtfully. This was not the first time people had expected a response from him at a level deeper than anything he really felt.

"We could help you tonight, show you the underlying meaning behind all this." Wallace spoke smoothly. "There is danger, you know. This whole earth has built up evil karma and negative vortexes of energy."

"If there is danger, and I'm not denying there is, what can you do about it?"

Wallace was thoughtful. "Well, if we stick together, pool our resources and information, we might deal with some of

229

the negatives—like the rise in the death rate after a close encounter. Suicides go up, too. Also mental illness. And on the very practical level, the government has a regulation that now makes it an offense to release information about UFOs—fines of $10,000 and up to ten years in prison. Of course, they're not really enforcing it."

"This is supposed to get me to join you?" Vinnie asked. "Showing me all the benefits you have to offer?" He was beginning to wish he'd opted for LeRoi's cartoons. As always, a conversation with Wallace unsettled him.

Wallace smiled again. "I guess you're right; this probably isn't doing much to attract you. But, Lord, man, you can't just ignore the power you have, make no effort to understand or control it! You don't don't want to be like him." Wallace jerked his head contemptuously toward LeRoi. "He's not the least bit curious where the power comes from, why he was chosen, what is really required of him! You can't stay neutral, you know!"

Vinnie looked up in surprise. This was the second time today he'd heard this. Maybe it was true, maybe he did have to pick a side. Wallace was leaning toward him intensely, his face serious, he eyes burning. He looked almost exactly as Josh had looked earlier when Josh had said the same thing: "You can't stay neutral!"

Vinnie rose and shoved the chair back under the table. He felt almost as though he were suffocating. "I'm going to take a walk." He retrieved his jacket from the kitchen doorknob, and without waiting to hear Wallace's answer hurried outside.

Malcolm Brown sat at the desk in his office and looked at his notes, refreshing his memory of this particular case and reassuring himself that everything was being done properly. He disliked funerals under the best of conditions and this one was far from ideal.

The parents were young and not religious people. As a

matter of fact, the only reason for a Christian burial at all was because they had asked him to make all the necessary arrangements. When he had suggested they follow the traditional routine, they had agreed.

The quiet, almost private service was to be held in the main hospital chapel which was best for that small a group. Then they'd drive out to the grave site, the transfer made smooth by the supervision of the funeral director and his men.

So everything was under control, all attended to except the funeral message. No eulogy, of course, not for a 22-month-old baby. What did one say about a baby who'd died so unexpectedly, and for no apparent reason?

His mind flashed to another of Brookshire's patients, the strange, haunted woman who'd peered into his eyes so forcefully and asked, "Where is my little boy now? Can you tell me, Preacher?" And now that mother was also dead, like her son. Could he safely say she was with her dead child now?

He shook his head in annoyance. This was not the time for metaphysical musings; he had a speech to write. Ten to fifteen minutes, understated, gentle: that was the ticket. The parents were still in shock at the death of their toddler.

He sat thoughtfully for a few minutes, then began composing the speech. He began with the word he'd just used, *toddler*. A baby that age couldn't walk very well, but he could take a few steps, take that next step, the step beyond this life. A toddler took hesitant, unsteady steps, but eventually got where he was going. And if he fell, he would get up again. Yes, there were possibilities here for a good talk.

He took a clean sheet from his notebook and began to write. He titled it, "One Step Beyond."

Sue and Josh had begun to meet regularly during Sue's coffeebreak at 10 a.m. They would arrive separately at the staff dining room and find a table for two in a corner. The only problem was that fifteen minutes gave them so little time to cover the subjects that concerned them.

The day after the Task Force meeting Sue quickly related to Josh details of the three unexplainable deaths. Josh was whitefaced when she finished.

"It confirms my worst fears. Brookshire has been picked as the scene of all-out spiritual warfare."

"What does that mean?"

"That these deaths will continue. Plus the mistakes, the wrangling, the bad scenes."

"Why, Josh? Why? You'll never convince me that all hospitals are this bad."

"No. This is unusual. I'm afraid Brookshire has opened the door to Satan and literally all hell has broken loose."

"Because of Project Truth?"

"Partly. But there's more involved here than these five psychics, although one of them could be the catalyst for the chaos."

"Which one?"

"I don't know. Wish I did."

Sue sipped her tea while Josh downed the rest of his orange juice. Both were deep in thought.

"I'm afraid the worst is yet to come," Josh said slowly.

"What can happen?"

"I'm not sure. But there's a build-up here to some kind of explosion." He paused, reflecting. "Do you have any vacation time coming?"

"Yes—two weeks."

"How soon could you get off?"

"I don't know. Why?"

"I'd like you to get away from here as soon as possible."

Sue felt her senses quicken. "I have no particular place to go. Nor do I care to take a vacation by myself."

Josh reddened slightly. "I was thinking of your safety."

"I hoped you were thinking of coming with me."

Josh was silent, obviously uncomfortable. Sue decided to speak frankly.

"Josh, there's no point in our playing games with each other. I'm no good at it, and you're too straightlaced. The last thing I'm going to do is leave the battlefield, as you call it, by myself. If you'll come with me, fine. I'll do what you say and live by your rules."

Josh studied his empty glass. "You've lived in the world all your life, Sue. I'm not sure you'd be happy away from it."

"What does that mean?"

Josh looked up at her. "As you say, I'm straightlaced. You could become very unhappy in my world."

"I guess I would never know until I tried, would I?"

Josh continued to look at her directly. "I would never be interested in an affair."

Sue felt anger rising in her. "That's a pompous, self-righteous statement. It's so typical of the Josh I first met."

Josh did not lower his eyes. "Sue, answer me truthfully. If I asked you to go away with me for the weekend, would you do it?"

Sue sighed and looked at her hands. "Yes."

"That's what I mean. I can't do that sort of thing."

Sue pushed her tea back and rose from her chair. "The reason I said yes, Josh, was because I knew that if you invited me to go away with you for a weekend, I'd be as safe with you as if I were inside a church." And she turned and walked off.

Every Friday at Brookshire Memorial Hospital the week began to wind down; many offices and departments closed or began operating on skeleton staffs until Monday morning. By afternoon there was a hint of holiday atmosphere. Most of the staff had just been paid. Many would stop on the way home and spend part of it. The Roadhouse Pub on the highway just outside the entrance of the medical center would be overflowing for the next twelve to fourteen hours. The clubhouse at the mobile home park would see a similar increase in activity. The hospital would settle down to a slower pace, a decreased census and a slightly different routine.

And every Friday afternoon Don Oliver Franklin took an elevator to the eighth floor. There he would view his kingdom from the top, watching the quickening tempo in the parking lot as cars sped away from the hospital into town. Usually there was a look of benign satisfaction and pride on his face as he looked out over the many acres of buildings, walkways, gardens and parks of Brookshire.

This particular Friday his face was solemn, intent, the main focus of his attention centering on the mobile home park, where the participants of Project Truth were housed.

Book IV

Deliverance

October changed to November as Project Truth completed its fifth week.

Dr. Isabel Nebo felt that at least another month of testing would be needed. There was so much to learn. The subject of charms, for example. One evening she spread out before her on the table a collection of books, dolls of all sorts and description, as well as amulets, medals, jujus, icons, totems, statues and idols. She was determined to learn how it was that an Oriental fertility god and a modern Barbie doll, so different in appearance, could both hold within their inanimate little bodies some type of supernatural power. These objects had one common factor: they were all images. Images of either humans or humanoids, or of geometric shapes that Isabel sensed also had a potential for housing power.

She picked up a small and very ugly statue and compared it with the picture in her book. Could this thing really channel extrasensory power from the supernatural realm into the world of men? She was willing, even eager, to believe. The book said so; so did increasing scientific evidence. And so did Joshua Kingston. But he'd say it was demon-possessed, Isabel thought scornfully. She picked up a second book and read the title: *The Use of Dolls in the Practice of Witchcraft.* It would not appeal to a wide audience but it certainly appealed to Isabel. She began reading avidly.

Joshua Kingston, best-selling author, minister of the gospel and head of the religion department of Project Truth, had spent the afternoon preparing his specialty, Irish stew, to serve his dinner guest. After stirring and tasting the contents of the large pot, with all due modesty he pronounced the result a masterpiece. He turned the stove to simmer and carried silver and plates into the living room to set the little table. Sue Dunn was due soon and she would be prompt. Josh had discovered that promptness was one of her many virtues.

Dr. Charles Fortuna was dressing for a date with Barbara Simmons, a big date in town, including dinner and dancing at one of the local spots. As he dressed, he found his hands were shaking with excitement. *Get hold of yourself,* he thought as he brushed his dark hair. *It's just a date, for crying out loud.*

Barbara Simmons, dressed in navy blue slacks and a blousy shirt of pale blue Thai silk, touched cologne to the hollow of her throat and her wrists. *I need to make up my mind about this joker,* she told herself. *If he's leading to a dead end, I'd better cut it off now. He's taking so much of my time, I couldn't see anybody else if I wanted to.*

Wanda and Glenda Simmons watched as their sister dressed. Although Barbara was too wrapped up in her own thoughts to notice, the twins were out of sorts. The interchange of thoughts that was so natural to them was impeded this day; they were out of harmony and it marred the synchronicity of their telepathic communication.

It wasn't the first time in their lives they'd disagreed, but it was extremely rare. And even when they disagreed in thought or attitude, they always acted in unison: They always did what Glenda wanted. So they would again this night; they would join Wallace Graham as he rendezvoused with his alien friends. Wanda would stifle her objections, her fears and resistance; and as she had every other time they disagreed, she would again surrender her will to Glenda.

But that would have to wait till Bebe was gone.

LeRoi Williams dressed formally for his night. He wore a shiny purple shirt with huge baggy sleeves and skin-tight black pants that he stuffed into the tops of high-heeled snakeskin boots. He added a white fur vest and a broad-brimmed hat and then beamed in total joy at his reflection in the mirror. He poured out a handful of Vinnie's cologne and applied it briskly to his face and beard and the scent enveloped him like a fog. *You some kind of a he-goat, man,* he told himself cheerfully.

He glanced at Vinnie's clock. Over an hour before time to meet his new girlfriend, and he would never commit the social gauchery of being early; he knew the beneficial effects of making girls wait. He'd get into the mood for his night by listening to Vinnie's music and smoking a joint or two, all he had left. It was a good thing he was going to meet his girl tonight; he could replenish his grass.

Wallace Graham paced his small bedroom. The anticipation of seeing the Zorans again swept his being with waves of excitement. They would be pleased about the Simmons twins. Before they'd finished, the Zorans would probably want to meet all the psychics, but so far they'd asked only for the twins. And how delightful it was that he'd been able to persuade the twins to meet them!

Wallace knew a lot about what the scientists called E.T.I.s— extra terrestrial intelligencies. The twins had wanted to know all about them, of course, and he'd been asked countless times to describe his Zoran friends. But even using all the right words, he knew he failed to communicate their real nature. It was so hard to explain. They were humanoid, certainly, bipeds with recognizable facial features, hair, that type of thing. But they were also undeniably non-human, and no verbal description did justice to their strangeness.

He could say they were giants, bigger than humans, but thin; that they were ethereal, pale, bloodless, like cadavers or ghosts. He could explain that they sometimes appeared to be only semi-solid, transparent, shadowy, like an apparition. But still they could talk, move about, handle matter, make contact with humans on the sensory level.

These creatures whose intercourse with mankind was as old as history—whose presence had always been acknowledged, if only stories or myths, as angels, goblins, spooks, zombies, spectres, phantoms—were incredibly, astonishingly, overwhelmingly real. More real and more alien than anyone could believe except those few chosen to be their human consorts. And he was sure no human experience could compare with the thrill of such an encounter.

Vincent Ponder, musician extraordinaire, was delighted that both his roommates had plans for the evening. How great it would be to have the trailer to himself without their constant arguing.

Sue Dunn prepared very carefully for her dinner with Josh Kingston, dressed herself in a pastel print dress of soft, flowing material, with a full skirt and graceful neckline. She brushed her hair carefully and applied a little lipstick, then examined herself critically in the mirror. The dress was pretty, but it seemed to hang a little on her thin frame. Her face needed more color. *I wish I could be beautiful just for one night,* she thought wistfully. *I wish he could look at me and just once see a woman, not a soul that needs saving.*

And then what would I do? she asked herself. *Be honest. If he really wanted me, would I give up my career, join him in whatever crusade he goes on next? Watch him being ridiculed, hurt, hated . . . all the things that seem to be his lot in life?* She wasn't sure.

Anyway, it's all just an academic question. She shrugged. His main interest was elsewhere. She looked again at the pale, thin reflection in the mirror. *What fun to be really great-looking, just once, and knock him for a loop!*

Wallace was startled and took an involuntary step backwards. Then he recognized Josh and smiled slightly. "I didn't see you at first. Hope I didn't scare you."

"I don't scare so easy," Josh replied calmly.

They were standing on the path between their adjoining trailers. Josh held a paper sack of garbage; he stood politely as Wallace made no move to leave.

Wallace disliked Josh Kingston and under most circumstances he would have left after a few polite remarks. But on this particular night, Wallace was full to overflowing with the excitement of his scheduled meeting with the Zorans; he had to talk to somebody about it and Josh was a better choice than LeRoi or even Vinnie. Josh at least had a belief in the supernatural.

"I was trying to see the sky but there are too many trees," Wallace continued.

"Looking for your friends?" Josh asked. "Do you know when they're coming?"

"Usually. I do tonight." Wallace was dressed in neatly pressed slacks and a warm leather jacket. He shoved his hands into his pockets; he felt vulnerable, afraid his shaking hands would reveal his excitement. "They'll be here but probably not till later."

"You ought to tell the Project people. They'd love to take some measurements. Magnetic field, that kind of thing."

"I don't think so. Not this time."

"You'd have to get the Zorans' permission, I take it?"

Wallace nodded. "They want the—well, initiative or control, for themselves. A lot of researchers don't understand that."

"I do." Josh set the garbage sack on the ground. His unruly black hair shaded his face from the dappled moonlight and Wallace could see only the gleam of Josh's intense black eyes.

"You know about aliens?" Wallace asked.

"I know the spirit realm," Josh said simply. "You do, too, but from a different viewpoint. We both agree the spirit

241

realm is real, powerful. It's like a parallel universe, like you read in science fiction, and it's eternal; and we both know its influence is growing."

"But you do believe we've had contact with extraterrestrial intelligences?" Wallace realized suddenly that in the few talks he'd had with Josh, the young minister had been quiet and Wallace himself had done most of the talking.

"Sure. Nothing new about that. It's been going on for ages."

"You mean the ancient astronaut thing? Chariots of the gods and such?"

Josh nodded. "That too. They're all the same thing."

"I must say I'm surprised. I'd have thought you considered my UFOs an hallucination."

"Well, maybe I do. Let's define hallucination. If we agree it's a false view of reality, caused by a force—a strange, spiritual force—that can distort our perception of reality and give us a counterfeit comprehension of time and space and matter, well, I guess I do."

"But you agree they're real? And you just think I'm seeing a distortion of them as they really are?"

"Exactly!" Josh nodded. "There's all kinds of stuff around that we don't perceive with our senses. Like in the natural realm there are radio and television waves, light and sound waves, electricity. . . . The brain is selective in what we can perceive. And our understanding of what we perceive is based on how we look at reality. So, this is how I see it. You are in contact with something—something extraterrestrial, hyperdimensional, supraluminal, something that has some degree of power over matter and certain minds. But you're hallucinating in that you perceive them as good. That's where the deception comes in."

"Since I'm the one they contact, maybe I'm the best judge of their character."

"No way. You're under so much deception you're seeing just what they want you to see. Those things are not visitors from another planet. They are demons."

242

"Oh, come on now." Wallace kicked the ground in disgust. "You have a one-track mind!"

"I have a proposition for you," Josh pressed. "A little wager that might help illustrate my point. Hear me out and remember what I say. At some point they'll bring in sex, and in particular perverted sex." Josh peered at him suddenly. "If they haven't already."

"That's disgusting," Wallace said shortly.

"Just remember what I predicted. Because demons are evil and they will eventually show it. Their true nature comes forth."

"I don't intend to dignify that with a response," Wallace said angrily.

"You speak as a true science-fiction fan. 'If they're there, they're good,' looking to the sky for your second coming, your salvation. But they're evil, diametrically opposed to everything good and decent and wholesome on this planet."

"Too bad you're the only one who knows that." Wallace was too angry to maintain a facade of politeness.

"Maybe the only one you've met, but hardly the only one. Some people are waking up. Jesus didn't ignore demons; He knew demons and evil spirits were real. Jesus told us to try the spirits, to see if they're of God. That doesn't sound like He wanted us to act as if they didn't exist! Our problem is conceit. We feel we don't need His admonitions—"

Wallace's irritation finally overwhelmed him and he interrupted Josh in the middle of his speech. "All that doesn't apply to me. I have a different viewpoint and I'm not really interested in yours, if you know what I mean."

Josh fell silent and stared at Wallace for a long time. Suddenly he threw back his head and the moonlight fell across his face. His eyes pierced Wallace and he spoke in a tense whisper: "How dreadful it must be to believe in the supernatural without believing in God!"

Wallace suddenly backed away. Then he gave a scornful

little laugh and hurried back to the trailer he shared with Vinnie and LeRoi.

It was twenty minutes after seven when the laboratory boys finished the final report for the Task Force on the three unexplained deaths. They were still unexplained. None of their studies had revealed a cause of death, and there were almost no similarities in the three victims. They did have the same blood type, Type A, but that proved little. And all three did have a certain amount of inflammation of the gastric mucosa, but again, what did that mean? The vast majority of the tests that had been done on the blood, tissue samples and slides had been negative.

Of course, they'd have to bring in the medical examiner, the pathologists all agreed; no way to avoid it. And almost certainly he'd notify the Center for Disease Control in Atlanta—the glamor boys, the highly publicized medical detectives. They would dig in here as they had done with Legionnaire's disease that killed so many starting in that Philadelphia hospital. But so far it was still Brookshire's own problem and the front office people, as well as Hal Givens from public relations, were doing all they could to keep it that way.

The report was finished, typed and delivered to the administrator's office at twenty minutes after seven Friday night.

At seven-thirty they discovered the body of Number Four.

The odd thing was that Charlie could see Bebe's faults. From the beginning, he'd been aware that she wasn't very bright. He recalled some of the twins' little digs: "Bebe doesn't have too much power under the hood," and, "Bebe's thinking isn't really on the tournament level; she gets washed out in the preliminaries." He realized her conversation was limited. It was almost impossible to discuss an abstraction with her. And he had quickly learned that his lady love had no sense of humor. She offered no witticisms of her own and seemed unable to appreciate them from others.

And she was so passive about everything. Charlie was a fighter. He'd pushed and shoved himself from a lower-class background through medical school, internship and residency, all the way to a position of respect in a tough and competitive profession. He possessed a sharp mind, drive and courage. So Bebe's placidity, her almost total lack of intellectual effort, were foreign to him.

But even when he went all the way and admitted she could be a crashing bore, he was still totally captivated by her. She displayed the unconscious attitude that she needed only to grace a scene with her beauty, and with this unspoken belief, Charlie agreed wholeheartedly. If she had indeed possessed any additional faculties of wit or intellect, he would have been overwhelmed. As it was, he still approached her with awe.

This Friday night he had made reservations at an elegant and expensive restaurant. The meal was delicious, served with all the trappings of glamor—soft candlelight, music and deft service. Bebe looked wonderful, a fit jewel for such a setting. As they lingered over brandy, Charlie realized he was enjoying what many men dream of but few possess.

"Can't we go somewhere else? This place is dead!" Bebe complained. "Let's go to a disco."

Charlie had no fondness for discos. During his marriage to Margie, he had often been dragged into this garish, strobe-lighted scene. The crowd was younger and he had felt a vague embarrassment for those over 35 who tried to maintain a place in the frantic crowd of fun-seekers. He had usually ended up sitting alone, getting blind, staggering drunk while Margie danced with a variety of college boys, openly flaunting her availability to them. Discos brought him bad memories, but he lacked the courage to deny Bebe any request. He paid the check and they drove to the most notable of the town's nightspots, the All-Day Sucker.

As they entered, their ears were assaulted by loud music, and Charlie fought his way through the standing-room-only crowd to find a small table next to the side wall. Bebe was smiling in pleasure, coming alive in response to the music and the crowd.

"I'm really going to let go tonight," she said brightly. "Forget all my responsibilities."

He shook his head in amusement. She had almost no responsibilities, no home, husband, children, job—nothing but her younger sisters who were very independent of her.

"Come on, let's dance," she urged, and because he had no heart to refuse her anything, he joined her in a heavy-footed and barely adequate attempt at dancing. Since she gave continuous advice as they gyrated around the floor, he was panting with exhaustion and frustration when they returned to their table.

"You don't dance much, do you?" she laughed.

"No, I guess not." He despised himself for staying in this setting in which he made so poor a showing. If she could only see him in his own milieu, he thought, in the hospital where his competence and position were accepted. He was somebody there; here he was a tired, aging man who looked more than a trifle foolish. But he sat meekly, dancing at her invitation, drinking too much, watching her with an admiration that approached reverence.

"You people have this trailer smelling awful." Wallace Graham entered the living room from his bedroom with his usual display of bad temper. "It's not just a mess anymore. Now it stinks like marijuana."

LeRoi Williams roused himself from his slouching position on the couch. "And a cheerful good evening to you, Wallace," he said.

Vinnie was playing his flute, the thin, silvery notes hovering high above the pall of grayish smoke that floated in layers on the air. "Open a window. There's a breeze."

"That might intoxicate the whole compound," Wallace snapped. "And don't you think there's a limit to what they'll allow? You can't just flaunt your lawlessness."

"I'm not smoking pot," Vinnie protested mildly.

"Who died and left you in charge, man?" LeRoi asked in annoyance. "I'm damn sick and tired of folks bossing me around. You getting bad as Isabel."

Glenda and Wanda Simmons were sitting on the floor, dressed in identical blue slacks and gray sweaters. Glenda squinted her eyes and drew deeply on the tattered end of a home-rolled cigarette. "Don't sweat the small stuff, Wallace," she smiled through the smoke.

Wallace turned to scowl at the twins and Wanda spoke in annoyance. "Hey, you invited us, remember? We're going UFO hunting."

Wallace's scowl disappeared. "O.K. It's time to leave."

Glenda scrambled to her feet, childlike in her eager excitement. "'Night, Vinnie. Next time you see me, I'll be speaking Zoran. Keep cool, LeRoi. See you later." Wanda rose more slowly and nodded without speaking.

They followed Wallace out the front door and down the steps. The moonlight spilled along the path, dappled by the shadows of the trees. It was a beautiful sight. At the path they turned left, toward the deep woods.

The Irish stew was a success and the conversation relaxed. Realizing that he had not come off so well at their last meeting in the staff dining room Josh deliberately stayed away from the subject of Project Truth in particular and religion in general. He asked Sue about her childhood.

Sue looked at him in surprise. "I grew up in Sacramento, California. My father has been an accountant in the statehouse for thirty years; Mother's a practical nurse. My older brother Fred was an aircraft engineer. He died in an automobile crash ten years ago, I decided to be a nurse when I was just a little girl.

As Sue talked Josh studied her intently. He found himself warming to her candor, her good humor, the occasional volatile reactions. Seeing her as a person this way stirred something deep within him. He found that the graceful curve of her neck and the trimness of her body attracted him. Vitality always seemed to flow from her—especially from those hazel eyes with flecks of gold. He liked the spare way she used makeup, the simplicity of her attire.

When Sue paused in her recitation, Josh abruptly changed the subject. "I'm sorry about our last talk. I was very self-righteous."

Sue looked startled. "What makes you say that?"

"I've thought about it since then, I tend to say things before I think."

Sue shook her head. "You say what you think and feel in a very forthright way. Often it does come across as self-righteous and it can hurt. But truth often hurts."

"Did I hurt you?"

She paused reflectively, "Yes, you made me feel like a loose woman. I'm not really. But I'm not as straightlaced as you are."

"I don't think you're a loose woman or I wouldn't be sitting here with you now." Josh was surprised at his vehemence.

Sue's smile lighted her whole face. "Those are what you might call healing words, Josh. I have strong feelings about my integrity as a person, but they are not tied to any moral or religious beliefs."

"Then what are they tied to?"

Sue shifted about in her chair. "I feel we're about to head into one of those unequal discussions where the weight of your convictions is too much for me."

Josh's smile was almost boyish. "That's a disarming statement, Sue, which stops me. But before we drop the subject

248

let me ask this one question. Does your personal philosophy—or call it your value system—completely satisfy you?"

Sue's reply was quick. "The answer to that is no, because things change too fast in our world today to hold onto any value system rigidly." A thought suddenly came to her and her face grew troubled. "I see something that bothers me, Josh. Your value system rooted in Christianity is not subject to change; mine is. I'm in the weaker position."

"And more vulnerable." The telephone rang and Josh arose from the table to answer it. It was Vinnie.

"Josh, something awful is happening. Can you come over? It's the music. It's acting strange."

Josh could hear the sounds of Vinnie's music clearly over the phone; actually, he had been hearing it faintly through the windows for some time. It was hard rock and now it did sound strange. It would pour out very high and shrill, then slow down into a deeper bass tone as though someone were speeding up and slowing down the revolutions of the record on the turntable.

"What's happening? Who's doing that?" Josh asked.

"I'm by myself. The music's acted funny before, the volume changing. Now the speed is acting up. I—I tried to turn it off, and Josh, it wouldn't stop!"

"You turned the switch off and it's still playing?" Sue was up from the table and standing close to Josh, staring at him with wide eyes.

"Vinnie, grab the cord and pull out the plug. Unplug it."

"Josh, it *is* unplugged!" Josh almost never felt fear, but a lick of ghostly dread raked him now. He put an arm around Sue, who was shuddering, and spoke as calmly as he could to Vinnie.

"I'll be right there. Stay calm."

He hung up the phone and smiled at Sue. "I have to go over there. You understand. I'll be right back."

"I'm going, too."

"Come on then." They left by the kitchen door and

started toward the psychic's trailer next door. It was cooler now and the wind was rising. Josh could hear the music over the other sounds, now high-pitched and garbled. It raised goosebumps along his arms.

Poor Vinnie, he thought. *Alone in the face of these bizarre happenings without understanding the cause.*

Vinnie opened his back door as Josh and Sue walked into the yard and his face showed his enormous relief. "Hello, Sue. Sorry to interrupt your dinner."

"Don't be silly."

Josh walked past Vinnie into the kitchen and on into the living room, Vinnie and Sue trailing behind. The lights were dimmer than usual, and as Josh stood there they began to flicker. He stared at the stereo; the lid was off and on the floor. He could see the cord, unplugged.

The music dropped suddenly to a normal speed and then lower and slower. The throbbing bass tones pounded on their eardrums as the music dominated the room.

Josh could hear words within the sound of the music. Not the lyrics of the song; those words were now too slow and deep to understand. These new words were only now audible, as the record slowed down. He couldn't understand the language.

With a sudden influx of energy born of anger, he strode across the room and yanked the arm from the record-player. It was suddenly, blissfully silent. The record continued to spin and he took it off the turntable and put it on the couch.

"Is it over, Josh?" Vinnie whispered.

"Probably, for now." He wasn't sure the episode was over. Or when it would return.

"I never saw anything like that in my life," Vinnie said weakly. "You guys want to stay here till the others get back?"

"I have a better idea," Sue said. "Why don't you come with us back to Josh's place? I don't know about you, but I want to get out of here!"

"Great! Let's go!" Vinnie smiled for the first time.

LeRoi liked the Roadhouse Pub. He fitted into its atmosphere and crowd comfortably. He had spent only one evening at the clubhouse in Brookshire's trailer park and had never been back. Among doctors and other professionals, he was afforded no respect. No one sought him out to hear his opinions, no one looked up to him as an expert in any field. But here at the Roadhouse, things were different. He liked the music played, the management policy of ignoring minor transgressions of the law, like smoking pot and gambling. Best of all, here at the Roadhouse LeRoi was somebody.

By careful implication and crafty deception, he had painted a distorted picture of himself and his role at Brookshire. To his listeners he was the gifted consultant and advisor, brought to the Project for his psychic skills. The group to which he had attached himself at the Roadhouse, the group to which his new girlfriend belonged, had seemed awed by his knowledge and experience in a field that was new and fascinating to all of them.

This night had started like the others, with LeRoi dominating the conversation, answering with absolute conviction any questions they asked. But now a new couple had joined them, a couple who looked askance at LeRoi, even challenged some of his pronouncements, and he was soon seething with anger.

The girl, called Red in deference to the violent and blatantly artificial color of her hair, sipped beer and studied him closely with cynical, small eyes. Her boyfriend, a stocky young man with a serious, scholarly face and horn-rimmed glasses, was called for some unknown reason, "Wolf."

LeRoi was pontificating on the subject of witchcraft. "Now I'm not a witch myself; I'm not into that. But some people I know are and I learned about it from them. They know how to cast spells on people, put a curse on you, stuff like that."

"You think it works?" asked his new girlfriend.

251

"Honey, I know it works."

"You know anything about voodoo, LeRoi?" she asked.

"Yeah, man. That's a big thing."

The young man called Wolf leaned forward. "You really know people who cast spells and all?" he asked skeptically.

"Sure, man. Witchcraft's the fastest-growing religion in America." He settled back confident he had their attention and continued. "There's black witchcraft and white witchcraft. I could tell you some real stories."

"Have you ever seen anybody cast a spell?" his girlfriend asked.

"Sure, lots of times. You need to know some astrology, and you need music, got to have that beat going, and—"

"I don't think you know anything about it," Wolf interrupted.

"You want me to prove it?" LeRoi cried, stung. "Want me to lay one on you?"

LeRoi's girl shushed him and he calmed down slightly.

"I can see why people might like that kind of religion," Red said, amused. "It promises all this power and secrets but it doesn't make any demands on you. No 'thou shalts' and 'thou shalt nots.'"

"You don't know the half of it," LeRoi boasted.

"You've got a big mouth," Wolf said. "And you sound like something out of the Middle Ages."

LeRoi bristled and stood up. "You asked for it, man." His eyes narrowed to slits and he pushed a fist toward Wolf who had also stood up. "Drop dead, man."

To his surprise, Wolf fell to the floor as though he'd been struck by lightning.

As the others crowded about the stricken man, LeRoi walked rapidly toward the front door of the inn, then out into the silvery light of the full moon.

Wanda felt strangely alone, mainly because Glenda's thoughts came through very dimly to her. Glenda was busy talking to Wallace, but that alone couldn't account for the weakness in her messages to Wanda. Wanda found it all very disconcerting.

"Josh said it was a haunting," Glenda was saying. "So I looked the word up in the dictionary. It doesn't mean what you'd think." They had left the path behind the mobile home compound and were now in the forest itself. "It only means to return or reappear."

"I know the Zorans are going to reappear tonight because they told me. But that can't be classified as a haunting," Wallace answered.

"Josh says it's been a haunting all along, starting even before the Project began," Glenda countered.

"I don't like the connotation that hauntings are evil or frightening. The Zorans aren't either one," Wallace said.

"Funny how nobody but you sees them," Glenda said suspiciously.

"Don't you read the papers?" Wallace retorted. "Hundreds of people have seen them."

"They see stuff in the sky, lights and flying saucers. Not many have seen people."

"Are you doubting my word?" Wallace bristled.

"Or maybe your sanity," Glenda teased.

Wallace stayed calm. He often erupted at LeRoi, but with Glenda he was only annoyed. "You'll see. Just wait."

"How much farther?" Wanda asked.

"About a mile more." They were trudging up an incline, through undergrowth, approaching a hill. It was full dark and growing colder. The moonlight was a shimmer of light through the enormous trees overhead. They had walked completely out of the medical center complex into the deep woods, much farther than the twins had gone before. In this direction they could go for miles and miles into almost-untouched forest.

As they walked on, Glenda spoke again. "Have they ever told you why they're so strange?"

"Well, you'd expect them to be different, wouldn't you? Coming from another world?"

"But even so, it seems they'd be more logical."

Wanda listened in bewilderment. Glenda's interest in UFOs and her information about them was all new to her, an unsuspected facet of her sister she neither shared nor understood.

"It seems if they're so advanced and all, capable of building craft that can travel from another planet, even another planet in our solar system, it seems like they wouldn't be so playful," Glenda persisted. "They wouldn't come all that way just to tease us, would they? That's not logical."

She continued.

"Seems they don't actually hide from people, but they don't really reveal themselves, either. They have all these abilities to defy gravity and other laws of physics; they can appear and disappear; they can go at impossible speeds and make impossible maneuvers; but they don't do anything. No outright contact, no scientific research; they don't even observe us in an orderly, logical way. It's like they're— what's the word, capricious? Like they traveled light-years to get here and now that they're here, they're just playing around."

"Just because you don't understand them doesn't mean they're illogical. Maybe their logic is based on a plane you can't even comprehend."

Glenda said firmly, "They aren't consistent, they're strange."

How do you know so much about them? Wanda thought, but Glenda's mind shrugged her off.

They walked along in silence for another half-hour. Then Wallace called a halt and began flashing his light around. "I think we're in the right place," he said softly. "Yes, look!" His light revealed broken branches on some of the undergrowth and an area on the ground that looked burned and he nodded in quiet triumph. "This is it."

He sat down crosslegged on the ground, Indian style, and hunched his shoulders against the chill.

The twins sat down near him. Wanda moved closer to Glenda, her only comfort in this strange, chilly and clandestine adventure. "Can we light a fire?" she asked. "I'm cold."

Wallace shook his head. He kept looking upward, totally engrossed in the impending rendezvous.

You got any more grass? she thought to Glenda.

No, it's all gone, Glenda thought back. *LeRoi didn't have enough to give me any.*

I don't like this, Wanda thought. *I really feel funny about it.*

It's going to be great. Glenda's mind revealed her excitement. *Just think, a whole new race of beings! And they want to meet us!*

Wallace stood up suddenly and whispered, "They're coming!"

Sudden fright assailed Wanda. She stood up and found she was dizzy; she leaned against a tree and looked around.

Because of the woods, she couldn't see much of the horizon, but there were patches of open sky through the trees. In one such open space, in what Wanda thought was the direction opposite the medical center complex, she could see lights. There was no sound. The lights grew brighter. She wished at that point she hadn't smoked that reefer at LeRoi's. It was hard to evaluate anything so strange and different with her perception already distorted.

In the glow of the lights Wanda could see Wallace's face. He looked ecstatic.

"What's happening, Wallace? Will they land?" Glenda asked in a whisper.

"No, there are too many trees. They bring down a little hover-craft, like a lifeboat or something. Just three of them."

"Is that what burned the ground?"

"Yes, the exhaust." He was staring up at the lights. They could hear a sound now, a whirring, humming noise. Wanda shook her head to clear her thinking.

The woods were bright now with the lights from whatever it was that whirred and hovered overhead. Wanda tried to get some conception of its size but the trees and the strange lighting distorted the view. It seemed enormous, though. Wallace was standing in perfect stillness, listening.

255

Suddenly, the Zorans were there.

Wanda felt their alien presence throughout her body; a cold, tingling, prickly sensation touched her, not just her skin but deep within her as well. The temperature seemed to drop sharply, as though a door had been opened into a giant refrigerator. The wind was rising, howling through the trees, its sound clashing in painful dissonance with the humming of the enormous, overpowering, smothering thing that hovered over them.

Wanda had a sudden sense of being controlled, of heart-pounding fear and the nauseating, enervating terror of being in the presence of something unspeakably alien and powerful beyond imagination.

Her body reeled under the onslaught; her teeth chattered, tears welled up and she reached instinctively for Glenda's hand. Then the worst thing of all occurred—the most shocking, mind-numbing, fearful thing of all.

Within her mind she heard a new voice. All her life she had felt Glenda's mind with her own; their thoughts were almost totally in tune and it was a perfectly natural thing to hear Glenda. This was someone else.

There is much to do. We must get started.

"Are we going aboard?" Wallace asked. Even in her terror, Wanda was able to spare a thought of contempt for Wallace who had no abilities at all in telepathy and had to speak aloud.

Two of you, Wallace Graham. You and the one named Glenda. We need only one of them.

Glenda was standing as though paralyzed, her face absolutely blank in the reflections of the flashing lights. *Glenda, don't go with them*, Wanda thought desperately, but there was no answer. The chill, tingly, somehow metallic voice spoke instead.

Be silent, Wanda. You have no understanding of what is happening here. What do you know of "The Nine"? "The elementals"? "The Elohim"? Leave your sister and go.

Wallace turned to Wanda and spoke urgently. "Don't

256

argue with them, for God's sake! Glenda has to stay; they want her. Can you find your way home?"

"By myself?" Wanda's voice sounded shaky to her own ears.

"We're going into the ship," Wallace said. He was quivering with excitement, eager to have her gone. Glenda was still frozen, paralyzed, her mind silent to Wanda.

"I'll get lost, Wallace," Wanda whimpered.

"It's not far to the path," he encouraged her. "Look, we paralleled that ridge about a mile-and-a-half. The highway's just on the other side, or you can follow the valley by the ridge and you'll run right into the path."

"But Glenda—" Wanda was crying now. The atmosphere was still frightening but her thoughts were so full of her sister that she was able to ignore the strangeness that had assaulted her senses and the three pale, luminescent, spectral beings who stood nearby.

"She'll be fine. I'll bring her home when this is over." Wallace turned again toward Glenda. He was almost dancing in his eagerness to have Wanda gone. "They're ready to take us," he hissed. "Go on!"

"Wallace, don't do this to me!" Wanda howled.

"You'll be fine," he urged, then turned one last time and walked away from her toward the thin, shadowy figures.

Wanda blinked her tear-filled eyes and suddenly stifled a scream, covering her mouth with both hands. In the strange, shifting light, it seemed to her that both Wallace and Glenda were being lifted from the ground. She wanted very badly to scream.

Leave!

The cold voice terrified her. She turned in horror from the sight and ran as fast as possible, back the way they'd come.

For the first time in her life, Wanda was truly alone.

By two o'clock Saturday morning, most of the residents of the Brookshire mobile home compound were asleep for the night. Only a few, like Charlie and Bebe, were still out on the town. All the fun-seekers had left the clubhouse. A still, early-morning fog was beginning to haze the moonlight and the temperature had dropped to forty. All seemed peaceful; nocturnal animals were bold in scurrying around garbage cans and the heavy forest seemed to hover closer, able to reassert its ancient claims to this ground now as the human intruders slept.

But in the far corner of the mobile home compound a light shone in Josh Kingston's trailer. Sue Dunn, Vincent Ponder and Josh were still deep in conversation, each unwilling to break up the cozy comradeship, no one wanting to be alone in the stillness of this particular night.

Sue had taken off her shoes and sat in the small armchair, her feet tucked under her full skirt. Vinnie and Josh shared the couch and all three were sipping hot tea.

"Okay," Vinnie was saying. "I'll accept that it was some kind of evil spirit. Believe me I know it was evil! But I don't see why it picked on me."

"For starters, evil spirits hate all humans," Josh explained. "We really have what they've always wanted, dominion of the earth. Make no mistake, their purpose is to rob, kill and destroy. But if they can't do that, they'll just try to scare us or hassle us. They probably got a real kick out of our fright."

They were interrupted by a pounding on the front door. A breathless, frightened voice called out.

"Mr. Kingston, it's me. Wanda Simmons!"

Josh opened the front door and stepped back as Wanda exploded through the opening. She was disheveled and dirty, her face tear-stained, her teeth chattering and her blue eyes enormous with fear behind her steel-rimmed glasses.

"Thank God you guys are still up! I saw your light from the woods." She sank in a shuddering heap on the couch while Josh brought a blanket from his bedroom and put it around the twin's hunched shoulders.

258

"What were you doing in the woods this time of night?" Josh asked. "Where's Glenda?"

"Glenda and I went with Wallace to meet the Zorans. It was awful! The flying saucer thing was big and weird and I got cold and was so scared! I tried not to even look at the Zorans; they were so creepy. They didn't want me, just Glenda, and they made me leave."

The three could only stare at Wanda. It was the first time they'd seen a weakness displayed by one of the Simmons twins, usually so arrogant and superior. It made her surprisingly human and likable.

"Wallace said he's been with the Zorans many times and that Glenda would be O.K. Do you think he's right?" Wanda pleaded.

"I certainly hope so, Wanda," Josh replied. "But it seems strange they'd let you leave. They don't usually like somebody to witness a close encounter who's not a participant."

"They told me I didn't understand them." Wanda took a deep, shuddering breath. "They told me to go home. I started walking, then I ran until I got lost. I wandered around for hours! I was so scared! Then I finally saw your lights and came here." She sighed a huge sobbing sigh and began to relax a little.

"Wanda, where's Bebe?" Josh asked finally.

"Out with the Tuna."

"You haven't been home yet; maybe they're there, worried about you. Why don't you and I walk over to your trailer and if nobody's home, I'll wait with you."

Wanda nodded without enthusiasm.

"I'm going too," Sue declared, snapping off the kitchen light.

"And me," Vinnie agreed. "I wasn't too eager to go home alone before this, and I'm sure not now."

Josh shrugged, turned off the rest of the lights and led the way out the front door and along the path toward the Simmons' trailer.

It was late before Bebe was willing to leave the All-Day Sucker, and Charlie walked out with a feeling of great relief. While driving back to Brookshire, he became his old jovial and confident self.

It was after 2 a.m. and the car was a haven of warmth in the chilly night. Bebe rested her head against the back of the seat and closed her eyes. "I wish we didn't have to go back," she murmured. "I'd like to party and dance forever."

"Aren't you tired?" he asked.

"Oh, I guess so. I guess I'm ready for sleep."

Charlie parked in the long-term parking lot and they walked as quickly as they could through the still, moonlit woods. Ahead they saw lights in the Simmons' trailer. Bebe turned to Charlie with annoyance. "The twins should have been asleep hours ago." They walked into the living room and stopped in surprise.

Josh Kingston and Vincent Ponder were sitting at the table, talking softly. Sue Dunn was sitting on one end of the couch, and Wanda lay next to her, her head resting in Sue's lap. As the door opened, Wanda turned to look at Bebe but she made no move to sit up. She was dressed in pajamas and snuggled into a little ball. She looked, to Charlie, about three years old.

"This could get old," Bebe said resentfully. "Coming home and finding a bunch of people in my living room." She looked around again. "Where's Glenda?"

"Glenda's with Wallace Graham," Josh said calmly. "We were waiting with Wanda till you got home."

Bebe sank gracefully into the large armchair. She fixed her younger sister with cold blue eyes and asked, "What happened?"

Wanda told her story again, calmer now. They all then looked at Barbara.

"I don't think we need to do anything," Barbara said calmly. "I'm sure Wallace will bring Glenda home safely." She turned back to Wanda and with some concern, said "You go to bed. I'll give you a pill to help you relax."

Wanda rose obediently and started down the hall toward

the bedroom. Barbara explained, "She has some Dalmane, her own perscription from home. I'll give her a couple."

As the Simmons left the room, Josh turned to Sue Dunn. "I think I can supply Don Oliver Franklin with one of his sought-after common factors. I believe all these psychics use drugs regularly."

"I don't use them," Vinnie protested.

"Did you ever?"

"When I was in therapy I was on mellaril and equinil. They zonked me out good. But I quit taking them as soon as I quit going to the doctor."

"The fact that you quit may explain why you're different from most psychics. And may explain how you've been protected as much as you have from the dangers around you."

Dr. Fortuna was reviewing Josh's suggestion in his mind: LeRoi, certainly. Drugs were a part of his lifestyle. Wallace took tranquilizers routinely, Charlie knew, mostly Valium. And now the twins with "their own" Dalmane. But he wasn't willing to let Josh's statement stand without contradiction.

"These are medications, prescribed by a doctor," he protested. "That's different. And these kids are highstrung, under tension. They need something to relax them."

Josh didn't reply and Charlie was annoyed at himself for feeling so defensive about his own profession.

Bebe came back shortly, her face relieved. "She'll go to sleep now."

"Bebe, are you sure we shouldn't do something about Glenda?" Josh asked again.

"Oh, no," Bebe replied. "She'll be all right. She'll come home."

The four walked slowly back to their separate trailers, each facing solitude with much disquiet.

At twenty minutes after seven Saturday morning, a large, very bold cockroach strutted across the faded vinyl floor of

261

the motel room, and Wallace Graham crushed it firmly beneath the toe of his well-polished Italian shoe. He looked around in distaste, observing the sagging bed with its thin chenille spread, and the dusty furniture placed at irregular intervals around the walls of the room: two chairs, a small table, a painted brown dresser and a coin-operated television set. What a dreary place! But for his purpose, it would serve.

It was far better to rent this room, which was all he could afford with the money he had on him, than to return to Brookshire for more cash and face questions. No one must know of his plans; they would try to stop him.

He took off his jacket and folded it neatly on the dresser. Then he sat on the edge of the bed and removed his shoes. Next he stretched out on his back, adjusting the thin, sour-smelling pillows under his head. He closed his eyes against the feeble glare of the bulb in the ceiling fixture and began to slow and deepen his breathing. For it was his purpose to prepare for the most momentous event of his life, possibly of all human life.

He was going to Zora!

For the past several hours he had been in counsel with three of his alien contacts, in a sort of extra terrestrial pre-briefing. He had sat enthralled in the bowels of the Zorans' mothership, answering questions. His head was aching, his heart pounding, his breathing labored by the time he had run the gauntlet of their questions, but the result would be worth any price. They were taking him not merely into the ship for a tour; they were taking him home. He would be the first human to visit a strange world, in the first true and open encounter between *homo sapiens* and an alien race since the days of the ancient charioteers. And Wallace Graham was the man selected.

He had left the ship in a daze, taking upon his unworthy shoulders the mantle of responsibility and glory.

Glenda had been found wanting and sent back home to her sister. It wasn't that she lacked ability; actually, at one time her enormous capabilities had almost persuaded the

Zorans to accept her in spite of the problems, but in the end they decided against her. She was far too stubborn to be a suitable vessel.

Wallace brought his thoughts back, settled his mind firmly on the job at hand. It wouldn't be quite as simple as a visit to the ship; the Zorans had explained that to him. He had to prepare himself spiritually, for this was not merely a physical journey.

He remembered what the Zorans had called it; their simple, beautiful explanation of his forthcoming journey would be "The Ascension." It was the same journey taken by all the ascended masters: Buddha, Krishna, Vishnu, Rama, Christ, Sanat Kumara. And now Wallace himself. And because he was a being composed of both body and spirit, he would take a journey with both his physical and his spiritual self. He was moving *beyond*, ascending into another plane, his body traveling in the spaceship to Zora, his spirit evolving into the next stage.

Again his excitement threatened to overwhelm him and he fought it down urgently. The Zorans had explained that he must enter an altered state of consciousness. He knew that such a state was a part of the doorway to the beyond. And there were many ways to reach it: drugs, the breathing and relaxation techniques of the Yogis, contemplation and meditation like the Hindu mystics, trance states like mediums and other occultists, hypotism, catatonia, astral projection . . . all were just a way into a state where control of self was surrendered to others, in this case the higher beings from Zora.

Wallace used a combination of meditation, self-hypnosis and biofeedback. He closed his eyes and pictured in his mind a brilliant red cube floating against an inky-black background. As he chanted the syllable "ba," slowly and softly at first, gradually growing faster and louder, the cube began to whirl faster and faster. And while the sound and the image increased, Wallace's pulse slowed, his blood pressure dropped and his basic metabolic rate slowed.

" . . . and there was another one on 11-to-7, so that's five in all." Carleton Phillips ran a restless hand through his thinning hair and faced Don Oliver Franklin across the broad fruitwood desk. "I've checked with Children's and Jocelyn Cannon Hospital. We're the only hospital having trouble. And I think it's getting beyond us."

Franklin nodded. "I'm glad you called me. We must stay on top of the situation."

It was the first time these two men had both been present at the hospital before eight on a Saturday morning. But Phillips had responded to a call from his Chief of Staff and Franklin had responded to the call from his administrator. Now they sat in Franklin's office, sipping coffee, discussing the latest additions to the death count.

"I have an appointment with the Medical Examiner at ten," Phillips continued. "The Chief of Staff is going with me. Do you want to join us?"

Franklin was lighting a cigar, turning it slowly in the flame from his lighter. He shook his head. "No, that's not necessary. I have every confidence that you two will do what has to be done." He rose ponderously from his chair, indicating the conversation was over.

Barbara didn't even wake up when Glenda returned home around daylight. It was Barbara's habit to sleep eight hours or more from the time she went to bed and only very extraordinary circumstances could alter her routine.

Wanda had been awake since 5 a.m. She tossed and turned, tired but unable to sleep well with Glenda gone. Where there should be a reflection of self, an answering spirit and companionship, there was now only silence. Wanda felt as though a part of her had been amputated.

Then she heard Glenda's mind as her sister approached on the path from the forest. She was alone.

Where have you been so long? I missed you, Wanda thought. Glenda's mind reached out, but Wanda could tell she was drained completely in body, mind and spirit. *I'm okay. I saw the Zorans' ship. I'll tell you about it later. I need to sleep.*

Where's Wallace? Wanda asked.

He's going back with them to their planet. He's gone off somewhere to prepare. Did Bebe get mad that I was gone?

She was irritated but not really mad.

Glenda closed her mind and entered the trailer. Wanda was relieved to have her sister back. It was the first time in their lives they had spent so many hours separated; she wondered if it would affect their relationship.

Suddenly Glenda's mind projected another thought: *You didn't like it when they didn't want you, did you?*

Wanda was suddenly angry. *I didn't want to have anything to do with them! I just went because you wanted to.*

They wanted to meet us, Glenda thought. *Especially me.*

And you wanted to meet them, Wanda challenged. *I never did.*

It started when I got hit on the head by that limb. Remember?

Of course Wanda remembered. That had been their first separation, a brief but even more frightening one. And now that she thought about it, Glenda had been different ever since then. And she was even more different now.

What did they do to you?

Nothing much, Glenda retreated; her mind was once again a distant dim voice. *I don't feel like talking about it.*

Wanda was annoyed with her sister. Glenda was different. But at least she was home.

To her surprise, Sue slept soundly after the frightening events of the night and didn't awaken till about 10 a.m. on Saturday. It was not a good awakening; she felt disquieted, depressed. And for some reason, guilty. Her telephone call to the Simmons' trailer was sleepily answered by Bebe. Yes, Glenda had returned safely, around 6 a.m. Bebe hung up without another word.

Suddenly Sue was thoroughly fed up with supernatural

265

happenings and discussions about them. She wanted most of all to return to that time before Josh, the psychic kids, the Project and the strange occurrences around the hospital. She wanted no more conversations about stereos that wouldn't turn off, about Zorans, about demons or PSI factors. She wanted her old life back.

To avoid meeting any of her neighbors, she stayed inside all day, fixing her meals at home instead of walking to Brookshire's dining room. She wrote letters to her aunt in Savannah and her uncle in New Jersey, something she rarely did. She watched a televised football game, something she never did. And she went to bed early Saturday night.

Sunday dawned crisp and bright and she attended a service in the hospital chapel. Dr. Brown's sermon was based on Rudyard Kipling's poem "If," and the minister presented a neatly outlined summary of the poet's requirements for manhood. She found it pleasant listening, a soothing contrast to the recent events at Brookshire. She knew it was straight psychology, but so what?

"If you can keep your head, when all about you are losing theirs. . . ." Malcolm wound up his sermon with a few practical thoughts and the people filed out of the church in a warm, jovial mood. Sue drove back to her trailer feeling more like her old self.

It was early Sunday afternoon when Isabel knocked at her door, looking very glamorous in brown plaid pants and a burnt orange over-blouse. She relaxed in Sue's armchair and kicked off her high-heeled shoes.

"What a beastly weekend," she began. "And you've been hiding away in here like some bloody cave-dweller."

"I've had a lot to do here," Sue said defensively.

"Are you interested in what's been going on?"

"Sure."

"Well, LeRoi and Wallace have been missing since Friday night." Isabel looked pleased over this bombshell.

"You're kidding. Both of them? Is anybody looking for them?"

"You mean the authorities? No, nobody's reported it. Glenda Simmons came back from her close encounter saying that Wallace was going to Zora on a flying saucer. Seems the Zorans were looking for a specimen and chose Wallace. They rejected Glenda, which of course any right-thinking alien would do. She's such a dreadful little snot. And as far as LeRoi is concerned, he's probably spending the weekend with his girlfriend. Anyhow, they're both adults, free to do as they please. I expect they'll be back by tonight."

"You heard about Vinnie's stereo?"

"Oh, yes. We've talked it through at meals."

"How is Josh taking all this?" Sue asked awkwardly.

Isabel's answer was without a smirk. "He's preaching to everybody who'll listen that evil spirits are in control. All we need to do is become fanatical Christians like him; then we can command them to leave." She laughed again, her face scornful.

Sue wearily mustered up support for Josh. "Do you think he could be right?"

"Oh, for heaven's sake, Sue, don't be a fool! I know he's a sexy-looking man, but don't let that blind you to his fanaticism."

"Are his theories any farther out than Wallace's—or any of the psychics, for that matter?"

"Yes," Isabel said firmly. "Because they go against scientific truths."

Sue suddenly realized what was happening. Only a few weeks ago she and Isabel had stood in about the same position in regard to this whole business, a position of almost total ignorance. Since the first ripples of supernatural activity, they had both been learning, thinking, making decisions. And moving in opposite directions: Isabel toward the realm of the occult, Sue toward the Christian perspective. She seemed to be facing two choices—believe as Isabel did or as Josh did. The middle ground of forming no opinion at all seemed to have been washed away.

It was not what she wanted. She was not ready to make a commitment to either side. Yet she sensed deep down that soon she must choose.

The trailer park was a neat place to live, Charlie thought, very handy to the hospital. But it wasn't handy for things like parking. He hurried along the footpath through the woods, balancing a large square box of pizza, hoping to reach the Simmons' trailer before it cooled.

Charlie was a little irritated this Sunday evening. He was, after all, a successful member of the most honored profession in modern society. He was attractive, personable, affluent and looked up to by others. Yet here he was trotting along with pizza-to-go like some high school kid, for crying out loud, bringing his small offering, reeking of pepperoni, to his lady love.

The beautiful girl wasn't the least bit domestic. She'd made coffee a few times, but that seemed about as far as her culinary talents extended. In fact, he realized suddenly, she was bone-lazy.

He balanced the box carefully in one hand while he knocked on the Simmons' front door. Bebe opened it quickly. His annoyance faded and the familiar dry-mouthed, urgent longing for her was back.

"Oh, good. I'm really hungry." She smiled. Bebe wore a casual robe of gray and white striped denim. Charlie thought her enchanting.

"Where are the twins?" he asked, pleased as always when they were gone.

"They're out with Castor and Pollux. They're driving me crazy!"

"The kids or the dogs?" he asked, grinning.

"The twins. They're snapping back and forth at each other. They've never done that before."

Bebe sat at the table and they ate in silence for a while. "Do you ever feel you want to get away from here?" she suddenly asked.

"I just got here a few weeks ago," he protested.

"I want to leave everything, not just Brookshire." She reached for his hand and held it in her own, her red nails making painful points of contact along his palm. "I get so tired of the turmoil! I want to get away, not have to be responsible. You can't have any fun if you're always responsible."

"The twins, you mean?"

"Well, them and my folks and my life back home. I just hate it! It's boring and I have to have a job and I hate that, too!" Her voice was a whisper of intensity. "I want to get in a car and just drive away. Maybe California. I've always wanted to see the Pacific Ocean."

A wild hope plunged through Charlie's mind, dragging in its wake a series of pictures. He could see the two of them swimming together in the Pacific, hunting for an apartment together, going together to all the tourist spots in southern California. The key word was *together*. Was she merely confiding in him her resentment and fatigue over the upsets of the weekend? Or was she perhaps making a very subtle offer?

"They say California is a lot of fun."

"I don't ever want to go back home. It's not exciting like California." Bebe looked into his eyes. "I really want to go there, Charlie." Her voice grew dreamy and his heart raced with excitement as his idea took hold. "I'd like to get some new clothes, see some new sights. Does that sound good to you?"

"I think we all have our own Shangri-La somewhere." Her face was blank and he adjusted to the idea that she'd never heard of Shangri-La.

She talked on, outlining her dreams of a larger world,

one that did not make any demands on her time and energies, one that would never bore her. As she talked, he watched her face, already memorized by his eager mind but still an endless joy to behold. Would he leave his position at Brookshire, pull up roots again to take this girl to California? How long could such a relationship last? How deep a commitment would she be willing to make, she who was eager to break a commitment to her family after years of blood kinship and love? Was he willing to upset his entire life and professional status just for a transitory, superficial and probably one-sided affair with Barbara Simmons?

Of course he was.

At 24, Hal Givens was the youngest department head at Brookshire. Until now it had been relatively easy to direct the Public Relations Department and maintain a good image for prestigious Brookshire Hospital.

No longer.

He sat in Don Oliver Franklin's office at one o'clock Monday afternoon and nervously made his presentation: "So it's bound to come out, Don Oliver," he concluded. "There's no way we can keep it under wraps. It's news, and more than that, it's unusual medical news, and that's always big."

"I'll accept your judgment," Franklin gestured blandly. "So we release the story of our strange deaths. What else did you have in mind?"

"Well, it's this dinner you want for the Project. I thought maybe we ought to toss that idea back and forth and see if it's really the best thing to do."

"We opened with a dinner; I thought it would be a nice gesture to close with one." Franklin took a long black cigar from his pocket and rolled it gently between his hands. "Is there some problem about the dinner?"

"I don't know if you've been told, but two of your psychics have been missing for nearly four days. It might be very awkward if they don't show up again."

Franklin laughed heartily. "My dear boy, don't worry about that. They'll return. This is only Monday. If we have the dinner on Saturday, they'll surely be back by then."

Hal Givens shifted uneasily in his chair. "I hope you're right, sir. LeRoi Williams had a fight with another man at the Roadhouse Pub last Friday night, then disappeared. The man was taken to County Hospital in a coma. Didn't seem seriously injured, though, and was due to be released today. No one has heard a word from LeRoi since.

"I've been told that Wallace Graham is somewhere on an alien spaceship heading out of the solar system! I shudder to think what this kind of thing would do to us publicity-wise if it got out."

"Then we must be sure it doesn't." Franklin smiled genially.

"Graham's situation is much harder to explain than the deaths. People have read about medical mysteries before: Legionnaire's Disease, the Seaport Plague. But to lose a patient to a flying saucer?"

"Mr. Graham is not a patient. He is a guest, and free to do as he pleases." Don Oliver Franklin was just a shade less genial.

"Well, you're the boss." Givens said hesitantly.

"Indeed I am," Don Oliver Franklin laughed, jovial again. Then he stood and walked around his desk and clapped a friendly hand on the publicist's shoulder. "Don't worry so, Givens. Our image will remain untarnished! The people need us too much to get upset for long about their hospitals. They have to trust us; they don't have any choice so get cracking on plans for that farewell dinner Saturday night."

The word spread rapidly through Brookshire that Project Truth was folding up, that there would be a final farewell dinner the end of the week. When Isabel Nebo told Sue Dunn late Monday afternoon, Sue was startled. "Well,

271

thank heavens things can get back to normal again." As the words came out, she knew she didn't mean them.

She went straight home after work and stood in her kitchen looking out the windows toward Josh Kingston's trailer. That was the real problem, she knew. It wasn't that they'd all be leaving; it was the fact that *he* would leave. And despite her low period over the weekend when she wanted life to return to what it had been before all the multiplied, distressing, inexplicable problems at the hospital, Sue ached inside to think that by this time next week Josh would be gone.

As she watched, he walked out the kitchen door of his trailer, dressed in jeans, casual shirt and boots. He stood on the top step and looked around, his face intense and un-smiling. He hunched his shoulders in the cold wind and walked rapidly toward the psychics' trailer, now occupied only by Vinnie Ponder.

As Vinnie opened the door and Josh disappeared inside, Sue realized she hadn't talked to either of them since they'd separated on the path in the chill pre-dawn of Saturday. She herself had avoided company over the weekend and neither Josh nor Vinnie had been at meals today.

With sudden determination she changed rapidly from her uniform into casual clothes and walked briskly over the same path to knock on the same door Josh had just entered. Vinnie opened to her with a smile.

"Come on in, Sue. We're just talking."

She could tell Josh was glad to see her even though there was no big welcoming smile. She took a seat by Vinnie on the couch.

"What am I interrupting?" she asked.

"We call it a 'leaven hunt,'" Josh was saying. "Before Passover the Hebrews went through their tents getting rid of any leaven, a symbol of corruption. So when a person has had a deliverance session, we go though his house making sure there isn't anything left which the dark forces can hang onto. Nothing that gives them a legal right to stay."

Vinnie turned to Sue and explained it his way. "Josh has been telling me that after you command the demons to go, you have to go through the house and get it spiritually clean."

"How?" she asked.

"Well, let's see." Josh was leaning forward speaking with his usual intensity. "You get rid of anything to do with the occult, horoscopes or zodiac things. Drugs. Things that have been connected with sin, like stolen property. Statues, especially statues of false gods. And the wrong kind of music, that's a big one for Vinnie."

"What's wrong with music?" Vinnie looked distressed. He had not yet made a decision to seek deliverance, and a sacrifice of music would be quite a drawback.

"Music is worship, Vinnie. And music that's written under the influence of drugs or dedicated to evil forces can be destructive." Josh gestured. "Look at the album covers. Can't you just see how sick they are? I always tell parents that their kids don't listen to that kind of music because they're rebels; they're rebels because they listen to that kind of music."

"And it's addictive, too," Sue added. The others looked at her in surprise. "The more hooked on it you get, the louder you need to play it."

"That's right," Josh agreed.

"I don't understand, Josh," Vinnie protested. "Are you saying my music caused the stereo to keep playing?"

"Your having that kind of music here gave the evil spirits a legal right to be here. It's like you opened a door and gave them permission to enter. Look at it this way. You can't get rid of a spirit of lust if you keep pornography around the house. And if your problem comes through music, make sure you don't have any music around that glorifies Satan. That stuff is deadly. If members of a family fly into a mur-

273

derous rage, then you need to get rid of any weapons of violence like guns and knives. Don't give that spirit of violence any ground."

Vinnie was still unconvinced and he was starting to reply when the living room door burst open. It was LeRoi. His dapper clothing was filthy and torn. His long hair was wilder than usual and his face wore an expression of tightly controlled fear. Barely nodding to them, he hurried down the hall toward his room.

"Hey, LeRoi, where you been?" Vinnie asked. When there was no answer, they all followed LeRoi to his room, where he was throwing clothing into a suitcase.

"Are you all right?" Vinnie asked.

"Yeah, man. I'm just fine. Just that I'm leaving."

"Why? You liked it here."

LeRoi nodded. "I did, man. But now I gotta go! They got me in a real box."

"Who's trying to hurt you?" Sue asked.

"I don't know. Somebody's setting a trap for me but I found out about it in time so I'm leaving. When they ask, you tell them I left for parts unknown. I ain't going back to Huntsville, in case anybody wants to know."

"What kind of a trap, LeRoi?" Vinnie asked.

"A real cute, neat trap," LeRoi answered. "But I ain't the onliest one they after. They gonna get every one of you before it's through. I was just the head of the list." He closed the suitcase and snapped the locks. He looked around the room one final time.

"I can help you, LeRoi," Josh said quietly. "I think it's a mistake to run off like this, no matter what kind of circumstances you're facing. The enemy you're fighting will just go with you."

Slowly and majestically, LeRoi rose to his full height and glared at Josh. The lines of his face altered. He suddenly seemed older, stronger, and he spoke softly in a clipped, grammatically perfect Bahamian English.

"Tread carefully, Dr. Kingston. Follow the rules. You may

274

function only where you have been invited. Your side always follows the rules."

Josh's eyes narrowed and he nodded in recognition. "What have you done to LeRoi?" he asked. "What sort of trap is he in?"

A refined laugh emerged from LeRoi's body and the British voice chided, "You don't really want to know. It could involve you in a messy situation with the authorities and would do no good whatever to you or to LeRoi. Just mind your own business for a change."

Sue and Vinnie were watching the exchange with open mouths. The smooth British voice continued addressing Josh. "He'll be all right. I have no wish to see him locked away and I certainly know how to avoid it."

Josh stood aside and LeRoi's still erect and dignified body marched calmly down the hall, suitcase in hand. The others trailed after him.

At the front door of the trailer, the figure turned again and spoke one final time, now including Sue and Vinnie in his audience. "LeRoi was right, you know. He is merely the first of many here who will be snared by the fowler. Mark my words, the trap has been set for each of you."

"Don't count on it," Josh retorted. The tall, thin figure turned and left the trailer, walking briskly down the path toward the hospital. They watched him until the trees hid him from sight.

"Well, what's that all about?" Sue asked in a shaky voice.

"Don't let him upset you," Josh replied. "One of the main things about demons is, they lie a lot."

Effie MacAllister expected to be alone Monday night, but shortly after supper two of her sons dropped by. They joined her in the kitchen where she was washing dishes and sat at the big round table.

We're concerned about you, Ma," the older boy admitted. "That nurse's job is too much physical labor with your legs bothering you so much."

The younger son nodded. "We've all seen you coming home from work just worn out, and we don't like it, Ma. You don't need the money."

"I don't work just to make a living, son," Effie said mildly. "I like my job."

"How can you like wearing yourself out every day taking care of people who don't appreciate what you do for them?" Mac asked.

"I've been a nurse all my life," Effie said. "I don't think I'd feel right if I wasn't."

The two sons looked at each other. "Guess we'd better tell it straight," said the older. "The news is out about Brookshire, Ma. People are dying there like flies! And nobody knows why! You could catch it same as the patients."

"Please, Ma," the younger son said gently. "We don't want anything happening to you. That hospital's getting too dangerous for you."

Effie sat up straight, touched by their concern, but quite determined. "A good nurse doesn't flee when people get sick and die, my sons. The Lord has protected me all my life. When my time comes He'll take me, but right now He wants me where the action is. And the action is at Brookshire."

Effie suddenly smiled at her sons. "You're both good boys and I'm real touched you came over. Now, how about some spice cake? It's fresh, still warm. . . ."

Wearily, they both nodded.

" . . . chance of rain and a low in the mid-thirties. . . ."

Sue snapped off the television and sank back in her chair, unable to rouse herself to walk down the hall to the bedroom. She was still depressed over the day's events: the workload had never seemed more burdensome and she found the whole hospital routine distressing. The episode

276

earlier with LeRoi had been deeply upsetting and now at 11:30 Monday night, she still sat in the living room of her trailer, too overwhelmed to get up and go to bed.

A thought entered her mind: maybe she should sleep on the couch, not bother to walk down the hall to her room. But this was something she never did. The idea was so unusual and silly that she pondered it. And as she took it apart, investigating the motive and rationale behind it, she was suddenly aware of a startling fact.

She was afraid to go to her bedroom.

Why in the world would she be afraid? She'd never been a fluttery, dependent female. She'd lived alone for years and had never been nervous. Now suddenly she was reluctant to walk down a dark hall into a dark room, sensing some danger; or, more precisely, some evil.

I'm not afraid, she thought defiantly. Then, as if in answer to her boast, there appeared in her mind a parade of the few things she was afraid of. The list began with spiders.

There was no logical reason for fearing spiders to the extent she did. It was undoubtedly a phobia, an unreasonable fear, but knowing that her fear had no basis in logic did nothing to diminish it. The very thought of spiders overwhelmed her reason. She hated the sight of them, so obscene with their jointed, hairy legs; and the idea of being touched by one was abhorrent to her.

And for some reason, she felt this horror would come on her if she went to her room.

I'll just stay here and they won't come down the hall, she thought firmly.

But as the image of spiders faded, a second, stronger fear thrust itself into her mind. Sue also had a fear of knives. Because of it, she had never been able to work in surgery. The idea of a sharp, cold blade slicing through sensitive skin made her physically nauseous. She sat now, racked with shudders as her mind played out the fantasy of knives, thin and razor-sharp and frosty-cold, slicing thin strips of flesh from her arms while her blood flowed unabated onto the floor. Whatever presence she had sensed in her room, it was armed with knives. She gulped and swallowed repeatedly, forcing down the bile that rose in her throat.

Get hold of yourself, she commanded. *What's the matter with you? You're just imagining all this. Stop it!*

She recognized the effects of adrenalin, racing pulse, raspy, shallow respirations. She calmed her breathing by an act of her will, sitting up straight, assuming a posture of bravery and self-control. But the next attack crushed her against the back of her chair, whimpering in terror, beyond the reach of self-discipline.

For the thing she feared the most was being in a confined place. Claustrophobia. From childhood, the horror of being held close, smothered, shut in, had overwhelmed her. As an adult, she had overcome certain aspects of her problem. She was now able to ride in elevators; she could go into a crowded movie theater and not demand the aisle seat; she could sit in a room crowded with medical personnel and not want to flee, although she felt uncomfortable.

But this enemy had not been truly conquered. As it rode in now in all its fury, crushing her mind in terror, she realized it had been lying dormant for all this time, waiting to strike out at her in unabated strength.

The living room lights were still on. She could see the darkness beyond the cold glass of her windows, and the night seemed somehow more than the absence of light; it appeared to her fear-crazed eyes as something palpable, a thick curtain of deepest black velvet, wrapping itself around the trailer tighter and tighter, blocking out the air. And as she watched, it seemed the walls were coming closer, the floor rising, the ceiling sinking, certain to crush her soon.

She sat in her chair, sobbing wildly, chewing a knuckle until she tasted the metallic saltiness of blood, totally unable to rise against this enemy. *I shall die of fright,* she thought in desperation. *I've heard that expression but I never believed it before. But it's true. If this doesn't stop, I'll die.*

278

She drew her knees up, hugging them to her body with one arm while she continued to cry and chew her hand. And through her chattering teeth she managed to whisper: "Jesus!"

"Well, look who's here," Isabel said brightly. "To what do we owe this honor?"

"Oh, can it, Isabel," Charlie snapped. He took a sip of a drink that was almost completely rum and sat down next to her. Isabel was sitting before a fading but still warm fire in the trailer park's clubhouse. At midnight on Monday, the room was almost empty. Charlie was glad to see a friend; it had been impossible to sleep and nothing seemed worse than his own solitary company, the treadmill of thoughts about Barbara Simmons and the possibilities of going away with her.

"Well, seriously. Why are you here?" Isabel asked. "Trouble with Miss Bebe?"

"Look, can you be just a friend for a while? Not dedicated to cutting me down?"

Isabel stared at him stonily for a moment, a glint of firelight on her dark glasses making him wince. Finally she smiled, a genuine smile, and nodded. "Sure. You got a problem?"

"Well, I need to make some decisions and I can't seem to get anywhere."

She nodded. "Yes, we all do. With the Project ending, we'll all need to make some decisions."

"Mostly it's Bebe." He shifted his gaze to the fire, where a few yellowish flames flickered above a bank of cherry-red coals. "I swear I don't know what to do about her."

"You're not considering marrying her, are you?"

"Bebe doesn't believe in marriage. But I am considering hooking up with her. I'm considering it seriously."

"Oh, Charlie, no!" Isabel spoke so violently that Charlie looked at her in surprise.

279

"As bad as all that?"

"She'll destroy you," Isabel replied, her face grim. "She is shallow, immature, intellectually poverty-stricken, overwhelmingly selfish, boring, dull. . . . Oh, I could go on and on. But there's one more thing I don't think you're aware of, and it might have an effect on your decision. It is my considered, professional opinion that the girl is as frigid sexually as she is emotionally. I think she is totally poison and you should run in the opposite direction as fast as your legs will carry you."

Charlie stared at the flames while he considered this. Surprisingly, he didn't resent these attacks on his lady love. Isabel was obviously motivated by jealousy, but some of what she said was probably true. Yet it had no effect on him; the devastating description of Bebe did not reach Charlie in his emotions.

With all her faults, Barbara Simmons was still all he wanted in life.

"She's in my blood, Isabel," he finally said. Now that the door had been opened and the first admission made, Charlie found it impossible to stop. He poured out his aching soul to Isabel, the indignities Barbara forced on him, the slavish submission he yielded, the constant pain of desire that was never fulfilled.

"You poor jerk," Isabel said finally. "You poor, stupid jerk! I had no idea it was that bad."

"Yeah, well, it is."

Suddenly she rose and stood before him, blocking his view of the fire. He looked up at her hesitantly. He had been utterly exposed to her and he was now utterly vulnerable.

"Come on, Charlie," she said gently.

"Where?" he asked, suspicious and defensive.

"We're going back to your place. Back to Charlie's back room. Let's see if we can't do something to bring back the old Charlie."

"Oh, Isabel, I don't know. I don't think—"

"Hush. You just relax and trust me."

"Well, if you think—"

"I do think. Come on. If one woman could wipe you out like that, maybe another woman can restore you."

Charlie rose, embarrassed but beginning to feel a flicker of excitement. Maybe it would help, at that. At least briefly.

He shrugged into his jacket and helped Isabel with her wrap. Then they walked down the path toward his trailer.

Malcolm Brown looked around the kitchen surreptitiously and then poured the remainder of his milk back into the plastic carton and put it in the refrigerator. His wife deplored this habit; called it unsanitary. But it was after midnight, she was sleeping and he could do as he pleased. For despite a good income, Malcolm was constantly worried about finances. He was, in fact, bound to a myriad of little economies that bewildered his wife and irritated his servants. He simply hated to throw away two ounces of milk.

It was a black and cold night, a good night to be indoors. The creamy milk spread its balm in his angry stomach and rest should now be sweet. But Malcolm knew sleep would not come so easily to him. He had no desire to return to his comfortable early-American bedroom, crawl into his too-soft bed beside his warm little wife, to hear and be annoyed by her peaceful snoring. No, that would just get his ulcer riled again.

He padded quietly from the kitchen into his den, seating himself behind the desk. He turned on no lights, preferring the dark. He propped his elbow on the desk, rested his head in his hands and braced himself for the attack.

He'd tried to name this enemy. It was an old, familiar foe by now; certainly they had known each other long enough to be on a first-name basis. Was it just depression? No, it was too specific. Depression might be the family name, but not the first name of his nemesis. Discouragement? That was closer, for it included a feeling of hopelessness and told him that everything he did was vain, done in vain, of no lasting value.

He could understand perfectly the countless suicides committed by those who had achieved their goals. All those wealthy, handsome, talented, successful, beloved young people who each year overdosed on drugs, crashed in cars and planes, cut their wrists with razors . . . he knew the voice that had pointed their way down this dead-end street. This voice spoke to him, too, and said over and over, *Things will never be better. Why continue to toil along for rewards that shrivel in your hand and honors that turn to ashes?*

Just let go. There's no point in going on. There are those sleeping pills; take them, fall asleep and you'll never have to worry again. Rest. Peace. Quiet.

"No!" he muttered through clenched teeth. "I have responsibilities." He rose from the chair and began to pace the den, fighting back.

It was only after several hours that he did win a victory of sorts. He couldn't quiet the voice and he never did rise out of the misery that threatened to swallow him whole. But he did learn the name, and for some reason, that fact was a real comfort to him.

Its name was Despair!

Josh was awakened suddenly only a little while after he had gotten to sleep. For a brief moment he lay there listening, then threw back the covers and bounded from the bed. He knew the Voice that had awakened him.

"Go to Sue."

Why? he protested. *She'll probably misunderstand. The neighbors will see me sneaking over there after midnight and there'll be talk. And I won't even know what to say when I get there.* All the time his mind was arguing he was dressing, preparing to obey.

It was bitter cold as he hurried along the path to Sue's

trailer. He was relieved to see her living room was lighted; at least he wouldn't have to rouse her from sleep. He knocked on the door and called softly.

"It's Josh, Sue. Let me in."

The door burst open immediately and she threw herself into his arms as he entered. She was shivering, crying, teeth chattering in fear and cold and she whimpered against his chest, "Oh, thank God you've come!"

Once again he felt the relief of vindication. No matter how often he heard and recognized the Voice, it was always satisfying to have its instructions confirmed. He held Sue gently, patting her back and murmuring soothing words. She was nice to hold, a comfortable height, and her hair smelled like sunshine and fresh air.

She calmed down slowly, the sobs growing farther apart, and at last she pushed him back, humiliated by her display of weakness.

"I don't know what got into me," she apologized.

"I think you had a visitor. A visitor named Fear."

She looked startled, then nodded in agreement. Suddenly the idea of receiving help seemed more important to her than a restoration of her dignity, and she took his hand and led him to the couch.

"I've never had anything like that happen to me. Visions of spiders and men with knives, things I'm already afraid of. Then it seemed like the trailer was wrapped in some thick black substance and it was getting tighter and tighter. It was awful!" She shuddered and then spoke shyly. "I prayed, Josh. I prayed and then you came."

Josh pondered the situation. There were so many things he didn't know about Sue. What was her relationship to Jesus? Was she in a position to take the authority and the weapons provided for humanity to use against the spiritual enemy? "Sue, have you ever made Jesus your Lord?" he asked.

"I don't know," she answered honestly. "I go to church, I

believe in God and I've tried to keep the Ten Commandments."

He smiled gently and patted her hand. "God has a first name, Sue. It's Jesus. And He's the only way to heaven, or to anything else good, for that matter, like peace and joy and power and freedom. He's what you really need."

She stared at him, her tear-stained face serious. For the first time, he noticed how smooth and clear her skin was, how the soft golden freckles exactly matched the copper-gold of her lashes and brows. Her hair was the consistency of spun gold, soft as a baby's.

"Tell me what I need to do."

He explained the simple, beautiful, infinitely loving plan of salvation, and led her through a short prayer. As she sat obediently repeating his words, her eyes closed, he felt an overwhelming tenderness for her. This was the truly child-like faith that so few Christians could maintain. When she finished her little prayer and opened her eyes, he smiled and hugged her shoulders.

"Now you're in the Kingdom and all the promises are yours. You have power over all power of the enemy. Go get 'em, Tiger."

"I guess it's not very spiritual but all I want is sleep. I'm just worn out."

"Not afraid anymore?"

"Well, not with you here." She was holding his hand and it seemed very natural. "Maybe you could pray for me once more before you leave."

He nodded and took authority over the spirit of fear that had plagued her and then patted her arm. "Go to bed. I'll see you in the morning."

"Thank you, Josh."

He walked home in a glow of victory and joy. The night wasn't a bit cold to him now.

County Hospital was in the city, right in the heart of the

downtown section, and for about ten years it had been going downhill. Now it was almost exclusively a tax-supported psychiatric center and a receiving hospital for drunks, indigents and "John Does." Rarely did they admit a patient with a challenging, unusual medical problem.

One such patient was now on their census, one Wallace Graham of New Orleans, Louisiana, no local address.

Wallace was far better-dressed and better-fed than the majority of County's patients. He was clean, well-groomed, no signs of alcoholic intoxication or serious drug abuse. He had not been mugged or in an accident. There were no marks anywhere on his body. All his lab tests were normal. But he was in a coma, a steadily deepening coma, and had been for three days. The doctors were puzzled.

The chief resident stood by Wallace's bed and studied his chart. The pulse was hovering around 40. Should he consider a cardiac consultant, possibly a pacemaker? Respirations were between 10 and 12 and blood pressure was steady at 80 over 50. Rectal temperature was recorded at 96, dropping slowly since Wallace's admission. He was unresponsive on all levels, even painful stimuli.

If we don't do something, this guy'll die, the resident thought uneasily. He walked back to the chart rack, where a nurse stood chatting with a technician from X-ray.

The doctor interrupted their talk. "Look, on bed 6, anybody ever reach his family?"

"They tried calling his New Orleans number, from the ID in his wallet. No answer. The motel clerk said he came in early Saturday morning without luggage and rented a room. They found him the next day, passed out. They thought it was drugs, so they called us."

"We did a drug screen—gastric contents, urine and blood. He had some meprobamate, but nothing like enough to cause this," the resident mused.

"Strange, isn't it?" the nurse said.

"This is no skid row bum. This fellow's clothes cost more than mine do. He's somebody. We can't just let him sink away from us." The resident had visions of the family arriving with attorneys, demanding his hide.

The X-ray technician had followed the exchange with interest. "No identification at all?" he asked.

"We know his name—Wallace Graham."

The technician looked surprised. "That sounds like the guy who's been up in a flying saucer. It was in all the papers."

"I read that," the doctor said. "That's the man's name."

"Then he belongs at Brookshire," the nurse suggested.

"Lord, yes! Tell them to come get him." The resident suddenly felt much better.

One of the reasons Charlie liked his position with the Project was that with only five patients, and none of them sick, he didn't have to work very hard. One of the few things he had in common with Barbara Simmons was a strong distaste for hard work.

But now suddenly he had a sick patient; a very sick, bewildering, difficult patient. It wasn't fair!

Wallace Graham arrived from County Hospital via ambulance with a very inadequate history and physical, no lab reports, an I.V. of 5% dextrose in Lactated Ringer's, a Foley catheter in place and the beginnings of a bedsore on his coccyx. Charlie ordered him put to bed in a private room on Four South and began a battery of tests.

Why did it have to be this one, for crying out loud? The one with money, family connections. A fellow like LeRoi Williams could die a mysterious death without raising a stir, but Wallace Graham was too substantial to hope for such an outcome. No, he'd just have to get well or Charlie and the Project would be in a sling.

He was standing by the bed, watching the shallow, slow respiration of his patient, almost willing him to improve, when Isabel walked in. She looked tired, her face drawn, and

286

the harsh flourescent lights turned her frosted hair a sick greenish-yellow.

"How's he doing?" she asked, her voice a whisper.

"I don't know much yet. I started him on some stimulants."

"Well, I don't envy you," she said with a shake of her head. "Things are going to hell in a bucket around here. Did you hear that LeRoi came back? He was an emotional basket case, according to Vinnie. Packed his things, took on his alternate personality and said we were all in some kind of danger. Then he split."

"Terrific. You've made my day," Charlie said sarcastically. "I have this coma business to handle, and now you come predicting our doom. Thanks a lot."

They stood together looking down at Wallace, and Charlie fought off a feeling of panic. It was just one more reason for leaving and going to California.

Josh just picked at the dinner Sue had prepared. He took a few bites automatically, then pushed his plate back and turned to her with a expression of urgent intensity.

"What do you think of Vinnie Ponder?" he asked.

Sue wanted to scream at him, "I don't care about Vinnie right now! We only have a few more days—it's Tuesday night and you'll be leaving Sunday. I want to talk about me! You! Us!" But she said none of this and managed to keep her face calm.

"Vinnie's a charmer," she said lightly. "He's pleasant and sweet and handsome."

"That's what bothers me," Josh said, nodding in agreement. "That doesn't figure."

"It bothers you that he's so nice and wholesome?"

"Yes, it does. Look at the rest of them, the twins, LeRoi, Wallace. That's what most people are like when they're possessed: unpleasant, unhappy, twisted in some way, and almost always the kind of people you don't like. That's not true of Vinnie."

"What does that mean?"

Josh shook his head in bewilderment. "I don't know. But I've never seen anybody as useful to the enemy as someone who is charming."

He stared at his food for a long moment. "Satan can transform himself into an angel of light. Of course. Why didn't I realize that?" he muttered.

"Josh, what are you talking about?" she asked.

"There's someone here involved with the Project who is totally sold out to Satan and also his chief helper."

"Who?" Sue asked, eyes wide. "Surely not Vinnie!"

"I don't know. That's what bothers me."

They became silent, each with thoughts speeding in different directions. It was Sue who spoke first.

"Josh, will you stop thinking about demons and look at me?"

He looked up from his plate, startled by her shift in tone.

"Were you not hungry—or is my food unappealing?"

Josh chuckled self-consciously. "Everything is delicious, Sue. I guess when my thoughts are elsewhere, my hunger goes away."

"That I can see. Will you try to bring your thoughts back to the here-and-now, please, and eat. Then I have some questions."

After Josh had cleaned his plate, Sue began nervously. "You came in here the other night like a ministering angel when I was beset by fears. You calmed me and you did something else. You explained the plan of salvation to me, then asked me to repeat some statements after you. I did so, feeling quite right about it."

Josh nodded, his eyes brightening.

"Since then I've thought a lot about it, I've gotten a Bible, but I've become confused."

"That can happen."

"You see, Josh, I joined the church years ago and repeat-

288

ed many of those very same vows, which made me a Christian, right?"

"Not necessarily. Vows made in becoming a church member can be done so casually as to be meaningless."

"Well, I'm not sure if what I did the other night was any different than when I joined the church. I don't feel any different."

"Feelings have nothing to do with it."

"Josh, that statement doesn't help me. Feelings are what I live by. I feel tired, I go to bed. I feel hungry, I eat. I feel thirsty, I drink something."

"Yes, Sue, but if you wake up in the morning feeling blah, you don't go back to sleep. You get up and go to work whether you feel good, average or poor. You *will* yourself to work because you're a responsible person. In the same way, you've made a decision in your will to love and obey Jesus Christ, to belong to Him forever."

"I have?"

"You sure have."

"But I did it all before, too, if I remember correctly."

"You may have said the words, but the decision may not have been made in your will."

They had both finished eating. Sue stood up, started to clear off the table, then stopped. "Let's sit on the couch together and finish this. It's too important to be interrupted."

Josh nodded and led her over to the couch. She sat down and took his hand. "I want to confess something, Josh. When you ran through that whole plan of salvation and asked me to make those vows, I was so frightened I think I would have said or done anything you asked."

Josh looked startled. "I should have been sensitive to that."

"You were doing what you thought was right. But I was not commiting myself to Jesus, I was just clinging to you. What I did was make the vows to you."

Josh looked crestfallen. "Are you saying you don't believe you're a Christian?"

"No, I'm saying I don't feel any different from before. Maybe feelings shouldn't be involved, but with me they are. If I make a commitment to do something or be something, I want to feel it."

"Do you want to give your heart to Jesus Christ, Sue?"

"What exactly does that mean?"

"What do you know of Jesus?"

"Not a great deal, except what's in the Bible. I think I know more about demons than I do about Jesus."

Josh looked stricken. "What a fool I've been! What an utter fool!"

"How, Josh?"

"I've been trying to win you and others here to the Lord in the wrong way. I've been focusing on the negative forces. No wonder there's been such resistance."

"But Josh, you didn't come here as an evangelist. You came as a specialist in—well, I guess you'd call it demonology." Sue suddenly wanted to reassure him; she took his hand in both of hers. "I want to be what you'd like me to be, but I won't be a phony about this. If I'm going to take a big step, I want my whole being to know it's a big step."

"All right, Sue. We're going to start all over again and this time be sure the emphasis is where it belongs."

"Start with your love for Jesus. I really want to hear about that."

For an hour Josh talked, about his boyhood, his early training in the Bible, then his first experience with the Person of Jesus. Sue interrupted him several times to ask questions. When Josh started talking about the Spirit of Jesus, she stopped him. "Let's save that for another time. Let me get to know the Person of Jesus first."

"You think we should leave it at that tonight?" Josh asked.

"Yes. If you promise we can continue on it tomorrow night. There isn't much time left."

"Why do you say that?"

"Because the Project ends this weekend."

"Do you think I'm going to flee this place and you when the Project is over?"

"What else would you do?"

"Take you out of here."

"Josh!" Sue stared at him so wide-eyed that he blushed.

"Don't get any wrong ideas. I haven't changed my thinking about that."

"Where would you take me?"

"To your home."

"Oh." Sue's tone of disappointment made Josh laugh.

"I want you out of here, Sue."

"I like the idea of your wanting to take me away from here. I'm not really sure that I can just up and leave, though."

"Will you pray about it?"

Sue felt a surge of panic. "I don't think I can, out loud."

"Why not? Just talk to God. Say what's on your heart."

Sue closed her eyes and took a deep breath. *Why is it so hard?* she thought. *Josh does it so easily.* Then a picture of Jesus appeared in her mind. He was smiling at her, encouraging her.

"Jesus, I'm sorry I don't know You very well. It's my fault. I never took the time. But I want now to change that. I want—" Emotion surged up inside her and she stopped for a moment. "I want to care about You, Jesus, to get to love You as Josh does. I want my life to be different. Help me."

Tears trickled down her cheeks. Then, to Sue's surprise, Josh took her in his arms and hugged her. "That was great, Sue." He hugged her again, kissed her hair, her forehead and then her mouth. The impact of this was like a bolt of electricity through Sue. She gasped and then her arms went fiercely around him.

Wanda Simmons had never known what it was like to have control of her own mind. She had always shared every feeling, every impulse, every whisper of emotion with her sister; and indeed, until recently, had never dreamed of any other kind of existence. But then had come Glenda's accident with the falling limb and her encounter with the Zorans.

As a result three things had changed. First, Glenda herself was different. Since her return from the forest early Saturday morning, there was an additional realm in Glenda that Wanda did not share. They had not discussed it, but it was there—new, different, alien and private to Glenda. Second, there was a stirring in the realm of Wanda's spirit that she vaguely identified with Josh Kingston. The heavy gray fog that surrounded her mind and will was being strained and altered. At times she could almost see a new light beyond the turmoil that heaved and roiled about her. Then she would sink back into the murky heaviness that all her life had encompassed her.

Now a third factor had entered. Something new was stirring in Wanda as a result of hearing Josh describe the mentally ill children whose case histories he had written about. "Before their healing, they were almost completely hollow, as though they weren't even real," Josh had explained. "Their language was just jargon, meaningless. They had no personalities of their own. They weren't real until after the Spirit had filled them and they had begun growing in the Lord."

Most of this had gone over Wanda's head. A lifelong rebellion against anyone in authority had given her a resistant mindset. But as distorted as Josh's words became as they filtered through deep layers of deception and prejudice inside her, one thought somehow penetrated. Within Wanda there was a new and deep longing to be real.

She sat with Glenda in the living room of their trailer Tuesday evening, watching television, building a careful wall of protection against the mental tentacles from Glenda that probed and penetrated her mind. She wanted freedom and privacy to explore her exciting new thoughts. She wanted to be real, and if that meant hiding a part of herself from Glenda, then she must learn how to do that.

Wanda had never succeeded in winning against Glenda and had quit trying many years ago. Glenda's will had always been dominant. But maybe if she were very, very clever she could hide her thoughts without Glenda's knowing.

At least she would try

Like Tuesday, Wednesday was cold, wet and dreary. The subdued little group who met for breakfast at the long table under the windows in the staff dining room looked out on a scene of dampness and fog.

There was almost no conversation on this drab morning. Barbara Simmons was busy with thoughts of Charlie Fortuna as a possible escape route from the tedium and burdens of her life. She knew he was completely under her spell. He would take her away anytime she chose. But did he have enough money? How badly had he been hurt by the divorce settlement? He had potential, she knew, but was he possibly a little too flighty? Should she commit herself to his keeping? She took a dainty bite of buttered toast and continued her deliberations.

Wanda Simmons sat in silence, eating without tasting her food. A shimmer of excitement hovered just below the surface of her mind, but she kept a tight rein on it. Any flurry would rouse Glenda. She slowed her breathing and murmured soothing words in her mind. *Calm down. Don't rock the boat.*

Glenda Simmons was also eating in silence between her two sisters. She knew they were both in deep thought, she could feel the stirrings within their mental climates as the winds of change whispered around their consciousnesses. She could hear their questions and considerations. It was hard not to smile in secret superiority; how helpless they were before her. Of course, Wanda had always been open to her, but it was a new power to have Barbara's mind revealed so clearly.

She was just developing this telepathy that would work with anyone, not just Wanda. But it was real, she was discovering. Ever since the aliens had probed her mind during the long hours of Friday night and Saturday morning, Glenda had recognized a new, untrained but very real ability.

Her mind moved down the table. Isabel Nebo. A jumble of thoughts—anger against Charlie, the new dress for Saturday night—a jumble, but not closed from Glenda. She sent a sly tentacle toward Vincent Ponder; she could read him . . . something about his music; how much would he lose if he built walls around himself against the intruders? His mind was not as open as her sisters' but neither was it silent.

She peered down the table—who was next? Joshua Kingston. Her mind withdrew quickly from that front. Glenda had no wish to tangle with him. She quit playing with her new talent for the time being.

Sue Dunn was experiencing something brand-new to her. At the moment she was feeling two diametrically opposed emotions. She was both supremely happy and deeply sorrowful. How could this be?

On one hand she sat encased in a bubble of joy, a shimmering, shining, sparkling orb of lightness and peace. All her life she had accepted disappointment and broken promises as being normal; nothing ever quite lived up to one's expectations. Reality usually damped down her hopes.

This time it did seem different. She was in love with two people she had not known at all a month ago. First, Josh. What a surprise to discover this feeling for him! Then the second—the One Josh always referred to by His first name, Jesus. She had now met Him as a Person and felt His love for her. And it was strange: while she wasn't at all sure how Josh felt toward her, she was completely sure of Jesus.

Yet there was sorrow, too. Josh would be leaving. He said he wouldn't leave her there at Brookshire, but those words hadn't rung with Josh's usual conviction. And she didn't know how she could look ahead to next week, envision her life without him, and not dissolve in tears at the thought.

So she sat in total joy and total misery and ate her egg and whole wheat toast.

Charlie Fortuna was trying to think about Wallace Graham. It was a very critical case, and he should be giving it his full attention, but thoughts of Barbara Simmons kept intruding. Would she really leave with him? Would this satisfy the craving he had for her? Or make it even stronger? Had he gone beyond the point of making up his own mind about it?

Vincent Ponder sat next to Josh, his mind on one question. Until it was answered, he could make no decision or move in any direction. If he were freed from the hauntings of his mind, delivered from the intruders who came to him and wrote music through his faculties, what would he find as his own true talent?

A trough of low pressure had descended on the Brookshire Mountains and settled over the medical center complex like a hen squatting on her nest. From deep within this pressure zone came fog, rain and cold, casting a pall of depression on all the residents of the complex.

It was late Wednesday morning. Charlie, on a break, had just sugared his coffee and taken the first sip when his name was paged. He went to the telephone and spoke.

"Yes, Dr. Fortuna? This is Compton of Four South. Your patient in 411 is awake and very upset. He's demanding to see you right away."

Charlie hung up the phone and stood for a moment in thought. His combination of stimulants had roused Wallace Graham from his coma. A little surge of pride filtered in; the doctors at County Hospital had treated him for days without effect while Charlie had been in attendance only 24 hours. But his satisfaction was overshadowed by the annoyance of having to face an angry and ungrateful patient. He left his coffee and went directly to 411.

Wallace Graham was sitting up in bed, his body stiff with indignation. Compton, the nurse, stood with arms folded across her chest, face carefully neutral. *They always like to hang around when somebody's reaming out the doctor,* Charlie thought with annoyance.

"Just what in blazes do you think you're doing?" Wallace demanded in icy tones. His arm gestured wildly, indicating the equipment surrounding the bed, and Charlie noticed a trickle of blood from the infusion site on the inside of his elbow, all that remained of Wallace's fluid setup. "Who gave you permission to do all this?"

"You were dying!" Charlie protested. "I was just trying to save your life, for crying out loud!"

"You had no right to give me all of this. Fluids and drugs and God knows what all." As Wallace raged on, Charlie considered briefly the disquieting thought that he had no "Consent for Treatment" signed. Of course, a court order could always be obtained; the courts were almost invariably on the side of the doctor as opposed to the patient. Judges almost always allowed doctors to treat the unwilling. But it was still disquieting.

"O.K., we'll unhook all the stuff, now that you're awake," Charlie said.

"This is what I'm going to do," Wallace continued, almost as though he hadn't heard Charlie. "I'm going to get dressed . . . and incidentally, where are my clothes?" He paused and glared at the nurse. She opened the closet and brought forth a heavy paper sack ticketed with Wallace's name.

"Good," Wallace nodded. He climbed from the bed and took the sack from the nurse and ripped it open. He was a little unsteady and Charlie realized that Wallace's sudden change of posture after days in bed had probably dropped his blood pressure, but he said nothing. Wallace still looked neat and tidy, even in his short hospital gown. His legs were surprisingly thick, muscular and very hairy, almost as though they belonged to a different body.

"I'm going to dress; then I'm going to the trailer and pack my things; and finally, I'm going to get in my car and leave. And you can tell the Director of Nursing, you can tell the administrator, you can tell Dr. Nebo, you can tell Don Oliver Franklin for all I care, that if they leave me alone and don't try to stop me I may—I just may—decide not to sue you."

"Oh, come on now," Charlie said reasonably. "All we did was try to help you."

"Suppose I didn't want help? Suppose I was doing exactly what I wanted to do and it was none of your business?" Wallace's face was tight with rage, but he was making an effort to control himself. "I am legally an adult, I am a taxpayer and a registered voter and a freeholder in the state of Louisiana. I am not an incompetent nor an indigent, and you had no right to interfere with what I had chosen to do with my own body." He leaned forward and hissed at Charlie, "You didn't have *informed consent!*" As he stressed the final two words, Charlie took a step backward. That was lawyer talk.

"Fine. You go ahead." Charlie spoke to the nurse. "Miss Compton, get a release form ready: Discharge against medical advice."

"Forget it," Wallace countermanded. "I'm not signing anything." He took his sack of clothing into the bathroom and clicked the door shut firmly behind him.

"What'll I do?" the nurse asked. "He's not fit to be walking around or driving."

"Don't lay a hand on him," Charlie ordered. "Chart exactly what's happened and note the time he walks out. He's not a prisoner, you know. He has every right to walk out if he wants to."

A few minutes later Wallace burst from the bathroom

dressed and tidy. His hair was brushed and he looked just as he always had except possibly a little pale. "I'm leaving now," he said defiantly.

Charlie's voice was cheery. "Good luck."

"They won't find me this time!" Wallace's voice was grim. "I guarantee you that."

He walked to the door stiffly and Charlie shrugged. So much for that. He'd have to tell Don Oliver Franklin and the Project people, but it was no longer his responsibility.

At lunch the talk was all about Wallace and his angry departure. To Wanda Simmons, the fact that both LeRoi and Wallace had made sudden exits made for a wild new hope. She didn't know whether the strangeness that had haunted those two young men for so long had been left behind when they departed. Be that as it may, they had broken free and she was encouraged by the fact.

If she were also to be real and her own person, she must come out from under Glenda's dominion. As carefully as possible, Wanda made plans.

The rest of Wednesday was spent in routine testing. The twins took the Minnesota Multi-Phasic Personality test, and toward the end Wanda carefully withdrew her mind from communion with Glenda, marking her own answers without sharing. Undoubtedly their answers would still be identical but each had reached the decisions on her own. This was not totally without precedent, but it was unusual. Glenda said nothing.

After dinner at the hospital dining room the twins walked back to their trailer; Bebe would be watching television and they'd fallen into the habit of joining her. It was at this time of day, with her stomach full of food and her mind diverted by television, that Glenda was weakest, the controlling spirits within her somnolent and placid.

They entered the trailer and took off their jackets. Their

sister looked up without smiling as they took seats together on the couch. The dogs whined their greeting.

"You get wet?" Bebe asked.

"It's not raining now," Wanda responded.

"Why don't you look out the window, Bebe?" Glenda asked sarcastically.

They sat in silence through the first scenes of the program; a commercial came, then the story began again. Glenda had been sucked into a total absorption with the story line when Wanda made her move. She rose slowly from the couch and spoke softly. "Come on, Pollux. Let's go outside."

The dog raised his head and looked at her. His expression was almost comical as he looked back and forth from Wanda to Glenda, then at his own twin as though to say, "Just us, Boss? Not them?"

"I want to go outside, Pol, come on."

Glenda said nothing but Barbara looked up from the screen. "Don't get wet," she said.

Pollux put his chin on his outstretched paws and watched Wanda with bright eyes. She opened the door and snapped her fingers at him, her call more urgent. "Come on, Pol!" Suddenly it seemed to her that this was the battle in microcosm: a sign of the way things would go. If she could entice Pollux away from Castor, separate these two Gemini twins, then it would be an omen that she could separate herself from her sister's control and become an individual entity.

She watched in rising hope as Pollux rose to his feet, stretched and walked toward her. She opened the door to let him out, heart pounding with victory. As she started out behind Pollux, she heard Castor rising also, and he pushed by her to go outside. She gritted her teeth in frustration but said nothing. Glenda seemed unaware of the activity.

Wanda closed the door behind her and took a seat in one of the redwood chairs on the concrete slab. It was cold and windy, the sky gray with scudding clouds of darker gray.

299

The dogs walked around the yard from tree to tree. *Well, I'm outside*, she thought stoutly. *And nobody said anything.*

It was then that the first cold, slimy tendril of thought from Glenda's mind found her. It was arrogant, harsh, compelling: Glenda at her worst.

Come inside.

No, Wanda's mind rebelled. *I want to stay out here.*

You'd better not try anything. They won't put up with it.

Wanda was suddenly afraid, afraid of being defeated and going back into the same trap as before. And even more afraid of something else, something she couldn't define but which she had sensed in Glenda ever since her Zoran encounter. She knew there was more involved now than just a battle of wills with her twin sister.

She knew Glenda was rising from the couch and walking into the kitchen.

I don't need you anymore. Glenda was aloof now, haughty, contemptuous of Wanda. *It was all right when you helped and made it stronger, but if you are trying to make it weaker, we don't need you.*

Glenda was opening a drawer in the kitchen cabinet, withdrawing a long, sharp knife. A feeling of unbelief overwhelmed Wanda and she made a violent protest.

Glenda! What's the matter with you? What are you doing?

The front door opened and Wanda could see with her eyes what had been obvious to her mind. Glenda walked down the steps carrying the knife, her face closed and expressionless. Castor gamboled up to jump and wiggle before her, to lick the slightly soiled hand of his mistress. She paid no attention to him.

Wanda stood up and stared with horror as her sister walked toward her. *Glenda!* her mind screamed, but there was no answer now. *Bebe!* Wanda tried to vocalize her cry for help but her throat was closed and no sound came forth.

You're trying to make it weaker, Glenda accused her in fury. *They won't stand for that!*

It should have been an even battle; they were almost

exactly the same size and strength. But it wasn't. There was really no battle at all.

Glenda slashed out with the eight-inch carving knife and opened Wanda's abdomen as neatly as a surgeon. Death came within minutes. Wanda made no defense and no outcry. Her strength ebbed rapidly as her blood gushed forth, and as she grew weaker, Glenda grew stronger. The last thought Wanda heard was, *That'll teach you!*

Discovery came as Barbara investigated the howling of the dogs. Then she collapsed in a faint as she saw that Wanda was dead.

Malcolm Brown approached Don Oliver Franklin's office with his stomach a hot, angry knot of pain, and he realized suddenly that this was his usual reaction to a summons from the great man. Franklin was his friend; why should an early-morning call to his office frighten Malcolm?

He opened the door and stepped into a room vibrating with tension. Dr. Isabel Nebo stood looking out the window, smoking furiously, her posture rigid and tight. She turned her head as he entered and Brown was shocked at the furrowed age lines etched on her face.

Joshua Kingston was seated in one of the twin chairs that faced the fruitwood desk. His head was bowed and his large, strong hands were clasped in his lap. He, too, glanced up at the chaplain and his face was etched with pain. Only Franklin was his usual benign self.

"Come in, Mal, and have a seat. We have a little problem here and I thought the four of us should discuss it and determine the best plan of action for the hospital. Then we can make suggestions to the authorities."

Malcolm took a seat next to Josh and waited.

"Last night Glenda Simmons killed her sister. Wanda's body is in the morgue, Glenda is in the locked ward on Eight Central and their sister Barbara has been heavily sedated." He turned to Isabel and asked, "Someone is with her, I suppose?"

The psychiatrist responded without turning from the window. "Yes. Dr. Charles Fortuna is there."

"Are we liable, Don Oliver?" the chaplain asked.

"The boys in Administration think probably not. But we need to decide what's the best step, and quickly. Mr. and Mrs. Simmons have been notified and are on their way here."

"Glenda needs to be transferred to the state hospital," Dr. Nebo said flatly. "Our facility here is for short-term, acute-care cases. We're not set up to handle anything like this. At least move her over to Children's."

Franklin turned his whole body to address Isabel's back and his tone was grave. "That wouldn't solve the problem. Children's is still part of the medical center. I think the state hospital is better."

Isabel turned to him and stretched out her hands pleadingly "I had her under professional observation. I should have known. I'm so sorry."

"Do you have any comments, Dr. Kingston?"

"What do you want me to say?" Josh asked. "I can understand how you feel—ship her out, get rid of the problem. But maybe we ought to assume some moral responsibility and try to heal some of the damage we've caused."

"You think we caused this?" Isabel asked stiffly.

"Certainly," Josh responded. "You think this would have happened if they'd stayed home?"

"We really don't know," Isabel said, shaking her head. "They were very unstable, have been for years."

"And you dug and pried and stirred up all the forces in them, and this is the result," Josh said bitterly.

"You should be very sure your own skirts are clean before you begin accusing others," Malcolm interposed. "I don't see that you offered any great help, either."

Josh opened his mouth to speak, then stopped.

A silence fell and the chaplain spoke into it cautiously. "How is Glenda? Has anybody talked to her?"

"The officers took a very short statement, then security took her to Eight Central. Her older sister was quite hysterical and it seemed wise to separate them." Franklin turned back to Josh. "You have no further advice, Dr. Kingston?"

"You don't really want to hear what I have to say," Josh answered.

Malcolm Brown spoke up, anxious to demonstrate the difference between himself and Kingston. "I'd like to visit Glenda, see if I can offer her some comfort. Will you arrange it, Dr. Nebo?"

As Isabel walked to the desk and lifted the telephone, Josh suddenly turned to the chaplain and spoke in harsh and bitter tones. "What in blazes do you think you can offer that child? She's so full of demons there's almost nothing left of her, and you'll try to minister to her without even believing in them. And probably without really believing in God." He flung himself out of the chair, his dark, narrow face etched with new lines of pain. "You'll go up there and spout your little platitudes and she'll stay just the same. She needs *deliverance!* Not counseling or drugs or that ungodly collection of human wisdom called psychiatry!"

Malcolm's face was pale, but he rose with dignity and nodded to Isabel. "Make the arrangements, please. I'd like to see her."

As Isabel spoke softly on the phone to Eight Central, Josh leaned over Franklin's desk. "I wish I could tell you what to do, but I only know one solution to any human problem, and that's the healing power of Jesus Christ. If the idea of using Him is tossed out, then I have nothing else to offer."

He left the room without waiting for an answer.

Isabel hung up the phone and nodded to the chaplain. "You may see Glenda whenever a visit fits into your schedule. Maybe you can help her."

Malcolm felt a sudden rush of optimism. The insufferable Dr. Kingston had given up and Dr. Nebo had no confidence in her ability to solve Glenda's problem. Maybe now the Project would see and appreciate the worth of one Dr. Malcolm Brown. It would be a great feat to succeed where those two had failed. He maintained his expression of kindly concern and patted Isabel's shoulder. As he walked toward the door, his mind intent on the choice of an opening gambit, Don Oliver Franklin spoke again.

"Be sure you're at the little dinner party Saturday night, Mal. In the light of this problem, it's very important that we present a united front."

Dr. Nebo's mouth opened in surprise but she said nothing. Malcolm understood her concern; all the psychics except Vincent were gone now, but they both knew Franklin would have his way and the party would take place as planned.

"I'll notify the administrator that Glenda is to be moved to the state hospital as soon as possible. We can trust Dr. Fortuna to handle Barbara, I suppose."

Chaplain Brown nodded. If Glenda were to be moved soon, he might have only one opportunity with her, one chance to succeed where both psychiatry and Bible-toting Christianity had failed.

He left, tense with excitement.

Effie looked at the big wall clock. 2:15. Good, only one hour more to go. The death of Wanda Simmons was hanging heavy over all of Brookshire. The toll from that strange, fatal malady was now at seven, the tension and fear caused by those deaths growing. Everybody was defensive, upset, disturbed by the mystery as much as by the deaths. And this tension was a background for a multitude of errors, problems, delays, frustrations and the usual heavy workload.

She was just starting her charts, seated at the counter in the nurses' station, when she felt a hand on her shoulder.

"I need to talk to you."

She looked up to see Josh Kingston. His serious face was tightened with pain and his eyes were haunted with distress.

Without a question she set the charts aside and rose from her seat. "Let's go where we can be alone," she said quietly. She walked down the hall toward the linen closet. Almost certainly it would be deserted at this hour.

They shut the door behind them and Effie turned to him in concern. "What now?" For nearly fifty years, family, friends, patients and relative strangers had found comfort and peace through Effie MacAllister. It wasn't an unusual thing to have a distressed, pained young man turning to her for help, but it was unusual for the needy soul to be such a famous one as Josh.

"Wanda's murder by her twin sister is a shock, but I knew something like this was going to happen. And more of the same will happen before it's over. Yet nobody listens to me." Josh's voice was as agonized as his face.

"You've done all you could."

Josh brushed off her comfort. "I know it's not my fault. When light's been given and people reject it, then this kind of thing happens. But it's such a waste! And it hurts the Lord. He loves them."

"You look like it hurts you, too."

"Anything that hurts Jesus hurts me. I'm ready now to get out of this place before judgment falls."

"Judgment? On Brookshire?"

"Yes. We've had a Day of Visitation. After that comes the judgment."

Effie was shifting from one foot to the other, easing her sore legs, but the sudden quickening of her spirit drove away the awareness of discomfort. "You know, my boys

305

have been after me to leave here. But this has been my place of work so long I just can't imagine leaving."

"I think you ought to leave," Josh said firmly. "Why would you stay?"

"The reason I started here in the first place—to help people. To try and make it better. Isn't that what we're here for? To make things better?"

"No!" he thundered. "Jesus didn't come to make the world system better. He gave us reality instead of the system, which is a counterfeit."

"What system? What counterfeit? I don't understand you. Doesn't God want to heal people?"

"This whole medical system is a counterfeit of divine healing. It's actually a false god, setting itself up as a healer. It's a counterfeit of Jehovah Rapha, 'The Lord who healeth thee.' It's not godly, it's worldly, Egyptian. And the Bible says the Lord mingled a perverse spirit in Egypt. No wonder it doesn't work."

Effie stared at him as though he were deranged. All thoughts of her aching feet, her unfinished charts, the lateness of the hour, were gone. She forgot even where she was; she had to understand this strange young man and his startling ideas.

"God's early people never had doctors," he continued. "They had priests. The medical system started in Egypt and Babylon. That ought to tell you something. The system has never had faith in God as a healer. It teaches people to have faith in the system as a healer. Look at Asa in II Chronicles. He was lame and went to physicians instead of to the Lord and he died."

Josh paused for breath and Effie spoke quickly. "Even if the whole medical system is of the world, corrupt as you say, God would still want some of us Christians here in the system to help the sick and wounded."

Josh shook his head. "What about alcoholics who can't stop drinking? Does God want Christian bartenders and cocktail waitresses to tend to them?"

"It's not the same thing," Effie said with quiet dignity. This strange, wild-haired young man was so different from the quiet, gentle pastor of her church. *He's like an Old Testament prophet*, she thought.

"There is no way you can make this system holy," he said more quietly. "No matter how many Christian doctors and nurses you bring in, you can't take a system based on the belief that man heals, which operates from motives of greed and fear as much as from motives of helping people, which dedicates itself by an oath to false gods, which uses drugs when God has forbidden the use of drugs, which is now engaged in legalized, sanctioned killing of unborn children. . . . You can't make that system holy. Read in Haggai what happens when a holy thing touches an unclean thing. Does the holy thing make the unclean thing holy? No! The unclean thing contaminates the holy thing. And I didn't say that, God did!"

Effie felt almost assaulted by the words. Her chin was quivering and she was fighting back tears. She was so tired, so frustrated by the workload and the intolerable strains added to that workload, and now this all-out attack on what she had spent most of her life doing.

"The Lord has placed me here to serve Him," Effie finally answered. "I will stay here until He tells me to leave."

Josh stared at her for a long moment. "I'm sorry. Bless your heart, you were just minding your own business out there and I came to get a sympathetic ear and maybe a prayer partner and it turned into a sermon. And one you didn't want to hear, I know. I'm sorry."

"No, don't apologize. I think you were supposed to tell me all those things. I really do. I need to go back to the Word and be sure that God still wants me here. And I think it helped you to sound off." She took his hand. "I will be your prayer partner. Let's pray that God will clean out the evil here. Expose the corruption. Kick Satan out."

Josh smiled at her. "I can sure pray for that."

It was 7 p.m. when Sue walked slowly toward Josh's trailer, wondering at the roller-coaster flow of her emotions. Tuesday night had been sheer exhilaration. Wednesday night had been a continuation of talk with Josh at a deep, satisfying level until interrupted by that moment of horror—the killing of Wanda. Since then a series of incidents had numbed her.

She knocked on Josh's front door. He opened it at once, his face not disguising his eagerness to see her.

"Are you still in a state of shock?" he greeted her.

Sue nodded without answering. He took her coat and led her to the sofa. "I didn't have time to fix much for dinner. Hope a cold platter will be O.K. I did get you one extra little fillip."

"What's that?"

"Later—when we eat."

Josh's face was haggard, Sue noticed, and a flicker of tenderness stirred within her. What an ordeal they had all been through! But for the first time in many days Sue found it difficult to talk to Josh. Her thoughts were so jumbled. How was she to sort them out?

"You seem almost lifeless, Sue. What else has happened today?"

Sue looked at him with a wan smile. "Let's eat first. Then talk."

Josh brought in a platter of coldcuts, some cole slaw and potato chips. When Sue was seated, he placed a juice glass in front of her, went to the kitchen and returned with a bottle of white wine.

"Josh, this is a surprise!"

"I knew you liked wine." He filled her glass, obviously pleased by her reaction.

"Where's your glass?"

"You know I don't touch alcohol, Sue."

The joy left Sue's face. She started to reply, then checked herself. Josh went back to the kitchen to pour himself a glass

308

of milk. He returned with it, seated himself, bowed his head and blessed the food.

"It's my understanding that Jesus drank wine," Sue said finally.

"That's true, although it was probably unfermented grape juice."

"Do you really believe that?"

Josh looked uncomfortable. "It's not worth arguing about. I made a decision years ago not to touch alcohol."

"I wouldn't for a minute try to change your mind, Josh. You have a right to your convictions. It's just that—" Sue's voice trailed off.

"Just that what?"

"You always come across as so self-righteous."

Josh stared at her for a moment. "You're in a foul mood, Sue. What happened today?"

Sue sighed, then pushed her plate away, the food hardly touched. "A lot of depressing things, Josh. Several affect us and our relationship."

"Like what?"

"Like the talk I had with Isabel this afternoon. She's never been a booster of yours, Josh. Today she was so mad at you she could hardly talk."

"Everything is coming unglued with Project Truth, including Isabel."

"What she had to say concerns an encounter you had with Malcolm Brown today."

"I was sort of rough on him," Josh conceded.

"Why?"

"Because he was going to try to minister to Glenda Simmons when he was totally unqualified to do so."

"Josh, he's the hospital chaplain."

"He's an incompetent."

"He's a respected pastor and author. He tries to do his job. You blasted into him and, according to Isabel, accused him of not believing in God."

"I don't think he does."

"Who are you to judge? Are you God? Why are you so obnoxious, Josh? Do you want everyone to hate you?" Tears suddenly welled up in Sue's eyes.

Josh looked down at his plate and went on eating.

Sue regained control of herself and continued, "I did the best I could to calm Isabel. I explained how upset everyone is over Wanda's death—"

"You don't have to defend me to these people," Josh interrupted.

"I know that, but I do anyway."

"Well, stop doing it."

"You really are a loner, aren't you, Josh?"

"I guess so. If the Lord gives me a job to do, I do it."

"And trample people in the process."

"If necessary, yes. But go on—you said there were several incidents."

Sue took a deep breath. "There was one more. I had a talk with Effie MacAllister just as she was going off duty. You managed to upset her, too."

"I just told her she should leave Brookshire before she got hurt."

"You did more than that. You dumped your total hatred of the hospital system onto her and left her feeling wretched."

"I like Effie. She is a real Christian and I hate to see her smashed."

"Josh, I think your attitude toward hospitals is warped. Granted, most are poorly run. Granted, the medical profession is more concerned with making money and protecting itself than caring for people. Granted, the killing of babies is a horror. But that's no cause to wipe hospitals off the face of the earth. If you had a ruptured appendix, your only chance is a hospital operation; if you were seriously injured in a car wreck, your only chance would be emergency treatment in a hospital."

310

"I don't necessarily agree," interrupted Josh. "I think I'd prefer asking God to heal me rather than trust Brookshire."

"All right, let's say you'd do that," Sue continued evenly. "But most Christians don't have that kind of faith. Their only hope is the hospital and the skill of some doctor. They have no other alternative. You can't just write off all hospitals because they're imperfect. We live in an imperfect world. Churches are imperfect. All Christians are imperfect, including you."

"Especially me," Josh said calmly. "I never claimed perfection. But I hate evil and I see it running rampant in hospitals."

"So you want to pull out all the Effie MacAllisters so that things will be even worse. Why, Josh? Why? She's doing good; she's committed to helping people, even if many other nurses and doctors and technicians aren't."

Josh got up from the table and began to carry the dishes into the kitchen. Sue sighed again and arose to help him. They didn't speak for several minutes until the table had been cleared.

"Want me to wash the dishes?" Sue asked.

"No. Let's continue talking." He switched off the kitchen light and led Sue back to the living room couch. "Why are you so worked up about all this?" he asked.

"It's been building, Josh. I've given twelve years of my life to hospital work. Despite all that's wrong with the system, I feel it's where I belong."

Josh was shaking his head. "There's more to it than that, Sue. I've come to know you pretty well. You're not wedded that much to your hospital work."

Sue felt the tears coming again and struggled for control. "You do know me well, Josh, and you're right; there is more to it." Long sigh. "I'm not good at doubletalk so I'll—I'll be honest. I love you, Josh. That's why I want to defend you. That's why I've dared to have hopes about us for the future. I built a new world for myself and you, a beautiful world.

Well, it all crashed down around my ears today. I don't know when it happened—just before I came here tonight, I guess. But I saw clearly that you had built a world for yourself and there was no room in it for a person like me. Effie gave me the key. She said you were an Old Testament type prophet come to warn people to repent—or be consumed. I guess that's true."

Josh nodded. "She's right. I'm called to battle here and I can see why it's frightening to you."

"I admit I'm scared, Josh." She gulped. "If you would be a little more normal it would make all the difference."

"And drink wine with you."

"That's not it so much. It's more to do with the way you deal with people."

"Be nicer, you mean?"

Sue sat back on the couch and closed her eyes. "It was hard for me to say these things, but I had to. Something inside compelled me. You're a great man in many ways, Josh, and I'm sure it takes someone as hard as you to battle all these evil spirits. I wish I could help you, really help you. I'll die inside when you leave here, but I know that's the way it's got to be."

Josh was silent, his face inscrutable. When Sue arose slowly, he got up, too, and stared at her. "So you really came tonight to say goodbye."

"We'll see each other again before you go."

Josh retrieved her coat and helped her into it. The tears didn't come in a flood until she was back in her own trailer.

Malcolm Brown awoke Friday morning with a firm resolution. He would make his visit to Glenda Simmons the first order of business. He drove to Brookshire, parked his car and walked smiling into the front entrance.

The elevator took him to the eighth floor, and while being passed into Eight Central through the locked doors and red tape, his mind was busy. He would not make the mistake

Isabel Nebo had made of offering nothing beyond the human realm. Kingston was right about that; it almost never really worked. But neither did he plan to insist that God alone would be sufficient. That would be the other extreme. For while man did need God occasionally, Malcolm felt it was wrong to say that he needed only God.

A combination of the two viewpoints was needed, and he, Malcolm Brown, would merge the two into a reasonable, effective combination. Glenda needed a mixture of divine and human succor.

Glenda sat alone in a locked room, a bare cell without windows and very plain furniture. She was sitting on the floor in a far corner, dressed in a shapeless blue garment. She looked up as the door opened and he walked toward her with a friendly smile.

"Hello, Glenda. Remember me?" he said. "I'm Dr. Brown."

"I know who you are," Glenda said, her voice deep and throaty. "Paul we know, and Jesus we know, and we've heard about you."

"Well, I'm here to help you." He felt uncomfortable standing, so he reluctantly took a seat on a chair opposite her. "This isn't very pleasant here, is it?"

"Sitting on a cold floor will crucify the flesh and give you hemorrhoids," Glenda responded.

"Would you like to talk?" he asked, embarrassed. "It must be lonely in this room all by yourself."

"Oh, bug off!" Glenda snapped, her voice even deeper and less childlike. "If we get lonely, we can talk to ourselves." She laughed then, and the sly, impish thing that had hidden behind her words was more open. "We all fellowship together. You know what fellowship is? A bunch of fellows in the same ship. That's us, all in a ship. Rub-a-dub-dub . . . a bunch of us in a tub . . . She is a little tubby, isn't she? A ship is a tubboat, a tugboat. . . ."

The chaplain stared at Glenda uncertainly. Was she joking, teasing with her bizarre patterns of speech, or was she insane? He watched her through narrowed eyes and she continued her confabulation.

"Tub, tub, rub-a-dub-dub . . . tubby little boat full of all us fine fellows." She stopped suddenly and peered at him slyly. "You don't even know who we are, do you? Josh said you didn't know. Josh, Josh, by gosh, big old Josh comes from Oshkosh. But he does know." She giggled like a little girl, then her voice dropped back to its former deep tone. "He knows but nobody believes him. You don't, do you?"

"How do you know what Dr. Kingston said to me, Glenda? Can you read his mind like you did Wanda's?" It occurred to him that it might be a mistake to mention Wanda, but Glenda hardly noticed.

"Oh, we keep a very close eye on Dr. Kingston. Dr. Joshua Kingston: award-winning-author-and-all-around-fink. We know what he does." Suddenly Glenda stood up and started clapping her hands rhythmically. "Rain, rain, go away, come again some other day, little fellows want to play." She stopped and peered at him, and for the first time spoke in her own voice. "Can you take me out of here? I don't like it in this place. They won't let me watch television."

"I think you'll have to stay here a little longer, Glenda." She was walking around her cell-like room and he twisted to follow her with his eyes. He felt very uncomfortable if she were behind him. "Is there anything else I can do for you?"

"You can go to the devil." She snapped this in anger, then hooted with laughter. "That's funny, isn't it? But it's later than you think. It's stronger than you stink. You're blinder when you blink." Her voice chanted on in a singsong and he was totally at a loss to respond.

She sat down again, closer to him, and murmured confidentially, "I'm going to tell you my name. I know yours and it's only fair for you to know mine. Now don't tell anybody but this is my name." Her eyes were large and blank, staring into his with diabolical glee. "My name is *Madness*."

She leaned closer and closer to him. "Do you want to know your name? Your names, rather?"

He leaned as far away from her as he could and for the first time felt a chill of fear. She was, after all, a murderer. She wasn't very hefty for her age, but he'd always heard the insane were inhumanly strong. What if she grabbed him? He stood up and began to edge away from her, moving surreptitiously.

"You're named Dull and Useless and Lukewarm and Self-Righteous and Proud. Those are the names of some of the cousins. But maybe the main name is Pharisee. O ye hypocrites, vipers, woe unto you!" She threw back her head, opened her mouth and howled like a dog. Malcolm was covered with gooseflesh and his heart was now pounding in fear. She dropped her head and peered at him again, sly and secretive. "Do you realize that all you've ever done is useless? It was all vanity, vanity! Wood, hay and stubble which will burn! Vanity!"

The chaplain jumped up from the floor and began pounding on the door, calling loudly to the nurse. Glenda laughed in glee, her voice a cackle of derision. As he was ushered out and sped down the hall away from her, he could hear her scornful words: "Lukewarm, lukewarm. Vanity, vanity!"

He passed through the locked doors almost without noticing, and found himself in the hall. There he staggered like a blind man, seeking solitude to think, to adjust to the attack, but there were people all around. Two reporters had got wind of the murder and were trying to gain entrance through the locked doors; a tall, officious security guard was countering their plans with a firm tone. A psychiatric aide was pushing along a wheeled cart containing fruit juice and other nourishments. Malcolm stumbled away down the hall and without thinking turned down the south hall and entered the testing rooms that the Project had used for psychic investigations.

Isabel replaced the phone on Don Oliver Franklin's desk and gave him a relieved smile. "Well, we don't have to face them," she said gratefully. "They're going right to the State hospital at Parkland."

She had just spent a very uncomfortable half-hour on the phone with Mr. and Mrs. Simmons. All the delicate, involved plans were made concerning the shipment of Wanda's body, the various contingencies in case the coroner's inquest didn't go as predicted, and when and how Barbara would meet them at the state hospital at Parkland. It was all settled and Isabel had several pages of notes in her large, untidy scrawl.

"They really took it well," she continued. "Very calm. Almost too calm."

"Possibly they were relieved," Don Oliver Franklin suggested.

"That's quite likely," she answered, not at all shocked by his suggestion that the Simmons felt no grief over losing two daughters so traumatically. "Those two girls must have been a dreadful burden for years."

"We've been fortunate," he continued. "It appears there will be no trouble from the family, probably no difficulty with the authorities if they do as they have indicated they will, and Hal Givens assures me it will be played down in the media. Miss Barbara Simmons is evidently going to be sensible about things, like her parents. All in all, we have been most fortunate."

Isabel nodded. Most fortunate.

The anteroom was deserted and Malcolm Brown passed through into one of the inner offices used by the Project for testing. It was also deserted. He sat at one of the tables and rested his head in his hands, shuddering still from fear at the venom of Glenda's attack.

That filthy little brat, he breathed, hoping to drive away fear by increasing his fury. But over it all, over the fear and anger and embarrassment and the knowledge of failure, was the horrible suspicion that he had been wrong.

Like a bilious, gibbous sun rising from dark, roiling clouds in a sickly sky, there rose in his mind the unwelcome thought that all his life and ministry he had been wrong in his convictions. He knew now that Kingston had been right about one thing. The creatures that had addressed him from Glenda's mouth were not merely abnormalities of her personality, not just the evidence of a human distortion. He had been conversing with an evil, alien spirit, possibly many of them. Was this error typical of his whole ministry? Had all the books, the sermons, the counseling, been off target? He shook his head from side to side to escape the bright glare from this hideous new sun inside him.

And if Kingston had been right about this, he must be right about all of it: Yes, it had come out of Glenda's mouth, too, in undeniable reality: he was Useless, Vain, Proud, Lukewarm, totally without value to himself or his fellow man. Josh Kingston on the one hand and the evil spirits on the other had agreed on this. Malcolm Brown was a failure.

The call came again from inside himself, insistent as always. This time he would obey.

He rose on shaking knees and walked to the window. He couldn't raise it; it had been locked for years and had been repeatedly painted shut. And it was very difficult to break the glass, which was one solid, heavy pane with chicken wire meshed within its glass. But he lifted the chair and struck the glass until it did eventually break.

Then he climbed up on the windowsill and stood a long moment, looking down the eight stories to the pavement. He could see the tops of the trees all around, dulled by the dreary weather but still colorful. He lifted his eyes and looked at the cloudy gray sky and could see no sign of the sun. He sighed in relief.

It would all be over now, all the efforts without gain, all the trials without rewards, all the battles without victory. He balanced himself delicately on the windowsill with one hand on either side. Then he closed his eyes, took a deep breath like a little child on a high diving board, and stepped off into nothingness.

"This place is cursed—or something!" Barbara Simmons stared at Isabel Nebo, pacing the living room of her trailer while she twisted her hands in distress. Her long nails were very red against the paleness of her hands. It was Friday afternoon and the news of the chaplain's death had sent new shock waves through the hospital.

"Wanda's dead. Glenda's crazy. Now Dr. Brown's dead, LeRoi and Wallace are gone. What else can happen?" Barbara turned to Isabel and demanded an answer.

Surprisingly, Isabel found herself reacting almost favorably toward Barbara. For the first time since she'd met her, Barbara was showing strong honest emotion. For the first time she seemed real to Isabel, a three-dimensional woman instead of a plaster doll with nothing inside.

"I don't know. I agree it seems more than a coincidence," Isabel replied.

"Did you hear what LeRoi said when he came to get his clothes?" Bebe asked. "He said something awful was going to happen to all of us! He prophesied!"

"Well, there's no reason for you to stay here, if you want to leave. Glenda doesn't need you anymore, and your father is planning to meet you Sunday night at the hotel in Parkland."

Barbara glared at Isabel, her blue eyes snapping in rage. "Why in blazes should I go to Parkland? There's nothing for me there!"

"I'm just passing along your father's instructions. What you do about it is your own affair."

"You know, there are two things I don't like: I don't like responsibility and I don't like being so bored I'm cross-eyed. If I go back to my folks, I'll just be asking for both. A dull job, living at home and having them criticize every guy

318

I date. I'm old enough to be on my own and I should have left home years ago."

Isabel watched her with interest, making professional observations. This pretty child had expressed no grief or concern about either Wanda's death or Glenda's breakdown. It seemed that one hundred percent of Barbara's interest was centered on Barbara.

Isabel arose from the table, leaving there the paper with the address of the hotel in Parkland. "I just came to give you the message and to express my sympathy and regret about your sisters. I certainly don't mean to be advising you in any way. You must do what you think is right."

"Yes," Bebe answered a little breathlessly. "I'll have to make up my own mind. But one thing's settled: I'm not going to Parkland or back to Wichita. If I can't do any better than that, I'll just shrivel up and die. I'd rather be dead than back in that old rut."

Strange choice of words, Isabel thought, considering the recent turn of events. She'd rather be dead. Better not tempt fate, Miss Bebe.

It was 3 p.m. and Charlie arrived breathless at Barbara Simmons' trailer. The urgency in her voice had translated itself into a summons: *Come.* He obeyed.

Bebe's hair was still damp from the mist and curlier than usual. She was wearing a nubby blue sweater with tight-fitting jeans and Charlie's eyes clung to her. He felt like a starving man outside a restaurant, breathing hard and fogging up the window.

"You heard about Reverend Brown?" she asked as he sat down next to her on the couch.

"Yes," he nodded. She was more emotional then he'd ever seen her, twisting her hands in agitation.

"I can't stand it here anymore," she was saying. "Bad

things are happening to everybody, just like LeRoi said. I feel like a curse or something is hanging over me."

She gripped Charlie's arm with her red-nailed hands. "I want to get away from here!"

"Is that an invitation?" Charlie asked, trying to keep his tone light.

"Yes! Let's go to California! Now! Tonight!" Bebe jumped up and began pacing the length of his living room. "We can just throw something into a suitcase and leave. Get away from this everlasting rain and cold."

"I can't leave tonight. I have to finish up the Project stuff. It's closing down, but I still have all their records to update, reports to write, statistics to file—"

"You don't have to do all that! Just leave it! You said you loved me and you'd take care of me. All right, get me away from here before anything else happens!"

"Bebe, please. I have a contract, responsibilities. I can't leave tonight; all my things are in the office at the hospital, my books and things. Plus there's the matter of money; I have to close out my bank account. . . ." Charlie was trying to plan as he spoke.

"We can use a credit card or something to get there, then you can write for your money and your equipment. And you can work out there; you're a doctor."

"Bebe, I'm not licensed to practice medicine in the state of California. That kind of thing takes a while. And it costs a fortune to set up a practice, unless I try to get on staff somewhere like I did here." He was standing now, trying to reach her with rationality and logic. "And I can't walk out on my commitment to Brookshire. You just don't do that."

Her heard himself with a mixture of amusement and contempt. *You can flop on the hook, Charlie,* he thought sadly, *but you're one fish that's caught.*

"O.K. then," Bebe said coldly. "I'll go by myself." She started toward the door, her slender body erect and stiff with anger.

"Where are you going to go?" Charlie asked. He caught

320

her and held her by the shoulders. "You going back to Wichita? Because I can wind up here in a few days and I'll drive there and pick you up. We can be married and leave from there for California."

Bebe stared up at him, eyes level and voice flat. "No."

"Look, be reasonable," he pleaded. "Can't you wait just a week or so, for crying out loud?"

"No. I don't intend to wait. And I don't intend to get married. I'm going to California; I'm leaving tonight, and if you won't take me I'll go by myself." Bebe turned from him and pulled her shoulders free. "Or I'll find somebody else, somebody who isn't tied to a silly old job."

Charlie stood for a moment in an agony of indecision, weighing the effects of abandoning his duties at the hospital against the effects of losing Bebe. The issue was never in doubt; he capitulated and took her in his arms again.

"All right, you win. We'll go tonight in my car. But I need a couple of hours; I have to pack, get somebody to take over things that are pending at the hospital. Two hours. Okay?"

Bebe smiled graciously, her perfect teeth gleaming behind her perfect lips; her perfect blue eyes sparkling. She rose on tiptoe to give him a perfect little kiss on the cheek. "Two hours," she agreed. "Then you pick me up at my place and we leave."

Charlie stumbled out the door, breathing hard. *It's over now,* he thought. *I've been landed, gutted, scaled and filleted. Charlie the Tuna is ready for tuna casserole.*

Sue returned to her trailer Friday night totally spent. Malcolm Brown's death had shocked her at a deep level, more so because of her confrontation with Josh the night before. She had gone through her afternoon responsibilities numbly, her face a frozen mask, avoiding conversation, especially determined not to run into Josh.

How had *he* taken it?

She might never find out. People were fleeing

Brookshire. Sue saw Charlie loading Bebe's bags in his car. Was he taking her home? Or away? Who was left? For all she knew Josh might be gone, too. The Project was a disaster. A catastrophe.

Sue picked at some food, cleaned up her kitchen and tried to read a magazine. Her mind wouldn't focus. She tried writing a letter. It was useless and she crumpled the sheet of stationery in her hand after one paragraph.

A return to the old life prior to Project Truth was before her. Last night she had looked forward to it, but tonight it seemed dismal. And lonely. Lonely.

In a panic she turned on television and forced herself to look at several programs. Then she glanced at her watch. 9:30. *Only 9:30!*

Well, she was tired so she would get a good night's sleep. A long shower relaxed her. She dried herself and reached for her old nightie on the hook behind the bathroom door. Then a thought struck her. She went to her bureau, rummaged among her lingerie in the second drawer and pulled out her new pink nightgown.

"If I'm going to be lonely, I'll do it in style," she said to herself, viewing her soft new purchase in the mirror. It did look good on her, she thought. A bit revealing, but so what?

Before turning out her light, she read two chapters in the Gospel of John. She had promised Josh she would study the New Testament. It was turning out to be anything but a chore.

Sleep was slow in coming. Her thoughts churned for at least an hour, then she dropped off.

"Sue." The voice was soft, urgent. She awoke with a start. "Sue, are you awake?"

The shadow of a man was standing in the doorway of her bedroom. For a moment she was frozen in fear.

Then she recognized him.

"Josh!"

"Yes. I must talk to you."

"How did you get in?"

322

"I have a key. Remember?"

Suddenly she did. Following the night of her terror a week ago, Sue had pressed her extra key on him in case he ever sensed again that she was beset by an assault of fear. He might need a key to get in if it was late at night. She reached over to her bedside table and switched on the light.

"I'm all right, Josh. But I'm grateful you came."

"Well, I'm not all right."

Sue looked closely at him and was shocked. His face was more haggard and drawn than she'd ever before seen it. His hair was a tousled mess. He had a bathrobe on over his pajamas and an overcoat over his bathrobe. He had on only one slipper. Concerned, she scrambled out of bed and went to him.

Josh put his arms around her, his body rigid, his face a mask. "I couldn't sleep. I kept seeing those pathetic eyes of his, those sad, pathetic hound-dog eyes seeking attention. But I had such contempt for him. He disgusted me and I showed it. I not only acted superior; I knew I was superior. I put him down and stomped all over him. I clobbered him. And then he went and committed suicide. Can you understand what I feel, Sue?"

"Yes."

"No, you can't. You're gentle and kind and loving and simple and clean. You care about people. You could never do to Malcolm Brown what I did to him. You're not made that way."

"I feel for you, Josh."

"Yes. I'm sure you're sorry for me. But that doesn't help me. Only God can help me. For I've committed the kind of sin that must disgust Him as much as Malcolm Brown disgusted me. I'm in agony, Sue. My spirit is in torment and the Lord has turned His back on me."

"How can you say that?"

"Because I know when His Spirit is with me and when He isn't. He's gone from me."

Sue was becoming alarmed now. The torment was real,

the suffering more intense than any physical pain she had ever witnessed. She had to do something to snap him out of it.

"Josh, let's go in the kitchen and get you something hot to drink."

"Food or drink won't help me." He stared at her, his face softening. "You must think I'm mad, busting in this way. I'm sorry to wake you, but I've been wrestling with my thoughts all evening. Finally I knew I had to talk to someone. And I realized something startling. I've achieved success and fame with my book; I've been on all the talk shows; and there's only one person I really enjoy talking to. You."

A flood of warm feelings flowed through Sue. She hugged him, then suddenly became aware of her sheer nightgown. "I'll put a bathrobe on and we'll go to the living room and talk," she said hastily.

Josh seemed hardly to notice. "Sue, I've gone through hell tonight and seen myself as never before. It's been ugly. I've prided myself on my discernment and wisdom and knowledge. God showed me how I looked—like a prancing horse, a sounding brass, a tinkling cymbal. Or even worse, a Pharisee! I have vaunted my position and power; I've been harsh, critical, unloving, contemptuous of others. That's not just weakness or error, Sue, that's sin. And God has left me."

They moved to the living room where he removed his overcoat. As they sat together on the couch, Josh continued to berate himself: "God once said 'A smoking flax I will not quench and a bruised reed I will not break.' All I've done here at Brookshire is quench flaxes and break reeds."

The tears came. Soon Josh's body was racked by sobs. Then came a chill and he began to shake. This was too much for Sue. She threw her arms around him.

"Josh, please. Let me get you a blanket."

He shook his head, but pulled Sue closer to him. "I think I'm all right now."

"Want to talk some more?"

324

"Yes. I need to unload, if you don't mind."

"Go right ahead." Sue snuggled closer into his arms.

Josh talked while Sue listened. His voice was quieter now and he began to reminisce about his boyhood. As the story rolled on, she was amazed at the pain and rejection Josh associated with his youth. No wonder he was so brusque with people, so defensive. It all poured out in a flood tide.

An hour went by, perhaps two. Sue was getting sleepy and Josh's voice had stopped. Was he asleep?

"I love you, Sue."

Startled, she looked up into his eyes. He was very much awake and pulling her head toward him. Tremors of excitement shot through her as he began kissing her. Suddenly she realized he did not intend to stop with just a kiss.

"No, Josh!"

Sue pulled away from him gently but firmly.

He straightened up in bewilderment. "Why did you stop me?"

"I was told to."

Josh stared at her, a mixture of emotions on his face. They arose from the couch and went into the kitchen where she poured each of them a glass of milk. Then the two sat down together at the table.

"Tell me exactly what you heard," Josh asked.

Sue took a drink of milk and chuckled. "First, you tell me what happened to your other slipper. You arrived here with only one, you know."

"I did?" Josh seemed surprised. He looked down at his bare feet.

"The other's gone, too."

"It's under the couch."

"Oh. Well, I must have lost it coming over here. I was pretty upset!"

"I know."

"I'm sorry I awakened you."

"I'm not."

"Tell me what the Voice said."

Sue smiled at him. "It wasn't a voice, actually. More like soft words dropped gently into my mind. To be honest, I wouldn't have stopped you otherwise."

Sue was almost startled by the change taking place in Josh. The haggard look was gone from his eyes, which stared intently at her.

"Josh, there is something else I almost hesitate to tell you."

"Don't, then, unless you're sure."

Sue was reflective for a moment. "Yes. I'm supposed to." She sighed. "The other words I heard were, 'He needs his strength.'"

Josh became excited. "Sue, don't you see what that means? He plans to use me again in the battle."

Sue's eyes were cloudy. "I guess so. But I don't like to think that I can subtract strength from you."

Josh's thoughts were elsewhere. "The truth is very humbling for me, Sue. God broke me tonight. He smashed my ego to pieces and showed me what a weak creature I am. He humiliated me before you. He not only exposed my weakness to you, He then gave you the strength to retrieve the situation."

"It's ludicrous for me to be strong and you weak," Sue said uncertainly.

Suddenly tears slid down Josh's cheeks again, though the excitement remained in his eyes. "He's back with me, Sue. I feel His Spirit in me. For some reason He finds me worth using again."

It was 2 a.m. when Sue kissed Josh tenderly at the door. She looked at the one slipper he carried in his hand, then at his bare feet, and shook her head. He may have the Spirit of God back in his life, but he surely did need her.

Josh had promised Sue he would meet her for an 8:30 breakfast in the staff dining room. She arrived on time, selected a small table, then dawdled over her tea and toast while she waited with tremors of excitement. He was twenty minutes late.

One look at Josh's face sent Sue's spirit plummeting. His eyes were bloodshot and pain-etched; deep crevices lined his forehead and cheeks; his hair looked like a shock of wind-tossed hay. He sat down without smiling.

"What's wrong now?" Sue cried.

There was misery in his look. "I couldn't sleep."

"Why?"

Josh didn't answer right away as he examined his bacon and eggs carefully before taking a bite. "Satan has been winning all the rounds, and now that we're down to the final confrontation, I'm not sure I'm ready for it."

"I don't think he's won everything." Sue's voice was strained. "What about last night?"

Josh nodded. "You're the only good thing to come out of this mess. Thank God for that."

"What about Vinnie?"

"He still could go either way."

"What do you mean about a final confrontation?"

Josh ate silently for a few minutes. "I think it's going to take place tonight, and I'm—" He didn't finish.

"You mean the dinner tonight hasn't been canceled?"

"It sure hasn't!"

Josh and Sue were startled by the intruding voice, then quickly made room for Isabel at their small table. The psychiatrist was dressed in a natty beige suit with a green scarf about her throat.

"Just three of us left? Where's Vinnie?" she asked.

"Probably sleeping in," suggested Sue. "The rest are all casualties, I'm afraid."

"Terrible about Chaplain Brown," Isabel said matter-of-factly.

"Anyone been to see Mrs. Brown?" Josh asked.

"She's handling it pretty well. Don Oliver called on her last night." Isabel paused. "Charlie resigned and is taking Bebe to California."

"She'll make his life miserable," Josh remarked.

Isabel looked at Josh carefully, then studied Sue's face. "You two planning something similar?"

"Not like that!" Josh's voice was abrupt, then it softened. "I think Sue should leave, though."

"Please wait until after tonight's dinner," Isabel said. "Don Oliver is determined to go ahead with that."

"With so few project people left, what will he say? How will he explain the terrible things that have happened?"

Isabel laughed mirthlessly. "Don Oliver will give a speech. I'll give a report and we'll conclude that Project Truth has greatly advanced scientific knowledge."

Josh snorted. "The operations were all successful. Unfortunately, the patients died."

Sue sat on one of the uncomfortable, high-backed benches under the bookcases in the medical library, once again trying to be inconspicuous, hoping her claustrophobia wouldn't rear up. Despite the fact that this emergency meeting of the Task Force had been called for a Saturday morning, the room was full. As before, Don Oliver Franklin opened with a few remarks and then turned things over to Carleton Phillips who had one new fact to present: the eighth death had occurred.

Once again there was the usual round of scientific questions and answers. To Sue, it was all futile. And then a strange new emotion stirred inside her. It startled her, scared her, but she couldn't shake it off.

She had something to say!

That's ridiculous. I have nothing of importance to bring before these learned people!

But the idea could not be squelched. It was there.

I'll stammer and stutter and forget what I want to say right in the middle of the sentence.

But the new inner Voice was quietly persistent.

The battle raged inside her as the administrator was fending off a suggestion that the hospital refuse all new patients for one week while a complete review of all procedures was made.

Sue raised her hand. The administrator nodded to her doubtfully.

"As a nurse I'm hardly qualified to offer any scientific suggestions to solve this problem," she began. "So I'll offer a spiritual suggestion instead. I think that evil forces have been let loose in this hospital. I think the answer is a new practice call exorcism . . . some call it deliverance. It's not really new, though. Jesus did it 2,000 years ago."

Everyone stared at Sue in astonishment. Most of the medical men looked pained. "Well, thank you, Miss, uh, Miss Dunn," said Mr. Phillips stiffly. "I don't think we want to get into that area."

He turned away from her to seek another question. Sue felt mortified. Why had she done it? She wanted to sink through the floor.

Then she heard another voice in the back. The new young head of pediatrics, Dr. John Bedford, was speaking. "I'd like to go back to Miss Dunn's comment. I think what she said is quite significant. I have felt the presence of something heavy and oppressive in this hospital ever since I arrived two months ago. I never could put my finger on it until Miss Dunn spoke. I would like to ask her to enlarge upon her statement, if she would."

The administrator was obviously annoyed. "Does anyone else really think there is anything to this idea of evil spirits at work in this hospital?"

"Yes . . . worth investigating . . . let's hear more." Six or eight people either spoke up or raised their hands.

Sue stared about her in utter amazement. Who were these people? Why had they kept silent for so long? Panic tore at her as the administrator nodded stonily in her direction. "Miss Dunn. They want to hear more. Better stand up so we can all see you."

Sue couldn't believe what was happening to her. What

could she possibly tell them? She flicked a glance at Don Oliver Franklin, hoping for a sign of encouragement. He was staring at her in surprise, as were the others she knew.

And suddenly she was completely calm. None of this was her doing, she knew, so she would just trust the inner Voice. For ten minutes Sue poured out the story of how only a few weeks before she had been as skeptical as anyone else about the supernatural world. Then she ticked off what had happened to her, to patients under her responsibility and to the people in Project Truth. She then made a strong plea that they look into the whole area of exorcism, referring to Josh Kingston. She was surprised at the fervor and passion of her words. When she sat down, a number of people were nodding their heads.

A firestorm of words followed as the chief medical men one by one loftily denounced Sue's idea. As one put it, "We don't want our hospital dropping to the level of some monastery in the Middle Ages." But Sue's remarks dominated the discussion for the next hour as questions were asked about Project Truth. At this point Sue expected Don Oliver Franklin to take over. She looked in his direction. His seat was empty.

The meeting ended in confusion and disorder, and as they filed out Sue felt herself the recipient of mixed reviews. But Dr. Bedford spoke to her warmly. "You're a Christian, aren't you?" he smiled.

"I sure am," Sue heard herself reply.

"Don't let them intimidate you," he said, patting her on the shoulder. "I'm with you one hundred percent."

Sue and Josh found Effie in the nurses' lounge where she was relaxing over a cup of tea. Effie stared at them in surprise. "I didn't expect to see you here this afternoon— especially you, Sue, after you tore into them at the Task Force meeting this morning."

"What was that?" Josh asked in astonishment as he and Sue sat down with Effie.

"Sue didn't tell you what she said at the meeting?" This time it was Effie who was surprised. "It's the talk of the whole hospital. No one can believe that the quiet, good-humored Miss Dunn has suddenly turned into a tiger. What have you done to her, Josh?"

Josh stared at Sue in amazement. Sue fought down her embarrassment. "I don't know what happened to me. I never talk at these meetings; in fact, I don't know why I'm invited. Today that inner Voice could not be ignored, but I'm afraid all I did was make a lot of people angry."

"You did that, Sue. But you got them talking and thinking. Some want a full investigation of Project Truth. And for the first time I've heard real criticism of Don Oliver Franklin."

"That's significant," mused Josh.

"Even more significant is that I've uncovered a Christian at the top echelon," Sue interjected. "Dr. Bedford, head of pediatrics."

"I know him and I like him," exclaimed Effie. "But I didn't realize he was a Christian."

"Well, he is, and I think there are others we don't know about," Sue continued. "I was amazed at how many of the Task Force were open to the ideas I presented."

"You presented ideas?" asked Josh.

"They asked me to stand up and enlarge on my statement. I told them about deliverance, Josh, and about you. They didn't throw me out although I know some of the top medical people wanted to."

Josh sat there, shaking his head. "It always amazes me the way God works."

"Well, He's going to do something about this hospital," Effie added. "He has to or it will become a disaster area."

"It is already, Effie," Josh said firmly. "God doesn't usually restore and redeem a corrupt place or a sick society. He destroys them. Like Sodom and Gomorrah. And those pagan countries promised to the Israelites. You and Sue may think God will heal the medical system, but I don't. It's too corrupt."

"What should Christians do who are in it?" asked Effie.

"They should get out."

Sue shook her head. "I can't agree, Josh, but I understand your position better now. You're a modern prophet and I would never want to change that in you. I guess it's your role to call attention to corruption in the medical system. It will start people thinking. And if enough people get concerned about something that is wrong, the next step could be action to change it."

"It goes deeper than that," Josh replied. "Medicine is just one part of the cosmos, the world system. There are seven parts to this system: government, commerce, education, medicine, religion, the arts and science. The only one we're told to accept is govenment; we are supposed to submit to the government. But these seven parts are the world's substitute for things we're supposed to be getting from God.

"In the Bible God tells us over and over again that *He is the answer to our every need.* The world system was set up by Satan to counterfeit this, to make God unnecessary. Then Satan divided the system into these seven areas, which are nothing but a substitute for the seven special things God says He is. Like this whole medical system is nothing but a counterfeit for Jehovah-Rapha, 'I am the One who healeth.' And the system of commerce and banking is a substitute for Jehovah-Jirah, 'I am the One who provides.' The religious system, which isn't of God at all, is a substitute for Jehovah-Tsidkenu, 'I am thy righteousness.' And the system of education. . . ."

Sue shook her head in amazement as once again Josh was off and soaring like an eagle, his ideas and insight so far beyond her that she was left behind, limping and gasping. She wanted to reach out and smooth back the unruly black hair, and caress the intense, passionate face, but she could only stare at him in empathy.

"Every one of these satanic counterfeits is based on the same lie," Josh continued. "They have the same father—Satan. And they have the same purpose—to deceive, to deny the Bible and the gospel of Jesus Christ, to dethrone God and put man on the throne instead . . . in short, to counterfeit the Kingdom of God with a man-made system."

Josh wound up his monologue as Effie rose to go back on duty. She paused a moment before leaving and stared at Josh and Sue in a motherly way. "You two could make a good team; I hope you realize it."

"I realize it," Sue smiled. Josh was silent.

As Effie turned to go, Sue took her by the elbow. "I'm putting together a list of several other names, in addition to Dr. Bedford, who I think are with us. They've been very quiet about it, but the time has come for Christians at Brookshire to get together and mount a counteroffensive against the forces of evil that are trying to destroy this place."

Josh was shaking his head as he and Sue walked out the door. "You don't believe anything I've said about the medical system, do you?"

"Everything that's happened here backs up your beliefs, Josh. But you operate at the highest spiritual level in all this. I don't and can't, so I have to operate on the level where I am. Which means doing whatever little things I can."

Josh took her hand and squeezed it. "I can't argue with that."

But his eyes were still pain-wracked. And Sue hurt on the inside too, for both him and herself. And she wasn't really sure why.

Gloomily, Vinnie looked out the window of his trailer. It was another dreary day, with intermittent rain, and his view of the outside was distorted by the wet glass. As he stared at the dripping trees, suddenly there seemed to be a haze over the view, a gray, smoky blur that dimmed his vision.

Oh, no! he protested mentally. *Not again!* For this was the aura, the warning sign that preceded his trance states. It was like the calling-card of those entities that replaced him at the controls during these periods.

A gentle, faint strain of music wound its way into his mind, a simple tune that grew louder and louder as Vinnie's sight dimmed and his control lessened. Somebody had asked him if it was like going to sleep. No, he had replied, it was very different. He drifted into sleep, whereas he was sucked down into this thing. He was never afraid of normal sleep, but this trance state frightened him more every time.

The song was louder, fully orchestrated now, the strings and woodwinds playing a contrapuntal rendition of the tune. He knew how it would be; he would lose consciousness for some indeterminate period and awaken with the music so powerfully imprinted on his mind that he had no choice but to play it, tape it, write it out on sheet music. And his very being protested this intrusion again, right when he was thinking about other matters.

His last thought, before he lost the ability to think, was that when he came out of it, he was going to see Josh.

So it was that late Saturday afternoon he rose from the chair, pulled on his Nebraska Cornhusker sweatshirt, took a deep breath and walked through the chilly rain to Josh's trailer home. The short walk next door seemed like the crossing of some invisible boundary.

Josh was alone, sitting at the table with a book in his hands. The Bible. He looked up as Vinnie walked in without knocking.

"I made up my mind."

"About what?" Josh asked.

"I think you're right. I think my whole problem is demons and I want you to cast them out."

Josh sat waiting, and as Vinnie said nothing more, his face fell. "Is that all, Vinnie?"

"Well, I believe all that other stuff you said, about getting rid of the wrong kind of music and zodiac stuff and cleaning up the place I live."

"No, I mean, is that all you've made a decision about?"

"What do you mean?"

Josh groaned and shook his head. "Is that all you have learned from me? Look, I'm sorry, but you've only got half the message, and the dark half at that. There's nothing worse than just believing in evil spirits without believing in Jesus and His power to overcome them. It's like going to war and seeing the enemy but not having any weapons to fight him. It's like knowing the world's coming to an end but not realizing that you don't have to go down the tube with it when it does end. If that's all you got from me, then I need to ask you to forgive me."

"You mean am I ready to accept Jesus?" Vinnie asked. He was suddenly becoming aware of many things about Josh that irritated him. The intense, commanding voice, the unsmiling face and penetrating eyes. And suddenly he was aware that Josh had a large Adam's apple in a neck that was never properly shaven. Vinnie noticed now some coarse black whiskers that Josh's razor had missed and that were an affront to him.

"We can make the demons go, but then you have to fill up the vacuum with something more powerful than demons or they'll just come back with seven more." Josh was leaning toward Vinnie, forcing the point home, and a fine thread of saliva quivered in the corner of his mouth. This infuriated Vinnie so much he felt like hitting Josh.

"That power stronger than demons is Jesus," Josh insisted.

Pious, pompous ass, Vinnie thought in contempt. *You won't catch me.* He pictured himself suddenly as a target for Josh's trap, which he would escape by clever and adroit maneuvering.

"Stop it right now!" Josh's voice thundered out. "Quit lying to him! In the name of Jesus, I forbid it."

The thoughts scurried away and Vinnie shook his head in

amazement. With the scales pulled from his eyes, he saw now that Josh was not an ugly, offensive man; he was as good and decent as any man Vinnie had ever met.

"What's going on?"

"I discerned that they were lying to you about me, trying to set you against me and anything I said. Was I right?"

"You sure were. I was noticing everything wrong with you." Vinnie grinned. "You'd be surprised how ugly you looked."

"That was just a little demonstration of how they work and how Jesus works against them. You didn't even recognize that it was an enemy talking to you in your mind until I made him shut up." Josh laughed. "And that wasn't casting them out; that was just taking authority over them. Just wait till they're gone! Then you'll really see what freedom is like."

Vinnie sat in silence, his thoughts a jumble. So they not only put their music into him; they could manipulate his thoughts as well.

He realized he stood at a crossroads. No matter how he chose, things would never be the same. There was an urgent voice clamoring for attention, repeating to him, "Let's don't be like Josh. Let's just be normal, not far out. People are always laughing at Josh."

Suddenly Vinnie realized this, too, was a voice talking to him, no longer pointing out Josh's faults but trying to exert influence against him nonetheless, trying to manipulate Vinnie's thinking again and force him into a decision against Josh. He was suddenly very tired of being manipulated. And if the manipulators were opposed to his choosing Josh's way, then maybe that was the right way after all. He took a deep breath and forced his will to a new direction.

"All right," he said. "I want what you have. I'll do whatever you say."

Immediately the voice howled at him, *Fool!* Vinnie ignored the voice and fixed his eyes and mind on Josh's face.

"Remember, this isn't something you're doing with the

336

emotions, Vinnie. We're dealing in the area of the will. So set your will and your purpose and keep your mind focused on me for a minute." Then as briefly as he could, he reviewed for Vinnie the plan of salvation.

"Vinnie, I want you to repeat after me: Jesus, I ask You to forgive my sins and come into my life as Lord and Savior and remake me in Your image."

Vinnie closed his eyes and stuttered out the words. It was agony. He was assaulted by every negative emotion he'd ever felt, running the gamut from fear to humiliation. But he clenched his fists and forced the words out and when he was through, he sagged back in exhaustion.

"Good. Now, I'm going after some of those enemies. You're going to feel all kinds of things and you may want to cough or throw up. Just be aware that the words for spirit and breath and wind are all the same in the original language in the Bible. Lots of times when the spirits leave, they go out like a breath. So you might yawn or cough or even holler. Don't let any fear or embarrassment stop this; this is a real, genuine act of spiritual warfare and when it's over you'll be different. Not just feel different; you'll *be* different. You'll be free. So don't be concerned with how you're feeling. Just set your will against them. That's the battleground."

"O.K." Vinnie said softly. His eyes clung to Josh's and he took several deep breaths.

Josh cleared his throat. "I come before the throne of God boldly because Jesus said I could, and I proclaim my position as a son of God, an inheritor of the Kingdom and more than a conqueror in Christ. The Word of God says I have been given authority over all the power of the enemy, and I command all the powers of darkness to be bound, powerless against my brother Vinnie here, and I remind you the Word of God says whatever I bind on earth is bound in heaven. . . ."

As the prayer continued Vinnie hung his head. The giggling little voice chattered in his mind as the powerful words continued to pour from Josh in ringing tones. It was a mocking, joking little voice and occasionally Vinnie was afraid he would laugh. He suppressed it as well as he could.

"Now, I take authority over the spirits of evil music and I command them to come out now, in the name of Jesus."

Vinnie felt a great stirring within him, almost a scurrying, like bugs running to hide when a rock is turned over. Then he felt an irresistible urge to cough. He remembered Josh's words and obediently yielded to the urge and began to cough. It was a tremendous coughing fit; it went on and on, now totally out of his control. Josh leaned closer, so that he could be heard over the noise of the coughing.

"I bind the strong man over the field of music, and I strip him of his armor, for I intend to rob his house and reclaim this captive. I bind you, Pan. I command you to loose him."

At last the coughing stopped and Vinnie wiped his face with a trembling hand. "Wow!" he said weakly.

"Yes. Wow, indeed." Josh grinned. "That one's gone, brother. The music that's left is your own. And never forget that music is worship; be careful what kind you let in. You don't want to worship the wrong side."

"Right," Vinnie agreed.

"You've been into drugs a little, haven't you? I know you were in psychotherapy counseling a few years back and they almost always use drugs. Now that opens a wide door for demons. As I explained before, in deliverance you're usually dealing with a three-strand cord: a natural weakness, a sin and a demon, all intertwined. Let's deal with these drugs, which the Bible calls sorcery; it needs to be renounced and cast out."

Vinnie nodded and Josh began again, addressing the spirits in a calm, forceful voice. "I bind you, Pharmakia, you strong man over drugs." He spoke with authority and Vinnie again felt a stirring in his body. *This is real!* he thought. *There are evil spirits inside me and they're coming out! I never believed it till right now. But, man, I'm glad they're going!*

As the deliverance continued, his gladness grew. It was

shocking to realize the contamination he'd held within his soul, but how glorious it was to see it going, going, gone!

Josh wound up the session with this prayer: "Jesus, the temple is now empty. I ask you to fill Vinnie with Your Holy Spirit." Vinnie repeated the prayer, then felt a sudden urge to go over to Josh and hug him.

Since Don Oliver Franklin had requested that the closing dinner for Project Truth be a formal affair, Isabel had chosen a floor-length dress of *cafe au lait* silk. She viewed herself in the mirror with satisfaction. Since this would be a trying night, she needed every advantage.

The rain had started again and she heard it pounding on the roof of the trailer. She bundled up in a slicker, boots and hood, raised an umbrella and took off through the woods to Brookshire.

The doctors' dining room was tastefully decorated. There were cut flowers everywhere and candles shone from the dining tables, sideboards and wall sconces. The chandelier lighting was as soft as the candlelight and she was grateful for the way it flattered her.

She was a little early; only Don Oliver Franklin and a few staff members were there when she arrived. He crossed the floor to greet her, moving majestically in his dinner tails.

"We're sitting next to each other, my dear, and I'd like you to help me greet the guests."

She stood with him at the door, smiling confidently, mentally reviewing his plan for the evening. "I'll say a few words," he had told her. "Then you can give your report. Add some human interest touches. Tell the people what you've learned."

Mostly I've learned that the whole thing was probably a big mistake, she thought.

"I had an interesting call this afternoon," he whispered confidentially as they walked to the entrance. "Something in the way of a reference check. You're being considered for a post with the A.F.P.R. Quite a plum; you'd be one of just three women on their staff."

Her mind raced, trying to sort out the letters, and he came to her rescue. "The American Foundation for Psychic Research. Top of the line, my dear. They maintain a continuing exchange with the Soviet Union. You'd be stepping into a position that might earn you an international reputation."

"It would mean leaving Brookshire."

"It would remove you from any, er, lingering bad effects from some of our little upsets here." He turned to greet the first arriving guests.

Isabel knew many of the guests; her position gave her entree into the upper strata of society and it was always heady stuff. About 25 had been invited. There were a few from the world of publishing, as well as bankers, educators, leaders in the medical profession, a sprinkling of politicians and two military men.

Sue and Josh arrived with Vinnie Ponder, all a little damp from the rain. Isabel pointed Vinnie toward the head table and told Josh, "Sorry to break up your trio. You'll find your places over by the wall."

Her thoughts went back to the A.F.P.R. Was this the next step for her? Would it satisfy the drive of ambition within her? She'd be very glad when this dreary dinner was over and she could be alone to think about it.

Josh and Sue found their placecards at the very end of a back table and took their seats. Sue looked at Josh proudly. He had flatly refused to wear a tux, but he looked good in his dark suit. She had gotten him to run a comb through his hair. It helped some. His face was still tense.

"Whatever happened to Castor and Pollux?" he asked suddenly.

"Bebe didn't want them, so Isabel called the pound. Sorta sad. Those poor dogs didn't do anything wrong."

Josh nodded, a flicker of pain in his eyes. It wasn't harshness, she realized suddenly, but pain that tightened his face into a mask of intensity. "All creation is groaning under the weight of man's sin," he said sorrowfully.

"Well, take heart. At least this Project is over."

"Glory to God for that," he agreed. But his face looked more troubled than ever.

A soup course was served and being cleared when suddenly the conversation in the room died down. Sue and Josh looked up to see what had so captured the attention of the diners.

The double doors to the hall had been thrown open and standing in their center, magnificently upright and bold despite being disheveled and dripping wet, was LeRoi Williams.

Up to now there had been only showers, but there was a blinding flash of lightning and a crash of thunder to punctuate LeRoi's dramatic appearance.

LeRoi still wore the clothes he'd donned eight nights before when he left for his Friday night date at the Roadhouse Pub. He was filthy and wet and unkempt, totally out-of-place in this gracious, elegant, candlelit room. Nevertheless, he walked boldly toward the head table. The broad brim of his black hat shaded most of his face but his eyes glittered through the shadow. He reached the head table and spoke directly to Don Oliver Franklin.

"I have some things I want to say." LeRoi's voice was harsh, compelling, attention-grabbing. Don Oliver nodded slowly. LeRoi turned to Isabel, seated next to Franklin, and began to speak in a still louder voice. "I know some things about you, Miss—or shall I say—Dr. Nebo. I could tell these people why you hate men so much and I could tell them the

341

very interesting little story about your father and the brown car. Then they'd all understand you better."

Isabel sucked in her breath, eyes narrowing in horror as she shook her head.

"You're so interested in the occult, aren't you? The dark, hidden things. That's what occult means. So I'll tell you some hidden things."

LeRoi turned to survey the room, his shrouded face with its glittering eyes moving in a slow pan down the tables from one to another. "This is the gift of clairvoyance . . . clear vision. I have clear vision about all of you." He gave a high, cackling laugh and started toward the nearest table.

"Here's Mr. Banker, our respected financial man . . . who also just happens to be an adulterer. Why don't you tell your wife about the little receptionist in the loan department?

"And next to him we have one of the town's leading society matrons, a whiz at bridge. You're on the board of the Literary Society, too, I believe. And you can't make it through till noon without that flask of vodka you carry in your purse."

The guests watched LeRoi with glazed, incredulous faces, rooted to their chairs. Josh, too, listened in fascination. A familiar spirit, he decided. A spirit guide who was passing along information about these people to LeRoi, the demons exchanging information like nasty kids snitching and tattling. No sin was safe from their eyes or awareness except the sins that had been repented, confessed and forgiven.

"And Colonel Jonas, why don't we tell the good people about your fine collection of magazines? Such wonderful photography! Photographs of little boys and girls, pretty children doing some very unpretty things."

The room was transfixed and LeRoi moved down the table. His voice was clipped and precise, higher than LeRoi's normal tones.

Another clap of thunder roared out and the sound startled the mesmerized audience. As the spell was broken, several people jumped from their seats and moved toward the door.

"Oh ho, afraid of what I might say about you, huh?" LeRoi laughed at the departing guests. "I particularly wanted to talk to you, Dr. Parrish. I wanted to warn you to change the place you hide your dope; your partner has found it and he's getting ready to dump you."

Josh leaned over to Sue and whispered, "This is what comes of putting the spotlight on demons and asking them to perform. They won't follow the script; they put on their own show."

"Can't you make them stop?" Sue asked.

"If you want me to," he agreed. He rose from his seat and walked to LeRoi, placing a firm hand on the thin, damp shoulder and speaking in a low but firm and audible voice. "In the name of Jesus, you spirits be silent!"

LeRoi suddenly sagged against him, teeth chattering and body quivering. Josh put a supporting arm around LeRoi and the tall frame seemed matchstick thin, brittle and fragile.

"Oh, Josh, man, I need you! I came all the way back to see you. I want free, man. They got a grip on me like never before and I can't stand it no more!" He was crying now, clutching at Josh in desperation. "You hear all that I said? That wasn't me, man. I don't know what got into me. I didn't know all that stuff! Can you help me?"

Josh felt a sudden excitement tempered only by his underlying sense of foreboding. Another victory! Three now led to safety. "Sure, LeRoi. Let's get out of here, go back to my place. I'll round up Sue and Vinnie."

Josh turned to Sue, who nodded. Then he signaled Vinnie. In the confusion and sudden hubbub, it was surprisingly easy to gather them together. He smiled reassuringly at Vinnie, who was white-faced. "It's all right," he said. "LeRoi came back for some ministry. You ready to help, Vinnie?"

Vinnie's handsome face broke into a grin. "Sure! Let's go." He turned to his former roommate and spoke as the four of them hurried from the room.

"You sure know how to break up a party, LeRoi!"

The rain had slackened a little but the wind still howled as Josh strode back along the path toward the hospital. His heart was pounding and he wondered how much of this was due to physical exertion, how much a result of the adrenalin pumping through his body. The time had come. At last he would see the face of the enemy without the mask.

From the moment he accepted the offer to be a part of Project Truth, Josh knew it was a fateful decision. The warfare in the heavenlies swirled about Brookshire. Satan considered this hospital his turf, and he was defending it with every weapon he had. Now Josh was to confront the enemy head-to-head and prepare to lay down his life in the process.

The parallel between his lonely battle against strong entrenched forces and what Christ suffered during his last days in Jerusalem had been in the forefront of Josh's mind over the past few days, including the fact that both reached this climax at age 33. Several times he examined himself. Was he a megalomaniac to compare himself to the Savior this way? Was it an absurd, arrogant assumption of importance? Was he an insufferable egotist who in some unhealthy way yearned for martyrdom?

Josh looked at these questions carefully and dismissed them one by one. Reduced to its simplest form, he was a disciple, an instrument of the Lord. And quite a flawed one at that. His personality not only bruised people, which action he knew grieved his Master; he was as inherently weak as those he condemned. All this had come out so clearly the other night with Sue. The Lord had taught him a great lesson then. Josh was comforted by the parallel again between himself and the mortal Jesus, who had sensed the physical pain he must soon suffer and groaned his anguish, "Lord, take this cup from me."

The Lord didn't remove the cup from Jesus and Josh did not expect it to be withdrawn now from him. From the beginning he had known he was to die in this battle.

What had devastated Josh over the past 24 hours was the conviction that he had failed so miserably in his assignment. Nothing had gone as he expected. He had hoped to confuse and deter the enemy from reaching his objective. He had expected to win for the Lord some new followers. As of last midnight the tally read: victories—one nurse; uncertain—one possessed young musician; defeats—all else.

His heart had been lifted greatly by Vinnie's decision for Christ that afternoon, and then, only moments before, a similar action by LeRoi. Both had been delivered of their inner torment through intensive prayer. His fear allayed that he had killed a man in the Roadhouse Pub by psychic power, LeRoi was now snoring in Josh's spare room.

Falling in love with Sue was certainly not in the plan; in fact, another indication of his weakness. Then he corrected himself. No, he felt the Lord's approval of his feelings for Sue. It was unfortunate that it had happened during this final stage of his life.

Then the inner message had come. The confrontation was to take place back in the doctors' dining room!

It had not been easy to leave Sue. She sensed the tension, the urgency in Josh and was almost hysterical in her determination to go with him. When he told her she needed to be with Vinnie and LeRoi, she remained unconvinced. Only when he commanded her to stay did Sue quiet down. The fear in her eyes was so naked as he walked out the door of his trailer that he told her, "I'll be back soon." He shouldn't have lied to her.

He burst through the side door of the hospital and strode along the corridor, leaving wet tracks along the terrazzo floor. He paused at the dining room door and took a deep, steadying breath. The final, face-to-face encounter was upon him and he brought his body under control before thrusting open the door.

His nemesis was waiting for him.

The candles still flickered, burning low and unsteadily in this dim and almost deserted room. The wind rattled the long windows and rain bounced noisily against the darkened panes. No attempt had been made to clear the dishes away and uneaten food remained at every place. Josh peered through the candlelight, moved around the room and then saw the one lone figure still seated behind the spread of white linen, china, crystal and half-eaten food.

"So it is you," Josh said softly.

Don Oliver Franklin inclined his regal head slightly and gestured grandly with his hand. The candlelight caught the flash of his diamond ring. "Dr. Kingston, you have been a worthy adversary. Our warfare has truly been on a heroic plane. Come, have a seat. Let's talk."

Josh walked toward Franklin as though in a trance and took a seat opposite him. He shoved aside a plate of cold rare prime rib, shuddering at the sight of partially congealed fat swimming in the blood that surrounded the remains of the dinner. He stared at Franklin, seeing suddenly all the earmarks of the enemy's presence. How had he been blinded so long, unaware of this man's spiritual allegiance?

Of course he was the most logical one. The very top man, at the upper levels of the hierarchy at Brookshire, a part of the power structure of society in this area. As Satan stood before the very throne of God to bring accusation against mankind, so Don Oliver Franklin was seated in the high places, wielding his satanic influence.

"At first I thought maybe Glenda was the one," Josh said.

"A mere tool, totally owned," Franklin said with a contemptuous wave of his hand. "But even there, a battle.

Somebody must have been praying." His genial face was almost playful as he pointed a finger at Josh. "Wanda almost got away. If she had not been so submitted to Glenda, so tied together in the soul realm since before birth, she might have escaped. As it was, she had to die."

"That must have been horrible for Glenda," Josh said.

"It was really a form of suicide," Franklin said.

Josh looked up suddenly, his eyes narrowed with the intensity of his thoughts. Of course! It all fell into place. "Suicide," he exclaimed. "That's the strong man, right?"

It was this enemy that had caused Malcolm Brown's plunge from the eighth floor, ending a life that was only a performance played upon a stage. Behind the mask of the busy, contented, purposeful man was the reality of a lonely, shallow, despairing soul who had gained what the world offered and found it not enough.

Charlie Fortuna had given up his life, too. He was no longer his own man; he was totally bewitched, now the slave of the lust he had fed and fanned and savored all his life. In total slavery Charlie had left his profession, his friends, his interests and preferences behind, and at the whim of another's will, driven docilely away, his life reduced to one primal, addictive urge: to be with Barbara Simmons and worship at her shrine. It was an unconditional surrender, and it was a suicide.

"Am I right?" Josh insisted.

Franklin nodded, as a professor with a bright student. "Yes, every single attack was in the realm of suicide. Some were subtle, however. And Miss Simmons will leave Dr. Fortuna, you know," Franklin smiled. "She has no constancy and no loyalty. She will leave him, and at that point he may well commit physical suicide. That is our plan, at any rate."

"Wallace Graham?"

"Certainly! He lies in his small, hidden room, willing his life away moment by moment. He thinks he is preparing himself to go to Zora. It will be quite a surprise when he

347

discovers where he is really going." Franklin chuckled softly, his broad body rocking slightly in mirth.

"And Isabel Nebo?"

"Dr. Nebo is eating of the fruit which tempted Mother Eve: knowledge of good and evil. She has been enticed into trying to understand evil in her intellect. And without recognizing that it is evil, her intelligence will become more and more darkened and she will eventually drop into our hands like ripe fruit. We've had many professional ladies like this; they begin with an intellectual interest in something, like grief or death, for example, and they end up as our instruments."

Franklin leaned forward confidentially. "What I enjoy the most is when we manipulate a person into evil while he still thinks that he is doing a good, even noble thing."

Josh took a deep breath. The atmosphere in the room was tense. There wasn't enough air. He spoke again, his voice forceful and strong, counteracting the weakness that was creeping into him.

"So Glenda's in a mental hospital, Wallace is dying, Isabel is entrapped by circumstances and deception. Charlie is heading for California, dancing attendance on Bebe. Malcolm Brown is dead. But what about the rest of us? What about Sue Dunn? Vinnie Ponder? LeRoi Williams? Myself?"

Franklin's genial good humor was gone. He lowered his gaze, staring into the plate of spoiled food before him. His large white hands formed into fists, one on either side of the plate and he pounded the table in anguish. "We did not anticipate defeats. I spoke for you personally, sure that your ego and arrogance and knowledge would make you fall like a ripe plum into our hands. It didn't work out the way I planned it, so now there is a different ending—"

"The deaths, Don Oliver. What about the nine unexplained deaths?" Josh asked, wanting to postpone the climax.

Franklin nodded. "There would have been ten tonight if you had stayed and eaten your main course. Too bad. But the deaths will continue. They haven't been easy to cover up, but we have managed so far. One of the ladies in Dietary, a kitchen aide, has a husband in the Navy. He recently returned home on leave from the Mediterranean. And he had been in Egypt where he was touched by a pestilence. She now has it and when she touches certain foods, assigned for certain patients, it is fatal. It's a new scourge, designed for these modern times, neoteric, serving our purposes."

Franklin paused to light a cigar, puffing the smoke as he turned the Panatela in the flame of his lighter. "And, of course, this is only the beginning. It will spread. But we had to start somewhere."

"And all the other stuff, the accidents, the poltergeist activities, the strange things, the weird happenings?"

"Yes." Franklin inclined his head, a hint of pride on his face. "That, too."

"But some of them seemed so pointless. Do you know the reason behind all of it?"

"No, certainly not. I just do as I am led. You must understand that." Franklin straightened his broad body and spoke forcefully, almost as a lecturer. "To corrupt any society, we must follow certain steps. We must take God out of things first. Then we create new gods, write new laws. We must give the people *our* answers to their questions and *our* substitutes for their needs. And at some point we must corrupt their institutions. Look at history. Rome, Greece, the Third Reich. Take the legal system. We divert them from their true goal, justice, and turn their attention to some other, lesser goal, like the protection of rights. Soon we make the protection of rights a higher good than the preservation of justice, and at that point the legal system becomes corrupt."

Josh nodded, his eyes fixed on the big man.

"We make the medical system a dealer in death rather than life," Franklin continued. "It began when we substituted 'medical care' for 'health' and so confused the people that they didn't even realize the two weren't synonymous. Through the legalization of abortion we've gained the right to use death—execution—as an answer to social problems. Now we practice infanticide in almost ninety percent of American hospitals. Soon we will implement mercy-killing; in time, our doctors will have the legal right to determine who lives and who dies. Now we stress the quality of life rather than the sanctity of life. Oh, we have come very far!"

"What happens to you now, Don Oliver?"

Franklin raised his regal head and stared at Josh. "I will stay here. I have much work to do here. Especially right now."

The inner Voice spoke to Josh and he leaned forward and shouted.

"You lie, Don Oliver! You're a defeated man. You're finished at this hospital and you know it. Satan has cast you out as he does everyone he has finished using."

The composure was gone from Don Oliver and his eyes glittered at Josh, who was now leaning forward with great intensity.

"Come out from among her, my people, that ye be not partakers of her sins, and that ye receive not her plagues, for her sins have reached unto heaven . . . and she shall be utterly burned with fire. Alas, alas, that great city Babylon is fallen, for in one hour is thy judgment come."

Franklin turned pale as Josh thundered out the apocalyptic words. A whimpering sound came from his throat as Josh leaned even closer. "You are not only a defeated man, Don Oliver, but your master has prescribed your verdict. The strong man will soon be coming for you. That's why you do not want to leave this room."

Then the big man placed both hands on the table and glowered at Josh. "You are wrong, Dr. Kingston. I will soon be leaving this room, but you will not—alive, that is."

Don Oliver reached under his napkin and pulled out a

heavybore Colt revolver, which he aimed carefully at Josh's forehead.

So this was to be the enemy's final desperate attack! The battle in the spiritual realm had taken on a temporal reality that would have appeared ludicrous, were not the peril so great. Josh stared at the deadly metal pointed at him.

"Suicide is on your mind, Dr. Kingston. I can promise you that this will be made to look like suicide. For I still do control the authorities in this area. And I do have witnesses to your distraught condition of late."

As Josh looked into the round open end of the weapon, he was calm. "Do what you have to do, Don Oliver."

"Stop! Stop!"

The agonized cry came a split second before the sound of the gun. Josh felt the impact of the bullet in his head and slumped forward.

The darkness came for a while, but behind and above it were the voices—insistent, sometimes incoherent, emotional, persistent. Then light filtered through and the cloudy shape of a room appeared about Josh.

It was a bedroom, his bedroom in the trailer.

Faces now came into view—anxious but not sad or fearful. Sue . . . Vinnie . . . LeRoi . . . several others in hospital attire.

"You gonna be all right, man."

Who else but LeRoi?

He felt pressure on his hand. Sue. He squeezed back. *What had happened? How could he still be alive?*

Sue sensed his questions. "The bullet creased the side of your head, Josh. Dug in enough to knock you out. Lots of blood, but nothing serious."

"Don Oliver?"

"I came screaming into the dining room just as he shot you. Then he turned the gun on me. At least, he did at first.

351

Then on himself. When the gun went off, he dropped over dead."

"Suicide," Josh muttered weakly.

"And attempted murder," Vinnie finished.

"I owe you my life, Sue."

She shook her head. "It's my new inner warning device. The message came: *Go to Josh in the doctor's dining room.*"

Josh suddenly became agitated. "I learned something very important. Don Oliver knew what was causing these mysterious hospital deaths." Quickly he told of the infected kitchen worker. Sue and the attendants then hurried to report this startling news to hospital authorities.

Later Josh and Sue were alone. Since Josh was still too weak to be up and about, Sue sat beside his bed and held his hand.

"The hospital is total bedlam," she reported. "Local police, hospital security, doctors and staff all milling about. With Don Oliver dead, no one seems able to take charge."

"This is a good time for you to pull out," Josh said seriously.

"That depends on what new offers come in," Sue replied with a slow smile.

"Tell me something," Josh said, suddenly rising up on his side. "How did I end up here instead of in a hospital bed?"

"We almost took you to Intensive Care. When it was obvious that the wound was not serious, we cleaned you up and I persuaded the medics on duty to carry you down here." Sue paused. "Besides, I didn't want you to wake up in a hospital bed, get mad and come charging out in your bare feet and nightshirt. It would have looked indecent."

Josh leaned back, a smile spreading across his face. "I'm glad you understand that my convictions about hospitals have not changed."

"Nor have mine," replied Sue, eyeing him steadily.

He reached for her hand and pulled her close. "Differences can make a marriage very interesting," he said.

"I'll accept that," Sue replied before his lips found hers.